Hunter:
SEASON OF THE WITCH

ART WIEDERHOLD

Order this book online at www.trafford.com
or email orders@trafford.com

Most Trafford titles are also available at major online book retailers.

Printed in the United States of America.

ISBN: 978-1-4907-2301-3 (sc)
ISBN: 978-1-4907-2300-6 (e)

Trafford rev.   01/02/2014

 www.trafford.com

North America & international
toll-free: 1 888 232 4444 (USA & Canada)
fax: 812 355 4082

CHAPTER ONE:
It's Elemental, my dear DuCassal

New Orleans during the Second Age looked and felt the same as the city had always looked and felt. The French Quarter was still the French Quarter. And the crowds of tourists and local drunks still made their nightly rounds of the clubs and restaurants on Bourbon, Royal, Decatur and Frenchman.

And parts of the city, especially those that were dimly lit at night, were still as dangerous as they had always been. Only now, the more mundane human predators competed for victims with vampires, rougarous and various other supernatural beings that prowled the shadows.

And the ancient cemeteries.

And many of the old homes.

This night was no different.

Jessica Harte, a pretty young waitress at Ralph and Kacoo's, had just gotten off work for the night. She was making her way down Dauphin to Esplanade to get to her apartment. When she crossed the dark street at Barracks, four tough-looking young men dressed in dark, dirty clothes emerged from a doorway and walked toward her. Jessica saw them quickened her pace. She hurried across to Esplanade only to find her path blocked by two more rough-looking men. One was holding a large butcher knife and grinning at her. She tried to run to the side but the men intercepted her. The man with the knife seized her by the hair and pulled her to the ground. Then he straddled her while the others gathered around.

"Where ya goin' in such a hurry, darlin'?" her attacker asked as he leaned over. "You don't wanna leave just yet cause the party's just startin'—ain't it boys?"

The others laughed and made crude comments.

Jessica was terrified.

Too terrified to even speak or scream for help.

Her attacker grabbed her blouse and pulled her to her feet. Then he shoved the knife in her face.

"Me and the boys wanna get laid. Since you're the only woman around right now, that means it's your turn to get raped. Play nice with us and we might let you live," he threatened.

"I'd let her go if I were you," said a man standing in the shadows of a nearby tree.

"Mind your own business, mister! She's out alone late at night. That makes her *fair game*," the knife wielder said.

"So are *you!*" the man said as he walked toward them.

Three of the men charged at him. The first got sent to the pavement by a quick kick in the throat that broke his neck. He died gurgling out his last breath. The second fell next to him with a bloodied face from a fist that was far too quick to block. The third attempted to stab the stranger. Instead, he got grabbed by the wrist. The stranger twisted is suddenly. The wrist snapped and the thug screamed as he dropped the knife. Next he was seized by the front of his shirt and hurled into the branches of a tree on the other side of the street. The impact showered the street below with leaves and twigs. He didn't move after that.

The stranger was dressed in a long, black leather mantle and wore a wide brimmed black hat. He moved with the speed of a cat and struck with the deadly accuracy of a cobra.

"I said let her go—now!" the man snarled.

"And I told you to mind your own business!" the man with the knife said as he lunged at the stranger.

The other two watched in disbelief as the man lifted their leader over his head with one hand and slammed him to the pavement with enough force to shatter several bricks. Realizing they were overmatched, they took off down Esplanade only to find their path barred by a tall, slender, red-haired woman in a black cloak.

When the woman wouldn't get out of their way, they attempted to run her over. The first hit the pavement hard after he received a right cross to the face. As he shook the stars from his head, he saw the woman grab his friend by the shirt and sink her fangs into his throat. He watched helplessly as his friend twitched for several seconds. When he became still, the woman let him fall to the ground. She wiped the blood from her lips and smiled at him.

Jessica stood and watched the entire scenario unfold. She knew who her saviors were. Everyone in New Orleans knew them. Everyone, apparently, but the hoods who attacked her.

The man in black dragged the surviving hoods to their feet and warned them not to try and flee if they wanted to stay alive. When they realized he meant it, they simply stood quietly while the woman dragged the other man over. Only four remained. The leader was so banged up; two of his friends had to hold him erect.

He stared at his attacker.

"Just who the Hell are you, mister?" he asked.

"My name's Hunter," the man replied.

"And I'm Lorena," the woman added as she bared her fangs. "And you men are very fortunate to be alive right now."

They stared at her fangs. One of them shook visibly as he realized they had attempted to fight a vampire.

"What are ya gonna do with us?" asked one of the hoods.

"We're going to take you to the Basin Street station and turn you in to Inspector Valmonde. If you know what's good for you, you'll come along quietly like good little boys. If you give us any trouble—," Hunter warned.

"We get the idea," the leader said.

Hunter turned to Jessica.

"Are you alright?" he asked.

"I sure am—thanks to you two," she answered as she hugged them both. "Thank you!"

Leon Valmonde was the head of the New Orleans Police Department. After dealing with Hunter for the last few years, he wasn't a bit surprised when he and Lorena marched their latest catch into the station. He smiled and put down his coffee mug when he saw them.

"And what do we have here?" he asked.

"A pack of would-be predators. We bagged them when they tried to attack a young woman a few blocks from here. Of course, this isn't *all* of them," Hunter said.

"The other three are still where we left them. They won't be going anywhere, so there's no need to hurry over to get them," Lorena added with her usual smirk.

Valmonde knew that smirk well.

He laughed.

"I'll send the meat wagon over to get them in the morning," he said as he nodded to his deputy, Sam.

Sam and two other officers seized the gangsters by their arms and took them downstairs to the holding cells. They'd be there less than a week. Then the local judge would hear the charges against them and decide if they should be tried, executed or sent to Angola, which was arguably the toughest prison on the continent. Going there was tantamount to a death sentence. Very few criminals ever came out of Angola alive.

"Where'd you leave the bodies?" Valmonde asked.

"The neutral ground on Esplanade between Bourbon and Royal," Hunter replied. "You'd better have the ambulance crew bring a ladder."

"Why would they need a ladder?" Valmonde asked.

"To get the one down from the tree I threw him into," Hunter said with a grin. "He might not be dead, but right now, he probably wishes he was."

Valmonde laughed.

"I'll tell the drivers," he said. "Where you folks goin' next?"

"I think we'll stop by the Dragon for a few drinks, then head home. It's nearly sunrise," Hunter said.

"And I didn't bring my sunglasses with me tonight," Lorena added.

Vampires could and did wander around in broad daylight. As long as they shielded themselves from too much direct sunlight and wore dark glasses, the sunlight didn't affect them. They preferred overcast days and they were at their strongest after sunset. But most did go about their normal business during the day.

Lorena was no exception.

New Orleans had a large vampire community. Most of them fed only off humans who frequented the clubs of the underground. And only if they were willing. Most got their "nourishment" from wine mixed with blood or plasma which also came from willing donors. The underground was very popular with locals and tourists alike who wanted to experience the world of vampires first hand.

The Dragon was the largest club on the circuit of about a dozen clubs. Ten of which were owned by Tony LeFleur, the unofficial "head" of the vampire community. Tony was a personal friend of Hunter and Lorena, who were well-liked by the local vampires for having rid New Orleans of a hybrid creature that had actually fed on vampires. They were so grateful to them; they made Hunter, Lorena and DuCassal the grand marshals of their Vampire Mardi Gras that year. They even donated money to have a stature erected in their honor in Armstrong Park.

The irony of vampires honoring Slayers did not escape anyone, especially not Hunter's employer at the Vatican. The Cardinal had found that to be quite amusing. Usually Hunter slew vampires. In fact, he was extremely good at it. But the large community of vampires in New Orleans posed no threat to the local humans. In fact, the two groups co-existed peacefully. When outside, predatory vampires disturbed that peace, Hunter, Lorena and DuCassal eliminated them—as well as anything else that preyed on humans.

When Hunter, Lorena and DuCassal (who had met them outside the station) entered the Dragon, Tony Le Fleur greeted them with a wave. They walked up to the bar and sat down. Tony brought them their usuals and stopped to chat as always. He smiled at Lorena.

"You look well nourished this evening," he remarked.

"I stopped for a quick bite on the way over. It was an impromptu snack, but very satisfying," she replied with a gleam in her green eyes.

Tony laughed.

"I can imagine. I've already heard about the incident on Esplanade. News travels fast around here," he said.

"Tell me about it," Hunter said as he sipped his Sazerac.

"Just like it did the night we finished the Baron, eh, Charles?" DuCassal said as he downed his cognac and placed the empty glass on the bar.

Tony refilled it.

"Merci, mon ami," DuCassal said as he raised it in salute.

"Just about everyone I know claims that they saw that battle, even those who weren't in town at that time," Tony said.

"Like Woodstock," DuCassal added. "It was this grand concert during the First Age that was attended by a half million people, but everyone for the next two generations claimed to have been there—even those who had not yet been conceived at that time."

"So how does it feel to know your true identity?" asked Tony.

"A little strange but I can deal with it. I just look at that as a long dead part of my life. I'm not that same person now," Hunter replied.

"Does the Cardinal know?" Tony asked.

"Not that I'm aware of. I know I didn't tell him," Hunter said. "I sometimes wonder what he'd say if he did find out?"

"What *could* he say?" Tony asked.

"Not a damned thing," Hunter replied as he emptied his glass.

Tony mixed him another and handed it to him.

"I don't care who you started out as centuries ago. That's in the past. To me, you're Charles Hunter and a damned good friend. And that's all that matters," he said as they clinked glasses.

DuCassal and Lorena clinked glasses with them.

"And a better man or friend I have never met," DuCassal added.

"I could not have wished for a better man to marry than you, mon cher," Lorena said.

A woman dressed in a short floral dress walked over. She had a tourist guide in her hands. To Hunters surprise, the cover photo was of him and Lorena standing outside of St. Louis Cathedral in Jackson Square.

"May I please have your autographs?" the woman asked nervously.

Hunter smiled.

"What's your name?" he asked.

"Madison," she replied.

He wrote "To Madison, Welcome to New Orleans," then signed it. Lorena and DuCassal also signed it. Madison gushed and thanked each of them.

"I'm from St. Louis. We've heard about you all the way up there. I wish we had someone like you in our city," she said.

"Oh? Are you having trouble up there?" Hunter asked as he ordered her a drink.

"Oh my, yes! Not a week goes by that someone isn't found dead on the streets or in their own beds. People are afraid to go out after sunset," she said.

"Vampires?" asked DuCassal.

"To be honest, nobody seems to know what's killing people. Some are found whole. Some are torn to pieces and others just up and vanish into thin air," Madison said. "I came down here to get away from it for a little while. I may just stay in New Orleans, too."

"Sounds like more than one nasty is prowling St. Louis," DuCassal said. "How long has this been going on?"

"I think it started about a year ago," Madison said. "I'm not real sure. St. Louis has always been a dangerous city to live in so it's hard to tell when this started."

"Sounds like St. Louis has a lot in common with New Orleans," Tony said as he refilled everyone's glasses. "But these are bad times we live in."

"No more so than they were during the First Age," DuCassal said. "Charles and I were kept quite busy in those days, too."

"Even without the Baron," Hunter smirked.

DuCassal refilled his glass and nodded.

"I still have several questions concerning you, Charles," he said.

"So do I," Hunter said as he took a sip of the Sazerac. "What's yours?"

"You turned the Baron out of revenge because he betrayed you to your enemies. But why did you feel that was a punishment?" DuCassal asked.

"I felt that being a vampire was the worst curse that could befall a man. I figured that since I detested my existence, I'd curse the Baron by making him just like I was," Hunter replied. "I thought he'd be tormented like I was. I never expected him to *embrace* being a vampire. Hell, he actually *relished* his existence. That surprised me."

"I'm sure that you've come to appreciate the *irony* in this," DuCassal said.

Hunter laughed.

"My entire life is filled with ironies," he said. "Not only did I make him a vampire, I spent over a decade trying to kill him. What was a curse to me proved to be a blessing to him. I detested what I'd become so much that I made a pact with the Devil to rid myself of the curse. That was another bit of irony. The Devil rid me of my curse then granted me forgetfulness and immortality. It was he who put me on the path to becoming a Slayer so I could hunt and kill the very things I once was."

"The Prince of Darkness is using you rid the world of evil things who prey on humans. Thanks to him, you have become an agent for good," DuCassal said. "That goes far beyond mere irony, mon ami. In fact, I cannot even think of a proper word to describe it."

Hunter laughed.

"And to add to the irony, the one great love of my life is Lorena. I'm a former vampire lord turned Slayer and I am married to a vampire," he said.

"Not to mention that you have also become a folk hero of sorts to the local vampire community. Your life—and through you, mine—is filled with ironic contradictions," DuCassal said. "You should write a book."

Hunter smiled.

"Maybe someone already has," he joked. "Maybe we're all just characters in a series of novels."

DuCassal grinned.

"That's absurd!" he said. "Any writer who could create the likes of us would have to possess a very sick and twisted mind. Not even Lovecraft, Poe or Derleth ever sunk to those levels. If we are characters in a novel, I don't want to know how it ends."

"Me neither," Hunter agreed as Tony refilled their glasses.

"There is one more question that begs to be answered, Charles," DuCassal said.

Hunter smiled.

He knew where he was going with this.

"I am certain that you have also wondered about this," DuCassal continued. "You were once Vlad Dracula, the most famous vampire of all time. But you were not born a vampire. Someone *turned* you. So the remaining question is: *who made you*, Charles?"

Hunter sipped his wine and looked at him.

"I've wondered the same thing. I also wonder if the one who turned me still walks the Earth," he said. "I also feel that the answers still lie hidden in some of my dreams."

"Any dream in particular?" Tony asked.

"There's one I keep having about me and my brother finding that crypt in the city that had been destroyed by the Turks. In the dream, my brother opens the crypt and goes inside. When I try to stop him, he knocks me unconscious and goes inside. Then I hear that dark, sinister laughter," Hunter said as he recalled the dream.

"You think your brother released a vampire from that crypt?" DuCassal asked.

Hunter shrugged.

"Perhaps. But I don't think I was bitten by *him*," he said. "I think I was turned by someone else."

"Whatever became of your brother?" asked DuCassal.

"That part of my memory is still a blank. I sometimes have short visions of him dressed in the uniform of a Turkish soldier. At least, I think it's him," Hunter said. "I also have a gut feeling that he has something to do with me becoming a vampire."

Madison finished her drink and thanked them for their kindness and autographs. Hunter asked where she was staying.

"The Cornstalk on Bourbon," she said.

"I'll escort you safely there," Hunter offered.

"We *all* will," DuCassal added as he finished his cognac.

"That's very kind of you all. Thank you," Madison said.

"See you tomorrow, Tony," Hunter said as they left.

Tony waved and watched them leave. It was four a.m. The Dragon would close in two more hours and his crew would start cleaning up. He wondered if the pretty young tourist would decide to stay in New Orleans. If so, she'd need a job.

"I can always use another waitress," he said.

As they strolled along Bourbon Street, several passersby stopped to chat with them as usual. Madison was also drawn into their conversations and began to feel like she'd been in New Orleans her entire life. She commented about this on the way to her hotel. Hunter laughed.

"That's just the way we are here," he said. "What do you do in St. Louis, Madison?"

"I work in a bank and wait tables at night," she said.

"If you do decide to stay here, I might be able to help you find employment," Hunter said.

"I know that Tony would hire you. He's always looking for help in his clubs," DuCassal said. "And I also know several bankers who may be of assistance."

"I'd have to work nights. I'm not very alert during daylight hours," Madison said.

"We know," they all answered at once.

The following evening, Elmer Wood, 76, of Treme, was taking a shortcut through Louis Armstrong Park. He had just left his job as the early shift bar tender at May Bailey's on Dauphine and was "bone tired".

It was a clear, starlit night and a soft, sultry breeze was blowing in from the west. He often cut through the park, but never this late at night. Tonight he was feeling kind of tired so he opted for the shortcut. The park was well-lit and deserted except for him. This put him at ease. Normally, the park was crawling with local thugs who liked to hang out and drink and shoot craps. Anyone walking through the park when they were around became a victim.

But Elmer was alone.

When he crossed over the bridge and walked across the meadow, something large, fast and menacing caught his eye.

But only for a split second.

Then just as quickly, it was gone.

Poor Elmer never knew what hit him.

The next morning, a pair of joggers happened upon a most grisly sight and hurried over to the Basin Street station to report it to Inspector Valmonde. He rounded up Sam and a couple of his best men and hurried over to the park. What they saw made them turn their heads in disgust and horror.

In the middle of the meadow was a long, deep rut where something heavy had plowed up the grass. In the rut were the smashed and splattered remains of Elmer Wood. His shoes were on the far end of the rut. The rest of him was scattered all through it, along with shredded clothing. The entire middle section of his body was crushed beyond recognition. His head, one arm and a shoulder lay at the other end of the rut. A quick search of the immediate area turned up his other arm and part of the other shoulder. The rest of him was gone.

Valmonde took off his hat and shook his head.

"What do you suppose killed him, Chief?" asked Sam.

"I don't even want to guess, Sam. I ain't ever seen anythin' like this in all my years on the force," Valmonde replied. "Go on over to the Garden District and fetch Hunter and Lorena. I think this is right up their alley."

Hunter, Lorena and DuCassal arrived an hour later. Sam led them to the crime scene and Hunter winced when he saw what was left of poor Elmer.

"The impact must have been horrific," Hunter said. "There are bits of bone, flesh and clothing smeared all through this rut."

They walked the length of the rut and stopped. Hunter examined the edge of it and shook his head.

"Whatever hit him was very large and heavy. It was moving at great speed, too. It hit him here and skidded. The skid created the rut and Elmer was either in front of it or beneath it when it happened. I imagine that it happened so fast he never knew what hit him," he said as he looked around.

"There are several tracks leading up to the impact site," Valmonde said as he led them toward the trees. "I've never seen anythin' like them. Maybe you can figure out what made them."

They came to the first set of prints. Hunter squatted down and put his hand inside the print. Each print had four long, pointed toes in front and a spike at the heel.

"It's at least ten inches deep. My guess is this is where the creature launched itself from. As for what made the tracks, I honestly have no idea, Chief. These tracks are from a creature that's a complete mystery to me," he said as he stood and looked around.

Valmonde led them to the three other prints they found. They were all at least 20 feet apart.

"From the looks of this, this creature came out of those trees at a run, then made at least three good leaps before it killed Elmer. From the depth and size of the prints, it must weigh at least 600 pounds," Hunter surmised.

"How can anything that big and heavy move fast enough to do this?" Valmonde asked. "It ain't natural!"

"No—but we could be dealing with something that's *supernatural*," Hunter said as they walked back to what was left of Elmer.

"Can you have the remains examined? I'd like to know if anything's missing," Hunter asked.

"I suppose. You think the thing that did this may have been huntin' him?" Valmonde asked.

"Like for food?" queried Sam.

"It's a strong possibility. If the thing attacked Elmer because it was hungry, then this park is its hunting ground. If not, that means someone sent that thing to kill Elmer either out of revenge or for sport," Hunter said.

"Sport?" asked DuCassal.

Hunter shrugged.

"Anything's possible when dealing with monsters," he said. "Maybe whoever created or conjured the beast was using Elmer for practice to see how effective his monster is. Or maybe there's something in Elmer's past that made him a target."

"That's crazy! Elmer was a musician. All he ever did was work the clubs and fairs in Louisiana. Hell, I don't think he's ever been in any kind of trouble. Most people who knew him liked him, too. I don't think he had a single enemy," Valmonde said.

"Just in case, I'd like you to do some checking for us," Hunter suggested. "Everyone has a skeleton or two in their closet they want to keep hidden. I'm betting Elmer also had a few."

"I'll check, but I doubt I'll come up with anythin'," Valmonde said. "Meanwhile, I'll double the night patrols on the park—just in case."

Hunter nodded.

"Tell your men to carry shotguns and keep ready to fire at all times. We don't need any of them to end up like *this*," Hunter said as he nodded at the rut.

"Do you think shotguns will be of any use against this thing, mon ami?" asked DuCassal as they walked back to his carriage.

"Beats me, Jean-Paul," Hunter replied.

They climbed back into the carriage. George, the driver, looked down and asked where they were going.

"Minerva's temple on Chartres," DuCassal said.

"Good idea," Lorena smiled. "Maybe she can help. Minerva knows all of the old legends of Louisiana."

"If this happens to fit into one of them," Hunter said.

Minerva DuPres was the reigning voodoo queen and high priestess of New Orleans. She was slender, dark skinned and of indeterminate age. It was her letter to the Vatican that had been responsible for bringing Hunter and Lorena to New Orleans several years earlier. She was a veritable living encyclopedia of local history, folklore, magic and other arcana and she had also helped them on several occasions.

Her temple was a three story townhouse on Chartres with a Spanish lace iron gallery and a courtyard in back. Minerva presided over all voodoo celebrations and ceremonies in New Orleans and was highly regarded by the locals.

She also had a knack for knowing when Hunter, Lorena and DuCassal were about to show up and usually had a pot of herbal tea and a platter of spiced cakes on the glass topped table in the front parlor.

This day was no exception.

Minerva was seated on her high-backed chair stirring a cup of tea with a silver spoon when they entered. She smiled at Hunter.

"I've been expecting you," she said. "I heard about Elmer Wood."

"News travels fast in this city," Hunter said as he helped himself to a cookie. "Then you know how he died?"

"I heard he was spread into a furrow in the ground as if something great and heavy struck him," she said.

"You heard right, Minerva. Whatever killed him must have been traveling at great speed, too," Hunter said. "There wasn't much left of him."

She sipped her tea as they explained what they saw at the scene. When they were finished, she sat quietly and stirred her tea as she thought. After a few seconds, she looked each of them in the eyes.

"I've lived here all of my life and I tell you that I have never heard of anything like this before," she said.

"Then you have no idea what killed him?" Lorena asked.

"Not exactly. I think I can guess what did this, but I want to be sure. I'll have to do some research. Give me a few days to look into this," she said.

"Can you give us a hint?" DuCassal asked.

She laughed.

"Not really. But I will tell you this: if what I'm thinking is right, we're all in for a very bad time," she said.

"That's not exactly what I wanted to hear," Hunter remarked.

"Too bad, Hunter. That's all I've got right now. You'd best pray that I'm wrong this time—*if* you pray, that is," Minerva said.

"I used to pray—way back when I believed there was a god," Hunter said as he finished his cookie.

"Oh, there *is* a god, Hunter. It's just not what folks think it is," Minerva assured him with her usual smile. "You can't deal directly with god. That's why I always use the go-betweens."

"Can your go-betweens help us with this?" Hunter asked.

"I'm not sure," Minerva said.

"What *are* you sure of, Minerva?" DuCassal asked.

"Just one thing, Jean-Paul. That thing that killed Elmer will be back," she said.

Four a.m.

Lester Marcel "Mad Max" Browne was asleep in the master bedroom of the old abandoned mansion on Clara and Josephine. The place had been empty for more than 50 years. Since the locals believed it was dangerously haunted, Lester used it as his hideout. The area was dark and rough. So rough, the New Orleans police never bothered to patrol it. This was fine with Lester.

Lester was one of the city's most vicious thugs.

He was wanted for several rapes, hold ups and two murders. The murders were particularly gruesome as he'd hacked his victims to death with an axe. He'd been on the run ever since. The last thing he wanted was to return to Angola. He'd spent 15 years there and it nearly killed him. When he got out, he vowed he'd rather die than return.

Lester was about to get his wish.

The sound of his bedroom window creaking open caused him to sit up. At the same time, he reached for his pistol. Just as he wrapped his fingers around the grip, he heard a soft swishing sound. Then he let out a scream as his hand suddenly became detached from his wrist. The last thing he saw was the grinning face of dark haired woman just before she sunk her fangs into his throat.

An hour later, Hannah Morii dumped the lifeless and bloodless corpse of Lester Browne on the front steps of the Basin Street station just as Valmonde and Lem walked up to start their tour. Lem turned the body over as Hannah watched. He looked up at Valmonde.

"That's Lester Browne alright, Chief. No doubt about it," he said.

Valmonde laughed.

Hannah followed him into his office and watched as he took out $3,000. He handed the reward to Hannah. She counted out $1,000 which she pocketed and returned the rest.

"There was a $3,000 bounty on that punk's head," Valmonde said. "It's all yours, Hannah."

"Give the other $2,000 to charity," she said.

"Which one?" asked Valmonde.

"Whichever one Father Paul prefers," she replied.

"I'll make sure he gets it. Thanks, Hannah. You did our city a great service—as usual," Valmonde said.

"I don't mind. Besides, a girl's got to eat," Hannah said with a satisfied smile as she left the office.

"That Miss Morii has sure been tracking down a lot of criminals lately. That's the sixth one this month. I think she feeds more than Lorena," Lem said as he entered the office.

"I believe that's a fact, Lem. Hannah's kind of new at this vampire stuff. I think she has more trouble controlin' her urges than Lorena does. As long as she keeps helpin' us out like this, I don't give a rat's ass how much she feeds," Valmonde said as he poured himself a cup of hot coffee.

It was nearly sunrise.

Hannah hurried back to the apartment above her shop and hung up her cloak and katana. Although Browne was a small, wiry man, he had more than enough rich, red blood to keep her satisfied.

At least for a few days.

Hannah smiled at her reflection in the old silver mirror. The myth about vampires not being able to cast a reflection was just that.

A myth.

For all intents and purposes, they were no different from anyone else. But they had certain other gifts that she was slowly but surely learning about that made them far superior to ordinary humans. The downside was they needed blood to survive.

At first, Hannah had felt repelled by this aspect or her vampirehood. She fought hard to resist the urge to feed. When she was finally forced to give in, she found out she actually enjoyed the taste of blood and how the sudden rush of it into her system made her feel. Each time she fed, she felt herself getting stronger and stronger. After a few feedings, she no longer fought to control her urges. She simply gave in to them.

And there were more than enough criminal vermin to keep her satisfied. Lorena fed once or twice every month. Hannah fed whenever she felt the hunger, which was at least once or twice a week.

She removed her clothes and walked into the bathroom to shower. As she did, she felt that sudden rush of energy and euphoria she always felt after a feeding. Lorena had told her about this. She just never was able to convey how wonderful it felt. It was almost orgasmic.

"At least now, I'm on equal footing with any vampires I hunt," she thought.

That was another one of life's ironic twists. She hated vampires for what they did to her parents and had spent her life hunting them down and killing them when she could. But she had suffered many injuries and had nearly been killed herself several times when she'd gone after the more powerful vampires. The only way she could change that was by becoming a vampire herself. Now, she was just like Lorena.

A vampire who hunted and slew vampires and fed on human criminals.

"What would my parents say if they saw me now?" she wondered as the warm water cascaded over her shoulders.

Dr. Julienne Sumner was the coroner at the city morgue. She'd been in the position more than 20 years and almost nothing ever surprised her. Then she examined the pitiful remains of Elmer Wood. In the middle of her exam, Hunter, Lorena and Valmonde walked into the morgue. Sumner looked up.

"I've been expecting you," she said as she peeled off the rubber gloves and tossed them on the tray with her instruments.

She walked over and looked at Hunter.

"What do *you* think did this?" she asked.

"Something large, heavy and moving extremely fast," Hunter replied.

"Exactly," Sumner agreed. "Elmer Wood was simply turned into road kill. There's no other way to describe what's left of him. Now, as for *what* did this, I'm open to suggestions."

Hunter paced, turned and walked back.

"I've been hunting supernatural creatures for more years than I care to think about. I've seen all sorts of twisted, mangled and crushed corpses. Yet I have *never* seen anything that looked like this," he said. "I can tell you one thing for certain—whatever it was didn't come from this world."

"I'd say you're right," Sumner nodded. "There's a theory that we share the same time and space with dozens of parallel worlds and dimensions. If so, what's to stop something from one of those worlds from crossing into ours and vice versa?"

"Portals or gates *can* be opened between the universes," Lorena said. "Either by accident or on purpose."

Valmonde scratched his head.

"Who in the world would bring whatever killed Elmer over?" he asked. "That'd be insane!"

"Or an accident. Sometimes, those gates open of their accord and fun ensues," Hunter said with a grin. "But right now, that's just a guess on our part. We won't know what killed Elmer until we find it."

"Then what?" asked Valmonde.

Hunter shrugged.

"We'll either kill it or end up like Elmer," he said.

Ten p.m.

Jason Mallory had just left his waiter job at Johnny's. It was a warm, muggy and somewhat misty night. He lived on the other side of Armstrong Park and he was tired. He decided to take a short cut through the park so he could get home and sleep.

Jason never made it.

The next morning, two young women who happened to be jogging through the park came upon a long, straight and unusual rut in the grass. Curious, they decided to follow it. When they reached the end, they both screamed in terror. It took them several minutes to calm down and several minutes more to run to the Basin Street station to tell Valmonde what they saw.

Valmonde grabbed his hat and hurried out the door.

"Sam—go and fetch Hunter fast. Tell him to meet me in the park!" he shouted on the way out.

Hunter, Lorena and DuCassal met Valmonde in the middle of the park. He shook his head when they walked up.

"Looks like that thing struck again," he said. "There ain't much left of this one, either."

Hunter and Lorena examined the pile of grass, mud and crushed human remains at the end of the rut. The only thing still recognizable was Mallory's head which had an astonished look to it.

"From his expression, he didn't see what hit him until it was right on top of him. Then he didn't have a chance," Hunter said. "Who is he?"

"I found his wallet about 20 years down. He was Jason Mallory. I think he waits tables over at Johnny's." Valmonde said as he handed the wallet to Hunter.

"Any connection to the first victim?" Hunter asked.

"None that I'm aware of," Valmonde said. "I guess there's no need for autopsy this time."

Hunter shook his head.

"I don't know what we're dealing with, Chief, but I think I know a way to find out," he said. "Before we do this, I want you and your men to warn everybody to stay out of the park after sunset. We don't need any more Mallorys."

"Will do," Valmonde agreed. "I'll send the meat wagon over to scrape this poor boy up. Now comes the part I hate most about this job— breakin' the news to his family."

"I don't envy you, Leon," DuCassal said.

He turned to Hunter.

"I know what you have in mind, mon ami. You want to set a trap for this monster," he said as they walked to Bourbon Street.

"And a trap needs bait," Lorena added. "I'll go first, mon cher. If anything shows up, I may be fast enough to get out of its way. Just in case, stay close."

"You can count on that," Hunter said. "I'll take the second night."

"That leaves the third night for me," DuCassal said. "What if that thing doesn't take the bait?"

"We'll keep crossing the park each night until it does. I recommend that we both load our weapons with the high explosive shells. We need to try and do enough damage to it to slow it down so we can finish it off," Hunter said.

"What if it's bullet proof, mon cher?" Lorena asked.

"We'll cross that bridge if we need to later. Right now, let's find out what we're up against," Hunter replied.

That night, Lorena began her patrol at nine p.m. It was a slightly rainy night and the park was deserted. She made several crossings of the open areas. The only thing that crossed her path was a wild hare which wriggled its nose at her and hopped away. She smiled at it and continued her walk. Hunter watched from the shadows of the trees. When the sun began to rise in the east, he stepped out and walked with her.

"I guess it doesn't like the bait," Lorena said.

"I don't see why. I've always found you totally irresistible," he joked.

"Let's go home and get cleaned up. We promised Jean-Paul we'd meet him at the Court of Two Sisters for brunch this morning," she said.

Hunter patrolled the next night with the same results—minus the wild hare.

Thursday.

It was DuCassal's night to be the bait.

Rather than walk through the park, he decided to take his carriage, "In order to provide the creature with a more tempting target."

With George in the driver's seat, DuCassal's carriage made its first pass through the park just after sunset. A few tourists and locals were still strolling along the paths and over the bridges as the concert had just ended. DuCassal opened a bottle of wine and poured himself a glass while he waited for the park to empty out. By 8:30, it was deserted and a light fog began to roll through it. The fog wrapped the street lights in a ghostly blanket and gave the park a creepier-that-usual atmosphere.

DuCassal pulled the bell cord to signal George to make another pass. They made it safely to the far side, then George turned the carriage around and headed back to the main entrance.

As the carriage crossed the park, an unusual sound, much like the roar of hundreds of freight trains, caught DuCassal's ear. He rolled down the window and called up to the driver to stop so he could listen. Before he got a single word out of his mouth, something large, dark and very powerful struck the carriage at tremendous speed. The blow landed just behind the driver's seat and the impact sent George flying into the air. The terrified horses whinnied and bolted across the park while the back half of the carriage flipped over and landed on its roof with DuCassal still inside.

He heard the sound vanish into the night along with the creature as he struggled to right himself. He kicked the door open and rolled onto the grass. That's when he saw the deep, wide rut in the ground the creature had made as it hurtled toward them. He dusted himself off and looked around.

"George! Are you safe?" he called out.

He watched the splintered remnants of the first half of the carriage stir and raced over. After he pulled away the shattered driver's seat, a hand reached up. DuCassal clasped it and helped George out of the wreckage.

"I'm fine, Sir. Nothing's hurt but my pride," George assured him with a smile. "What in God's name hit us?"

"I have no idea, mon ami. But I am determined to find out," DuCassal answered as they looked for their horses.

After an hour of searching turned up no traces of them, they decided to head back home. To their relief, they found both animals standing in front of the house. They were panting hard and covered with sweat, but otherwise unharmed.

DuCassal and George went over and patted them gently.

"Wash them down and put them up for the evening, George. I'm going to visit Hunter and Lorena and tell them what happened," he said.

Hunter and Lorena met him on the porch.

"I figured something was up when I saw your horses return without you. We were just headed out to look for you," Hunter said as they walked over to DuCassal's place. "What happened?"

DuCassal told them what happened. Hunter whistled.

"Jean-Paul, did you see what attacked you?" he asked.

"No, mon ami. It struck too quickly. It sounded as if a hundred freight trains were barreling toward us then WHAM!—it was gone and my carriage was scattered all over the park like so much kindling," he said.

"So there was no time to prepare?" Hunter asked.

"None at all. It was fortunate that neither myself or George was harmed, but my carriage will never be the same. It's good I have a spare in the carriage house," DuCassal said.

"Now what, mon cher?" asked Lorena.

"Now we visit Minerva to see if she's learned anything," Hunter said.

"I have nothing for you yet, Hunter," Minerva said as they walked in. "Whatever killed Elmer isn't in any of my books. I have ruled out anything from across the River and I'm sure that no voodoo was used to create it or bring it over."

"That means it's from someplace else," DuCassal said. "Whatever it is, it's very powerful and unbelievably fast."

He told her what happened earlier. Minerva looked him in the eyes and shook her head.

"Being the bait can be dangerous at times," DuCassal concluded.

"I think you'd best find another way to deal with this thing," Minerva warned. "There's no way any of you can react in time to fight it. And even *you* might end up like Elmer Wood if you make a mistake."

"But *what* is that thing?" Hunter asked in frustration.

"I'm still working on that, Hunter. Be patient," Minerva said.

"Let's go down to the Dragon, mon cher. Perhaps Tony or one of his clients may have heard something?" Lorena suggested.

"It's worth a try. I'm a little thirsty, anyway," Hunter agreed.

"So am I, mes amis. I'm buying!" DuCassal declared.

Two a.m.

Hannah stood on a rooftop overlooking Peniston. She rarely patrolled the well-lit and crowded streets of the French Quarter. Vampires didn't hunt those areas anyway. They liked to make easy, silent kills with no witnesses around. They preferred the more quiet and darker areas of the city.

That's why Hannah patrolled those areas, too.

She'd been at it since sundown without success. The street below was deserted now. She was about to call it a night when she heard the sounds of footsteps hurrying along the street. She could also hear the sound of a terrified heart beating. She watched as a short, dark-haired woman in a red dress crossed over from Pitt and turned west. She was running as fast as she could. As she did, she kept glancing back over her shoulder.

Hannah looked in the same direction and saw what was chasing her.

He was tall, thin and dressed almost entirely in black. And his heartbeat was very slow. Less than 35 beats per minute.

A vampire.

Perhaps the very same one who had left two other young women dead in the Uptown area. Perhaps the very one she had been searching for.

She watched and waited.

The woman crossed the street twice more. When she looked back, she saw no sign of her pursuer and slowed her pace. She took a deep breath, turned east and screamed as her pursuer suddenly appeared in front of her. He reached out and seized her by the throat, then pulled her toward him. She struggled and started punching him with all of her might.

The vampire laughed, then opened his mouth and bared his fangs.

Hannah had seen enough.

She launched herself from the rooftop and landed right next to the vampire. Startled, he let the woman go and turned toward Hannah. Then he smiled.

"You are like me. Don't worry, I will share her with you if you like," he said.

He never saw Hannah draw her katana until it was too late. A split second later and his head began rolling down the street. It came to rest at the corner of Peniston and Camp just as his torso struck the pavement and lay twitching. Hannah took a wooden stake from the leather case she carried on her hip, rolled the vampire over and plunged it through his heart. When the body became still, she doused it with a bottle of oil and set it ablaze.

The would-be victim sat on the curb and watched as Hannah retrieved the head and tossed it on the burning body. Hannah smile and sat beside her.

"Are you alright?" she asked.

The woman took several deep breaths to calm herself down and nodded.

"I am now. Thanks," she said. "Aren't you Hannah Morii?"

"That's me," Hannah said. "I'll escort you safely home. Where do you live?"

"Four blocks up the street," the woman said as Hannah helped her to her feet. "Just how many vampires are there in New Orleans?"

"Lots. Too many to count. But this one's not from around here. He had a foreign accent," Hannah explained as they walked along Peniston. "Local vampires rarely feed on humans without an invitation."

"You mean like those ones in the clubs?" the woman asked. "I've been in a couple of those places out of curiosity. I even watched a few of them feed."

"Have you even been asked to be donor?" Hannah joked.

"No. But nearly became one tonight," the woman said.

When they reached the woman's house, she thanked Hannah again. Hannah waited until she was safely inside then headed back to the French Quarter.

It had been a good night's hunt.

When they entered the Dragon, they were surprised to see Madison working behind the bar with Tony. They walked over and sat down. Tony mixed them their usual cocktails and had Madison bring them over.

"I see you've decided to stay in New Orleans," DuCassal said.

"I was going to leave but Tony offered me a job here. Since I feel at home here, I decided to stay. At least for a while," Madison said. "Tony's teaching me how to mix cocktails this week so I can fill in when one of the other bartenders are off. I didn't know so many different things mixed well with blood."

"My favorite is the red wine mix," Lorena commented. "It helps me get through most nights."

"That seems to be the most popular drink with the regulars," Madison said. "I've made more of that than any other drink since I started here tonight."

"Have you tried it yet?" Hunter asked.

Madison nodded.

"How long have you been a vampire?" DuCassal queried as she refilled his glass.

"Six years now," she said. "I was attacked in my bedroom by a terrifying dark man. I thought he was going to kill me. But for some reason, he didn't drain all of my blood. A few weeks later, I realized I was a vampire."

"How often do you feed, Madison?" asked Lorena.

"I don't. I mostly got transfusions at one of the blood banks or drank cocktails. I've never actually fed on a human being. So far, I've been able to keep myself under control," she said. "But it *is* getting tougher."

"Your willpower is remarkable," DuCassal said. "I am impressed."[1]

"Thank you," Madison smiled. "I think that's because of my schooling. You see, I used to be a nun. I gave that up when I moved down to St. Louis. I wanted to try other things for a while."

Hunter smiled.

"What order did you belong to?" he asked.

"I was an Ursuline. I grew up in Quebec. That's where the order originated on this side of the Atlantic. I was with them for four years when I realized that sort of life wasn't for me. So I resigned from the order and moved to St. Louis. Now, I'm here," she explained.

Hunter raised an eyebrow at her mention of the Ursulines. The order had also branched out to New Orleans in the 1750s and had developed a most checkered history. 1

She smiled at him and nodded.

---

[1]   See Hunter: Nightmare in New Orleans

"Folks here told me what happened," she said.

"It was something that needed to be done," Hunter said. "Have you been there yet?"

"I went there on my first day in New Orleans. It's a beautiful place. It's hard to imagine it had been a vampire nest," Madison said. "You couldn't tell by the way it looks now."

"That's because Hunter and I spent a lot of money to restore it. We even had the statues of the founders replaced so it looks exactly as it did during the First Age. It's a popular tourist attraction now," DuCassal said.

"And Father Paul sometimes performs mass in the chapel," Tony added. "But only upon request. I go there when he does."

Madison nodded.

"I've been to Guadalupe and St. Louis Cathedral. I still go to mass. Once a Catholic girl, always a Catholic girl," Madison said as she handed Hunter another Sazerac.

"I am happy that you like our city enough to stay," DuCassal said. "If you like, perhaps I can show you around on your off days?"

"I'd like that very much," Madison replied. "Thank you, Mr. DuCassal."

"Please call me Jean-Paul," he urged.

At that point, one of Valmonde's men, Sam, walked into the Dragon. He spotted Hunter and hurried over.

"The Chief sent me to find you folks. There's been another killing in the park," Sam said.

"We're on our way," Hunter said as he down his drink.

When they reached the park, they saw Valmonde and three of his men standing next to a shattered tree at the far end of another deep rut. They walked over and Hunter winced at the partial remains of them victim which was now embedded in the stump. His arms were to either side of the rut and his legs were at the far end.

"This poor fella got hit mighty hard," Valmonde said. "Hard enough to make him part of that tree."

"I thought you warned everyone to stay out of the park," Hunter said as he examined the remains.

"I did. But you know how it is. Some folks either don't get the word or they figure it won't happen to them," Valmonde said. "I don't know who this one is. He looks foreign. I figure he must be a tourist."

"That would explain why he was here. He probably didn't get the word," DuCassal said. "A few hours earlier and that might have been *me*."

"Let's go see Minerva. Maybe she's found something," Hunter suggested.

Twenty minutes later, they entered the voodoo temple on Chartres. Minerva was already seated in the parlor with the usual array of teacups and cakes. Hunter sat down and helped himself to a ginger cookie. Minerva smiled.

"I had a feeling you'd come by," she said.

"I guess you've already heard?" Hunter asked.

She nodded.

"Just what in Hell are we up against?" he asked.

Minerva put her cup down and leaned back.

"The closest I can come is an *elemental*," she said.

"You mean a nature spirit or demon?" Hunter asked.

"In this case, I'd say it's closer to a demon. I think we are dealing with some kind of earth elemental. But it's not exactly an elemental in the true sense," Minerva said. "Since it apparently hunts at night, I'll call it a *night ranger*."

"A night ranger?" Hunter asked.

"Since it prowls Armstrong Park, wouldn't that make it a *park ranger*, mon ami?" DuCassal joked.

Minerva rolled her eyes while Lorena groaned. Hunter simply shook his head.

"Why night ranger?" he asked.

"I can't think of anything *else* to call it," Minerva admitted. "Night ranger sounded like it fits."

"What are we facing, exactly? Is this a wild animal? A spirit? A demon? A monster?" Hunter asked.

"None and perhaps all of the above. From what you've told me, it seems to have the characteristics of all the things you just mentioned and a couple of its own," Minerva replied.

"Is it from this world?" Hunter asked.

"I don't think so," Minerva said. "Not unless this is another escapee from an old Opus Dei lab. You said they were trying to create some sort of killing machine."

"I doubt it's one of theirs," Hunter said. "If it was, it would be searching out specific victims. This thing kills whatever crosses its path."

"In that case, I think that this beast has been brought here from a world that occupies the same space and time as ours," Minerva said.

"You mean a parallel world of some sort?" DuCassal asked.

Minerva nodded.

"Something like that. I think it came from the Hell of that world," she said.

"That means it was *brought* here. Someone *gated* it in. But who in their right mind would want to do that?" Hunter said. "It's not like they could control the beast."

"It was probably an accident. I think this was unintentional. And whoever did it is probably dead," Minerva answered.

"Why is it stuck in the park?" Lorena asked.

"I think that's where it entered our world. Someone was in the park when they opened the gate. I bet they used a Ouija Board. That's the easiest way I know of to open a gate," Minerva said.

"Maybe the board is still in the park somewhere?" DuCassal suggested.

"We can always go and look for it," Lorena added.

Hunter nodded.

"If a board was used, I'll need that same board to try and send that thing back. If not, you'll have to find a way to kill it," Minerva said.

"And just how do we do *that*?" Hunter asked.

"I'm not sure you can," Minerva replied.

"Come again?" Hunter asked.

"I believe that beast draws its strength and speed from the night itself. It's probably from an eternally dark world. It appears to be solitary and highly territorial. It attacks and kills anything that crosses its path. Since the night gives it strength, you would have to lure it out into the bright sunlight and try to kill it when it's at its weakest. I doubt you'll be able to do this. It's far too fast, too ferocious and too strong to be killed by your usual weapons. Taking it head on would be dangerous and suicidal," Minerva explained.

"You make this sound difficult," DuCassal said.

"That's because it *is*," Minerva said. "You're immortal, Jean-Paul—not *invulnerable*. That thing *can* kill you—any of you. If you can find that board, bring it back here so I can find out if it was used to open a portal—and if that portal is still open."

"If it is, that means something else could have crossed over," Hunter said. "Maybe something worse."

"Now *that's* a pleasant thought," Lorena said.

"If something else did cross over, I think we would have learned of it by now," DuCassal guessed.

"What are the odds of that happening, Minerva?" Hunter asked.

"Fifty-fifty," she replied.

"If something else did cross over, we'll deal with it when it decides to show itself. Right now, we have to get rid of this night ranger," Hunter said. "Let's go to the park and look for that board."

"And lets' do it before the sun goes down," DuCassal added. "I do not wish to have another encounter with that thing. I'm running out of carriages."

They entered the park with several of Valmonde's men and spread out to cover every bit of ground possible. DuCassal was at the easternmost edge of the park. As he approached a group of oaks adorned with ribbons of Spanish moss, he spotted a little used foot path. He followed the path to a small clearing. The ground had been torn up in several places and bits of splintered oaks were scattered over the entire area. He spotted a pit in the center of the clearing and walked toward it.

The first thing he saw was a partially decayed human arm.

Then he found a leg.

And another arm.

Then bones of a ribcage and another ribcage.

When he reached the center of the pit, he found three decayed human heads, several black candles, empty beer bottles, drug syringes and articles of clothing. He carefully perused the dirt around the edge of the pit. After a few minutes, he saw the sharp flat edge sticking out. He walked over and carefully pulled the Ouija board from the ground.

"Voila!" he exclaimed.

He called out to the rest of the search party. One of the officers ran to get Valmonde. He arrived minutes later in his carriage and raced over to where Hunter, Lorena and DuCassal were standing. The rest of the officers were combing through the remains in the pit in search of wallets or anything else that could identify the victims.

"There are three bodies here, Leon," DuCassal said. "Two males, one female. From the looks of this, they were drunk and using drugs while playing with the board."

"You think they're the ones who gated that monster in?" Valmonde asked.

"I don't think there's any doubt, Chief," Hunter said. "I don't think they did it on purpose. If they did, they were too drunk to deal with what came in. I don't think they ever knew what hit them."

"Probably not. Jesus Christ! I've never seen such a mess! Now what?" Valmonde said as he looked around.

"We'll take the board to Minerva and pray this is something she can deal with," Hunter replied.

When Minerva saw the board she instructed Hunter to place it on the table. She stood over it with her hands out and concentrated.

"I see three young people at a party in the park. They're drinking and passing a needle around like they haven't a care in the world. The girl has a backpack. She opens it and takes out this very board. They all laugh when she tells them about a spell she read in a book a long time ago. She tells them she can use the board and the black candles to open a gate and summon a demon. They laugh harder and dare her to prove it. I see her placing a candle at each corner of the board and lighting them. She takes a black covered book from her pack, opens it and reads a spell. After that, all I see is chaos and blood. Lots of blood," she said.

She sat down and shook all over.

"This is the board, Hunter. Those damned fools let that thing in," she said. "But there's something else. I saw two things come in."

"Two? What's the second one?" Hunter asked.

"I don't know, Hunter. It went away real fast. It could be anything," she replied.

"Let's tackle the night ranger first. How do we send it back?" Hunter asked.

"*We* don't. *I* have to be the one to send it back. There's a spell I can try. I've only done it a couple of times and only when dealing with spirits. If I make a mistake, I'll end up like those others," she said with a nervous edge to her voice.

"You're frightened, aren't you?" Lorena asked.

"More than you know, child," Minerva said.

"Can we help?" Hunter asked.

"You can come with me to the park and give me moral support. Other than that, I think you'd best stay out of the way," Minerva said. "We'll do it tonight. Exactly at the stroke of midnight. That'll give me enough time to prepare myself for the ritual."

"We'll meet you here at eleven," Hunter said.

Minerva nodded.

"Just pray that I'm right," she said.

At the appointed time, they met Minerva at the temple. She had the board wrapped in a white cloth tucked under her left arm and a small bag containing four golden candles and matches.

"I have to open a gate into another world and lure that thing into it. That means I'm the bait tonight. I have to place the board directly in front of me, open the gate and wait for that thing to find me and attack. If I'm off by so much as a split second, you can scrape what's left of me up with a shovel and toss it in the river," she explained.

When they reached the park, Minerva held up her hand.

"You'd best stay back. I need to find the most open area for this," she said.

Hunter nodded.

"Bon chance," Lorena said.

Minerva walked to the center of the park and placed the Ouija Board on the grass. She knelt and placed a golden candle at each corner of the board. After saying a brief prayer, she lit each candle and closed her eyes.

The others watched from a safe distance as Minerva began her spell. Several long minutes elapsed with nothing happening. Then, slowly but surely, the board began to glow. It was a soft, golden glow that rose upward until it formed a bright white arc directly in front of Minerva. As the arc closed at the top, they heard the sounds of a hundred freight trains getting closer and closer.

They watched as the heavy dark form made a rapid beeline straight for Minerva. It tore a furrow in the ground as it approached. The sounds grew even louder.

Deafening.

The creature launched itself straight at Minerva.

She flinched and covered herself with her arms as it struck the light—and vanished.

Minerva wrapped her arms around herself and shivered noticeably as Hunter, Lorena and DuCassal rushed over. Hunter helped her to stand. She smiled at him.

"It's back on the other side," she said. "We have one more thing to do."

She picked up the board and wrapped it in a white cloth and placed it inside the heavy box. They then hurried from the park and raced along the riverfront until they came to the ferry dock. The last one was about to make its final round trip for the night when they boarded. Midway to Algiers, Minerva tossed the box into the murky water and watched it sink from sight.

"That's that," she announced.

"Won't that thing come back?" Lorena asked.

"The only way it can is if some fool finds that box and uses the board. I dropped it into the deepest part of the river. There's over 200 feet of water covering it now, so that's not likely to happen," Minerva said.

Hunter nodded.

"The poor fool who gated that thing in thought the board was a parlor game. He and his friends paid the ultimate price for their stupidity and so did a few innocent people," he said.

"Folks shouldn't mess with things they don't understand. When they do, bad things can happen. Yet, they always do, don't they?" Minerva asked.

"The world is filled with idiots and they always seem to cause trouble for the rest of us," DuCassal said. "I guess that's why people like us are around. Someone has to clean up the mess, eh, mes amis?"

"So you're saying that we are like *janitors*?" Lorena asked.

"I prefer to think of us as *custodians*," DuCassal said with a grin. "What do you think, Charles?"

"I think I'm hungry. Let's go to Arnaud's. I'll buy," Hunter said.

"In that case, Arnaud's it is!" DuCassal agreed.

Two weeks later, at the Vatican, the Cardinal received Hunter's latest report. With it was a hand-written copy of the official marriage certificate that was issued by Father Paul of the St. Louis Cathedral in New Orleans.

It was customary—and mandatory—for all Slayers to provide copies of such documents to the Vatican when they married or sired children. It was a way of keeping track of major changes in the lives of their Slayers and of their bloodlines.

As he perused the certificate, Hunter's signature caught his attention. For some reason, he'd signed it Charles D. Hunter. He had never used a given name before or middle initial. The Cardinal knew that Hunter's friend DuCassal always called him Charles. That explained his first name on the certificate. But what on Earth did the letter D stand for? Why would Hunter select it as his middle initial?

He shook his head and passed the report and the certificate across the desk to his aide, Fra Capella. The priest looked it over and squinted.

"Why would Hunter sign his name in such a manner?" he asked. "Is Charles his given name?"

"I believe it is the name he has decided to give himself," the Cardinal replied.

"What does the letter D stand for?" Capella asked.

"I have no clue. Only Hunter himself knows the answer to that. You can ask him yourself if he ever returns to Rome."

"Just what *is* his real name?" Capella asked. "All I've ever seen in his file is the name Hunter. Do you know his true identity?"

"I do not," the Cardinal answered.

"Do you even have a clue?" Capella asked.

"Well, I will say that over the years, I have had my suspicions. In the grand scheme of things, it does not matter who he is or was as long as he keeps doing God's work," the Cardinal said with a smile. "Only one man knew and he took that to his grave many centuries ago. Hunter is Hunter. He is our best Slayer and that is all I or anyone else needs to know about him. Understand?"

Capella nodded and placed the documents into Hunter's file.

"Anything else, Excellency?" he asked.

"Yes. Send Hunter and Lorena their usual stipends. Get those out on the first ship to New Orleans. After that, you may have the rest of the day off," the Cardinal directed.

Capella smiled and bowed as he left the office.

The Cardinal stood, stretched and walked over to the large window. He stared up at the clouds and laughed.

"If someone had told me that my best Slayer would marry a vampire, I would have had him committed to an insane asylum and thrown away the key. And who would have imagined that Lorena would have become so instrumental in helping Hunter rid the world of creatures just like her? Truly, the universe has gone mad!" he said.

CHAPTER TWO:
Love Stinks

Friday night at Razzoo, which had become the number one dance club on Bourbon Street. As usual, the place was packed. Jake Wilson and two of his best friends had gone to the club in search of hot young women—or horny older women. It really didn't matter as long as they got laid. They arrived around eleven and looked around. Bob Thames, the "ruggedly handsome" one of the group, spotted a short, rather shapely woman sitting alone at the end of the long, white bar and ambled over. After a couple of drinks and several dances, they left the club arm-in-arm.

Jake and his other friend, Harry Weems, stayed behind to look for other single women. That's when Jake noticed a very pretty blonde seated by herself at a table. He smiled and she smiled back. Then she winked. Jake tapped Harry on the arm and nodded toward the woman.

"Looks like I'm being paged," he joked. "I'll see you later."

Harry watched as he walked over to the table and sat down.

"My name's Jake. What's yours?" he asked.

"Melodia," the woman replied as she waved to the waitress and held up two fingers.

Seconds later, the waitress hurried over with two tall drinks. Jake handed her a $20 and told her to keep the change. His eyes stayed on Melodia. After a little bit more chit-chat, Harry watched them leave the club.

"Lucky stiff!" he complained as he returned to the bar for another drink.

Jake took Melodia to his apartment on Chartres. He just couldn't believe how lucky he was this night. Melodia was the cutest woman he'd ever met.

"Maybe she's the one," he thought as he watched her undress.

When Jake didn't meet Harry and Bob for lunch the next day, they wondered what was up. After their meal, they walked over to his apartment and rang the bell. After several rings, no one answered. Bob saw his landlady returning from the French Market with several sacks and offered to help her. She handed him two of the sacks, took the key from her purse and opened the door to her apartment.

"Hey, Mrs. H.—did you see Jake this morning?" Bob asked.

"No I haven't. I did hear him go into his place last night. He had a blonde girl with him," the landlady replied as he put the sacks on her kitchen table. "Why?"

"He was supposed to meet us for lunch two hours ago but he never showed," Harry said. "That's not like him. He always keeps his appointments."

"We thought he might be sick or hurt," Bob added. "He didn't answer his bell."

"I can take you up and let you in if you like," Mrs. H. offered.

She led them upstairs to the second floor. She knocked hard on Jake's door. As she did, it opened inward with an ominous creak. She glanced at the others.

"It's not like Jake to leave the door unlocked," she said.

"Let's check it out," Bob said as they went inside.

They found Jake lying face up on his bed. He was stark naked and still. His eyes were wide open and staring at the ceiling. Bob ran over and touched his cheek.

"Damn! He's cold!" he announced.

Bob grabbed Jake's wrist and tried to find a pulse. There was none.

"He-he's dead!" he said as he stepped back from the bed.

"Do you think that girl he took home did this?" Harry asked.

"I don't know, but we'd better go to the station and tell the police," Bob suggested.

An hour later, Bob and Harry returned to the apartment with Valmonde and two of his men. Lem checked out Jake's body and shook his head.

"When was the last time you boys seen him alive?" Valmonde asked.

"Around midnight. We were at Razzoo. Jake left with this pretty blonde girl," Harry replied.

"You know who she is?" Valmonde asked.

"No. I never saw her before last night. I heard her tell Jake that her name was Melodia," Harry said sadly. "You think she might have had something to do with this?"

"If she was the last one who saw him alive, she either knows what happened or did this herself," Valmonde said.

Sam, the second officer, walked over with Jake's wallet and handed it to the Inspector. Valmonde opened it and counted of five $100 notes and several $20 notes.

"I think we can rule out robbery," he said. "Any marks on him, Lem?"

"None that I can find, Chief. No cuts, stab wounds, bruises—nothing," Lem replied. "No sign of anything violent at all."

"Maybe he died from natural causes, like a stroke? He have any health problems?" Valmonde asked.

"None that we're aware of," Bob said.

"At least he never mentioned anything," Harry added.

"I'll have the ambulance boys come over and take him to the morgue. Maybe the coroner can figure out what he died from," Valmonde decided. "Thanks for your help, boys. If I find out anythin' I'll let you know. If you can think of somethin' else, drop by the station."

As they left the building, Valmonde stopped and looked up at the apartment.

"If he died of natural causes, why didn't the girl report it to us? Why'd she up and run away like she did?" Lem asked.

"Maybe it happened while they were makin' love and it scared the Hell out of her. Enough so that she decided to leave and not tell anybody," Valmonde speculated. "The only way to answer that question, Lem, is to find that young woman—which is exactly what I want you and the boys to do. Bring her into the station in handcuffs if you have to, but I want to talk with her."

"Will do, Chief," Lem said.

But try as they might, they could not find the lady in question. Although several people who frequented the local watering holes and clubs claimed they saw someone who fit her description, no one knew who she was, where she came from or where she lived.

After a week of searching, Valmonde told his men to give it up.

"She's probably left town by now. If so, we have no way of findin' her," he said.

Things remained quiet for the next week or so. Then another body turned up. This time, it was at the Prince Conti Hotel. When one of the guests missed his checkout time, the manager, Troy Andrews, sent the maid to his room to see if he was still there. He'd had several guest sneak out without paying over the years and felt this young man might be another. A few minutes later, a pale, shaken main hurried back to the front desk.

"He's dead!" she cried.

Andrews sent for the police. Twenty minutes later, Valmonde, Sam and Lem strolled into the lobby. Andrews led them upstairs to the room and opened the door. The body had already started to decay.

Valmonde walked over and looked down at the lifeless body of a dark haired young man.

"Who was he?" he asked.

Andrews showed him the registration card.

"His name is Steven Dunjler. He's from Pensacola," he said.

"When did he check in?" asked Valmonde.

"Four days ago. He was supposed to check out this morning. When he didn't, I sent the maid up. Then I sent for you," Andrews said.

"Did anybody see anythin'?" Valmonde asked.

"Joe Larson is the night clerk. I sent for him when I sent for you. He should be here shortly," Andrews replied.

"Let's wait in the lobby," Valmonde said.

Larson arrived an hour later.

"Sure. He came in about midnight with some blond. She was kind of cute, too," he said upon questioning.

"Did you see her leave?" Valmonde asked.

Larson thought for a second and shook his head.

"Nope—and I was in the lobby until six this morning," he said. "I didn't see anyone come or leave."

"Don't you think that's a little unusual?" Valmonde asked.

Larson laughed.

"In New Orleans?" he asked.

Valmonde thanked him and had Lem send for the ambulance.

"Pack up all of his things, Troy. I'll write a letter to his folks and give them the bad news," he said as he left the hotel.

"This is just like that case a couple of weeks ago, Chief," Sam said as they headed back to Basin Street. "A young guy picks up a pretty young girl, takes her to his room and ends up dead. Think we have a serial killer on our hands?"

"I don't even want to make a guess until we find out what killed those fellers," Valmonde replied.

At three p.m. the next day, Valmonde walked into the city morgue. He saw Dr. Sumner seated behind her desk on the far side of long, cold room and ambled over. She wrinkled her nose when she saw him.

"Find anythin'?" Valmonde asked.

"I just finished the autopsy on the Dunjler boy an hour ago," she said.

"What's the cause of death?" he asked.

"I'm not real sure, Leon. I did find one unusual thing during my examination. After I finished with him, I compared the results to the autopsy I did last week on the Wilson kid. They both were the same, but I'm not sure it was the cause of death matched," she said.

"And?" he urged.

"I think you'd better bring Hunter over, Leon. I think he'll really like this one," she said.

"We'll be back in an hour," Valmonde said as he left.

Sumner was waiting at her desk when Hunter, Lorena and DuCassal walked in with Valmonde. She smiled.

"I think I have something that's right up your alley, Hunter," she said. "Has Leon told you anything about the cases?"

"He told me they were two young, healthy males who died for no apparent reasons," Hunter said. "What do you have?"

"Something really strange," Sumner said.

"I'm listening," Hunter said.

"Both Dunjler and Wilson were missing a certain bodily fluid," Sumner said.

"Blood?" Hunter asked.

"No. Semen," she replied.

"Semen?" Hunter asked in surprise.

"Yes. Neither man had a drop left in him," Sumner said.

"Did they have fang marks on their penises?" Lorena asked.

"There were no marks anywhere on either of them," Sumner replied. "What's more, all other bodily fluids were at normal levels. Only their semen was drained—and I mean totally."

"Interesting," Hunter remarked.

"Very," Lorena added.

"Not even the women I know can do that!" DuCassal joked. "Although they usually try their best."

"No vampire did this," Lorena said. "At least none that I'm aware of."

"I agree," Hunter said.

"Then what did kill them?" asked Valmonde.

"The actual cause of death in each case is still unknown," Sumner said. "Their hearts simply stopped beating."

"This is new territory for me, Chief. I've never come up on anything like this," Hunter said.

"I have never even heard of anything like this," Lorena added.

"I think I have—a long time ago. If I'm right, there will be more victims like them and they'll all be healthy young men," Hunter said after a while.

"I think I understand where you're going with this, mon cher. You feel they were killed by some sort of a succubus," Lorena said.

Hunter nodded.

"And I hope like Hell I'm wrong," he said.

"What's a succubus?" Valmonde asked. "It seems that I've heard that name somewhere before."

"It's a female demon," DuCassal said.

"They come from one of the lesser planes of Hell. They usually resemble rather pretty young women. In their natural forms, they have tails and bat-like wings. They normally attach themselves to a human male they're attracted to and draw energy from him through sexual intercourse each night," Hunter said.

"That doesn't sound so bad," Valmonde said.

"Usually, it isn't. The relationship is quite pleasurable for both her and her victim. If the man is strong and healthy, no harm is done and the relationship can continue for years and years with no complaints. But if, for some reason the succubus feels her chosen mate is the wrong one or he does something to piss her off or he has a health problem he's not aware of, the male ends up drained and dead," Hunter added.

"So that would make a relatively harmless demon deadly?" Valmonde asked.

Hunter nodded.

"So this young feller didn't meet her expectations somehow," Valmonde surmised. "Or he really did but something went wrong inside and he ended up dead."

"That's about it, Chief," Hunter said.

"Do you suppose that succubus is lookin' for another man to attach itself to?" Valmonde asked.

"I'd say that's 100 percent likely," Hunter replied.

"If she does, I hope that relationship goes better," Valmonde said. "We don't need to find any more bodies like these two."

"I agree. But just in case, we'll keep our eyes open. Can you send your men around to the clubs and ask if either of them left with a young woman the nights they were murdered?" Hunter asked.

"I sure can. I'll let you know what I find out," Valmonde said.

They left the Funky Pirate and cut across Bourbon to Dauphine. Once there, they turned right and walked toward St. Peter Street. She turned to him in the middle of the block and smiled. He leaned close. Her perfume was tantalizing.

Arousing.

When they kissed, she suddenly recoiled and stepped back. He stared at her and wondered what the Hell was up?

"You are not the one," she said.

"One what?" he asked, now totally confused.

"Him. You are not *him*," she stated.

He reached out to her. She glared at him.

"Maybe I am and ya don't know it?" he said with a smile, trying his best to be charming.

"No. Go away. You are not the one," she insisted.

"Well, I'm gonna be, even if ya don't like it," he insisted as he tried to grab her.

The slap to the side of his face sent him hurtling through the window of a small café and across the table of several diners. He skidded across the table and landed on the floor amid a crash of dishes, beer bottles and glasses. One of the diners looked through the broken window and watched as the woman headed toward Burgundy Street while the other three and several others helped the dazed man into a chair.

The commotion caught the attention of Hunter and Lorena who were only a block away. They hurried over to the café and saw the waiters cleaning up the broken glass and scattered food while the manager held an ice-filled towel against the victim's face. Hunter squatted in front of him and examined the bruise, which covered half his face. He squinted at Hunter.

"What happened?" Hunter asked.

"This woman came onto me while we were in the Funky Pirate. After a few drinks, she agreed to come up to my place for some more fun. All that changed when we kissed outside," he said.

"Go on," Hunter urged.

The man took the towel from the manager and held it to the side of his face.

"She turned mean and slapped me. She hit me hard, too. I never knew anybody could hit like that. That little gal sure packs a wallop," he said.

"Did she say anything before she hit you?" Hunter asked.

"Yeah. She said I wasn't the one. I wasn't him—whatever that means," the man replied.

"What did she look like?" asked Lorena.

"She was about five foot seven with a nice figure and long, dark brown hair and blue eyes," the man said. "I never saw her before tonight. Now I'm real sorry I did."

"Thanks," Hunter said. "Did anyone see her?" he asked out loud.

"I saw her walk up toward Burgundy," the waiter said. "She was in a hurry, too."

Hunter turned back to the man in the chair.

"You're very lucky that you're not dead—which you would be right now if you had pressed her," he said. "You'd best get home and stay there."

"You don't have to tell me twice!" the man said.

Hunter and Lorena walked up toward Burgundy. The usual night prowlers were out doing the restaurants and bars. They meandered slowly through the crowds but didn't see anyone who resembled the woman.

"That man said the woman who hit him had dark brown hair," Lorena pointed out. "Witnesses say the first man went home with a blonde. The second man left Pat O'Brien's with a redhead. Are we dealing with three of those creatures?"

"Either there's three of them or this one can change her appearance at will. If she can do that, it'll be next to impossible to locate her in New Orleans. She'll be able to hunt at will and the only way we'll catch her is if she tries to kill someone right before our eyes," he said as they walked toward Esplanade.

"How likely is *that*, mon cher?" asked Lorena.

"Not very—unless she becomes desperate. From what the last victim said, she's searching for a certain male. The 'one'. The first two that were killed might not have been what she's looking for but she used them for nourishment anyway. I wonder who that 'one' is and why he's so important to her," Hunter said.

"Since she let the last one live, she obviously wasn't trying to feed," Lorena said. "I must admit that I'm lost on this one, mon cher. *Very lost.*"

"So am I. I think we need to pay Minerva a visit tomorrow morning. Maybe she can help us figure out what she is and what she wants," Hunter said.

At ten the next morning, Hunter, Lorena and DuCassal walked into the temple on Chartres. As usual, Minerva was seated at the table waiting for them with the usual array of cups, saucers, tea and sweets. She sipped her tea as they sat down and helped themselves to the treats. Hunter explained what happened the night before. Minerva listened quietly.

"We need to know what she wants, Minerva. Why is she here?" Hunter asked.

"The answer to that is *obvious*. I'm surprised that neither of you thought of it," Minerva said as she put her cup down.

Hunter thought about it for a second then a light went on his mind.

"A mate! She's looking for a mate. Someone with the right biological makeup to reproduce with," he said.

"That's right, Hunter. The succubus is in heat. She needs to mate but only a man with the right genetic matter can help her reproduce or it just won't work. If her chosen victim doesn't have *exactly* what she needs, it just won't work," Minerva said.

"What happens to the man *after* she mates?" asked Lorena.

Minerva grinned.

"That depends on how much she likes him. They either live happily ever after or she kills him," she said. "After she mates, she really has no need for him. She'll drain his body of what she needs and leave him for dead."

"And the offspring?" asked Lorena.

"Ninety-nine percent are born female and become succubae. The rest are males or incubi, who prey on women. Lucky for us they can only produce one offspring per mating," Minerva said.

"But she already killed two men. Does this mean she's mated?" asked DuCassal.

"I doubt that, Jean-Paul. She probably thought they were the right ones but as soon as they began having sex, she realized they weren't and simply killed them. Or they died of other causes while in the act. The last man was very lucky or he would have been the third," Minerva answered as she picked up a ginger cookie and bit into it.

"How did she get here? Was she summoned?" Hunter asked.

"In a manner of speaking. I think she was that second entity I detected when I activated the board. She came in when the Night Ranger did," Minerva explained.

Hunter shook his head.

"Those fools opened the gates to more trouble than they bargained for. Did anything *else* come through?" he asked.

"I don't believe so," Minerva said. "But I can't be 100 percent positive. Some things can escape detection."

"You mean they could have opened the floodgates between this world and others?" DuCassal asked.

"That's a very real possibility. The gate is shut now. Nothing else can come through it to plague us," Minerva said.

"Plague is the right word, Minerva," Hunter said as he picked up the tea and sipped.

"Mon dieu! It's not as if there aren't enough nightmares wandering around Louisiana!" DuCassal said.

"We have three different descriptions of the women who were last seen with each victim," Lorena said.

"Succubae can change their outward appearance at will in order to attract potential victims. They can read a man's surface thoughts and figure out what type of woman attracts him most. Then they can become that woman and the pheromones they emit make them irresistible," Minerva explained.

"So how do we find her before she chooses her next victim?" asked Hunter.

"You *don't* find a succubus. You have to stay alert and hope she makes a mistake and shows herself before she strikes," Minerva said.

Hunter sat back and shook his head.

"I can also read surface thoughts. Maybe I can try to read hers?" Lorena suggested.

"It's worth a try," Hunter agreed. "You'll have to open yourself to receive a lot of thoughts at the same time. It might be next to impossible to filter them all and find the right one."

"Do succubae have hearts that beat?" Lorena asked.

"They live, so they have hearts. It may not look like or beat like a human heart," Minerva said.

"Well, if her heartbeat is *very* different, I may be able to tune in on that instead. I think that would be much easier than scanning hundreds of different minds at once," Lorena said.

Hunter smiled.

Lorena often used a person's heartbeat as a way of tracking him down. She could hear it from over 100 yards away and follow it to the source. It was another benefit of being a vampire. Once she homed in on someone, she never lost him.

"We'll try it tonight while we're on our usual patrol," he said.

A few blocks away, Hannah Morii stumbled out of bed. Her head throbbed painfully and the light filtering through the curtains hurt her eyes. She reached for her sunglasses on the night stand and slipped them on as she went into the bathroom. She looked at herself in the mirror. Her reflection shocked her.

She looked very pale and light green circles had appeared under her eyes. She had been up all night, drinking Bloody Marys at the Dragon in an effort to control the hunger that wracked her body. Although the cocktails did contain some human blood, they weren't enough to make the hunger go away. She had only fed a few nights ago. Usually, that kept the hunger at bay for a week, sometimes longer.

Now, it had returned much sooner than expected—and with a vengeance.

She sighed as she brushed her teeth.

"There's no way around this. Tonight, I hunt!" she decided.

She went downstairs to the shop and saw the paper on the counter. She unfolded it. The headline immediately caught her attention.

There had been a bank robbery the evening before. Five masked people, armed with shotguns, swords and axes had walked into the Picayune Bank in Metairie and robbed the place just before it closed. But the robbery was just the tip of the iceberg. Before they left, they shot and killed all four of the male clerks, then took turns raping the terrified young female teller. One of the men, probably the leader, knocked her senseless with the butt of the shotgun and left her for dead in a pool of blood.

The teller survived.

In fact, some passersby saw the bank door open and looked inside. When they saw the bloodied bodies on the floor, they raced to Basin Street and told Valmonde. Since none of the gang wore masks, the teller was able to describe each of her attackers in detail when Valmonde interviewed her at the hospital at 10 pm.

Hannah smiled.

"Tonight I feast!" she said.

She dressed and hurried over to see Valmonde.

"There's six of them—and I don't want any of them alive," Valmonde assured her as he provided her with the sketches. "They don't deserve to live after what they did. I don't want to waste my time and the people's taxes on a trial or anythin' like that."

"I wasn't planning to bring any of them back alive, Chief," Hannah said with a grin. "But I *will* bring you their heads if you like."

"You can bring back any body part you want as long as you make them go away," Valmonde replied. "Can you handle all six by yourself?"

"No problem. I'll hunt down one or two each night until I find all of them. That way, I won't have to gorge myself. A girl's got to watch her figure, you know," she joked as she walked out.

Lem and Sam watched her go and shuddered.

"Sometimes, Hannah scares the bejesus outa me," Sam said as he sipped his coffee. "I'm sure glad she's on *our* side."

"Amen to that!" Lem agreed.

Hannah looked over the list Valmonde had given her. There were six names. To her surprise, one was a woman. From the description, she was only 16, somewhat chubby and had tattoos running from her left shoulder to her wrist. Her hair was dyed three different colors and she had multiple piercings in her ears.

"A typical thug's bitch," Hannah thought. "She'll be the easiest to find. Once I find her, I'll know where the rest of her gang hangs out."

The men ranged in age from 19 to 32 and liked to dress in black. All were tattooed exactly as the woman. Two of the men were also wanted for a rape-murder in Treme but the police lacked the manpower to launch an all-out search and they'd melted into the seedier areas of the city.

All of them were armed and considered dangerous. The APB warned officers to be prepared to use deadly force in any encounter with them. At the top of the page, the words "WANTED DEAD" appeared in large capitals.

Hannah laughed.

But the gang wasn't the only thing prowling the city. Another article in Time-Picayune reported that a young woman was assaulted by someone who may be a vampire. He surprised her in an alley at three a.m. and attempted to bite her in the neck. She managed to escape from his grasp and flee toward Basin Street. For some reason, her attacker didn't pursue her.

Hannah though that was odd.

Vampires never let their intended prey get away. Even if they manage to escape from their clutches, they *always* go after them.

"Might be a vampire wanna-be," she thought as she read the article. "I'll ask Tony if he knows anything."

Lorena had also read the same articles. Less than an hour after Hannah's visit, she stopped by the Basin Street station to speak with Valmonde.

"Miss Hannah stopped by less than an hour ago and picked up the same information," he said as he handed her the bulletin with the descriptions. "I'll tell you the same thing I told her. I don't want any of those bastards left alive."

"What's the reward?" asked Lorena.

"Two thousand for each gang member," Valmonde said as he poured himself a cup of hot coffee. "That's more than enough for you and Hannah to split."

Lorena nodded.

"I'll stop by her shop to see if she'd like to team up," she said.

"With the both of you goin' after them, that gang doesn't stand the chance of a snowflake in Hell," Valmonde said with a smile. "I suppose there's no need to wish you bon chance?"

"It's *them* who will need the luck," Lorena said with a smile.

When she stopped in the Emporium, Hannah greeted her with a warm hug. Lorena followed her to the back of the shop and sat down on the sofa while Hannah got them refreshments.

"It appears that we are about to go after the same gang," Lorena said as she showed her the wanted bulletin.

Hannah laughed.

"I kind of expected this. Want to team up?" she asked.

"Those are my thoughts exactly," Lorena said. "I was thinking of going after the woman tonight."

"Wow! We certainly *do* think alike! I thought I'd go after her, too. That way, I'll be able to learn where the rest of the gang hangs out by reading her surface thoughts. I'm starting to learn how to do that now. I'm not as good at it as you are, though. I have trouble filtering out the noise," Hannah said.

"It takes time to discipline yourself. Don't try to force it, Hannah. Let your abilities develop naturally so you can gradually learn to use and control them," Lorena said. "If you try to force it, you could go insane."

"I didn't know this. I'm very happy you warned me about it," Hannah said. "I still have so much to learn, don't I?"

Lorena nodded.

"Don't worry, Hannah. You have an *eternity* to master them," she assured her. "This gang is just what I need. I'm starting to feel *hungry*. It's been two weeks since my last feeding."

"I don't know how you can go so long between feedings, Lorena," Hannah said. "I don't have such discipline."

"Oh? How often do you feed now?" Lorena asked.

"At least once a week," Hannah replied. "Sometimes twice."

"That's quite often," Lorena observed. "I remember how hard you tried to resist the urge after I turned you. You said you couldn't imagine draining the blood from another human being."

"It doesn't bother me anymore," Hannah said.

"That is quite obvious," Lorena said. "Maybe you will learn to control it better as time passes?"

"Maybe. But I'm not even going to try," Hannah said with a smile. "A girl's got to eat after all."

Lorena laughed, but deep down, she was beginning to worry about her friend.

They knew from the APB that the woman was normally seen in the Treme area, so that's where they started. The sheet listed the address of her parents as 744 Marais. When Lorena and Hannah arrived, they saw that the house had been abandoned for several months.

"Let's go in," Lorena said.

"Why? It's empty," Hannah said.

"To pick up a trail," Lorena replied. "It's time for another lesson in how to be a vampire."

Hannah smiled, then laughed.

Lorena walked up to the front door and gave it a push. To their surprise it opened easily. Lorena looked back at Hannah.

"This place isn't empty. I detect a heart beating in the side parlor," she whispered.

"So do I," Hannah said. "It sounds like a young woman's heartbeat."

Lorena nodded.

They silently made their way across the worn carpet to the door on the right. Lorena listened and nodded.

"It's her all right. I can read her surface thoughts," she said.

"I guess she came here because it was empty and she thought no one would come here to look for her," Hannah said.

Lorena stepped back and kicked the door. It flew off its hinges and crashed onto the floor. The woman inside screamed, then reached for a pistol that was on a nearby table. Hannah got there first and snatched it up. Then she tossed it over her shoulder.

"Guns are of no use to you now," Hannah said.

"You're wanted for murder and bank robbery," Lorena said as she stepped toward her.

The girl pulled a knife and lunged. Lorena seized her wrist and gave it a violent twist. The sound her bone snapping echoed through the empty rooms along with the girl's scream of pain.

"What's it to you? Are you cops?" the girl asked defiantly.

"No. We're far worse than any cops you can imagine," Lorena said as she grabbed her by the throat and lifted her off the floor. "Far worse!"

Hannah watched as Lorena pinned the struggling woman against the wall and bared her fangs. The moment the woman saw them, she stopped. She realized who Lorena was now and knew there was no way to avoid what was coming. Lorena sunk her fangs into her neck and drank. The woman twitched several times, sighed deeply, and went limp. Lorena finished and let her lifeless body fall to the floor as she wiped the blood from her lips.

"The others are hiding in an old, boarded up house at the end of Hannabel in the Old Metairie area," she said.

"How did you learn that?" Hannah asked.

"I read her thoughts while I was feeding," Lorena replied. "You'll soon learn how to do that. It's quite easy, actually."

"The next one's mine," Hannah said as they left the apartment.

"Of course he is, Hannah. I have already dined," Lorena said with a smile.

DuCassal sat on the porch with Hunter and watched the sun set as they drank wine and discussed way to try and locate the succubus.

"Something Minerva said is still bothering me," Hunter said as DuCassal refilled his glass.

"And what is that, mon ami?" DuCassal asked.

"She said those men may have died from other causes while in the act. Maybe this thing didn't really murder them. Maybe I should ask the coroner to check for other causes of death?" Hunter said.

"It can't hurt," DuCassal agreed. "It's only six. Knowing Dr. Soamers, I'd say she is probably still at work."

"Let's get over there," Hunter said as he finished his wine.

DuCassal told George to ready the carriage. Ten minutes later, they were on their way to the morgue. They arrived just as Dr. Soamers was closing up for the night. When she saw them pull up, she topped and watched them climb out.

"Must be something important for you two to come here at this hour," she said. "What can I do for you?"

"When you examined those bodies, was there anything else unusual besides their lack of semen?" Hunter asked.

"Like what?" she asked.

"Like some other health problems that could have caused their deaths?" Hunter asked. "The lack of semen doesn't usually lead to sudden death. You know that as well as I do. So there must have been other medical complications."

"I'm already checking into that. I can tell you this, the Wilson case had lots of fluid in his lungs," she said. "That's a sign of congestive heart failure, which isn't very unusual even in a male his age. I've already listed that as the cause of his death. I haven't examined Dunjler yet."

"So Wilson *wasn't* murdered?" Hunter asked.

"Nope. He probably never knew he had a problem. Most of the symptoms mimic those of a bad chest cold," Soamers said. "Good, hard sex just made his heart work too hard. You might say he came and went at the same time."

DuCassal laughed.

Hunter smiled.

"Thanks, Julia. Let me know what you find out about the other man," he said.

They climbed back into the carriage. DuCassal looked up at George and told him to drop him and Hunter off on Decatur Street.

"So it appears that we are *not* looking for a murderess, eh, mon ami?" DuCassal said as they drove off.

"Not in Wilson's case anyway," Hunter said.

The house was somewhat difficult to find. It sat at the very end of a little used street that was overgrown with swamp grasses, twisted trees and abandoned, mostly ruined houses. Several of the houses had vanished long ago, leaving only concrete steps and platforms or open foundations behind. The others were half ruins with no roofs, doors or windows. The area had been abandoned over a century ago when Lake Ponchartrain overflowed its banks.

But the last remaining house still had a roof.

And doors.

And windows.

There was even a light shining from a first floor window.

"I sense five men inside," Hannah said. "They're all laughing. They seem to be very drunk, too. The one at the head of the table is the leader. He's a real heartless bastard."

"Let's save him for last. I want him to watch us kill his friends," Lorena said.

She went to the back door and peeked through the window. All six of the men were seated at a large, round table. They were playing cards and drinking beer. The room was also filled with smoke.

"This will be easier than I expected," Lorena said.

Hannah watched as she knocked hard on the door. The door slowly creaked open and a muscular man with several large, ugly tattoos peered out at them.

"What do you want?" he demanded.

Lorena shoved him aside and strode into the room. The man tried to grab her from behind but Hannah kicked him across the table. Cards, bottles and chips scattered everywhere. The gang members jumped to their feet and pulled out their weapons. The leader remained seated and watched as Lorena and Hannah walked in. Lorena glared at him. Her gaze made him feel more than a little uneasy.

"Come to join the party?" he asked.

"Yes—but not in a way you'll enjoy," Hannah said as she watched the man she kicked rise slowly to his feet with one hand on the small of his back.

"You men are wanted by the police for various nasty crimes. We've come to bring you in—*dead*," Lorena said.

"Is that so? Kill them, boys!" the leader ordered.

The first one tried to raise his gun to fire only to have it snatched from him—along with his hand—by Hannah. Before he could react, she grabbed him by the shoulders, pinned him against the wall and buried her fangs in his neck. While Hannah was feeding, Lorena had already taken down two more gang members. The first tried to stab her with an old sword. She sidestepped it, seized him by the scruff of his neck and hurled him face first into the fireplace. He struck so hard that he shattered several bricks which landed on him in a cloud of dust and mortar and soot. The second one she sized by the hair. She gave his head a violent twist and broke his neck, then hurled his lifeless body through the window.

Hannah finished draining her man and let him drop to the floor. The other man tried to run for the door, but she pounced on him and sunk her fangs in his throat. He lay twitching violently beneath her as she fed once again.

Lorena walked over to the now terrified leader. He tried to pull a pistol from his belt only to have it slapped out of his hand. The slap was so powerful, it shattered every bone in his hand. She smiled and bared her fangs.

"I know you! You're that vampire dame who runs with Hunter!" he said with a quivering voice as she seized him by the throat and pulled him to his feet.

"Look into my eyes, vermin, for they will be the last thing you ever see!" she hissed as she buried her fangs in his neck.

Two hours later, Lorena and Hannah strode up to the Basin Street station with a burlap sack. They dropped the sack on the front steps and went inside.

"You won't have to worry about that gang any more, Chief, Lorena said. "We killed all six of them. We left a bag outside with their heads in it."

"I don't suppose they gave you much trouble?" Valmonde asked as he went to the safe and pulled out 12 $1,000 notes.

"No more than usual, Leon," Hannah said with a grin.

Valmonde handed the money to Lorena. She counted out six notes and handed them to Hannah, who handed three back to Valmonde.

"Give that to Father Paul," she said.

Lorena smiled at her generosity and handed two of her notes to the Inspector. Valmonde nodded.

"I'll see that he gets this tomorrow morning, he said. "Thank you. You ladies have done the city of New Orleans a great service—as always. I've half a mind to appoint you both to the force."

"No thank you, Leon. I couldn't handle the cut in pay," Hannah joked.

"Neither could I," Lorena added.

"Well, you *do* handle a lot of cases for us," Valmonde said.

"We don't mind. We know you don't have enough manpower to patrol the entire city. Besides, it enables us to satisfy our hunger," Lorena said. "At least it helps make the streets of the city a bit safer."

"Ever since you folks have started helpin' us out, the crime rate in New Orleans has dropped by almost 40 percent," Valmonde pointed out. "Until you got here, I was nearly at my wit's end tryin' to keep things under control."

"We appreciate the compliments, Chief. I'll see you around," Lorena said as they left the station.

"Are you sated now?" she asked.

Hannah nodded.

"Two in one night is more than enough to hold me for a while. I noticed that you also fed twice," Hannah replied.

"That's because it has been a while since I last fed," Lorena said. "I don't do that very often. Or at least, I try *not* to."

Hannah laughed.

Scott Crump was 46 years old and athletically built. He kept his head clean shaven because his hair was falling out anyway and he sported a goatee. He had just finished another long workout at a nearby gym and decided to drop into a bar on his way for a cold beer or two. He chose the Rawhide on Burgundy because it was on his way home.

He ordered a beer and sat down at the bar to sip it. To his surprise, a very pretty girl with long black hair walked over and smiled.

"Is this seat taken?" she asked in a voice that made his heart melt.

"No," he said.

Pretty young women didn't usually sit next to him in half empty bars. At least not any more. She smiled at him.

"Can I buy you a drink?" he offered.

"Okay. How about a whiskey sour?" she said.

Scott ordered the drink for her and another beer.

"My name's Scott," he said.

"Mine's Penelope," she said as they shook hands.

"I haven't seen you around here before," Scott said.

"I'm new to New Orleans," Penelope replied. "I moved here from Crete two months ago. I don't really know anyone yet. Perhaps you could show me around?"

"I'd love to," Scott said. "Er, of all the guys in this bar, why'd you pick me?"

"I'm not sure. There's something special about you. So I decided to introduce myself and see what happens," she answered. "I'm usually not so forward."

"I like your accent," Scott said. "It's very attractive."

"Thank you," she said. "So, will you show me around?"

"I'm free tomorrow. Maybe we can start then?" Scott offered.

"That would be nice. Yes. Tomorrow is perfect for me," she agreed.

"Great. Where would you like to meet?" he asked as he ordered another round of drinks.

"At your place, of course," she said with a smile.

"What time?" he asked.

"Whatever time we decide to wake up," she said.

He laughed.

"I think this is gonna be the start of something really nice," he said. "Really nice."

"I think so, too," she agreed.

A few blocks away, Hunter and Lorena were walking through the crowd on Canal Street. When they crossed University Place, Lorena stopped and held her hand up.

"What is it?" asked Hunter.

"I hear something strange. Something that doesn't sound normal," she said.

"A heartbeat?" he asked.

"Perhaps. It's very slow. Almost too slow. I don't think it's human," she replied after a few seconds.

"An animal perhaps?" he asked.

She listened a bit longer, then shook her head.

"No. Animals' hearts beat faster than humans. Especially small animals. I'm hearing less than 20 beats per minute," she replied. "It's low, too. I almost didn't hear it."

"Do you think it's the succubus?" he asked.

"I don't know *what* it is, mon cher. I do know that it's *not* human," she said.

"Can you tell where it's coming from?" Hunter asked.

"Burgundy Street," she said.

"Let's go," he said. "Even if it's not the succubus, we have to check it out. It might be something dangerous."

Scott and Penelope left the bar arm in arm. Scott couldn't believe his luck. Penelope was, by far, the most beautiful woman he'd ever met and he was amazed that she was going home with him. Penelope hung on his every word as he talked, She seemed enchanted with him.

As they crossed the street, Hunter, DuCassal and Lorena just happened to be coming from the opposite direction.

The second she saw them approaching, she stopped. Scott wondered what in Hell was going and why Penelope seemed to get tensed up at the sight of Hunter and Lorena. As they stood in the middle of the street, Hunter and Lorena slowly circled them. Hunter looked at Lorena and nodded. She stepped closer and listened.

"It's her. That's the beat I've been hearing," she said.

"What is this all about?" asked Scott.

"Just stay calm and step away from the woman," Hunter instructed as he drew his pistol.

"Why? Is she dangerous or something?" Scott asked.

"She is the demon who has already killed two men and assaulted a third. If you don't wish to be her next victim, you had better step away from her," Lorena said.

"Demon? You're mistaken. She can't be a demon," Scott said as he stood his ground.

"She's a demon all right," Hunter said as he made eye contact with Penelope.

"Prove it!" Scott said.

"If you insist," Hunter said as he took out a vial of holy water and threw it at Penelope.

Before the water could make contact with her skin, Penelope's skin turned dark purple, her eyes blazed red and she sprouted wings and a tail. She hissed at Hunter, turned and flew away.

Scott gaped in disbelief, then fainted.

Hunter leaned down to revive him. After a minute or so, Scott was conscious and seated on the sidewalk.

"I guess she really *is* a demon!" he said. "Would she really have killed me?"

"Only if you aren't the one," Hunter said.

"One what?" asked Scott.

Hunter explained the entire situation to him. Scott whistled.

"Looks like I dodged a bullet tonight—thanks to you two," he said. "So *that's* a succubus. You know, even with those wings and all, she still looked sexy. If I'm the right one, it might not be so bad being mated with her."

"She's killed two men. That makes her a threat to humans. We have to find her and kill her before she kills anyone else," Hunter said as he helped Scott to his feet.

He watched as they walked in the direction Penelope had flown.

"Just my luck. I finally get hit on by a beautiful lady and she turns out to be a succubus!" he said as he returned to bar.

They searched the entire Quarter for the next two nights. Around two a.m. on the third night, Lorena again detected Penelope's strange heartbeat. They followed the sound to the Krazy Korner on Bourbon Street. Although Penelope had changed her outward appearance, Lorena easily located her in the crowd.

Penelope watched as they approached. She just sat at the table and calmly sipped her drink. Hunter walked over and sat down. She smiled at him.

"I knew you would find me if I waited long enough," she said.

"You wanted us to find you?" he asked.

"Yes. I want to know why you are hunting me like an animal. I have done nothing wrong that I am aware of," she said as Lorena and DuCassal sat down, too.

"You call murder nothing?" DuCassal asked.

Penelope wrinkled her nose at him.

"Murder?" she queried. She seemed genuinely surprised.

"Yes. There is the matter of two young men who were seen in your company on the nights they died," Hunter said as he drew his pistol.

Penelope stared at the weapon and blanched visibly.

"I killed no one!" she said. "They died because they were too weak inside. They weren't the ones I seek. I was going to take their energy and leave them. I didn't expect them to die."

"But they were drained of semen," DuCassal said.

"Doesn't that usually happen when one of your kind ejaculates? Doesn't that normally drain you of your sperm?" the succubus asked. "They emptied their seed into me and died. But I did not kill them purposely."

Hunter lowered the weapon.

"Is that why you slapped the third one?" he asked.

"Yes. I did not want him to fall dead like the others. I slapped him to keep him away from me," she said.

"In effect, you probably saved his life," Hunter said.

"That was my intent," she said. "I did not come to your world to kill. I came here to mate. I came to find the right one."

"So far, you've had very little luck," DuCassal observed. "Just what type of man are you searching for?"

"I cannot explain with words. I will know him when I meet him," she said. "When I find him, I will become his mate and bear his children for as long as he stays true to me. If he strays, I will leave and take our children with me. He will never see us again. That is our way."

"That doesn't sound so bad, eh, mes amis?" DuCassal said. "In many ways, it sounds like an ideal arrangement."

The succubus smiled.

"We are not the monsters you think we are," she said. "Our natural form frightens most humans and this is why we are believed to be evil. We need human mates to survive and when we find the right one, things work well for us both."

Hunter holstered the pistol. He pushed the brim of his hat up.

"I believe you," he said. "But why did you show your true form when we approached? You scared the Hell out of the man you were with."

"We always revert to form when we feel threatened. I didn't want to show my true form to him but I could not help it," she said.

"Was he the one?" Lorena asked.

"Yes. Everything felt perfect. Now that he's seen what I really look like, that chance is gone forever. I'll never find a mate!" she lamented.

"I'm sorry we ruined everything for you. We just didn't want you to kill anyone else," Hunter said.

"What will you do?" asked Lorena.

The succubus shrugged.

"I'll return to the bar. Maybe I'll see him again. I'd like to explain— if he'll listen," she said. "After that, I'll move on. I'll keep searching until find someone. It's all I can do."

Hunter nodded.

"What is your true name?" he asked.

"It really is Penelope," she said.

"It's a pretty name. It fits you well," DuCassal said.

She smiled.

Hunter stood and straightened out his hat. He smiled at Penelope.

"Good luck," he said as he left the bar.

"Thank you," she replied as her knees stopped shaking. "Thank you so much."

Lorena gave her a hug, then followed Hunter. DuCassal tipped his hat and kissed her hand.

"Bon chance," he said on the way out.

As they walked down the street, Hunter stopped and looked back at the bar. He sighed and put his arm around Lorena.

"I hope she finds who she's looking for—like I did," he said.

"That's what I love about you, mon cher. You have a very kind heart. Someone else would have pulled that trigger. You allowed her to live so she could find her mate. The Cardinal would be very surprised at this," Lorena said.

"Shocked is more like it," DuCassal said. "But I would have done the exact same thing After all, what is life without love?"

"Nothing!" both Hunter and Lorena said.

Two nights later, Scott Crump again stopped by the Rawhide for a cold brew on the way home. When he walked in, he spotted Penelope sitting alone at a table. He ordered a beer and a whiskey sour, then walked over to the table and sat down with her. He handed her the sour.

She stared at him.

He smiled.

"So you're a succubus," he said.

"That's what human call us. We really don't have a name for our kind," she said a little hesitantly.

"I'm glad you decided to come back," he said. "I wanted to see you again.

"I thought I frightened you out of your wits the other night," she said.

"You did, but I got over it," Scott said. "You still want me to show you around New Orleans?"

"Are you sure you want to?" she asked.

"Yes," he assured her.

"But you know what I am!" she said.

"And you know what I am. So what? None of that stuff matters anyway," Scott said.

"In that case, I'd be happy to let you show me around," she replied as they clinked glasses.

CHAPTER THREE:
Bewitched, Bothered, Bewildered and Dead

Nine p.m.

It was raining steadily and a mist was rolling through from the harbor. The rain and the mist cast ghostly halos around the street lamps along Esplanade and bathed the city is shades of gray and white shadows.

Near St. Louis Cemetery Number Three, Hunter, DuCassal and Lorena slowly searched for their prey: another rougarou was loose in New Orleans. This one was particularly nasty and had indiscriminately murdered a young mother and her two small children as they walked home from Louis Armstrong Park only four days earlier. The day after, he tore a local barfly to ribbons and ate his heart at St. Bernard and Broadway. Less than 30 minutes earlier, he had attempted to attack Lorena while she was separated from Hunter and DuCassal.

Only this time, the rougarou was surprised as Lorena stood her ground and slapped him clear across the street. He slammed into a brick wall, bounced off and landed on his feet. Then he howled and bounded away toward the cemetery. Lorena watched as he leaped over the wall and vanished into the shadows beyond.

Hunter and DuCassal raced over to her.

"He went into the cemetery," Lorena said with a nod. "I didn't see him come out."

"There are two gates," DuCassal said as he checked his shotgun. "I will take the one on other side."

Hunter nodded.

They waited until DuCassal ran down the street then calmly walked to the gate. It was unlocked. Hunter eased the rusted iron gate open. When it creaked loudly he winced.

"I'm sure he heard *that*. It was loud enough to wake the dead," he said.

"Let's hope not, mon cher," Lorena smiled as they entered and looked around.

St, Louis Number Three was one of the older and more poorly maintained cemeteries. Many of the old vaults had fallen to ruin. A few even had large trees sprouting from them and the grounds were unkempt and overgrown with weeds and wild plants. Very few of the original families that were buried here remained in New Orleans. Those who did preferred to have their family vaults in Lafayette Number One in the Garden District.

There were no lights in the cemetery.

As a lone owl hooted in the branches of a nearby tree, they made their way along the main path. As they walked, they watched the shadows for signs of movement. Lorena held up her hand.

"I can hear his heart beating," she whispered. "And I can smell him. He smells just like a wet dog, too."

"How close?" asked Hunter.

"About a hundred yards ahead and to the right," she said.

"Can you hear Jean-Paul?" he asked.

"Yes. He's approaching from the west at a good pace," Lorena replied. "He'll get there before us."

"If you can sense him, I know the rougarou can. We'd better hurry," Hunter said as they quickened their pace.

The rougarou *did* see DuCassal. In fact, he'd been watching his every move from the shadows of a collapsed vault.

"This one will be easy," he thought as he crouched and prepared to strike.

DuCassal also sensed the rougarou's presence. He peered into the shadows and smiled as he made eye contact.

"Here doggy, doggy. Nice doggy," he said as he readied the shotgun.

The rougarou snarled and leaped.

Hunter and Lorena heard the double blast from DuCassal's shotgun. The blast was followed by a high-pitched yelp/howl/snarl.

They rushed over and saw DuCassal picking his hat off the wet ground. He grinned as he placed it back on his head.

"I wounded him, mes amis," he said. "I shot him in the left shoulder."

"Where'd he go?" asked Hunter.

"Over that wall and out into the street," DuCassal said.

They scaled the wall and looked around. Lorena spotted a trail of blood on the street and pointed north.

"He's running up Esplanade toward the park," she said.

"Can you track him?" Hunter asked as they jumped into the street and raced after him.

"Yes. All I have to do is follow the scent of his blood trail," Lorena answered.

They chased after the rougarou for several blocks. They ran at a steady pace. There was no need to hurry anyway. The rougarou wouldn't be able to hide even in City Park. Once Lorena was on someone's trail, she never lost it. The rougarou was as good as dead.

Just before the rougarou entered the park, it turned west down Carrollton and darted between two buildings. It stopped and looked back. As it did, it sensed someone behind him and turned . . .

Hunter, Lorena and DuCassal heard the blood chilling scream several blocks away.

"The only thing that sounds like *that* is a dying rougarou!" DuCassal shouted as they ran toward the scream.

When they got there, they saw the mangled remains of the rougarou lying face-down in the middle of the street. Its throat had been torn out and its chest was ripped open. Blood and bits of flesh lay scattered everywhere.

Hunter watched as a figure in a wide brimmed hat, opera mask and long cape emerged from a door way. He was smoking a large cigar.

"Alejandro!" he said with a smile as he holstered his pistol.

"At your service, my friends. I hope I did not spoil your hunt, but this fellow crossed my path," the man said.

"Thanks for the assist," Hunter said as they shook hands. "It's been a while. Where have you been these past weeks?"

"I spent some time at my estate near Natchitoches. It needed some repairs. I have only returned to New Orleans this evening," Alejandro said. "I was just going to Pat O'Brien's for some drinks. Would you care to join me?"

"It would be a pleasure, my friend," Hunter replied.

Gideon Lamar Alexander was a wealthy and flamboyant man about town. Due to a series of lucky (or unlucky) incidents, he had become a hybrid of a werewolf and a vampire. When he was thirsty, he hunted down and killed rougarous, then drank their blood. Sometimes, he killed them for sport. He sometimes joined Hunter and the others in their adventures. He wore an opera mask to hide his scarred face—the result of a tragic fire when he was only 12 years old. The fire killed both his parents. He also liked to wear the mask because it gave him what he referred to as "a phantom of the opera effect."

"You did us a great favor tonight, Alejandro. The one you just killed was a bad one. We've been hunting him for the last three days," Hunter said as they headed back to the French Quarter.

"Lucky for him I wasn't thirsty tonight. I was kind of easy one him," Alejandro joked. "I didn't even bother to eat any of his flesh."

"I could tell from the condition of the body," DuCassal said with a laugh.

"Anyway, it is good to see you again, Alejandro," Lorena said. "We haven't seen you since our wedding."

"I left three days later. My estate needed some serious attention thanks to an errant bold of lightning. It's fine now and my caretaker, Louis, is back on the job. I'll have you come out one weekend for one of my grand balls," Alejandro said as they walked back to the French Quarter.

At one p.m. the next day, Hunter, Lorena and DuCassal met Valmonde and two of his men at 116 Elmira Street on Algiers Point. The house was a small, neatly kept Creole cottage with white clapboard siding and a dark, gray shingled roof.

"I thought you be interested in this, folks," Valmonde said as they walked up the street.

"What do you have, Leon?" Hunter asked.

"Young, Caucasian female, age 26. From the looks of her, this is right up your alley," Valmonde said as they walked inside.

Hunter wrinkled his nose at the obvious scent of decaying flesh while Lorena and DuCassal batted the flies away. Valmonde led them into the back bedroom.

"Here she is. This is just the way her next door neighbor found her a few hours ago," he said.

Hunter turned her head as he held his breath.

"There are no bite marks or sign of any blood—anywhere," he said. "She also appears to be dry, like there's not a drop of any type of bodily fluid left in her at all. No wonder you called us in."

"Like I said, this looks like it's right up your alley," Valmonde said.

"Looks like she's been dead for at least a day or two," DuCassal observed. "That lamp was knocked off the table and several other pieces of furniture are out of place. She didn't go without a struggle."

They looked around the room.

The windows were intact and there was no sign of forced entry on either door. Hunter looked at Valmonde.

The Inspector smiled.

"What's more interestin' is that both doors were locked from the *inside*. Her neighbor had to fetch the landlady to open it. That's when they found her. I asked them if they heard anythin' but both said they hadn't. This must have happened durin' the afternoon when both ladies were at work," he said.

"Who was she?" Hunter asked.

"Her name's Catherine Angel," Valmonde replied.

"From the looks of the candles on the altar and the pentagram on the floor, I'd say she was a witch of some kind," Hunter said.

"She was. She belongs to a small coven. I've already notified the leader of their group seein' as how the two of them were close friends," Valmonde said. "Do you think a vampire got her?"

"I'm not sure, Leon," Hunter said after some thought. "It doesn't look like your typical vampire kill. I'll reserve judgment until you get the coroner's report. We may be dealing with something *different* this time."

"The meat wagon should be here to pick her up in about an hour. I'll have the report for you in a couple of days," Valmonde said as they walked back outside. "There's always somethin' different in this city. Things are never what you expect them to be."

"That keeps things interesting," Hunter said.

"Too damned interestin' if you ask me!" Valmonde said.

Desdemona Ruiz was dark haired, brown eyed and attractive. She also had a hot temper and a reputation for being mean spirited and vindictive. When she received the news of Catherine's murder, she tried to keep it from the other members of her coven. But the story found its way into the evening edition of the Times-Picayune where other members of her coven read it.

At eight that evening, Heather Purdee, the second most senior witch in her group, came charging into Desdemona's house with the rolled up paper in her hands. When Desdemona let her in, Heather unrolled the paper and showed her the article.

"Have you seen this?" Heather said in a panicky voice.

Desdemona poured herself a glass of dark red wine and nodded.

"One of Inspector Valmonde's men came by here earlier this morning and told me she'd been killed. He said that Hunter was on the case," she said calmly.

"You don't seem very upset!" Heather almost shouted.

"Of course I'm upset, but Catherine's been murdered and there's nothing I can do about that. It makes no sense for me to panic," Desdemona replied as she sat down in her wicker chair.

"How can you be so fucking *casual?*" Heather demanded as she walked back and forth waving her arms in the air.

Desdemona sipped her wine and watched as Heather paced. She'd never seen her so agitated. After a few minutes, Heather stopped and sat down on the sofa. Desdemona handed her a glass of wine.

"Do you know what date this is?" Heather asked nervously.

"Um, March 10th. So?" Desdemona replied.

"Think, Desi! Think what happened on this very day *six years ago,*" Heather urged.

Desdemona let her thought drift back and stared.

"Oh my!" she said.

"Exactly! Marcus said he'd come back. He said he'd come back to kill us all. And he had the power to do it," Heather said with a quiver in her voice.

"Don't be ridiculous! Marcus is *dead.* We killed him. We even burned his body and scattered his ashes in Bayou St. John. No one, not even Marcus, can come back from *that,*" Desdemona reasoned.

"But what if he *can,* Desi? You know what he was capable of when he was alive. What if he had the power to do the same things from the grave? None of us are safe now. Just look what he did to Catherine!" Heather babbled.

Desdemona sneered.

"Don't be silly. Everyone knows she was killed by a vampire," she reminded her.

"*Was she?* How can you be so sure?" Heather asked.

"Of course it was a vampire. The police said she didn't have a drop of blood anywhere in her body," Desdemona said.

"Nor any other bodily fluids! When they found her, she looked as if she'd been mummified. What sort of vampire does *that?*" Heather asked.

"You worry too much. A vampire *did* kill Catherine and Hunter will find him and finish him off so he doesn't kill anyone else. And that's the truth!" Desdemona insisted. "Like I said, you worry too much."

"Maybe *you* should, too," Heather said.

Two a.m.

Amanda Lowry, age five, was awakened from her slumber by a light tapping on her window. When she rolled over and looked, she saw a small, blond haired girl smiling at her through the window pane. Amanda sat up and, curiosity getting the best of her, she went to the window.

The girl smiled.

Amanda smiled back.

"Who are you?" she asked.

"My name is Natalie. What's yours?" the girl replied.

"Amanda."

"I'm new here. I'm looking for someone to be friends with. Will you be my friend?" Natalie asked.

"Sure. I'll be your friend," Amanda smiled.

"Great! Now open the window and let me in so we can play. I promise to be quiet so we don't wake up your parents," Natalie said.

Eager to play with her new friend, Amanda opened the window and helped Natalie climb into her room.

When Amanda didn't come downstairs when her mother, Georgia, called her for breakfast the next morning, she went into her room and screamed her lungs out when she saw the pale, lifeless body of her daughter lying on the bed staring blankly up at the ceiling.

An hour later, Valmonde, Hunter and Lorena arrived. Lorena examined Amanda's body and nodded when she saw the twin bite marks on her neck.

"A vampire killed her," she said. "She's been completely drained of her blood."

"That means he *wanted* her dead," Hunter said.

Georgia wailed louder as her husband, Mark, tried to console her without much success. He looked at Hunter.

"I've never heard of a vampire killing a child before," he said.

"It's very rare but it happens. Usually, it's done for spite or for revenge. Do you have any enemies?" Hunter asked.

"None that I can think of. Hell, I don't even *know* any vampires!" Mark said as Georgia leaned into his chest and continued to sob.

Hunter paced.

"Then we can rule out a personal vendetta," he said. "But this leaves us with an even uglier possibility."

Lorena nodded.

"A vampire who prefers to feed on children," she said.

"That's unheard of! At least, I've never heard of it happenin' here," Valmonde said.

"I've known it to happen in Europe. I once tracked a vampire through Poland who fed on children because they were just the right size to satisfy his needs. But he was a *real monster*. He always raped them before he killed them because he felt that fear added a better flavor to their blood," Hunter said.

Valmonde visibly shuddered at the mental images.

Lorena looked at Amanda's expression.

"She wasn't the least bit terrified," she observed. "Whoever killed her didn't frighten her at all."

Hunter walked over.

"An adult vampire would terrify a small child. There's no sign of forced entry. So Amanda must have *invited* the vampire in," he said.

That's when he spotted the small, bloody handprint on the pillow next to Amanda's head. He examined each of her hands. He turned to the others.

"That's not *her* print," he said. "There's no blood on her hands at all. From the size of it, I'd say this was made by a very young child. Someone who's five or six years old."

Valmonde stared at him.

"You mean the vampire's a *kid*?" he asked.

"Or one who can take the form of a child," Hunter said. "Have you had any other reports of a child being murdered like this in New Orleans lately?"

"No. This is the first one," Valmonde said.

"Let's pray to God she's the last," Hunter said.

At Hunter's suggestion, Valmonde gave the news to the editor of the Times-Picayune. He released the gruesome details to the press in order to alert the people to keep their eyes on their small children and to report anyone who might be paying too much attention to their children to the police.

When Hannah read the article that afternoon, her blood almost boiled over. The Lowrys were friends of hers. Georgia often purchased items from the Emporium to decorate her home with and Mark was building a collection of samurai swords. They had even invited her to their wedding and to Amanda's christening.

The vampire had made this whole thing very *personal* to her.

"Whoever you are and wherever you are, your ass is *mine!*" she vowed.

When Hunter and Lorena stopped by the store to pick up their shipment of throwing darts, Hannah went into a prolonged rant about the Lowrys being friends of hers and how she would take that vampire down any way she could.

"I *want* this one, Hunter. I'm going to kill this bastard myself, even if I have to hunt him down forever," she said.

"I hope you find him before he kills another child," Hunter said.

"You think he's going after children exclusively? Why?" Hannah asked.

"Children are easy targets and they can't put up much of a fight," Hunter replied. "But there's a possibility that the vampire himself may also be a child."

"If that's the case, then who turned her and why?" Hannah asked. "Who would purposely turn a small child into a vampire?"

"Someone with an incredibly twisted and evil mind," Lorena said.

"Is there anyone out there *that* twisted?" Hannah asked.

"You'd be surprised," Hunter replied. "In this day and age, anything's possible. Just be ready for it. If it is a child, she may have been turned to exact a weird type of revenge against someone. He might even be the offspring of vampire parents who no longer walk the Earth and is forced to fend for himself."

Hannah shook her head.

"I don't care. Whoever it is, he's going down hard," she said.

The rest of the day and night passed uneventfully. Hunter, Lorena and DuCassal made their usual patrol of the city streets while Hannah prowled Old Metairie in a fruitless search for vampire who killed Amanda.

After a short nap and lunch at Brennan's, Hunter, Lorena and DuCassal stopped by Valmonde's office. He squinted at them from behind a mug of coffee. Hunter saw his expression and smiled.

"Long night, Chief?" he asked.

"Kinda. I've been here since six last evening. Me and my men have been chasin' down petty thieves and rowdy drunks for the last eight hours. I was hopin' you'd stop by. I have that report you wanted," Valmonde said as he handed the coroner's report to him. Hunter read and whistled.

"It says here that there wasn't a drop of any type of fluid in her at all. She was completely drained of everything. If this was done by a vampire, he's a very rare breed," he said as he passed it to Lorena.

"Is there such a vampire?" Valmonde asked.

"Maybe one in every thousand," Lorena replied as she placed the report on the desk. "The good thing is, they can go for months between feedings. If she was killed by one of them, it may be a long time before he strikes again."

"That makes him harder to locate. They usually blend in with the local population or move on after a kill. They rarely stay in one place. They like to feed and disappear like a shadow," Hunter added.

"Then I suppose we won't have to worry about another one like Catherine turnin' up," Valmonde said.

"But there *was* something about the report that bothers me, Chief," Hunter said.

"Like what?" asked Valmonde.

"There were no wounds anywhere on her body. Nothing at all to indicate she'd been fed upon," Hunter said.

"And *that* is highly unlikely," Lorena added.

"That means our killer is probably still in New Orleans," Hunter said.

"I'll put more men on patrol tonight and have them keep their eyes open," Valmonde said. "Just in case."

"I would," Hunter agreed. "You know where to find us if you need us. I have a hunch we haven't seen the last of this one."

Hunter was right.

At ten p.m., Hunter was summoned to the small Creole cottage at 305 Burgundy. When he, Lorena and DuCassal arrived, Valmonde greeted them at the front door. He looked exasperated.

"We got us another one. The same M.O., too," he said as he led them into the back bedroom.

Hunter knelt beside the body of the young, dark haired woman on the floor and shook his head.

"Who was she?" he asked.

"Her name is Belle Arlette Desmond," Valmonde said. "Her roommate found her an hour ago when she came home from a date."

"She's dry as wood," Hunter said. "No marks on her, either. It's the same killer alright. Where's her roommate?"

"She's in the bedroom up front. She's a nervous wreck, too. Want to question her?" Valmonde asked.

Hunter nodded.

When they entered the bedroom, the young red haired woman was gulping down a shot of bourbon. She stopped in mid gulp when she saw them.

"I know you. Everyone knows who you are," she said as she sat down on the bed.

"What's your name?" Hunter asked.

"Carlotta Tawney," the girl replied.

"I know you," DuCassal said. "You work in that sex club on Bourbon Street. I've seen your act many times. You're very erotic."

She half smiled.

"Thanks," she said. "Did a vampire kill Belle?"

"That's what we're trying to determine," Hunter said. "What can you tell us about her? What did she do for a living? Where did she like to hang out?"

"Belle waited tables at the Napoleon House four nights a week. The rest of the time, she was castings spells and such," Carlotta said.

"You mean she was a witch?" Lorena asked.

"Yes. I think she belonged to some sort of coven. I never asked her. We were roommates but we didn't talk much. Hell, I hardly ever saw her. I usually don't get home until daybreak. Belle's always gone by then or sound asleep."

"Why'd you come home early tonight?" Hunter asked.

"I forgot part of my costume. When I got here, the door was locked as usual. I opened it and noticed that Belle's light was still on. I went back to say hi and saw she was dead. So I screamed my head off. The next thing I knew, the cops were here. I guess someone heard me and fetched them," she replied.

She looked at the clock on the wall.

"Damn! I've got to get back to the club. I'm on in a half hour," she said as she jumped up and grabbed her bag.

"Are you sure you're up to it?" Lorena queried, somewhat surprised by her actions.

"Hey! A girl's gotta eat! See ya'll later!" she said as she hurried from the house.

Hunter and DuCassal laughed. Lorena squinted at them. That made them laugh even harder.

"This is New Orleans, Lorena," DuCassal said. "People here stop for nothing, not even death."

"Still, she seems a bit heartless," Lorena said as they left the cottage.

"Not really. She told us that she and Belle weren't actually friends. I guess once they take the body away, she will have to find another roommate," DuCassal said.

"I'll have the meat wagon boys come and fetch her. What's next?" Valmonde asked.

"Tomorrow morning we're going over to the temple. Maybe Minerva can tell us something about this coven she belonged to," Hunter said.

Nine a.m.

Heather raced over to Desdemona's house to show her the morning paper. When she read the headline, she blanched visibly.

"That's the second member of our coven killed in two nights," she said.

"I think we'd best tell Inspector Valmonde what we know about this before we all end up dead," Heather suggested.

"We *can't* go to the police. Valmonde will throw us in prison for murder. We need to try and handle this ourselves—like we did before," Desdemona said as she folded the paper.

"Just how on Earth are we going to do *that*? If it *is* Marcus, none of us has the power to go up against him. It took all seven of us to kill him in the first place. Even then, we had to take him by surprise. Oh, how I wish I hadn't let you talk me into being part of that night!" Heather moaned as she wrung her hands.

Desdemona glared at her.

"But you *did* take part in it. You're as guilty as the rest of us," she said bluntly.

"Well, you're the leader of our group. I suggest you come up with a way to put an end to this before we all end up dead!" Heather snarled.

At that very moment, Hunter, Lorena and DuCassal were seated in the front parlor of the voodoo temple, snacking on spice cakes and sipping herbal tea. Minerva was her usual two steps ahead of them. She listened as Hunter told her about the victims.

"From what I've seen and been told, I'd guess that both women were into witchcraft or voodoo of some sort," he concluded.

Minerva stirred her tea and looked at the leaves swirling around in the dark liquid. After a minute elapsed, she looked at them.

"Both of the victims *were* local witches," she said.

"Witches?" Hunter asked.

"Yes. They belong to a coven somewhere out in Lakeview. If memory serves me, it was formed ten years ago by a warlock named Marcus Owenby and his daughter Melinda Mac. I knew them. They always attended our festivals on St. John's Eve. He was what we call a "gray witch", she said.

"That means he practiced both white and black magic?" Lorena asked.

Minerva nodded.

"Mostly white. Marcus was a rather benign person but he was very vindictive when crossed," she said.

"Where is Marcus?" Hunter asked.

"No one knows. He disappeared about six years ago. After that, Melinda was killed in an accident. At least that's what the police called it," Minerva said.

"You seem to have your doubts," Hunter observed.

"How does one get run over by her own carriage?" Minerva asked. "Valmonde said she reeked of rum, but I know for a fact that Melinda never touched alcohol. Neither did her father."

"What about Marcus' wife or other family members?" Hunter asked.

"His wife, Mary, died giving birth to their second child. A girl they named Hermione. She was such a frail little thing. She was always sick. I felt sorry for her, too. She was really nice when you got to know her."

"Does the coven still exist?" asked DuCassal.

Minerva nodded.

"Who leads it now?" asked Hunter.

"A witch named Desdemona Ruiz. She took over right after Melinda died. After that, the coven was down to nine members. I don't think any sort of vampire is stalking those women. I think it's something much worse. Something you might not be able to handle," Minerva said.

"Why are they being singled out?" asked Lorena.

Minerva smiled.

"I feel these are *revenge* killings. Someone very powerful is going after the members of the coven and I've got a sick feeling inside as to who it might be," she said. "A very sick feeling."

"Who'd want to kill them?" Hunter asked.

"They have a lot of enemies. Since Desdemona took over, they have become a very bad lot. They've gone completely over to the dark side. The other covens shun them and I've banned them from the festivals. Desdemona is an evil, vengeful bitch—even on her best days," Minerva replied.

"But you don't believe that another witch or coven is behind the murders, do you?" Hunter asked.

She shook her head.

"Nobody has that kind of power. Nobody that is, but one," she said.

"Marcus?" Hunter guessed.

"Yes. I've always believed that Desdemona somehow murdered Marcus and Melinda so she could get control of the coven. She also believed that she would inherit Marcus' powers once he and Melinda were out of the way. Unfortunately, that didn't happen. I think Marcus took his powers with him—and they were *considerable*," Minerva replied.

"So you think Marcus is behind the murders? Was he *that* powerful?" Lorena asked.

"Who can say? This is New Orleans. Anything is possible here," Minerva said with a grin.

"How many are in this coven?" Hunter asked.

"The last time I bothered to keep track of them, there were nine," Minerva said. "A normal coven has 13 but this one has a few vacancies."

"It looks like they're about to have a few more," Hunter said.

Midnight. Phoebe Bourgh, a young, thin woman with long black hair who was so much into the witch mode that she even painted her fingernails jet black, wore lots of black eye shadow and black lipstick and had various mystic symbols tattooed on her body, was awakened from her uneasy slumber by the unmistakable sounds of someone with heavy boots walking down the hall.

She sat up and listened.

The heavy steps stopped outside her bedroom door. Scared, Phoebe reached into her nightstand and took out the long ceremonial dagger she'd used in countless rituals with the coven. She took a deep breath and waited.

A mist filtered into her room from beneath the door. She watched as it slowly took the form of a tall, broad shouldered man with large red eyes and a clean shaven head. She dropped the dagger and stared in terror as the man strode toward her with a decidedly evil gleam in his eyes and his lips twisted into a deadly smile.

"It can't be! You're dead! I helped kill you!" she gasped as he stopped at the side of her bed.

She was petrified with terror. The man's gaze fixed her to spot. She was completely immobilized by his eyes. He reached down and wrapped his long, thick fingers around her throat.

"You may have killed me, my dear, but I am *not* dead. Not in the sense that you think of death. I told you I'd come back . . ." he said.

Two of Valmonde's patrolmen found her dried, pale corpse lying face-up on the steps of Our Lady of Guadalupe church an hour later. Thirty minutes later, Valmonde, Hunter, Lorena and DuCassal arrived in a carriage to examine her remains.

She had a note pinned to her chest.

"Here lies the remains of one Phoebe Elizabeth Bourgh, murderess."

"A revenge killin'?" asked Valmonde.

"So it appears," Hunter said. "This one even looks like a witch. Any connection to the first one?"

"I'd have to check on that to make sure," Valmonde said. "I'm almost certain they knew each other."

"She seems to be as dry as the first girl," Lorena observed. "There is no doubt that she was killed by the same person."

"You're tellin' me that we may have a serial killer roamin' around New Orleans? We already have enough of them. We don't need another one," Valmonde said.

"I think the body count will depend on how many people he's out to kill, Chief," Hunter said. "Why did he call her a murderess? What do we know about her?"

"I'll dig through our files and get back to you if I find anythin'," Valmonde said.

While they were examining Phoebe, Lem and Sam came running up. Valmonde asked what was up.

"We found another young lady, or rather her corpse, on the steps of St. Louis Cathedral," Lem reported.

When they arrived, they found another dark haired young woman, dressed in a nightgown lying on her back. She also had a note pinned to her chest. Valmonde pulled it off and gave it to Hunter.

"Here lies Lisa Ann Riccio, murderess."

"Another witch?" Hunter asked.

"Could be. I do know she liked to hang out with Phoebe in the vampire clubs. You may have seen them there a couple of times," Valmonde said as he watched Lorena go over the body.

Lorena looked up.

"She's exactly like the others, Leon," she said. "No fluids left in her at all and no marks on her body. I will say one thing for the killer—he's efficient."

"That makes three in two nights. Whoever it is, is moving quickly," DuCassal said. "He's a man on a mission."

"We have to find out who he is, what sort of mission he's on and stop him before he completes it," Hunter said as they walked down to Bourbon Street. "Make sure this gets into the paper, Chief. The news may force one of his potential victims to come forward and ask for protection. If that happens, we may find the answers to out questions."

"I'll make sure it gets into the early edition," Valmonde promised.

When Heather saw the headlines, she went into a panic. She immediately rushed over to Desdemona's house and begged her to do something.

"It's Marcus! I know it's him! He's come back and he'll kill us all if we don't stop him!" she almost screamed.

Desdemona watched her pace and rant for a few minutes, then stood up, grabbed her by the shoulder and spun her around. Before Heather could react, Desdemona backhanded her across the face as hard as she could and shoved her down on a chair.

"Get control of yourself, Heather! No one can come back after being cremated. Not even Marcus!" she said.

"Then how do account for that the killer is only going after the members of the coven? These are no random killings, Desi! That guy's out to get us!" Heather said as she wiped the blood from her lip.

"Let Hunter and the police handle this. Just keep your mouth shut and don't panic," Desdemona warned.

But deep inside, she feared that Heather was right. Marcus had vowed to come back and finish them. He said it might take time, but he had all the time in the world. Sooner or later, he said, he'd kill them all.

She'd killed him for several reasons. Mostly she did it to steal his powers. But that didn't work out quite like she'd hoped it would. Even after two more murders, she still didn't get what she wanted. Marcus had taken his powers to the grave with him. What's more, her *own* powers had become limited.

Perhaps it was some sort of divine punishment?

And if Marcus had returned to carry out his threat, would even Hunter be able to stop him?

Things were already spiraling out of control.

At one a.m., Valmonde sent Lem to find Hunter and bring him to a small brick house at the corner of St. Claude and Columbus in the lower part of Treme. Valmonde was standing on the front porch waiting for them. He scowled when they got out of DuCassal carriage.

"I got two more for you. Sisters," he said.

They followed him into the kitchen where two young women lay with the limbs akimbo, staring blankly up at the ceiling fan that rotated noisily above them.

"The one on the left is Irene Grohl. That's her sister Luanne on the right," Valmonde said. "One of the neighbors heard them screamin' and went to find one of my officers. He came and got me. Looks like the same guy did this."

"They're drained alright, Leon," Lorena said after she examined them.

"They're known witches—just like those other girls," Valmonde said.

"Minerva said there were only nine witches in the coven," DuCassal said.

Hunter looked at the dried corpses and shook his head.

"And then there were three," he said as they walked out of the house.

"Somebody really has it in for that coven. Can't say I blame them. They're a real nasty lot," Valmonde said. "Any idea who it might be?"

"Marcus Owenby," Hunter replied. "At least, that's who Minerva thinks it is."

"I know that name. He up and disappeared about six years ago. He had a daughter but she died in a really weird accident a week later and another one that went missin' a few days after that," Valmonde recalled.

"That was *no* accident, Chief," Hunter said. "And Marcus didn't just disappear. Desdemona and her group *made* him disappear. I'd be willing to bet they also did the same to Hermione."

"You mean they killed him? But we never turned up a body or anythin'," Valmonde said.

"You wouldn't if he was *cremated*," Hunter said. "My guess is they burned him and threw his ashes in one of the bayous."

"That makes sense. What about Melinda?" Valmonde asked.

"I'd exhume the body and do an autopsy if I were you," Hunter suggested.

"I'll do that right away. With any luck, there might still be enough left of her to do an autopsy on," Valmonde said. "If you're right about her bein' murdered, I'll arrest Desdemona and her bunch so fast their heads will spin!"

"Now what, mon ami?" asked DuCassal.

"We pay Desdemona a visit. After this, she might be open to a little chat," Hunter said as they climbed into the carriage.

"She'll talk—if she wants our help. If not, ces't la vie!" Lorena added.

An hour later, they arrived at the white columned home on St. Charles Avenue. When Hunter stepped onto the porch and rang the bell, a female voice called out from inside.

"It's open."

They walked in saw Desdemona sitting in a tall backed chair sipping wine from an ornate goblet.

"Are you Desdemona Ruiz?" Hunter asked.

"I am," the woman replied.

"My name is Hunter," he said.

"I know who you are, Mr. Hunter. Everyone in New Orleans does," Desdemona said with an air of haughtiness.

Her attitude visibly irritated Hunter and caused Lorena to sneer at her.

"In that case, you know why we've come here," Hunter continued.

"I can guess. Something has targeted our coven and you've come to save what's left of us from the same fate. Is that correct?" Desdemona replied.

"Something like that," Hunter said.

"A few days ago, I'd have laughed at your offer. Now, I'm not so sure that we don't need your help. I have no idea who or what's behind this or why we've become a target for extermination," Desdemona said.

Lorena made eye contact and smiled.

"You're lying," she stated. "You *do* know who is behind this and why your members are being killed. You also know that you can't deal with this alone."

Desdemona stared at her.

"Vampires are living lie detectors," Lorena said smugly.

"What are you hiding?" Hunter asked.

"Nothing at all! I swear it!" Desdemona replied.

"I don't like being lied to," Hunter said. "You either tell us what we need to know or you're on your own. Do you know who's doing this?"

"I—I have an idea. But I can't be certain," Desdemona answered meekly.

"Is it Marcus Owenby?" Hunter pressed.

Desdemona stared at him.

"How did you know?" she asked.

He stepped close and pushed her down on a chair. Then he leaned over and looked into her eyes. She was now visibly rattled. It was just the way her wanted her.

"I know more than you can ever imagine," he said softly. "Tell me about Marcus."

"Marcus Owenby started our coven about 10 years ago. He recruited me and I helped him recruit the other members. At first, there were 13 members. There was Marcus, his two daughters, myself and nine other women. He was our mentor. Our spiritual guide and our lord and master. I learned everything I know from Marcus," she began.

"You said there were 13 members, counting Marcus and his daughters. How many are left now?" Hunter asked.

"Three. There's myself, Heather and Winona," she replied.

"That makes only 12. What happened to the other one?" Hunter asked.

"Her name was Carrie Ann Langley. She died from some sort of fever just before Marcus disappeared. We buried her in her family vault in St. Louis Number Two. Poor thing. She was our youngest member. A beginner. She had some much potential, too," Desdemona said almost sadly.

Lorena squinted at her.

"You were *lovers*," she said.

Desdemona nodded.

"All of us coven members were lovers. We had sex with each other and with Marcus and his daughters. It was part of our rituals. Witchcraft is highly erotic and sensual. Sexual energy powers our spells," she explained.

"You were jealous of Marcus and Carrie Ann so you cast a spell on her," Lorena said.

"Damn you! Stay out of my head!" Desdemona shouted in frustration.

"That would be impossible. You're broadcasting your thoughts loud and clear. I'm not even *attempting* to read them," Lorena said smugly.

Hunter stood up and smirked at her.

"So, it was *your* spell that killed her?" he asked.

"That was an accident. I didn't want to harm her. I just wanted her to feel too sick for Marcus to bother with for a while. I don't know how it went so wrong!" Desdemona said. "It was all Marcus' fault! Had he left her alone, she'd still be with me now."

"Is that why you killed him?" Hunter asked.

Desdemona clammed up. Hunter sat down in front of her.

"Despite my better judgment, I've decided to try and help you. But when this is over, I'm going to turn you and what's left of your murderous little band over to Inspector Valmonde and let him decide what to do with you—although I think letting Marcus finish you all off might be much more pleasant than rotting away in Angola for the rest of your lives," he said.

"Either way, you're all dead," DuCassal added.

Desdemona sighed.

Angola was the oldest, harshest prison in the entire territory. Over 90 percent of the people sent there ended up in its ever-growing graveyard. She knew that women rarely survived longer than three years at Angola. Now, she had to decide between a quick death at the hands of Marcus or a slow one at Angola.

She chose Angola. Besides, she thought she could always leave New Orleans before this was over—once she was certain that Hunter had eliminated Marcus. She didn't give a damn about anyone else in the coven.

"I'll cooperate," she said. "What do you need to know?"

"Has there been any sort of pattern or order in the way he's killing you?" Hunter asked.

"He's started with the newer members and seems to be working his way up," Desdemona said.

"He's killing by seniority in the coven?" Lorena asked.

Desdemona nodded.

"That means he's saving you for last. Who is the most senior between Heather and Winona?" Hunter asked.

"Heather," Desdemona said.

"That means Winona is tonight's intended victim," DuCassal said.

"We'll cover her tonight and try to run interference before he can strike," Hunter said. "Where does Winona live?"

"She lives 928 Royal on the top floor," Desdemona answered. "She works three blocks down at a curio shop. She gets off at nine each night."

"Thanks. Let's get going," Hunter said.

She watched them turn and leave. Her knees were still shaking.

They pulled up in front of 928 Royal just in time to see a young, blond haired woman hurtle through an upper window and crash onto the street amid a hail of splintered wood and broken glass. The noise caused several people to leave the bars and restaurants to see what happened.

Lorena leaped from the carriage and rushed over. She turned the girl onto her back and examined her carefully. Hunter and DuCassal walked over as she shook her head.

"She's like the others," Lorena said. "She was already dead before she was thrown through the window."

"Why did he toss her through the window?" DuCassal asked.

"Spite. Maybe he had a special hatred for her," Hunter guessed as he looked around. "There's no sign of Marcus anywhere that I can see."

Sam and another officer came running up the street. They slowed when they saw Hunter.

"Hello, Sam," Hunter greeted. "Looks like we're all a little too late again."

"I'll tell Leon to send the meat wagon over," Sam said as the crowd dispersed.

"And then there were two," Lorena said.

"Heather lives ten blocks from here. We'll never reach her in time," Hunter said as they climbed back into the carriage.

"I asked Hannah to stand guard at Heather's place. If he goes after her, she may be able to stop him," Lorena said.

"Or end up like the others," DuCassal said as he gave the address to his driver, George.

When they arrived at the modest, blue painted cottage on Dauphine, they saw Hannah seated on the front steps with her arms wrapped around her body. She was visibly shivering. She looked up at them as they climbed out of the carriage.

"What happened?" Hunter asked.

"I don't know. This dark shadow suddenly rushed through me. I couldn't move. I couldn't even speak. And I felt so terribly cold. Colder than I've ever felt in my entire life. I was frightened, too. You might say I was frozen with fear," she replied in a shivery voice.

"Heather!" Hunter exclaimed as they charged into the house.

They found her lying on the living room floor with her arms spread out. She was staring blankly up at the ceiling.

"We're too late, mon cher," Lorena said.

"And then there was one," DuCassal said as they headed back to the carriage.

Hunter stopped to check on Hannah. She smiled at him and nodded.

"I'm alright—now," she assured him.

"We're going back to Desdemona's place. Tell Valmonde what happened here," Hunter said.

She watched them drive off. It was several more minutes before she was able to stand and walk.

Unable to sleep, Desdemona paced the floor of her living room while downing glass after glass of wine. She was so preoccupied that she failed to notice the wisp of odd smoke that drifted out of the fireplace.

"Why worry yourself, bitch? It'll all be over for you in a few seconds," said a deep voice behind her.

She stopped in her tracks. She felt the blood run cold in her veins and began to quake at the knees.

"You didn't look this frightened on the night you murdered me," the dark figure said.

"Marcus?" she gulped without daring to look.

"In the flesh. Well, *almost* anyway," he said.

Desdemona turned slowly and stared at him in disbelief.

"I thought I killed you," she said nervously as she sidled toward the door.

He waved his hand and the door moved. Desdemona turned only to run into a solid wall. She frantically looked for the door and realized it was some ten feet away. She turned and leaned against the wall.

"Leaving so soon? Is that anyway to greet an old friend?" he said as he stepped closer.

"I *know* you're dead!" she said.

"I was—but I got better," he replied smugly as he took a step toward her.

"You *can't* be alive. My spells *never* fail!" she insisted, unwilling to believe the reality of her own senses.

"I didn't say I was alive, my dear. But your spell *did* fail. Not only didn't I stay dead, but I have returned to show you the error of your ways," he said. "I didn't cross the river. *But you will!*"

Just then the door crashed open. Hunter, Lorena and DuCassal rushed in. The warlock turned and smiled as they raised their pistols. Lorena raised her hand to stop them.

"Don't. If you shoot, your bullets will pass through him and hit the woman. In effect, you will do what he came to do," she said.

"She's quite correct. Earthly weapons are of no use against me," Marcus said.

They lowered their weapons and looked their quarry in the eyes. The warlock grinned.

"You can't stop me, Hunter. No one can. No one, not even god, can save this bitch. I've returned from the grave to exact vengeance. She must pay for her crimes," he said.

Hunter looked at Desdemona.

"What does he mean?" he demanded.

Desdemona remained silent and looked at the floor. The warlock laughed.

"Six years ago, this power hungry wretch convinced the other members of our coven that *she* should be in control. In order to get that control, she had to somehow wrest it from me. She knew that she didn't have the power to take me on face-to-face, so they combined their powers and ended my life while I slept," the warlock explained. "Then they chopped me into bits and burned them. Before I died, I warned them I'd be back to make them pay."

Hunter looked at Desdemona.

"Is that true? Did you kill him?" he demanded.

"Yes. The only way I could take control of the coven was to kill him. I never expected him to come back," she answered. "Damn you! Why didn't you stay dead?"

The warlock laughed.

"I *told* you she was a murderess—and a very cold hearted one at that!" he said. He turned to Desdemona and seized her by the throat. "For six years, your crime went undetected and unpunished. The others are dead. Now, you must join them."

She looked at Hunter. He stepped back and holstered his pistol DuCassal did likewise. As they turned to leave, she struggled and shouted after them.

"Aren't you going to help me?"

"No. You committed the crime. Now pay the price," Hunter replied as he left the room without looking back.

"Revenge is a dish best served cold," Marcus said with a cat-like grin.

Lorena grinned and followed him. DuCassal tipped his hat and also left. Desdemona cried out and begged them to help her. Her cries fell on deaf ears as they left the house and walked back to the carriage. Just as they climbed in, Desdemona's final, blood curdling scream echoed through the trees as the house became pitch black.

"It's over, mon cher," Lorena observed.

"Payback is a bitch," DuCassal said with a laugh. "A very nasty bitch."

"Justice comes in many shapes, sizes and flavors. It came to Desdemona but not in the way she expected," Hunter said as they rode away.

Inside the mansion, the desiccated husk that was once Desdemona lay beside a pile of dull gray ashes as the warlock completed his work and finally crossed the river.

The next morning, Hunter explained it all to Valmonde. The Inspector sipped his coffee and nodded.

"Things always seem to balance out in the end, don't they?" he said. "They almost got away with three murders but they underestimated old Marcus."

"Now that Marcus accomplished what he set out to do, I hope he and his family can rest in peace," Hunter said.

"So do I. I have enough on my plate without havin' to worry about some dead warlock runnin' loose. I did some diggin' on that bunch and was able to link a couple of other mysterious disappearances to them. It seems a couple of their close friends just vanished into thin air. I have no idea what happened to any of them," Valmonde said.

"They're probably buried somewhere on the grounds of the mansion—along with anyone else who got too close to their secret or was sacrificed in one of their sick ceremonies," Hunter said. "Maybe you should send some men over to poke around?"

"Maybe I'll do that," Valmonde said. "One of the missin' was that warlock's youngest daughter, Hermione."

"Desdemona and her gang wouldn't have left her alive. They had to get rid of her before her father's powers transferred to her and she'd become strong enough to challenge them for the lead spot. When Desdemona killed Hermoine, she'd hoped her powers would transfer to her. When they didn't, she must have felt furious but there was nothing she could do about it," Hunter said. "Marcus took his powers to the grave with him. When he became strong enough, he returned to get his revenge."

"Be careful what you wish for, eh, mon ami?" DuCassal said.

"Exactly. Desdemona not only *didn't* get the power she craved—she lost what little she had. So did everyone involved in the murder. Marcus somehow managed to siphon their powers into himself over the years so he could return as he promised. You see what happened after that!" Lorena said.

"So it was all for nothin'?" Valmonde asked.

"Not really. They all got exactly what they *deserved,*" Hunter said.

"Did they *ever!*" Valmonde agreed. "I'll make sure that Marcus' remains are placed in his family vault with those of his wife. It's what he would have wanted."

Hunter nodded.

"That mansion that Desdemona lived in belongs to Marcus. I'll see if I can turn up any family members to sign it over to while I'm at it," Valmonde added. "If there aren't any, we'll have to auction it off."

"Good luck with that, Leon," Hunter said. 'It's a fine old home. I'm sure you won't have any trouble finding bidders."

"Hell, I might just purchase it myself. The missus and I have been wantin' to move out of that shack of ours for years anyway," Valmonde said.

"I think the house would suit you both very well," Lorena said. "But what if it's haunted?"

Valmonde laughed.

"Name me one single house in this city that ain't!" he said. "In this town, that's a sellin' point."

CHAPTER FOUR:
Bits and Pieces

Sunday morning, two a.m.

Hunter was having one of his restless nights. After a short, fitful sleep or attempt at getting some, he got up and dressed for his nightly patrol. Lorena was out hunting in the Lakeview area, so he was alone.

He left the Garden District and walked across Canal and into the French Quarter. It was a quiet, drizzly sort of night. He passed a few tourists along the way and greeted them like usual. It seemed that even out of towners knew who he was now. It was the kind of fame Slayers always avoided. Here in New Orleans, avoiding it was nearly impossible thanks to the coverage of their exploits by the Times-Picayune.

Hunter wondered what the Cardinal thought of this as he smiled to himself. The old man probably didn't like it. After all, Slayers were supposed to operate in anonymity for the most part. He, Lorena and DuCassal had become local celebrities.

He made his usual walk up St. Ann. Less than a minute later, the expected eerie fog rolled down the street and obscured everything but the dull glow of the street lamps.

Hunter smiled as a familiar form stepped out of the fog.

"Good evening, Marie," he greeted.

She beamed back at him.

"God evening, Hunter. It's good to see you again as always," she returned. "You don't dream anymore, do you?"

"Not much," he said as they walked together.

Madame Laveau had been the most powerful, respected and revered voodoo queen in the history of New Orleans while she lived during the First Age. She still walked the streets of the city on foggy nights and people from all walks of life still placed offerings at her vault in St. Louis Number One and asked her for favors. Her history with Hunter was a little more personal. And intimate.

"Strange and terrible things are stalking the city each night. You need to be more careful this time. Things are not what you think," she warned in her usual style.

"You mean the murder in Metairie?" he asked.

"Yes—and something else. Something that has the potential to be even more dangerous. And this time, it's someone you know very well— but not well enough," she said.

"Tell me more," he urged.

"Right now, she's a force for good but her hunger is great. Each time she feeds, her powers grow and so does her hunger along with it. This one bears watching, Hunter. *Close* watching," Marie said.

"Hannah?" he asked.

Marie smiled and nodded.

"She cannot control her hunger. Right now, it controls her. Lorena feared this might happen when she turned her," she said.

"Right now, she doesn't pose a threat to anyone but other vampires and the usual criminal vermin," Hunter said.

"That could change—*if* she runs out of her usual prey," Maria said.

Hunter laughed.

"That isn't likely here in New Orleans," he said. "There are more than enough vermin for Hannah and Lorena to feed off of for the next 200 years. But I *have* been watching her to play it safe. So have Lorena and Jean-Paul. I don't want to get to the point where I might have to take her down."

"Right now, Hannah Morii is the *least* of your problems. There are much worse things haunting the shadows and dark paces of this city right now. Be careful," Marie warned again as she slowly melted back into the fog.

Hunter smiled and continued his walk.

As he crossed over onto Bourbon Street, he bumped into Alejandro who had just stepped out of Johnny White's Pub and Grill. He had two very beautiful young ladies with him and all three were more than a little intoxicated. Alejandro was dressed in his usual flamboyant cape and opera mask. He greeted Hunter with a warm hug and a pat on the back.

The two women instantly recognized Hunter and giggled when Alejandro made the introductions. The redhead's name was Barbara. The dark haired woman he identified as Rose Marie.

"You didn't tell us you were friends with Hunter," Barbara said as she shook hands with Hunter. "I've heard all about you, even back in Natchitoches."

"Hunter and I are very good friends. We have even worked together on occasion. Haven't we, Charles?" Alejandro boasted.

"Yes, we have. I don't think we could have defeated the Baron without your help," Hunter said with a grin. "I see you've been out celebrating."

"As always. Would you care to join us? We're headed over to the casino to try our luck," Alejandro offered.

"Judging by these two lovely ladies you're with, I'd say you've already been very lucky tonight," Hunter said.

Alejandro laughed.

"Not yet—but I intend to get lucky before this night is ended, if you catch my meaning," he said with a wink as he squeezed each women's waist.

They laughed and told him he was a dirty old man. Hunter laughed, too.

"I'd like to but I'm on patrol," he said. "Besides, you don't need me around to cramp your style."

"Ah, you're quite right, Charles! I forgot that you are married man now. I would not want to see you get in trouble with your lovely wife. Maybe we'll get together again later?" Alejandro suggested.

"You can count on it," Hunter assured him as he took his leave.

Barbara watched him walk down the street and sighed.

"He's so much better looking than I thought he'd be. Did you say he's married?" she asked.

"Yes," Alejandro replied.

"Too bad," Barbara said as they all headed down the street.

Hunter laughed headed for the Dragon. As he approached the club, a tall familiar figure stepped out onto the street. Hunter stopped and greeted him.

"Lord Chaz! When did you return to New Orleans?" he said.

"Hunter! It's been a long time!" Lord Chaz said as they shook hands.

Charles Rutherford Smith, or Lord Chaz as he liked to be called, was over six feet tall, weighed around 300 pounds and sported a handlebar mustache, goatee and dark eye makeup. His hair was long and unkempt and he liked to wear an old fashioned beaver hat and an 1860s style, black frock coat with tall flared boots. He also carried a brass knobbed walking stick.

Lord Chaz was well known in the city as one of its more flamboyant tour guides. He led groups of tourists through the older section of the city and graveyards and regaled them with tales of ghosts, grisly murders and vampires. Hunter's exploits had become a prominent feature of his tours now, which added to the Slayer's renown.

Lord Chaz was also a vampire and he'd lived in New Orleans since the latter part of the First Age.

"I've been in Charleston for the past several weeks. A distant relative of mine left me a small piece of property which I disposed of. It wasn't easy, either," Chaz explained as they went into the Dragon.

"How come? Is it haunted?" Hunter asked as they sat at the bar.

"Very much so!" Chaz replied. "Or so the locals believe. But I couldn't swear to that as I didn't see a thing while I was staying there."

Tony spotted them and brought over their usual drinks. After an hour of small talk, Chaz bade them good evening and left. Hunter stayed to finish his drink.

"Lord Chaz is strange even for New Orleans," Tony joked. "I've known him for more than 2,000 years and he's been like that ever since he moved here."

"What did he do before he became a tour guide?" asked Hunter.

"He was an attorney up in Boston. But like he said, anyone who dresses like he does usually doesn't many clients. So he started a rock band and traveled around the world for a while. When the band broke up, he moved to New Orleans. I think he got turned on the road somewhere because he was already a vampire when I met him," Tony said.

"I met him—or at least I think I did—at the beginning of the 21st century. The circumstances are still kind of hazy but I'm sure it had something to do with business," Hunter said. "Jean-Paul said that Chaz used to work for us at times as a legal advisor. He's pretty sharp."

"I know. There are more than a handful of people who made the mistake of underestimating him and they all paid the price," Tony said. "Chaz is a pretty good guy, but God help whoever crosses him!"

Hunter had another drink then headed back to the Garden District. He arrived home just as Lorena returned from her hunt. She greeted him with a warm hug.

"How'd it go?" he asked.

She showed him the envelope with the reward money she'd gotten from Valmonde.

"This was almost too easy. That fool left a trail even a blind person could have followed. At least *he* won't be able to murder anyone again," she replied.

Hunter laughed.

"I met Marie again tonight. She said that we should keep close watch on Hannah," he said as they went inside.

"I'll stop by the shop and see her after breakfast," Lorena said. "Leon told me that she's been collecting many rewards lately."

"Are you tired?" he asked as they headed upstairs.

She smiled at him.

"I'd like to go to bed—but not to sleep," she said.

The next day, after they breakfasted at Brennan's with DuCassal, Lorena walked into the Pacific Emporium and saw Hannah seated at the counter. Hannah smiled and greeted her as she approached.

"I'm kind of surprised to see you, Lorena. Isn't Hunter with you? Those shiruken he ordered came in this morning," she said.

"He stopped to check on something along the way. He'll be here soon. While I'm waiting, we can have a little talk," Lorena said.

"Oh? About what?" Hannah asked.

"I've noticed that you've been feeding a lot lately," Lorena said.

"Just on the usual lowlifes and criminals," Hannah said.

"That doesn't matter. What matters is how often you're feeding," Lorena said.

"I feed once or twice a week and only when the hunger gets the better of me. I know that you feed only once or twice each month, but you did say that the hunger is different for each of us," Hannah reminded her. "I need to nourish myself more often than you."

Lorena nodded.

"Do you ever try to control it?" she asked.

"I did at first. I was afraid to do it. When a person spends most of her adult life hunting down and killing vampires, the idea of sucking the life from another human being can be quite repugnant. At first, I tried to satisfy myself with the cocktails at the Dragon. After a few nights, they no longer helped. I realized that I had to feed or die so I began hunting criminals like you do. My first experience was almost *orgasmic*! Ever since then, I haven't tried to control the urges," Hannah explained. "You seem a little worried."

"I am," Lorena admitted.

"Why? I'm not feeding on anyone who will be missed. I only go after the worst, most brutal kinds of criminals and I make our city safer by taking them out," Hannah said.

"It's not who you're feeding on that worries me. It's the *frequency*. You are letting the hunger control *you* instead of you controlling it. I don't want you to become the very thing we both detest and hunt," Lorena said.

"I appreciate your concern, Lorena. I really do. At first I was worried about it, too. But with each feeding, I find I'm able to do more incredible things. I grew faster and stronger. I can see even in the darkest places and I can hear things blocks away. I can even hear heartbeats at a distance and read heat signatures. Being a vampire is amazing!" Hannah said with a smile.

"You really like being a vampire, don't you?" Lorena asked.

"Of course I do. Don't you?" Hannah asked.

Lorena laughed.

"Yes. I like it far better than being human," she admitted.

"Then you understand what I feel?" Hannah asked.

"In more ways than I can explain to you," Lorena said.

"Then there's no need for you to worry about me. I'm fine. In fact, I've never felt better and I have *you* to thank for it. I promise that I won't feed on any innocent people," Hannah vowed.

At that point, Hunter entered the store.

"Your shipment arrived today," Hannah said as she placed a wooden box on the counter. "Six dozen of the regular silver edged ones and one dozen of the exploding type."

"Thanks, Hannah," Hunter said as he handed her three 100 notes.

"Have you used up your first shipment already?" Hannah asked.

"Only half. I've decided to stock up—just in case," Hunter replied. "I heard that you nailed the vampire that was working the Uptown area. He give you any trouble?"

"Not much. I caught him by surprise. He had a Slavic accent," she answered. "I think he arrived on some passenger liner last month. That's when the killings began."

"Slavic?" Hunter asked.

Hannah nodded.

"That would mean he was from the region *you* originated from, mon cher," Lorena said. "Maybe he was one of your creations from back in the First Age?"

"Or a creation of the one who made me," Hunter said. "Anything's possible."

"He looked kind of aristocratic," Hannah said. "Young, too."

"Young is relative with vampires since we remain the exact the age we are when we get turned," Lorena said. "The turning stops our aging process and we stay young as long as we are able to nourish ourselves with human blood."

"Immortality?" Hannah asked.

"In a manner of speaking," Lorena said. "But such an existence can become a curse if you let it."

"I was for *me*," Hunter said.

"Well, I don't feel it's a curse. In fact, it's the furthest thing from it," Hannah smiled.

"We have your back, Hannah. We'll make sure it never becomes a curse for you," Hunter promised. "Thanks for the shiruken. I'll see you around."

"Later," Hannah said as they left the store. "I wonder what Hunter meant by that?"

At one p.m., the Mississippi Queen riverboat eased into the landing dock next in front of the Riverwalk. Among the group of tourists and returning New Orleans natives were six young passengers. All were similarly dressed in light gray cloaks. All appeared to be in their early twenties and looked to be a group on some sort of religious pilgrimage. The apparent leader, a tall thin dark haired man, hailed a carriage.

"Where to, folks?" the driver asked.

"Take us to the Frenchman Hotel," the man said as they all climbed aboard.

The Frenchman was, appropriately enough, located on the corner of Frenchman Street and Decatur. It was built as a Creole family home but became a hotel sometime during the 20th century of the First Age and had remained so ever since. It was quirky and a little unkempt but very popular with tourists.

It was also much quieter than any hotel on Bourbon Street. That—and the cost per night—were the reasons that Henry had booked it for the entire group.

As they clattered down the narrows streets toward the old Creole mansion-turned-hotel on Esplanade, one of the female members of the group looked out at the scenery.

"What a dreary place. Why would Fink think she'd come here?" she asked.

"It's the only city between here and St. Louis with a population that's large enough for her to blend in with," the man replied. "Fink is never wrong. If he believes she's here, then she is here."

"How will we ever find her?" asked another member of the group.

"We won't have to. Once she realizes we're here, she'll find us," the leader said. "Then we'll have her."

"You saw what she did to Ted and Byron. What makes you think this won't go the other way around?" asked another man.

"Because there's six of us and another group on the way. She's not strong enough to fight all of us at once," the leader said.

"Are you sure about that, Henry?" asked the woman.

"I'm very sure, Alicia," he said confidently.

"But what if you're wrong? What if we end up like Ted and Byron?" she asked.

"Then Fink will deal with her personally," Henry said.

"And we'll all be dead," said the woman.

Their arrival did not go unnoticed. A small, cloaked figure watched them disembark from the upper windows of the mall. She knew who they were. In fact, she knew each of them intimately.

And she knew exactly why they had come to New Orleans.

"Welcome to my parlor," she smiled as she headed back to her apartment.

At that same moment, Laura Gates, age 77, left the First Bayou Bank. She had just made a small withdrawal from her account. She was going to use the money to pay her monthly house note and purchase groceries at the French Market with what was left. As she walked down towards the market, a burly man with blue shirt stepped out of a doorway and put a knife to her throat.

Laura stopped and began to tremble.

"I saw you come outa that bank. Gimme all of your cash and I might let you live," he threatened.

Just then, he felt a hard, metallic thing at the base of his skull. He heard twin hammers being cocked and froze.

"If I were you, mon ami, I'd drop that knife," said the man holding the shotgun. "Especially if I wanted to keep my head where it was."

The would-be robber dropped the knife. As soon as it hit the sidewalk, Laura kneed him in the groin as hard as she could. He grunted and dropped to his knees. That's when she struck him across the face with her heavy purse and sent him to the ground. DuCassal laughed as she walked over him and continued to the market. He reached down, seized the thug by his shirt collar and pulled him back up to his feet.

"I guess she didn't need my help after all," he said as he shoved the hood against a wall.

"What're ya gonna do with me?" he asked.

"I was going to beat you to within an inch of your life, but that will not be necessary. Instead, I am going to escort you to the Basin Street station and turn you over to the police. I think, perhaps, a stay in Angola will help you get your mind right," DuCassal said as he pushed him down the street ahead of him.

"Just my luck. That's the first time I ever tried to rob somebody and I run into *you!*" the thug lamented. "All I wanted was some money to eat offa."

"Don't worry, mon ami. You will be fed where you are going—although I have heard that the chef isn't exactly known for his haute cuisine," DuCassal said.

CHAPTER FIVE:
From Below

The house was one of those local legends. It was built during the late 19th century of the First Age and had managed to survive all sorts of natural and man-made disasters. Such houses, especially grand-looking ancient mansions like this, often become the stuff of rumors and legends.

At first, it was known as the Willingham Mansion. Now, those who knew it, simply called it "the house" of "that house". Like all relics from the First Age, the house had a long, checkered and somewhat supernatural history.

The grand Second Empire mansion stood on a bluff overlooking a bend in the Mississippi River just outside the old city limits of Baton Rouge and was less than forty miles from the Myrtles Plantation.

But it was much larger than the Myrtles.

The house itself was built to be magnificent.

An opulent showcase of shameless wealth.

It towered three stories and had a Mansard roof made of the finest slate available. The slate tiles were so well made they had survived into the Second Age with only slight layers of discoloration to show their age. The beams were made of the best cypress and oak available. The main supports were two foot by two foot square with cross beams and tresses of oak at least ten inches thick and 24 inches wide. They were securely attached to the main supports with a clever notching system and long, hand-made nails. The outside of the house was made of granite blocks backed by two layers of hard-fired red brick. The brick walls were covered with five layers of the finest plaster available. When finished, the exterior walls were 18 inches thick. The builders boasted that nothing, not even an earthquake, could knock the house down. Just in case, they added 20 anchor bolts capped with ornate fleur de lis instead of the usual stars.

The floors were also of oak, as was the ornate woodwork and grand staircase. All was especially designed for this one particular house. The woodwork was hand carved and planed to perfection by the finest craftsmen available. Most was shipped in from Missouri. It was so well-made that builders of later homes copied the style.

The house itself contained twelve large rooms with 14 foot ceilings. The windows were 84 inches tall, 42 inches wide and had hidden interior shutters. The windows at the back of the house were only slightly smaller and it even had three interior bathrooms, which was unheard of in those days. The two parlors were done in the French Second Empire style with hand-painted wallpaper depicting European canals, castles and Medieval towns. Each room had a crystal chandelier made in Austria, ornate ceiling medallions and seven marble fireplaces that stood eight foot tall. The dining room was very large and formal with built-in hutches and the original table could comfortably seat 20 guests. The kitchen at the rear of the house was also quite large and had a butler's pantry and icebox that were the envy of the neighbors.

The entry hall also had a magnificent brass and crystal chandelier, Greek-style columns on either side of the grand stairway that led up to the second floor and split off in both directions to wrap around the landing. Each post was adorned with a pineapple—the southern symbol of welcome and newel posts were one-of-kind millwork designed in Germany. Unlike most houses of the time whose floors were covered with oilcloth, hand-painted to resemble marble tiles, the entry to this particular was floored with real marble, imported from Italy. It had a definite "wow" factor to it, which was exactly what the owner intended.

The double front doors stood eight feet tall and three feet wide each. They were made of solid oak and were perfectly balanced on ornate red brass hinges. There was a highly stylized brass knocker and ornate door handles. These led to a small foyer and another large door with a leaded glass panel.

Behind the main house stood a carriage house that was so ornate, people mistook it for a second mansion. It was large enough to house three heavy carriages and six horses. The second story of the carriage house was the servants' quarters. It was built to comfortably house five servants and even had a private kitchen and bath.

In short, it was built to be the most magnificent house in all of Louisiana and the envy of all who saw it.

And it remained exactly that, at least for a short time. Then, inexplicable things began to happen to those who dwelled in it.

According to public records, the house was built by the very wealthy Doctor Irwin Willingham III as a wedding gift for his new bride, Julia. The couple planned to hold grand balls there every month that would be the talk of Baton Rouge society.

The happy couple moved in when the house was completed in the summer of 1878 and christened it with a huge party. Naturally, everyone who was anyone in Baton Rouge was invited. Naturally, they all attended and the party was a huge success.

Several more parties were held there. Each was well attended by the local elites. The local records say the Willinghams lived in the mansion until 1881—then suddenly abandoned it and moved away without any sort of explanation. Rumors flew that they moved to Boston or even Europe. But neither of them were ever seen again.

A month later, it was put up for sale—and was almost immediately purchased by a wealthy family from Atlanta named Harrison. There was a father, George, who had made his pile in the transatlantic steamship trade. His wife Edna and their six children. Rumors flew around that they got the house for a fraction of its value.

The Harrisons moved into it in July 1882.

They moved out in October 1883 after the husband went insane. His family thought it best he be treated in Boston, so they packed everything and left for the east. The local papers and rumor mills speculated wildly on what had driven Mr. Harrison mad. There was a rumor that he had seen or found something that made his mind snap. Perhaps it was the very same thing that caused the Willinghams to leave.

Most of the locals believed he lost his mind when his business began to fail. Some attributed that failure to the curse leveled on the house by an Indian shaman. Whatever the causes, the Harrisons vanished from Baton Rouge society just like the Willinghams.

The house stood empty for another seven years. Then a young couple from Pittsburgh bought it at a tax auction. By then, the house had become a little run-down from years of neglect. But the couple loved it and considered themselves the luckiest people on Earth to have gotten it so cheaply.

They moved in during the autumn of 1891—and out in December of that same year. No one ever heard from them again. They had left in such haste that they'd abandoned all of their belongings. They even left their uneaten dinner on the kitchen table.

That's when the house gained its reputation for being haunted.

It stood empty and unattended to for the next 54 years. Desperate to get it off the tax rolls, the parish assessor's office gave it to a real estate investor in 1946. The investor spent a fortune repairing and renovating the property. This took several years. During that time, he had to hire and rehire several work crews to complete projects that previous crews abandoned. It soon became apparent that no one wanted to work on the place. Those who did, demanded three times the going rates and even they walked off the jobs after a few days.

In 1949, the work was nearly completed. The investor sold the house to a man named Franklin Soamers. Soamers and his wife moved in on October 14 and left nine months later. It was said they suffered a series of accidents and illnesses that left them destitute. Soamers blamed their bad luck on the house. They all vanished in the middle of the night and were never heard from again.

The house ended up in the hands of the assessor again after sitting empty for the next eight years. After several disastrous rentals, it was slated for demolition. It was saved from the wrecking ball by a family who saw it and fell in love with it. They picked it up for next to nothing. Thus began another round of expensive repairs and restorations. This family, named Cloosen, numbered five, the husband, wife and three small children.

On Christmas Eve of that same year, the entire family suddenly fled from the house. They were so anxious to get away, they also left their dinner uneaten on the table and most of their belongings behind. A week later, their workmen returned to board up the doors and windows. The house sat empty for several more decades and the vines and moss of the swamp slowly obscured it from view.

DuCassal looked up from the newspaper.

Hunter sipped his wine. Lorena smiled.

"That's quite a story, Jean-Paul," she said. "Did that house actually exist?"

"It still *does* exist, Lorena," he replied. "According to this article, it has been rediscovered and rescued from its vegetation tomb."

"You mean someone's bought the place?" Hunter asked as he sat up.

"Yes," DuCassal said.

"Does the article mention his name?" Hunter asked.

"It says here that the house was purchased by Gideon Lamar Alexander one month ago," DuCassal said.

"Alejandro?" Lorena gasped. "Does he know of its history?"

"If he doesn't, he will soon discover it for himself," DuCassal said. "That house is every bit as haunted as people say it is—and worse."

"It does seem to attract an awful lot of hard luck to whoever owns it," Hunter said. "I hope Alejandro doesn't get himself into too much trouble with it."

"I'm sure Alejandro will be able to handle whatever comes up, mon cher. Nothing frightens *him*," Lorena said.

"I suppose you're right, my love," Hunter agreed.

Alejandro was all about panache and the brooding mansion atop the granite cliff overlooking the river appealed to his twisted sense of style. He'd stumbled upon it accidentally while tracking a particularly vicious vampire through the area. He'd been chasing the vampire along the Old River Road on horseback. The vampire suddenly veered his horse to the left and vanished into the thick woods. Alejandro remained in hot pursuit. An hour later, he noticed that the vampire had fled into a large, overgrown structure.

He tied his horse to one of the porch supports and carefully stepped through the half-open door. The mansion was very dark and unusually quiet. Normally, when a building has sat empty for so long, it became the nesting ground for swamp birds, bats and all sorts of vermin. But no animal sounds broke the eerie silence. It was as if nature itself shunned the place.

As he walked through the foyer, his boots crunched pieces of plaster that had fallen from the high ceilings. He glanced at the grand staircase and stopped as something white and ethereal sailed up the steps.

He smiled.

"Of course such a place would have spirits," he thought. "But I'm not looking for ghosts."

He walked into one of large side parlors. Something tall and black with red eyes stared at him from across the room. Almost immediately it launched itself at him and seized him by the throat. Alejandro responded with a boot to his testicles that doubled the vampire up. Before the vampire could recover, Alejandro drove him to the floor with a hard left hook then stomped on his groin with all of his considerable strength. The vampire lay on his back moaning in pain.

Alejandro laughed as he picked the vampire up and buried his fangs in his neck. After several minutes, the vampire stopped twitching. Alejandro tossed its drained corpse to the floor and wiped the blood from his lips.

"You'll not bother anyone again," he said.

He dragged the body out into the overgrown front yard, covered it with dry twigs and set it ablaze. When the fire had completely consumed the vampire, Alejandro looked back at the mansion.

"Now that I'm here, I might as well have a look around," he said as he went back inside.

The next afternoon, he went to the parish assessor's office and asked about the mansion. The man took one look at the man in the long black cape, black hat and opera mask and started.

"Aren't you that Alejandro fella? The one who's been hunting down vampires around here?" he asked.

"In the flesh. What can you tell me about that house at the bend of the river? The one on the bluff in the middle of the swamp?" Alejandro asked.

The clerk squinted.

"You mean that place near the Old River Road?" he asked.

"The very one," Alejandro replied.

"This'll take a while. I'm not sure we have anything on it at all," the man said as he walked to the file room.

It took the clerk nearly an hour to find the yellowed deed. He placed it on the counter.

"Here she is. Why do you want to know about that place?" the clerk asked.

"I wish to purchase it," Alejandro replied. "Who is the current owner?"

"Nobody. That's the Willingham Mansion. It's been empty for over 250 years. It'll cost a fortune to restore it," the clerk said.

"Yes it will. But cost is not a problem," Alejandro replied.

"That house has a bad history. Folks say it's haunted," the clerk warned.

"That makes it all the more desirable. What do I have to do to own it?" Alejandro asked.

"Just pay some back taxes and it's yours," the clerk replied.

After a bit of haggling, he and Alejandro agreed to the sum. Alejandro left and returned two hours later with several large bank notes which he handed to the clerk. He shook his head as he handed the deed over.

"She's all yours, Mister. But I still think you're crazy for buying that place," the clerk said.

"I have been called far worse things than crazy. Thank you. You've been most helpful," Alejandro said as he folded the new deed and slid it into his coat pocket.

Before moving in, he hired a crew of workers to cut away the vines, Spanish moss and trees that had grown up around and over the mansion. It took them several days to complete this. After that crew hauled the trash away, he hired a second crew to replace all of the rotted windows and to check the roof. Much to his delight, the roof needed no help. With the grounds and the outside of the mansion in good order, it was time to restore the inside of the house.

He decided to start with the plumbing. The five bathrooms were in total disrepair and the pipes creaked and squealed when he turned on a tap. But water—albeit brown and rusty—did eventually flow from it.

But when he tried to hire a plumber, only three men in Baton Rouge agreed to take the job. They were new to the area and knew nothing of the mansion's history. But Bob, Jim and Ray would soon become painfully aware of it.

The three men showed up for work early on Monday morning as promised. Alejandro gave Bob the key to the front door.

"I'll be in Baton Rouge all day arranging for other contractors. Lock up when you leave and put the keys in the mailbox," he said.

"Will do," Bob said as he took the key.

After Alejandro rode off, Bob turned to the others.

"I reckon the first thing we need to do is go down to the basement and see if everything's still in one piece," he said as he turned on his lantern.

They located the cellar door which was behind and beneath the grand staircase. Bob had to wrestle it open after years of neglect. The old hinges creaked and moaned. Ray squirted some oil on them. They stepped back and waited. Much to their surprise, the old door swung open. They looked at each other.

Bob shrugged.

"I guess the oil made it open," he said. "Let's check out those pipes."

The steps were creaky but well-built and led down into a large, cobweb cluttered room with stacks leading upward from the concrete floor and several lines of dust-covered pipes going in all directions. Ray and Jim turned on their lanterns and the three of them began to check the pipes. As they moved along, they knocked the dust from the pipes with their brushes and examined them for cracks and holes. Jim spotted something that might be a crack and marked it with chalk. Ray located the main valve and gently turned it. He head the water rush through the ancient pipes and told the others to watch out for any signs of leaks.

They found several small ones and marked each with chalk. This done, they started back upstairs. When they reached the bottom of the steps, Ray's lantern flickered and died out.

"That's strange. I just put new batteries in it this morning," he said as he played with the switch.

Bob's lantern also died out. So did Jim's.

They made their way slowly back upstairs. As soon as they left the cellar, their lanterns came back on. They stared at each other.

"If that don't beat all!" Jim exclaimed.

"I wonder what made them do that?" Ray asked as they headed into the parlor.

"Forget about the lights. Now that the water's running again, let's check all the faucets and drains in the place to see if any of them need to be replaced," Ray said.

They started with the kitchen sink and the smaller one in the butler's pantry behind it. The pipes creaked and groaned when Ray turned on the taps. A few seconds later, rusty water began to flow out of both. After a minute or so, the water gradually became clear.

"They're older than dirt but it looks like they still work," Ray said as he turned them off. "That's unbelievable in a place that's been empty for so many years."

They checked the bathroom on the second floor and the one on the third with the same results. Ray smiled.

"This'll be good news for Alejandro. We don't have to replace much of anything unless he wants us to. Let's get our tools and see if we can patch those leaks we found," he said as they headed downstairs.

When they reached the parlor they stopped and stared in disbelief. All of their tools were now neatly arrayed on the floor along with several long pipes and other attachments they had brought with them.

Thinking that this had been done by Alejandro, Bob called out his names several times. All he got was an echo of his own voice as it drifted through the empty rooms. They walked around the parlor and stared at the tools.

"How in Hell did they get here? We left them out on the wagon," Jim said. "They didn't just unload themselves."

"This is nuts, guys. This can't be happening," Ray said as he shook his head.

"Maybe the place is haunted," Jim suggested.

"If it is, then the ghosts did us a favor. They saved us a lot of time unloading this stuff. I don't care how it got here. We got hired to fix the plumbing in this house and that's exactly what we're going to do—ghosts or no ghosts!" Ray said. "Now, let's get to it!"

They worked as diligently as was humanly possible over the next five days. They did their best to ignore tools moving on their own and lanterns going dark, doors opening and closing and the heavy footsteps that echoed throughout the house. And they made real progress.

Rusted and broken pipes were replaced. Small leaks were located and repaired, new taps were installed in the sinks and tubs and long-forgotten and neglected drains and traps were cleared. As they worked, the paranormal activities intensified. The three men had learned to ignore them as most were relatively harmless pranks.

But on the sixth day, that suddenly changed.

Bob was carrying some fittings in from the wagon when he froze in his tracks. Ray and Jim saw him staring at something and stopped what they were doing. They looked in the direction Bob was staring and just about soiled their pants when they saw the apparition of a slender woman in a Victorian dress glide past them and disappear through a solid wall.

"That was a ghost! A real ghost!" Jim said almost in awe.

"I never saw one of them before and I sure as Hell don't want to see another!" Ray said.

Bob shook himself out of his trance.

"That was *different*," he said with a slight smile. "You'll saw that, too?"

The others nodded.

"Now what?" asked Ray.

"Nothing. We finish the job. So what if this place is haunted? Nobody's been hurt," Bob said.

"You're right. Besides, I'm not afraid of no ghost!" Ray said with mock bravado.

That when they saw a large, heavy wooden chair hurtle toward them. It crashed onto the floor and broke into several pieces right between them.

"But I *sure as Hell am afraid of that!*" Ray shouted as he bolted for the door.

Bob and Jim were right on his heels. The three men jumped onto the wagon and drove off just as Alejandro came riding up the path. They sped past him like every demon in Hell was chasing them.

"We quite!" Bob shouted as they clattered past.

Alejandro went inside. The men had left their tools and some fixtures. He saw the splintered chair in the middle of the parlor floor and sighed.

Alejandro had to pull a lot of strings, but he finally managed to bring another crew of workers from Baton Rouge. All went well for the first few days and the men managed to replace most of the old rotted windows and frames and a few inside doors. Alejandro watched over them and helped where he could. Mostly, he stayed out of their way so they could work.

About three weeks into the remodeling projects, a blood curdling scream suddenly echoed through the mansion. When the other workers heard it, they immediately stopped what they were doing and stared at each other.

"Jackson! Has anybody seen Jackson?" Joe the foreman asked.

"He went into the cellar to trace a pipe about five minutes ago, Joe," one of the men said.

"I'd best go and find him. Who's with me?" Joe asked.

"I ain't goin' down there!" one said.

"Me neither!" said another.

"Not after *that* fuckin' scream!" said a third.

Alejandro looked at Joe.

"I'll go with you," he said as he picked up a lantern.

They went down the ancient steps into the musty smelling dungeon-like cellar. They found a set of tools scattered on the floor near the bottom of the steps along with Jackson's cap.

"Jackson! Where are you? Answer me!" Joe called out.

Alejandro spotted something in the dirt floor and held the lantern over it.

"It looks as if something heavy has been dragged across the floor," he said.

"Jackson weighs nearly 300 pounds," Joe said as they flowed the strange marks to the other side of the cellar.

They ended at a blank brick wall.

"Now what?" Joe asked.

"Have your men come down here and break through this wall. Since the bricks do not match the others in the cellar, this was obviously sealed up after the house was built. If Jackson is on the other side of this wall, we must find him quickly," Alejandro said.

"But what coulda dragged someone his size through this wall?" Joe asked as he ran his hand over the bricks.

"Break it down and we shall find out," Alejandro said.

Before Joe could say another word, another, even louder scream came from behind the wall. Joe turned and flew up the steps three at a time. He moved so fast that his feet barely made contact with any of them.

Alejandro calmly followed him. By the time he reached the living room, all of the workers and their tools were gone.

"That's the second crew I've lost," he said as he looked around. "It's time to summon the cavalry."

He did.

Robert Behan and his men weren't phased by haunted houses. In fact, restoring old plantations was their specialty. A few years earlier, Hunter had hired them to fully restore the old Myrtles Plantation so it could once again be operated as a bed and breakfast. They had just put the finishing touches on the Myrtles when Alejandro rode up and offered them the job.

Robert grinned.

"Sure. We know about that house. That's one of the most haunted places in Louisiana. We heard some jackass bought it. I guess that'd be you, huh?" he said.

"Yes. I am the jackass. I would like that house restored to its former grandeur. My friend, Hunter, said that were the best in the business and that nothing scares you. I will pay you top dollar—if you're interested," Alejandro said.

"Mister, you've got yourself a crew!" Behan said as they shook hands.

Alejandro gave him the keys and told him he'd be back in a few days to check on their progress. Behan said he'd have his men work around the clock to get all of the major things taken care of.

Alejandro rode off toward New Orleans and left Behan and his men to their own devices, confident that the needed work would get completed.

When he returned five days later, he found the house empty and all of their tools lying right where they'd left them when they fled from the house. Alejandro walked around and shook his head.

"This is proving to me very disturbing," he said. "Very disturbing indeed."

He walked up to the third floor and noticed that the door at the top of the steps was boarded up. Curious, he tore the rotted boards down and forced the door inward. A blast of ice cold air struck him and chilled him to the marrow. The next thing he knew, he was thrown down the stairs by a powerful, unseen force. He landed at the bottom with a loud crash. He lay still until the stars faded from his brain, then got up and dusted himself off. Now angry and curious, he stomped back up the stairs, determined to confront whatever was in that room. Ten seconds later, he found himself at the bottom of the stairs again.

He got and walked over to his desk. He took out a pen, paper and an envelope and wrote a letter to Hunter.

"Since the cavalry didn't work, it is time to send for the Special Forces!" he said.

It took two days for his letter to reach New Orleans. Two days later, DuCassal's carriage came rumbling up the old path toward the ancient mansion. George, the driver pulled up in front of the main entrance.

Hunter stepped out of the carriage and looked up at the brooding structure as he helped Lorena down. DuCassal followed.

"This looks like the Addams Family mansion," he remarked.

"Yes it does," Hunter agreed. "I half expect to be greeted at the door by their butler, Lurch."

"Who or what are the Addams Family?" asked Lorena.

"They were a rather macabre aristocratic family in an old television series of the First Age. Their decaying mansion looked a lot like this one," DuCassal explained. "It was filled with strange artifacts, torture devices, hidden rooms and trap doors and it was surrounded by a swamp."

"Just like this house," Lorena said as she looked around. "This place gives me the creeps. Why would Alejandro buy such a place?"

"It appeals to my sense of the theatric," Alejandro said as he suddenly appeared next to them.

DuCassal started then cursed.

Alejandro laughed.

"You look like you've been thrown down a flight of steps," Hunter observed.

"That is because I have," Alejandro replied. "And more than once."

"By what?" asked Hunter.

"That I cannot say. I have never seen it. But whenever I open a certain door at the top of the stairs, some force hurtles me down the steps. I must say that it's becoming quite tiresome," Alejandro replied.

"You don't seem frightened of it," Lorena observed.

"I'm not. But even I can't fight what I can't see. There are entities in this house that are not all that pleased with my presence here," Alejandro said.

"Maybe they are worried that you will drive down their property values?" DuCassal joked. "They may consider you to be riff-raff."

"Considering the history and condition of this house, I doubt that I can do it any more harm," Alejandro said.

Hunter looked at him.

"Just how much *do* you know about this place?" he asked.

"Not as much as I should, obviously," Alejandro said.

"Weren't you aware of its reputation and history when you bought it?" Hunter asked as they followed him through the creaky iron gates and down the red brick path.

"Of course I was aware of it. That is precisely why I bought it. I also thought I could handle anything that might arise, but alas, I was wrong," Alejandro admitted.

"Bit off more than you could chew?" Hunter asked.

"More than enough to choke on, my friend," Alejandro said. "From what my workers and I have experienced, I feel there is more than one thing haunting this house. We have encountered full bodied apparitions, an entire universe of sounds, moving objects, voices, shadows, strange lights and even physical attacks."

"Why'd you call us in? Those sound like things you could handle yourself," Hunter asked.

"I thought so, too. Then something dragged me out of my bed in the middle of the night and threw me into the back yard," Alejandro said. "The following day, one of the workers went missing. When confronted with something *that* powerful and dangerous, I thought I'd best send for the cavalry, so to speak."

"We're here," Hunter said as they stepped onto the porch.

Alejandro pulled a long, ornate brass key from his coat pocket. He was about to put it into the lock when the handle visibly turned and the heavy door creaked inward. They glanced at each other and waited. When no one came to the door, Hunter smiled.

"That door was locked. I locked it myself when I stepped out a few minutes ago," Alejandro said.

"Is there anyone inside?" Hunter asked.

"Not after this morning. That's when the last of my workers quit," Alejandro said.

"Why did they quit?" asked Lorena.

Alejandro shrugged.

"They didn't stop to explain. All I know is when I returned from Baton Rouge, they were gone," he said. "Shall we go inside?"

"Let's," Hunter said.

As they entered the foyer, they saw that the second door was also open.

"That was also locked," Alejandro said.

"Interesting," Hunter remarked. "Apparently, someone's expecting us."

"Let us enter, mom ami. I wouldn't want to disappoint out hosts," DuCassal said with a grin.

When they walked into the hallway, they saw two saw horses had been set up in the middle of the hall and several tools lay scattered about. They looked around. Hunter picked a hammer up off the floor and placed it on a nearby table.

"Craftsmen don't abandon their tools unless they're *forced* to. Something scared them away. Something that was too terrifying for them to deal with," he said.

"Robert Behan and his men were tough and nearly fearless," Alejandro said. "You know them, Charles. You hired them to restore the Myrtles Plantation three years ago."

"Robert isn't afraid of anything," Hunter said. "Anything that could make him leave in such a hurry must have been something straight out of Hell itself. His men are just as fearless."

"Not any more, eh, Charles?" DuCassal joked.

"Everyone has a breaking point, Jean-Paul," Lorena said as she walked around the room. "There is always something that they fear enough to flee from."

"Even you?" DuCassal asked.

"Perhaps. I just haven't met it yet," she replied with a smile.

"I am more curious than frightened," Alejandro said. "I want to know what is here so I can figure out ways to get rid of it. But being thrown from a balcony in the middle of the night does tend to put a scare in a person."

Hunter laughed.

"What other ghostly manifestations have you experienced?" he asked.

"Just the run of the mill types. Ghostly apparitions, clanking chains, mysterious footsteps and wailing in the middle of the night are all things I can deal with. As long as the spirits don't become total nuisances, they are welcome to remain here. After all, they were here first.

But when something throws me down flights of stairs or out of a window, and when workers vanish into blank walls, that is another matter entirely and must be dealt with. That is why I've asked you, my good friends, for assistance. I want to know what is here and I want it evicted from the premises," Alejandro said.

"We'll see what we can do," Hunter said. "We'll have to spend several days here to get an idea of what's haunting this place. While we're here, we'll even try to get some of the work done. That's should stir things up a bit."

"Good idea. Spirits have been to known to get upset when their abodes are renovated. Robert and his men left behind plenty of good tools. Feel free to use any of them you wish. I'm sure they won't mind," Alejandro said.

"Does the plumbing work?" asked Lorena.

"Yes. It was the very first thing I attended to," Alejandro assured her. "The electricity is off so we have to use lanterns."

"But this chandelier seems to work fine," DuCassal said as he pointed to the one above their heads.

They watched as it flickered on and became brighter and brighter. Then it suddenly burst and they were forced to cover themselves as hundreds of pieces of broken glass rained down on them.

"Looks like something wants to let us know it's here," Hunter said. 'I think our stay is going to be very interesting."

"And fun!" Lorena smiled. "I've always wanted to stay in a haunted mansion."

"In that case, you should enjoy your stay immensely, Lorena," Alejandro said. "Now you know why I purchased this pace. The ghosts had better grow accustomed to my presence. This house is mine and I intend to restore it. If they don't like that, they can pack their bags and leave because I am staying!"

Alejandro gave them the grand tour of the house. When they reached the third floor, DuCassal stopped.

"Is this the room you referred to?" he asked.

"Yes. Open it at your own risk, Jean-Paul," Alejandro replied.

"Nothing ventured . . ." DuCassal said as he turned the handle and pushed the door inward.

They watched as he stepped inside and walked around. He stopped in the middle of the room and shrugged.

"There's nothing dangerous about this. IT's just an empty room," he said smugly.

That's when the sudden blast of icy wind gushed from the room. They watched as some unseen forced picked DuCassal up and pitched him head-first down the steps. They raced down just as he picked himself up off the floor and brushed himself off. Lorena picked up his hat and handed it to him.

"Something in that room does not care for visitors!" he said.

"I told you so," Alejandro grinned. "I have no idea who or what that is, but I do know that it has a very nasty temper."

Hunter looked up at the door and watched as it closed by itself.

"I say we leave whatever it is alone for now," he said.

"That's fine by me, mon ami. That was far from one of the more pleasant experiences I've ever had," DuCassal agreed.

"For now, I have no need to use that room for anything. If I should need it in the future, that will be a most memorable confrontation!" Alejandro said as they walked back upstairs to finish the tour.

When it was over, Hunter looked at Alejandro.

"Before we go any further, I think we need to consult with someone who knows more about this sort of thing than any of us do," he suggested.

"I know just the person!" DuCassal said. "She lives just three miles from here."

"Let's go," Hunter said as they climbed into the carriage.

Vernae Richardson was a Creole woman of indeterminate age. She lived in a modest brick house at the edge of the swamp and was the local voodoo priestess and leading authority of local history and things that go bump in the night. Everyone in Baton Rouge knew about her.

She was also an acquaintance of DuCassal's.

When they knocked on her door, she opened it and beamed brightly at DuCassal. Then she immediately scowled when she saw Alejandro.

"It's good to see you again, Jean-Paul," she said as they hugged warmly. "It's been far too long since your last visit, although I doubt that you're making a social call."

"It *has* been too long, Vernae," DuCassal said as they followed her into the back parlor where she conducted her ceremonies.

She told them to make themselves comfortable as she sat down in her high backed wicker chair. She studied Alejandro with a great deal of interest.

"You're that damned fool who bought the old Willingham place," she said. "I can just about guess why you've come to see me. If you'd have come to see me weeks ago, you might not have bought that place."

"I knew it was haunted. Such things only made it more attractive to me. But several very strange and potentially deadly things have occurred and now I want to learn just who or what is behind them," Alejandro said.

Vernae leaned back and shook her head.

"There are several things wrong with that house, Alejandro. Maybe more things than you and your friends would be willing to handle," she said.

"We are listening," Alejandro said.

She looked each of them in the eyes and took a deep breath.

"That house, or rather the earth it sits on, was cursed since day one," she said. "It was built smack in the middle of a native burial ground. When Willingham took over the land, the last shaman of that tribe told him the ground was sacred and that he is not permitted to build there or disturb the ancient graves. Instead of heeding the warning, Willingham had his men whip the shaman from his property and they told him that if he ever came back, they'd shoot him on sight. Then they started building it. As they dug the foundation, they found bones and graves. Hundreds of graves. In keeping with the customs of the time, the workers tossed the bones into the river and kept at it. Halfway through, some of the men got sick and had to leave. A few of them even died. Willingham hired more men and the house was finished.

That's when the shaman came back and cursed the place and anyone who would live in the house for as long as it stood. Willingham's men caught the shaman and dragged him to the house. That's when Willingham put a bullet in his head and had his men throw the body into the river.

That's when the fun *really* began.

One of the men who caught the shaman was found with his lungs filled with water. The doctor said he drowned—but he was miles from the river or any other deep water. The other man involved in the shaman incident was stung to death by wasps a month later—during the time of year when wasps are dormant.

Soon after that, Mrs. Willingham gave birth to twins. A boy and a girl. It was said they were so horrible to look at that they were locked upstairs in a large attic space. The servants fed them and taught them to read and write and they were otherwise taken good care of. But after a few years, they up and vanished. That's when the rest of the troubles started and the Willinghams abandoned the place. For some reason, they left two servants behind to care for it, but they soon disappeared. Their bodies were never found.

Since you saw the deeds, you know the house changed hands several times and it also stood empty several times," she said.

Alejandro nodded.

"It *does* have a colorful history," he said.

"Colorful is one way of putting it. I'd say it different," Vernae said with a grin. "Anyway, that house is haunted by those who lived and died in it and by even more souls who pass through it as they travel between the world of the dead and this world.

Your house is a *vortex*. It's a conduit for souls and other things between this world and the next. Hundreds, maybe even *thousands,* of souls have passed through it over the centuries. Since a vortex can't be closed, they will continue to pass through it for as long as it stands. It is *well haunted.*"

Hunter smiled at his friend.

"That's what you bought, Alejandro," he said.

Alejandro whistled.

"It appears that I have inadvertently purchased the gateway to Hell itself," he said.

"Not all who pass through it have evil intentions, Alejandro," Vernae said. "But there are *other* things beside spirits there. Things far more *dangerous*. You'd best take care."

"What sort of things?" asked Lorena.

Vernae shrugged.

"That's hard to say," she said. "There are stories and dark rumors about that place. I can't say for sure which are true and which aren't."

"Can you help us?" Alejandro asked.

"In order to help you, I'd have to set foot inside the house and *that* is something I will *never* do again," she said.

"You've been inside?" Lorena asked.

Vernae nodded.

"That place is filled with tormented souls. There's pain there. *Lots of pain*. And sorrow so deep it drains your soul. What happened to me that night still makes me shake all over. No. I will *not* help you. *You* bought the place, Alejandro. *You* deal with what's inside!" she said.

They thanked her and walked out into the street. Alejandro looked up at the darkening sky and sighed.

"It looks like rain," he said. "We'd best head back home."

"Are you sure that you *want* to go back?" Hunter asked.

"I purchased that house. I refuse to allow a horde of ghosts or anything else drive me from it," he said.

"In that case, we'd better go with you," DuCassal said. "Besides, I'm curious to learn what we are dealing with."

"That makes two of us," Hunter said.

"Three," added Lorena.

"I ain't afraid of no ghosts!" Alejandro joked.

CHAPTER SIX:
The Walls Have Ears, Noses, Eyes . . . .

Midnight.

Hunter sat in the living room sipping absinthe as he watched the storm rage outside. There was a small lantern on the table next to the sofa. Something white and shimmery caught his eye. He waited and watched as a woman in a Victorian era dress glided silently across the floor. She moved the foot of the stairs then stopped and looked back at him. He picked up the lantern and walked toward her. She turned and moved slowly to the top of the landing, then looked back and motioned with her finger for him to follow. Intrigued, he went after her.

She led him around the landing to the third story, stopped and looked back to make sure he was still following. When he reached her, she moved around the railing to the left, past the mysterious door, and waited again.

When Hunter reached her, she pointed to a spot in the wall, then vanished. He walked over and checked the wall, knocking as he did. Everything sounded solid except for a spot in the middle of the wall. He took a pen from his pocket and made an X on the wall. Then he went back downstairs to tell the others what he saw.

They had just walked out of the kitchen when he reached the bottom of the stairs. He told them everything that happened.

"What did she look like?" Lorena asked.

"She was about your height, slender with long dark hair that she wore in long curls. She looked just like a younger version of that woman in the portrait above the fireplace," he said.

"Spirits can take any form they wish. She obviously prefers to remain young," DuCassal said as they looked at the portrait.

"I'm sure that's the woman I saw," Hunter said. "She was trying to show me something very important to her. I suggest that we break through that wall and see what that is."

"I'm all for it, Charles," Alejandro said.

They headed up the stairs. Hunter went to the wall and tapped on it with his fist. When he found a hollow spot, he punched it as hard as he could. His fist went through the old plaster easily, then he and DuCassal began pulling away chunks of the wall until nearly half of it was open.

Hunter peered inside.

"What do you see?" asked Alejandro.

"A rather large bundle of some sort," Hunter replied as he reached into the hole.

He carefully pulled the bundle out of the wall and placed it on the floor. The others watched as he untied it to reveal the skeletal figure of a woman dressed in a tattered Victorian dress.

"Her hands and feet are tied and her face has been wrapped, probably to keep her from screaming for help," he said. "She may still have been alive when she was walled up."

"What a terrible way to die," Lorena said. "Whoever did this must have really despised her. He *wanted* her to suffer."

"Do you think she is the same woman you saw last night?" Alejandro asked.

"I'm positive. She led me directly to this spot. She wanted to let me know she was here, that someone had walled her up," Hunter replied.

"I wonder who she is?" asked Alejandro.

They suddenly heard a loud crash come from the parlor. They hurried downstairs and saw that the portrait above the fireplace was now lying in the middle of the room.

"I think *that* answers your question," Hunter said as he picked up the portrait and hung it back over the fireplace.

"Now we know why Willingham left so suddenly," Alejandro said.

'And why no one ever saw Mrs. Willingham again," Lorena added. "Her husband murdered her and left the area to cover up his crime."

"But why, exactly, *did* he kill her? And why did he do it in such a horrible manner?" asked DuCassal.

"I think the answers to both questions are somewhere in this house," Alejandro said.

"It's your call, Alejandro. What do you want to do with Mrs. Willingham's remains?" Hunter asked.

"I think we should give the poor woman a proper burial here on the grounds. She deserves at least that," Alejandro replied.

"We can build her a coffin from the lumber on hand. We'll try to make it as nice as possible, too," Hunter said. "Later on, you can go into Baton Rouge and purchase a proper headstone."

"Let's do it," Alejandro agreed.

They buried her beneath an ancient live oak tree about 200 yards from the house. Hunter said a prayer over her grave and they walked back to the house to continue their work. A heavy rain was falling as they stopped for the night. Lorena went upstairs to shower while Hunter again retreated to the living room and sat down on the sofa. He poured himself a glass of absinthe and stared up at the portrait. He raised his glass to toast her.

That's when he felt a presence next to him. He turned and smiled as Mrs. Willingham materialized. He finished his toast. She smiled and nodded her head to acknowledge it.

"Thank you, kind sir," she whispered in a voice that was barely audible.

"Rest easy, Madame," Hunter said.

"Look beneath," she said as she faded away. "Look beneath."

He recapped his bottle and called out to the others. They quickly joined him in the parlor and he told them what happened.

"Look beneath what?" asked Alejandro.

"I think she meant beneath the house," Hunter said. 'If I'm right, there are other secrets here. Deep, dark secrets and they're all connected to the Willinghams in some way."

"I'm game. I'll try anything to get to the bottom of this. Where would you like to start?" Alejandro asked.

"We can start with that brick wall in the cellar," Hunter said.

They grabbed two sledge hammers from the pile of tools in the living room and followed Alejandro down into the cellar. They could see the marks on the floor which were made when the workman was dragged through the wall. Hunter stopped and examined the wall carefully.

"There's a door alright," he said as he ran his fingers along its edge.

He and DuCassal searched for a lock mechanism. After several minutes, they gave up. Hunter rammed his shoulder against it but it refused to budge.

"Let's get to it," he said as he raised the sledge hammer.

After several strong blows, the ancient stones gave way. Alejandro and Lorena cleared the debris from the opening while Hunter peered inside.

"It looks like some sort of passageway," he said. "This is where that workman was taken."

"If he's in there, I doubt that he's still alive," Alejandro said. "He may have already been dead when he was dragged in."

"I'd say that's a strong possibility," Hunter said. "Shall we?"

"Let's," Alejandro agreed.

DuCassal turned on his lantern and they entered the passageway. It was at least ten feet high and several yards wide. It was constructed of limestone and granite blocks and the floor was made of red brick. Hunter followed the marks on the floor.

"The workman was dragged through this passageway," he said, "But the trail ends here."

"Whatever grabbed him probably carried him the rest of the way," Alejandro said. "That means our adversary is very strong. The worker was over 300 pounds."

"But why would it grab him?" DuCassal asked. "What use could he have been?"

"Food?" Lorena suggested.

"You mean they are cannibals?" Alejandro asked.

"Only if they eat their own kind. This could be some kind of animal. A highly intelligent one that eats flesh. To some species, humans are just part of their food chain," Hunter said.

About two hundred yards in, they spotted an arched opening. Hunter raised his hand and looked around. DuCassal stepped in front of him and shone the lantern into the opening.

"It's a room. A rather large one, too," he said. "And it's got a vaulted ceiling."

"Let's check it out," Hunter said.

They stepped into the vaulted room and looked around. There were sealed vaults imbedded in the walls on either side.

"This is a crypt," Hunter said as he counted the vaults. "There are 22 people buried here and they all have the same last name. Willingham."

"Look at the dates, mon cher," Lorena pointed out. "None lived past two years. These are the graves of children."

"Could this be the result of the curse?" Hunter wondered as he looked them over.

"The first died in 1884. The last only six years ago, Charles," DuCassal said.

As Hunter stepped back, his foot hit something he turned and picked up a bunch of flowers, neatly tied together with a ribbon. He sniffed them and handed them to Lorena.

"These are only a few days old," she said.

"Someone still visits this crypt. Someone still mourns," Hunter said.

"Just what are we dealing with, Charles?" asked Alejandro.

"I'm not sure—but I'm beginning to understand a little," he said. "I have a feeling that we're being watched."

"Yes we are, mon cher," Lorena said. "I can hear a faint heartbeat nearby."

"They won't try to do anything if we stay together. They're probably waiting for us to split up so they can pick us off one at a time," Alejandro said as he looked around. "The rest of this labyrinth is pitch dark."

"Let's lure them into the open. We'll split up," Hunter said. "I'll take the passageway on the right. Lorena, I want you to go straight ahead."

"Alejandro and I will take the left passageway," DuCassal said. "Bon chance!"

Hunter nodded.

Lorena smiled and started walking. He waited until she vanished into the shadows, then went to the right. DuCassal nodded at Alejandro and they entered the remaining passageway.

Lorena walked along what seemed to be a nearly endless passageway. As she walked, she took time to study its construction. Like the first passageway, it was constructed of limestone blocks and felt cool and a little bit damp.

She smiled.

"It's almost got the feel of a grave to it," she thought.

That's when she detected the faint sound of someone breathing. She stopped and concentrated. Now that she and Hunter were married, they had developed a telepathic link between them.

"I hear one of them behind me," she thought.

"How far into the passageway are you?" Hunter asked.

"About one half mile," she replied.

"I'm on my way. Let it capture you so we can locate its lair," he said.

"That should be easy enough," she replied as she broke contact.

She continued walking a few more yards. As she did, she sensed something drawing closer. She knew the creature was behind her but she pretended not to notice. She slowed her pace and waited as it crept closer. The creature raised the club it was carrying and swung it. Lorena let it strike her without actually letting it strike her. She fell forward and feigned unconsciousness. As she lay with her eyes shut, she allowed the creature to shackle her wrists with a heavy chain. Once this was accomplished, the creature dragged her to her feet and pushed her ahead of it down a long passage. They stopped at heavy arched door. Her captor knocked and waited. A moment later, a larger creature opened the door and Lorena found herself being pushed into a large, square chamber with a high ceiling.

Her larger captor stepped close and sniffed. Lorena waited calmly. Puzzled, the creature stepped back and scowled.

"I sense no fear in you," it growled, much to her surprise.

"I fear *nothing*," Lorena stated.

The smaller creature, which was obviously female also sniffed her. After a few seconds, she stopped and turned toward the male.

"She is not like the others. Her scent is different. We should free her," she said.

"No. We need her," the male said. "We have nothing to fear. Her hands are chained. She can do us no harm."

"I would not be so sure of that, Hector," the female said. "She makes me nervous, mostly because she is *not*."

"You worry needlessly. She cannot escape her chains," the male assured her.

The female glanced at Lorena who had walked over to examine a pile of bones in the corner as if captors weren't even in the same room.

"I feel that this one can escape any time she wishes," she said. "Be careful."

The male shuffled over to Lorena while the female left the room. She looked at him.

"You seem fascinated with the remains of our meals," he observed.

"I see several human skulls mixed in with animal bones. You're cannibals," she said.

"We eat whatever becomes available to us. Whatever we can easily hunt and kill," the male said.

"So, do you plan to eat *me*?" she asked.

"In due time," he replied.

"Why wait?" she prodded.

"One does not eat the bait before the trap is sprung," he said with a grin that showed off hi jagged, yellowed teeth.

"Bait?" she asked, although she knew exactly what he meant.

"There are others in the house. They search for you even as we speak. I want to be sure they can find you. I've left a trail even a blind man could follow. Once we trap and kill them, I will deal with you," he said confidently.

Lorena laughed.

It unnerved her "host".

"We'll see who traps who," she said.

It looked her over with renewed interest.

"You speak very well. How is this possible?" she asked.

"Books. There are thousands of them in the library. All are quite ancient. Some are too ancient and their pages crumble to dust when they are touched," he replied.

His tone was gruff, as were his manners. But Lorena could easily tell that both he and the female were of above average intelligence.

"You have a library?" she asked, her curiosity piqued.

"I will show you," he said as he led her through another large chamber. They reached a heavy wooden door with ornate paneling. He tapped it.

"It is in there," he said. "Want to see?"

She nodded.

The creature turned the ancient handle and pushed the door inward. It opened into an even larger chamber with a tall, marble fireplace, a long table, two wing backed chairs with rotting upholstery and several shelves packed with books of all shapes and sizes. Lorena stepped inside and walked around. As she did, she examined the titles.

"Dickens, Poe, Heinlein, Lovecraft, Adams, Verne, Shakespeare, Doyle, Twain . . ." she read aloud, "This collection would be the envy of any library I can think of.

He smiled.

"I have always enjoyed the classics. I particularly enjoy Edgar Rice Boroughs," he said.

"There are even works by Moliere, deMaupesant, Victor Hugo. You've actually *read all of these?*" she asked.

"Several times over. So has *she,*" he said as he nodded to the female who had just entered the room.

"What manner of beings *are* you?" asked Lorena.

The male shrugged.

"To speak the truth, we do not know any more. We have lived in these caverns for more centuries than I can remember. I think we once looked more like you. Over the years, this is what we have become. Monsters. Creatures of the night who shun the light of day and love the night. We rarely travel beyond the grounds of this mansion and even when we do it is because local game cannot be found," he said.

"Wait. How is it that you can also see in the darkness like us? Other humans cannot do that," the female observed.

Lorena smiled at her.

The smile made her more nervous.

"I can do *many* things most humans cannot," Lorena said as they made eye contact. *"Many things."*

The way she said it made the female's heart race slightly. Lorena heard the change in its rhythm as the female looked away. That's when Lorena detected a *second* heart beating within her.

"You are with child," she said softly.

"The latest in many failed attempts. All of the others were stillborn or died within days of their birth," she said with a tremor to her voice.

"This one's heartbeat is strong and steady," Lorena said.

They both stared at her, stunned by the revelation that she was able to hear their hearts beating within them.

"I *told* you this one was different, Hector," the female said. "She frightens me. Let her go. I beg you."

"It is too late now, my sister. The other one is close. I can smell him approaching," the male said. "We must prepare ourselves for battle."

The female nodded.

Hunter left the main passageway and took one that veered to the left. After walking several yards, he stopped and looked around. He found himself at the entrance to a long, high passageway that had been crudely carved through the granite cliff. It ran straight ahead for hundreds of feet and it was pitch black. He looked around. When he sensed he was alone, he began walking.

The floor was level for the most part. About two hundred feet in, he noticed beads of moisture running down the rock walls. After a few more steps, he heard the unmistakable drip-drip-drop of water hitting puddles.

"I'm beneath the river now," he thought. "Just where on Earth *does* this lead?"

He began to notice broken bones scattered on the floor. Some were obviously animal. Others were unmistakably human.

"They eat meat," he thought. "And they're not too particular as to the type."

"Lorena! Where *are* you?" he thought.

A few seconds later, he received her mental response.

"Here, my love. I'm less than 200 feet ahead and to your left."

"Are you safe?" he asked.

"What do *you* think?" she responded.

He laughed and quickened his pace. When he entered the room, he stopped to study the two, unkempt ape-like creatures standing to either side of Lorena.

"I see you've found them," he said.

"They fell right into our rap," Lorena said.

The creatures glanced at each other then looked at Lorena, obviously puzzled by her statement.

To the creatures' astonishment, Lorena's chains slid from her wrists and clattered to the floor. She smiled, then bared her fangs at the male. He bellowed with rage and lashed out with his fist. She evaded the blow and drove her boot into his groin. He yelped in pain like a puppy and reeled backward—right into Hunter's waiting fist.

The punch sent the male staggering but he remained on his feet. He glared at Hunter as he wiped the blood from his split lip with the back of his hand.

"It's on now!" he said much to Hunter's surprise.

"You talk!" Hunter exclaimed as they warily circled each other.

"So do *you*," the creature said. "I prefer my meals to remain silent."

"Try to silence me, then," Hunter challenged as he delivered a punch to its face that shattered its nose.

In return, the creature landed a punch of its own to Hunter's jaw. It was so fast, Hunter couldn't avoid it. He stepped back, then lunged forward and lashed out with his fist. The creature blocked the first. The second landed on its already shattered nose and sent blood flying in all directions. The blow caused him to spin completely around and Lorena struck him with the back of her hand. Her blow sent him reeling back into Hunter who again punched him toward Lorena. The creature ducked under her swing, turned suddenly and tackled Hunter.

Lorena and the female watched as they exchanged several hard punches while they rolled around on the floor. Lorena looked at the female. She blinked, turned and fled from the room.

"Do you need help, mon cher?" Lorena called out to Hunter.

"No. I can handle this myself," he shouted back as they rained even more blows on each other.

Just then, Alejandro and DuCassal entered the room. They watched Hunter and the creature slug it out like prize fighters in a ring. Both had regained their feet and were trading punches in the middle of the room. Lorena walked over to them and smiled.

"So this is what has been haunting this place?" Alejandro asked.

"Among other things," Lorena replied. "They are the only *living* things haunting it. The rest are all dead. Long dead. I doubt that you will be able to get *them* to leave."

"Is Charles toying with that thing or is it really so difficult to subdue?" DuCassal asked as the wild battle continued.

"A little of both, I think," Lorena said.

"What *is* it?" Alejandro asked.

"I have a theory," Lorena said.

Before she could finish, the creature seized Hunter's mantle, lifted him off the floor and hurled him into the others. As they struggled to untangle themselves, the creature limped from the room and headed down the passageway. They righted themselves and went after it at a slow, deliberate pace. There was no need to hurry as the creature had no place to hide.

They followed him through a large wooden door. Hunter watched as the creature bolted through a door on the other side. Instead of chasing him, he stopped to look around.

The room was large, square and high ceilinged. There was one large, thick posted, canopied bed against the side wall and two tall armoires, a small side table with a basin and pitcher of water and a shelf with several ancient books. There was a steamer trunk at the foot of the bed and a threadbare rug on the floor. The room was clean and neatly kept.

Hunter walked over to the trunk and lifted the heavy lid. It was filled with ancient papers and parchments. He picked one up, perused it, and passed it to Lorena. She read it and nodded.

"It is just as I thought," she said.

"What is?" asked Alejandro.

"We'll explain later. Let's find those things first," Hunter said as he returned the parchment to the trunk and shut the lid. "Keep cool. I'd like to take them alive if possible."

"Why is that, mon ami?" asked DuCassal.

"I'll explain later," Hunter said.

They walked to the next door. Hunter raised his hand.

"I'll go in first. Wait here until I call for you," he instructed as he turned the handle.

When he entered the room, he was surprised to find himself in a comfortable Victorian era living room, with a large sofa, two wing backed chairs, a fireplace, book shelves and a large family portrait above the mantle. He was also surprised to see that the creature had donned a shirt and pants. He was also armed with an ancient dueling pistol.

"I always expected that it would come to this. Nothing lasts forever," the creature said. "This was my father's pistol. Besides my books, it is one of the few things he left to me. It has not been fired in a long time."

"Put down the weapon. I don't want to kill you," Hunter said.

The creature grinned and raised the pistol.

"You have no choice!" he said as he pulled the trigger.

The shot narrowly missed Hunter's hat. He raised his revolver and fired twice. Both shots struck the creature in the chest.

The creature staggered backward and fell into the old wing backed chair that was directly beneath the ancient portrait. Hunter holstered his revolver and walked over to him as the light slowly faded from his large, dark eyes and the blood stained the tattered ruffles of his moldy shirt.

Lorena and the others rushed in. Hunter turned and removed his hat.

"The female escaped. I don't know where she went. I can't pick up her scent or heartbeat," Lorena said with a wink.

Hunter nodded.

The dying male managed a crooked smile.

"Then the line will continue after all," he gasped as his head fell to the side and the life left his body.

"What did it mean by that, mon ami?" asked DuCassal.

"The female is pregnant. I sensed two heartbeats in her," Lorena explained.

"Mon dieu! We must track her down and kill her before she gives birth. We don't need more such monsters plaguing the locals," DuCassal said.

"Don't worry, Jean-Paul," Hunter said. "I doubt the locals will have anything to fear from her or her offspring."

He looked up at the painting. It was very old and dusty and depicted a middle aged couple with two small children standing in front of them. It had been painted sometime during the middle of the 19th century of the First Age. The faces of the children were painted in such a way that one could not clearly make out their features.

"If I were her, I'd get as far away from this place as I could. I'd flee into the swamps and find someplace where I could raise my child in peace," he said softly. "I'd go where no harm could come to my unborn child."

"At least I have my house back, thanks to you. But now, I'm not sure that I wish to keep it. It is still very active with spirits and other supernatural things. I doubt that I'll be able to get much sleep here," Alejandro said.

He looked up at the painting.

"What was he, Charles?" he asked.

"Not *what—who*," Hunter said as he ran his fingers over the tarnished brass plate on the frame of the painting.

"Ah, the missing twins!" Alejandro said as he looked at the portrait.

"Yes. They've been in these tunnels all this time, surviving on anything and anyone they could catch and shunning contact with the outside world," Hunter said.

"They were either the victims of a genetic birth defect or the shaman's curse. Either way, such children would have been considered a disgrace to the family and hidden from view.

My guess is that Willingham hired workers to construct these tunnels. When the children were old enough, he forced them inside. No one knew because he likely paid the workers and servants off to remain quiet. He had the servants bring them food and fresh clothing daily. Although they were a disgrace to the family, they were his children after all and he couldn't just kill them outright," Hunter added.

"Willingham objected and tried to prevent it, he killed her and walled her up, too," Lorena said.

"She probably threatened to expose his cruelty to the public. He couldn't allow anything to tarnish his reputation, so he killed her to protect his good name. Then he abandoned the house but left two servants behind to feed the twins. I think the servants left after his checks stopped," Hunter said.

"Willingham was the only *real* monster in this house," Alejandro stated in disgust. "They should have walled *him* up!"

"He succeeded in killing his wife but not the twins. They managed to live on all these centuries. How do you account for their longevity, Charles?" DuCassal asked.

Hunter shrugged.

"How do you account for ours?" he asked as he looked down at the lifeless body of Hector Willingham. "Let's give him the dignity of a proper burial, Alejandro. We can place him next to his mother. I think they'd both like that."

"I agree. What about the woman?" Alejandro asked.

"She's out in the world someplace. Frightened, alone and pregnant. Wherever she goes, I wish her and her unborn child well," Hunter said.

The others nodded.

They carried Hector's body out of the chamber and up into the living room. Hunter and DuCassal constructed a coffin from the lumber the workers had left behind and gave it several coats of lacquer like they did when they built the one for his mother. Lorena found Alejandro's razor and shaved the rough whiskers from Hector's face. When he was shaven, she sat back and looked at the strong, lantern jaw and deep set eyes. His nose and lips were twisted and deformed, but he otherwise looked fairly normal.

"It's too bad Willingham didn't have enough love and patience to raise his children. If he had, he would have been pleased with the way his son turned out," she said.

"He's no more a monster than *I* am," Alejandro observed. "What a tragedy."

Hunter nodded.

They placed Hector in the coffin and lowered him into the grave they had dug next to his mother's. When the grave was covered, Hunter said a prayer over them.

"I think I will have a granite marker placed on their graves. It is the least I can do," Alejandro said. "Maybe then they will be able to rest in peace. This solves one mystery. But what about the room at the top of the stairs?"

"I suggest you avoid it for a while," Hunter said. "Unless, of course, you enjoy being thrown the stairs."

Alejandro laughed.

It took some doing, but eventually Hunter and Alejandro persuaded the Behan and his crew to return and finish the job on the mansion.

Three days later, they piled into the carriage and headed back to New Orleans. On the way out, they rode past the graves. On each was a fresh bouquet of flowers. Hunter smiled and tipped his hat.

That same night, Alejandro once again opened the door at the top of the stairs. This time, instead of the usual blast of frigid air that had greeted him before, a gentle, warm breeze filled the room. He stepped inside and inhaled, expecting to be hurled down the steps. Instead, the light scent of lavender permeated the room and filled him with a sense of peace.

Alejandro smiled and nodded.

CHAPTER SEVEN:
The Killing Moon

Two a.m.

Hunter was awakened by an all-too familiar dream. It was the same one he'd had many times before. The dream where he and his brother found that ancient vault in the ruins of the city that had been devastated by the Turks.

It was always the same.

His brother opened the vault and he tried to stop him, only to get knocked unconscious. When he woke, the vault lay open and his brother was gone. Then he heard the laughter. He saw the dark figure emerge from the smoke that drifted from the vault. Then everything went dark and he woke.

He sat up and ran his fingers through his hair while Lorena watched. She reached up and touched his shoulder. He took her hand and smiled.

"The dream again?" she asked.

He nodded.

"It's always the same," he said. "At least it doesn't leave me in a cold sweat like the other ones did."

She looked at the clock on the wall across from the bed and sat up.

"It's time for our walk," she said. "Jean-Paul's been out by himself since midnight."

"Let's go find him," Hunter agreed as they dressed.

Ten minutes later, they left the house and headed for St. Charles. As usual, the streets were still crowded with tourists and the local party crowd. The clubs and bars had no official closing time in New Orleans. Most shut down between five and seven a.m. in order to throw out the remaining drunks and clean the places up. Then they reopened for breakfast. This was a centuries-old custom in the Crescent City. One that no one had any desire to break with.

They followed St. Charles until it crossed Canal Street. On the other side of Canal, it became Royale. Canal was the dividing line between the original French inhabitants and the new tides of Americans that flooded into the city after the Louisiana Purchase. The Americans built their mansions in the Garden District and settled west of St. Charles while the French remained in the Vieux Carre in their elegant Creole mansions or built even grander ones along Esplanade and Bayou St. John. Although New Orleans had become a real melting pot over the centuries, the street names never changed and Patois or Louisiana French, became blended with English so the two were nearly inseparable.

The more New Orleans changed, the more it remained the same.

It was this stubborn resistance to remain and preserve their ancestral homes that enabled New Orleans and several other towns and cities in Louisiana to survive the Great Disaster. Only a handful of North American cities had survived intact. New Orleans was the largest.

They strolled along Royal as they usually did. A few of the locals stopped to chat and say hello. Everyone in New Orleans knew them and appreciated what they'd done for the city and its people. Even tourists knew them on sight. Sometimes they asked for their autographs or to pose for photos with them.

"I guess it goes with the territory," Hunter said. "It's the price we pay for staying in one place. It's a little embarrassing at times, but I'm getting used to it."

"So am I, mon cher," Lorena said. "At least we are not bothered very often and most tourists are polite enough to ask first. But they always seem so surprised when I tell them that I actually do show up in photos."

Hunter laughed.

"I guess they've heard the old myths about vampires not being able to cast reflection in mirrors or showing up in photos," he said.

"I don't know how that ever got started. After all, we are solid living beings like everyone else. We cast shadows like every living thing. Some people think vampires are some sort of *ghosts*!" Lorena said with a smile.

"You mean like the myth that you sleep in coffins and can't go out in sunlight?" Hunter joked.

"Yes—like that," she said. "They believe we are animated corpses, which is absurd," she said.

"You can blame that on European folklore," Hunter said. "And Bram Stoker."

"Monsieur Stoker had it all *wrong*. But it was not his fault. He just based his writings on the legend that revolved around a certain Transylvanian nobleman," she teased as she hugged him.

Hunter laughed.

"I've often wondered where those outrageous stories came from," he said. "Superstitious people will believe almost anything they're told. Still, those stories came in handy at times. They kept would-be Slayers at bay."

"And now you *are* a Slayer, mon cher," Lorena said with a smile.

"Did I ever tell you that you have the most beautiful smile on Earth?" he asked as he pulled her closer.

"Many times. And I never tire of hearing it," she said.

When they reached Bienville, they saw DuCassal strolling toward them. They stopped and waited. He grinned as he greeted them and they walked down Royal together.

"It's been a most quiet evening so far," DuCassal said. "I have been along almost every street in the Quarter. All seems well in New Orleans."

"Let's head up to Rampart and check out the cemeteries and park," Hunter suggested.

"That's fine with me," DuCassal agreed.

They turned north on St. Louis to Dauphine. There were only a handful of small bars and restaurants on this street. Most were already closed and the street was deserted. They continued to Burgundy, which was a little busier. Burgundy was lined with long Creole cottages and some two and three story town homes. There were at least a dozen bars and eateries between Canal and St. Ann. The rest of the street was quiet.

A light rain began to fall. Hunter pulled up the collar of his mantle while Lorena adjusted her cloak and hood. When they reached Rampart, they crossed over to Basin Street and stopped in to check with Valmonde.

The station had been a tourist center during the First Age. There was an older police station across the street where most of the force gathered. Valmonde's office window looked out upon St. Louis Cemetery Number One. Most of the time, he kept his blinds shut so he wouldn't see it. He was standing at the counter making a pot of coffee when they strolled in. He smiled.

"Coffee will be ready in a few if you want any," he offered as he shook their hands.

"That'll be fine, Leon," DuCassal said as he sat down. "It's a quiet evening anyway and I could use a break."

"Same here. So far, we've made no arrests. Not bad for a Friday night," Valmonde said as he sat down. "It'd be real nice of it would stay like this for a few nights."

Hunter nodded.

"We could all use a break, Chief," he said.

Valmonde smiled.

"Lorena, you and Miss Morii sure made short work of that gang. I don't know how to thank you properly for that. You did the city of New Orleans a great service when you took them out," he said.

"The rewards are enough thanks, Chief," Lorena said. "At least I won't feel hungry for a while."

Valmonde laughed.

"I hope we can say the same for Miss Morii. It seems to me that she feeds a lot more than you," he said. "Is that normal?"

"For some," Lorena replied. "Each of us is different. We have different needs. Are you worried about her?"

"Kinda," Valmonde admitted. "She seems to be a lot more enthusiastic about it—if you know what I mean."

Lorena nodded.

"We're keeping an eye on her, Chief," Hunter assured him.

"The first year or two are the most difficult for a vampire. Each passing day brings changes in her metabolism, her abilities and her strength. In order to keep up with it all, she needs to keep nourishing her body. I think this will level off once her transformation is completed," Lorena explained.

"What if it doesn't?" Valmonde asked.

"In that case, you'll have a real shortage of criminals in New Orleans," Hunter joked.

Five a.m.

Imelda Cruz worked as a housekeeper at the old Frenchman Hotel. She was making her rounds of the courtyard and sweeping up loose trash when she noticed a dark liquid seeping out from beneath the door of room 102. She stopped what she was doing to check it out. She leaned over and watched as the brownish-red liquid oozed over the stone step and vanished into the muddy grass. Curious, she knelt down and put her finger in the liquid. When she examined it closely, she realized it was blood.

Her subsequent screams woke everyone in the hotel.

Joe Barnes, the manager rushed out to see what was happening. He saw Imelda standing outside room 102 shaking and sniveling. He ran over and asked why she was screaming. All Imelda could do was point at the liquid.

"Mother of God!" Joe exclaimed. "That looks like blood!"

"You go and get the police," he told Imelda. "I won't open this door until they get here."

A terrified Imelda burst into the station while Hunter and the others were drinking coffee. She caught her breath, gasped, and took a few more breaths before she could talk.

"You've got to come to the Frenchman right now!" she managed to say.

Then she fainted.

DuCassal caught her before she hit the floor and laid her on a nearby couch. Valmonde grabbed his hat.

"Look after her, Sam!" he said on the way out.

Thirty minutes later, they arrived at the Frenchman in Valmonde's buggy. Joe was waiting outside when the pulled up.

"What's up, Joe?" Valmonde asked.

"I'm not sure, Leon. All I know is you'd best have a look at this," Joe replied as he led them to room 102.

Hunter looked at the ooze and leaned down. He ran his finger through it and looked it over.

"That's blood," he said.

"Open that door, Joe," Valmonde said.

Joe used his pass key to open it. They stepped inside and were immediately repulsed by the unmistakable stench of decaying flesh. Joe went to the window and pulled the curtains open to let the light in. Then he opened it to let the smell out. The sunlight streaming into the room shone upon a most horrifying sight.

There were five bodies, all in various states of dismemberment. There were three men and two young women. One of the women, or what remained of her, lay on her back on the bed. The second, minus her head and legs, lay across her. One of the men, his face just about ripped off and an arm dangling from a single tendon, sat upright in a nearby chair. Another lay on his side against the wall. His chest was ripped wide open and his intestines had exploded across the carpet. The last man was found in a bloody fetal position in the bathtub.

"Jesus Christ! Look at these people," Valmonde said as he looked around. "They look like they've been put through a thresher!"

"There's blood and body parts scattered all over the room. It'll take months to clean this," Joe complained.

"Who were they?" asked Hunter.

"According to the register, this room was reserved by Mr. and Mrs. Henry Blanco. I'm not sure which of these is them," Joe said.

"What about the other three?" asked Valmonde.

"Beats me, Leon. Probably friends of theirs who came in for a drink. There's several beer bottles laying around," Joe guessed.

DuCassal searched their pockets. The men both had wallets. He handed them to Valmonde.

"The one against the wall is Lucas Manning. According to his I.D., he's from St. Louis," he said. "The second man is Browning Baer, also from St. Louis."

"Interesting. What about the Blancos? Did they mention where they were from?" Hunter asked.

"When they signed the register, they listed St. Louis as their home address," Joe said.

"What about the second woman?" Lorena asked.

"According to the I.D. I found in her purse, she is also from St. Louis," DuCassal said. "Her name was Linda Manning."

"Manning? She must be related to that fella over there," Valmonde said.

"When did they sign in?" Hunter asked.

"Five days ago. They took the room for ten nights," Joe said. "We don't usually have people stay that long."

"Were these others guests in the hotel?" Valmonde asked.

Joe shook his head.

"None of them show up on our register. Maybe they came from another hotel?" he said.

Hunter turned to Valmonde.

"I know what you're goin' to say. I'll check with every hotel in New Orleans to see if any of them registered and when. I'll have that information for you this afternoon," Valmonde said with a smile.

Hunter laughed.

Lorena bent down and examined one of the bodies. She looked back at Hunter.

"This one's a *vampire*," she announced.

"So's this one, "Hunter said as he pried the lips apart to reveal the fangs.

"Same here," said DuCassal.

"In fact, they are *all* vampires," Lorena said. "What could be fast enough and strong enough to do this to an entire room of vampires?"

"I'm almost afraid to guess," Hunter said. "Whatever did this was really pissed off, too."

"Rougarou?" Valmonde suggested.

Hunter shrugged.

"It sure looks like the work of one, doesn't it?" he said. "But looks can be deceiving, Chief. I don't see any prints, hair or other signs that point to a rougarou. Besides, a single rougarou wouldn't stand a chance against five vampires."

"Unless they were taken by surprise?" DuCassal asked.

"Some surprise!" Valmonde said.

"Not the sort of surprise *I'd* like either," Hunter said. "Have your men keep their eyes and ears open. Whatever did this must still be around and they may be more bodies like this. If they do come across anything, tell them not to try to take it down by themselves—not unless they have no other choice. Just let us know about any sightings and we'll handle it. We don't want any of your men to end up like these people."

Valmonde nodded.

"Meanwhile, I have the meat wagon come and take these people to the coroner's. Maybe she can tell us a little bit more about what killed them and why," he added.

"Was there anything special about last night?" DuCassal asked.

"There was a full moon, but you couldn't tell by the cloud cover we had," Valmonde said. "You think that might have somethin' to do with this?"

"Anything's possible, Chief," Hunter said. "Whatever did this tore them limb from limb. It's like they were attacked by a wild animal or worse. Joe, do you know if anyone heard anything?"

"I'll ask the night manager. If there was a ruckus, he'd sure as Hell know about it," Joe replied.

"I'm still thinking rougarou, mom ami," DuCassal said.

"I'm thinking the exact same thing," Hunter said. "But there's no sign of a violent entry. In fact, the door was still locked from the inside. No windows are broken either. In fact, the only window in this room was shut and locked. A rougarou would have shattered the window or door to get inside—or out."

"I don't see any prints on the floor or walls," Valmonde added.

"There's one," Lorena said as she walked over to a pool of blood near the window. "It's small, too. Like a woman's."

"Maybe one of these ladies made it?" DuCassal suggested.

"One way to find out," Valmonde said.

He looked around. He found two different women's shoes and carried them to the print. Hunter watched as he laid each shoe next to it. The second shoe seemed to match the size, but when Valmonde turned it over and compared the sole markings, they were completely different. He looked up at Hunter.

"This print doesn't appear to belong to either of the women," he said.

"That means there was a third woman in this room. Why wasn't she killed with everyone else? What happened to her? Where did she go?" Hunter asked.

"Serche la femme," Lorena said.

"Can you track her?" Hunter asked.

"I can try," she said as she walked over and concentrated on the print. After a few seconds, she smiled.

"Let's go," Hunter said.

The trail led them to Washington Square Park. Lorena stopped and looked around.

"What's wrong?" Hunter asked.

"The trail is gone," she said. "It ends right at this tree."

Hunter looked up and whistled.

"I can see why," he said as he pointed to the mangled body of a woman high in the branches. "I'd be willing to wager that she's Alicia Manning."

"This doesn't make sense," Hunter said. "Why drag her all the way out here and then kill her when she could have easily been killed with the others?"

"Perhaps she was used as a warning of some kind?" DuCassal suggested.

"Against what?" Valmonde asked.

"Can you find out what line of work those people were in, Chief? That might give us a lead," Hunter asked.

"I can sure try," Valmonde said. "I'll send the wagon out to get her. This sure as Hell turned into one nasty night!"

Lorena spotted three deep scratches midway up the tree and pointed.

"Those are claw marks—and they're deep," Hunter said.

"Very deep. They look as if they are a quarter of the way into the trunk," Lorena said.

"Rougarou!" DuCassal said. "It *has* to be."

"Maybe," Hunter hedged. "We might know more after the autopsy. Any idea who this girl was?"

"None," Valmonde replied.

"I'd be willing to wager that she's from St. Louis, too," Hunter said.

But the autopsy turned up nothing more than the fact that they had been torn to pieces by something with incredible strength. Several of the bodies had deep claw marks and just about every bone in their bodies had been broken.

"No organs were eaten or missing. They still had blood in them and they were all vampires. So I had their bodies burned in the usual manner to keep them from causing any trouble later on," Dr. Sumner explained. "I'd say whatever did this really detested these people."

"Or vampires in general," Hunter said.

"I don't think so, Hunter. Whatever did this specifically targeted this bunch for some reason. Something tells me that we haven't heard the last of this, either," Sumner said.

"You're probably right, Julia," Hunter said. "Right now, there's nothing we can do about it. We'll just have to wait for the creature to make its next move and try to track it down. Meanwhile, I suggest that you burn their bodies. We don't need any of them to come back to haunt us later."

"Will do," Valmonde said.

The Vatican—Two days later.

The Cardinal paced the floor of his office as Fra Capella sat and watched. He turned and looked at him.

"You're positive about this?" he asked.

"Yes, Excellency," Capella assured him. "Quite positive."

"I see. Then we have lost another one to this beast. That makes three Slayers who have met their end at his hands. Where was he last seen?"

"Nelson telegraphed us that the beast had left Budapest and was traveling southeast towards the Thulian Peninsula," Capella said. "He informed us that he would follow as quickly as he could. The last message we received from him came one week ago. He wrote that he had followed the beast to a large grassy plain called the Yboe. That's in the western part of Thule."

"That was it? There were no further messages?" the Cardinal queried.

"None," Capella said. "I've made several attempts to contact Nelson to no avail. He has simply dropped off the face of the Earth—just like Ramstein did last summer."

"And it was Nelson who determined that the beast had killed Ramstein," the Cardinal stated. "And I, like a fool, sent Nelson after it, only to meet the same fate."

"How dangerous is this thing you call the beast, Excellency?" Capella asked.

"Dangerous enough to kill three of my better Slayers and at least one thousand innocent people," the Cardinal said. "That monster has been on the loose for ten years now. It has butchered its way from Berlin to the Middle East and shows no sign of slowing its killing rampage. We must find it and kill it before it slaughters more innocent people."

"But it appears that none of our Slayers is up to the task," Capella said.

The Cardinal sat down and smiled.

"There is one . . ." he said.

Nine days later, Hunter and Lorena spotted the bright yellow envelope on the floor of the hallway when they returned from brunch at Brennan's. She picked it up while he hung his mantle on a nearby hook.

"It's from the Vatican," she said as she handed it to him.

"It has the Cardinal's official seal on the back. It must be important," Hunter said as he opened it with his finger.

He perused it for a few seconds then passed it to Lorena. She read it and stared at him.

"It's a new assignment. An *urgent* one. He wants us to travel to Thule and track down some sort of monster that's killed three other Slayers. He states that we are the only ones who might be capable enough to kill this thing," she said.

Hunter nodded.

"It also says that another information packet and travel documents will follow. I want to know more about this beast before I decide whether or not we should go after it. Regardless, when it's over, we're coming back home," he said.

DuCassal had been listening the entire time as he poured them each a glass of port from the bottle he had brought back from the restaurant.

"Do you wish me to travel with you, mon ami? I am available if needed," he volunteered as he passed out the drinks.

"We may be gone for several weeks, Jean-Paul. That would leave only Hannah here to safeguard New Orleans," Hunter said.

"She is more than capable of handling anything that arises. If need be, she can ask Alejandro for assistance or Tony. New Orleans will be in good hands," DuCassal countered.

"In other words, you're going no matter what we say," Hunter said.

"Exactly!" DuCassal replied with a smile. "Besides, I have never been to Thule. The change of scenery might provide me with a different perspective on certain things."

"Or it might make you dead. If that thing's killed two Slayers, you can bet it's no joke. We might not survive an encounter with it. Do you still insist on going with us?" Hunter warned.

DuCassal smiled.

"Try and stop me," he said.

Hunter smiled and shook his head.

"All right. You're in, Jean-Paul. But don't say I didn't warn you," Hunter agreed as they shook hands.

"And since when has Jean-Paul DuCassal ever heeded a warning?" DuCassal joked. "Many years ago, a certain young lady we were both fond of warned me that you would be nothing but trouble. She was right, of course. Fortunately for you, mon ami, I relish trouble."

Hunter raised his glass.

"Here's to trouble," he said as they clinked glasses.

St. Louis Cemetery Number Three was one of the oldest and most little used Cities of the Dead in New Orleans. Most of its vaults were falling apart and the paths were choked with weeks. Rats, rabbits and the occasional alligator called the place home. Several of the ancient vaults lay open, the victims of grave robbers and looters.

It was a sorry sight.

Alejandro was on the hunt. Two hours earlier, a young woman on the way home from work had been attacked near Florida Avenue. She had barely managed to escape with her life. Fortunately for her, she had run headlong into Alejandro as she darted down a side street. Their collision sent both to the ground and caused the rougarou to stop his pursuit.

Alejandro helped the woman to her feet and apologized for knocking her down. She told him why she was running and pointed back up the street.

And the hunt was on.

He'd heard rumors of a rougarou prowling the area and had decided to track the beast down. His keen senses immediately picked up the scent and he easily followed the trail to the gates of the cemetery.

The rougarou knew he was being followed. That's why he darted into the cemetery and hid himself in the deep shadows between the vaults. He expected his pursuer to enter the cemetery. Once he did, he would attack and kill him.

Alejandro was expecting an ambush.

As he entered the cemetery, he removed his hat, cape and mask and placed them atop a nearby vault for safe keeping. His laced shirt soon followed, along with his boots.

"It is time to fight fire with fire," he said as he followed the scent to the center of the graveyard.

He stood still and waited, watching the deep shadows for any signs of movement. He heard his quarry breathing and smiled. Then he turned his back.

The rougarou snarled and leapt at him. Alejandro turned quickly, seized the creature by the throat and slammed him to the ground with enough force to crack the ancient concrete and send dust and weeds flying in all directions.

As the stunned rougarou stared up at him, Alejandro began to change into the very thing he had been hunting. Seconds later, the rougarou's dying howls echoed through the moss encrusted vaults.

After he had torn the rougarou to pieces, Alejandro changed back to his human form. He dressed and left the cemetery, feeling sated by the blood he had just gorged himself on. But rougarou blood always left a bitter after taste in his mouth which he had to wash out as quickly as possible.

"It is time for a nightcap or three," he decided as he walked down the street.

One week later, the information packet arrived from the Vatican along with travel tickets and an envelope filled with Thulian currency. When Hunter, Lorena and DuCassal read the file, their blood nearly ran cold.

The Cardinal went into great—and gory—detail of the trail of murder and mayhem the being he called the beast had left from the Teutonic Empire to the borders of Thule. The only description of the being was that of a floating or drifting black mass that tore anyone it made contact with limb-from-limb and left the victim drained of all bodily fluids and marrow and stripped of flesh and organs.

"We have no further information about this being as all eye witnesses are now deceased. The only real trail it leaves is a trail of dead and it appears to vanish and reappear at random. I advise you all to take the utmost care when confronting the beast and, if possible, to enlist the aid of a powerful magic practitioner when you reach Thule. Please advise me of your decision as this assignment is of a purely voluntary nature."

"This is the first time he's offered us a voluntary mission," Hunter said. "That means he feels that this thing is *very* dangerous indeed."

"A black mass that can vanish and reappear at will? Just how on Earth do we kill something like that, mon cher?" Lorena asked. "Also, what exactly *is* this thing? Is it a demon? An evil spirit?"

"Or another experiment of Opus Dei gone terribly wrong again?" DuCassal asked. "How *do* we go about handling this?"

"By taking the Cardinal's advice and enlisting the help of a powerful witch," Hunter said.

"Do you know of anyone like that in Thule?" asked DuCassal.

"Just one. The question is, will she help us?" Hunter said.

"Then we are taking the assignment?" Lorena asked.

"Pack our bags. We'll leave on the first ship to Europe," Hunter said.

"What if this witch won't help us, mon ami? What do we do then?" asked DuCassal.

"I'm all for returning to New Orleans and waiting for it to come close enough for us to figure out how to deal with it. The only problem with that is thousands more people may die in the meantime," Hunter replied.

"If it's somewhere in Thule now, this witch will be forced to deal with it," DuCassal said. "She would have no choice."

Hunter nodded.

"It's a long journey. We'd better get some rest," he said.

CHAPTER EIGHT:
The Not So Grateful Dead

The next morning, they boarded the steamship La Joliet for the long trip to London. Six days later, they transferred to a small clipper ship bound for Malta. When they disembarked, they decided to spend the night at a local inn called the Crusader's Hole which had existed in one form or another since the 14th century of the First Age.

Their arrival didn't go unnoticed.

As they settled down for their evening meal at the inn, a tall, reedy man with an upturned mustache entered. He was dressed in the uniform of a constable and had a sword in a sheath on his left hip. He looked around, spotted Hunter and his party and strode over.

They stopped eating and looked up at him.

"I am Inspector Giles Maisson of the Gibraltar Constabulary Force," the man said with a slight bow and tip of his cap. "Are you the Slayer known as Hunter?"

"That'd be me. Care to join us, Inspector?" Hunter replied as he extended his hand.

Maisson shook it and sat down in the empty chair.

"I was informed by your employer that you would be here this evening," he began. "Your reputation is well-known."

"We're only here for tonight," Hunter said.

"In that case, I pray to God it will be enough time," Maisson said.

"Enough time for what?" Hunter asked.

"We need your help. Something terrible is happening here lately. That's why I was happy to know you'd pass through here," Maisson said.

"Just what is happening here?" asked DuCassal.

"We have a small problem," the Inspector replied. "It seems that our recently deceased refuse to stay buried."

Hunter swiveled his chair and faced him.

"Tell us more, Inspector," he urged.

"This all began two months ago with the untimely death of Edwardo Leech. He was only 30 at the time and in the prime of health," Maisson said.

"What killed him?" Hunter asked.

"His wife, Nilda. She caught him the throes of passion with another woman and buried a hatchet in his skull the next morning over breakfast," Maisson explained.

"That seems reasonable to me," Lorena said.

Hunter laughed.

"It would to *you*," he said.

"But I would not have used a hatchet," Lorena said.

"We buried Mr. Leech in St. Francis Cemetery two days later. When the caretaker went out to check the graves a week later, he discovered that it had been dug up. The coffin lay open inside the grave and Mr. Leech was gone," Maisson said.

"Body snatchers?" DuCassal asked.

"We have not had an incident of that in several hundred years. Besides, there is no profit to it anymore," Maisson said. "We sent out a party to search the grounds. They found a set of tracks that lead from the grave to the gate. The tracks vanished after that."

"You said there were more than one?" Hunter asked.

Maisson nodded.

"Yes indeed. We tried and convicted Mrs. Leech for murder and hanged her a week later. We buried her in the same grave as her husband. The following morning, she, too, was missing. A very terrified caretaker claimed he saw her claw her way out of the ground and walk toward the gate. Again, we followed her tracks. Again they vanished at the gate," he said.

"Interesting," Hunter said.

"Very," DuCassal agreed. "Were there others?"

"Yes. There were five more after that. All vanished within 72 hours after being buried," Maisson said.

"That's one common denominator," Hunter mused. "Any other similarities? Did any of them die of old age or natural causes?"

"Let me think," Maisson said. "No. All seven were in their early 30s and all had been murdered or killed in terrible accidents. Besides Mr. and Mrs. Leech, Gregor Millner was murdered by a would-be robber. The murdered, Sandor Billings, was arrested and hanged a week later. Victor Martens and Sheila Homs died in falls at their homes less than a week apart and the town drunk, Herman Zeiller was run over by a beer wagon. And each of them walked out of their grave soon after burial."

"So all were in their 30s, in good health, and all met with violent ends—and all of them walked out of their graves after being buried in St. Frances Cemetery—and all of their tracks ended at the gate," Hunter summarized.

"That covers everything," Maisson said.

"Have any of them been seen since?" Hunter asked.

"Not that I am aware of," Maisson replied.

"Since all of their tracks ended at the gate, they either vanished into thin air or someone picked them up in a carriage," Hunter said.

"The latter would be the most logical explanation, Charles," DuCassal said. "But then again, we rarely deal with anything that is logical."

"Dead people simply don't get up and walk away. They were either disinterred by grave robbers or something *compelled* them to leave the cemetery. But why?" Hunter asked.

"It sounds as if someone is in the market for fresh young corpses," DuCassal said.

"But what purpose would they serve?" asked Maisson.

Hunter shrugged.

"God only knows. Perhaps someone needs body parts for some kind of experiment or there's a market for fresh bodies outside of Malta," he said.

"This sounds like something our friends in Opus Dei would have their fingers in, mon cher," Lorena said.

"I'm sure the cluster that was destroyed was only a single head of the hydra. A splinter group may still be operating under a different name. In any case, this is far too interesting to pass up," Hunter said with a grin.

"Then you will help us?" Maisson asked.

"Definitely," Hunter replied as they shook hands. "I will need some help from you, too."

"Anything!" Maisson agreed.

"First, we need to interview any eye witnesses you may have—like that caretaker. Then we'll need to check out every inch of that cemetery, including the grave sites," Hunter said.

"We also need to be informed of any recent burials, especially of anyone who fits into the pattern," DuCassal added.

"Consider it done, my friends," Maisson agreed.

They checked into the inn and went upstairs to unpack. Before Hunter could take out a fresh change of clothing, he heard a knock at the their door. Lorena opened and smiled as Maisson entered.

"I don't want to disturb you but you did say I should tell you of any recent burials," he began.

"That's right. How recent are we talking?" Hunter asked.

"The coroner, Dr. Francisco D'Abo, informed me that a woman named Nadia Bellini was interred just two days ago," Maisson said as he read from the small notepad he took from his pocket.

"Interesting. Does she fit the profile?" Hunter asked.

"Yes. She was just 30 years old when she died from food poisoning in her home. Unfortunately, the family physician was unable to save her and her parents had her buried one day later," Maisson replied. "They buried her in her favorite gown, minus her shoes as is our custom."

"Let's check out her grave," Hunter suggested.

"My carriage is just outside," Maisson offered.

As they approached the cemetery, they saw several people running toward them. Maisson stopped and waited as a middle-aged couple ran over. The woman was a total wreck and sobbing uncontrollably. There were four other people with them. Some were holding bundles of fresh flowers.

"Giles! We are so glad you are here. Something terrible has happened!" the man said as he pointed toward the cemetery gates.

"Compose yourself, Frederico. Tell me what has upset you and your lovely wife so," Maisson replied.

"She's gone! Our daughter is gone!" the man said.

"Gone? How?" asked Hunter as he rightfully assumed the couple were the dead woman's parents.

"I do not know, Monsieur! We came to place flowers on her grave only to find that the grave is opened and her body is missing," the man said.

"Just like the others!" the woman wailed.

"You mean she just *walked* out of the cemetery?" asked DuCassal.

"I don't know!" the man shouted.

Hunter looked at Maisson.

"Who *would* know?" he asked.

"Perhaps the caretaker saw something," Maisson said. "His house is just down that street."

"Let's pay him a visit," Hunter said.

Maisson led them down a narrow, twisting street to a small, white-washed masonry cottage that looked like it had seen better days. Maisson walked up to the door and knocked hard several times. After a few minutes, the door creaked open and a broad shouldered man with a handlebar mustache and thick brown hair greeted them with a yawn.

"This is Bernard Marquand, the caretaker of the cemetery," Maisson said as he introduced him.

"I have some questions for you," Hunter said.

"Who are you?" Marquand asked as he eyed Hunter suspiciously.

"They are friends of mine. They have agreed to help solve the mystery of our missing corpses. I suggest you co-operate with them," Maisson said sternly.

Marquand nodded.

"What's do you want to know?" he asked.

"It appears that another of your recently buried has come up missing," Hunter said.

"Again?" Marquand asked.

"Did you see anything?" Maisson asked.

"No, Monsieur. I did not see a thing," Marquand replied.

"Why not?" asked Hunter.

"I was not there last night," Marquand said.

"Where were you?" Hunter asked.

"Passed out drunk in my parlor, like I am every payday," Marquand grinned. "It is my custom."

"I see. I guess that's all. Thank you," Hunter nodded.

Marquand smiled and watched as they walked back up the street. Maisson scowled.

"That does not make any sense," he said.

"What doesn't?" asked Hunter.

"Bernard said he was passed out drunk at home like he is every payday," Maisson said.

"Is that so strange?" asked DuCassal.

"It is when you consider that he does not get paid for another six days," Maisson replied.

"Interesting. Does he have another source of income?" Hunter asked.

"Perhaps. Being a gravedigger and caretaker doesn't pay very much. He likes to gamble, too. Mostly, he loses. Or so I have heard," Maisson said.

"That kind of makes me wonder about him," Hunter said.

"Yes, it does," DuCassal nodded.

"Now what?" Maisson asked.

"Now I want to have a look at that grave," Hunter said.

"Bon chance. I will be in my office if you need anything," Maisson said as he took his leave at the carriage. "I have other important matters to tend to."

They walked over to the cemetery. There were several sets of wagon tracks just outside the gate.

"This is no help. Any one of these could belong to the wagon that drove off with the bodies. It's impossible to tell which one or what direction it went in," Lorena said as she looked at the ground.

"Maisson said the grave was about three hundred yards up the main path. Let's check it out," Hunter said.

The cemetery was very ancient. Many of the more ornate vaults and markers dated back to the First Age. Some even bore the symbols of the Knights Templers. Most had crosses on them. A few had the Star of David.

They followed the path until they came to what appeared to be a freshly dug grave. Hunter looked around, then jumped in to examine the casket. He lifted the lid and looked on the inside, then shut it again and jumped back out.

"There's nothing that indicates anyone dug their way out of this grave. Nothing at all," he said as he checked the dirt around it.

"That's interesting," Hunter said as he squatted down and examined the ground.

"What is, mon ami?" asked DuCassal.

"There's a set of footprints leading up to the grave and a set of prints going away from it," he said.

"Perhaps the first set belongs to the gravedigger and the second was made by the corpse?" DuCassal suggested.

"Ordinarily, I'd agree with you, Jean-Paul. But something blows that theory away," Hunter said as he pointed to the second set of prints. "See for yourselves."

"Both sets of prints were made by the same person!" Lorena said.

"Exactly!" Hunter smiled.

"If the person who was buried here actually escaped from this grave and walked away, the second set would be different, especially when you know that this is the grave of a young woman who was also buried without shoes. The prints were obviously made by a heavy set male wearing work boots," he added.

"Ergo, the corpse did *not* crawl out of this grave and walk away. It was dug up and *carried* off," DuCassal concluded.

"Bingo!" Hunter smiled.

"Now who around here wears work boots and is heavy set?" Lorena asked with a grin.

"You *already* know the answer to that, my love," Hunter said.

"Marquand, the caretaker!" DuCassal said.

"But why would *he* lie about such a thing?" Lorena asked.

"What's more important is why is he doing this and who does he work for?" Hunter asked as they left the cemetery.

"I'll find out, mon cher," Lorena said.

Hunter nodded.

"Be careful," he said.

Lorena smiled and nodded.

Two hours later, a rather nervous Marquand knocked on the heavy wooden door of the crumbling abbey that overlooked the waves of the sea as they crashed and broke against the granite rocks below. A hunchbacked, malformed semi-human creature shuffled to the door. He opened it, studied Marquand with his one rotating eye and led him through the dank halls. Several minutes later, they reached the only well-lit room of the structure.

A tall, reed-like man in a long white frock was busy uncovering the lifeless body of young woman that lay on a table in the center of the room. Marquand's escort cleared his throat.

The man in the white frock glanced over his shoulder at Marquand and nodded. The hunchback shuffled out and closed the door behind him.

"What brings you here?" the man asked.

"Three strangers have arrived, Dr. Lerrante," Marquand said as he watched Lerrante examine the young woman's corpse. "They might be trouble."

"Oh? Why do you think that?" Lerrante asked.

"Maisson asked them to find out what's been happening to all these bodies," Marquand said. "I think they are Slayers or something."

"Who are they?" Lerrante asked as he turned to face him.

"I don't know their names. The leader is a tall man dressed in a black mantle. With him is a beautiful red haired woman and another man," Marquand replied. "The word going around the city is that the woman is a vampire."

"A vampire? How interesting," Lerrante said with a smirk. "It seems to me that I have heard of such a couple before. If your description is correct, I believe the Slayer's name is Hunter and the woman with him is Lorena. They work for the Vatican."

"But what are they doing here?" Marquand asked.

"The Vatican has its nose everywhere. Most likely they have come here to find out about this place. Watch them closely, my friend. Let me know every move they make," Lerrante said.

"Will do. But why would the Vatican send them here?" asked Marquand.

"The Vatican frowns upon anyone who tries to play god. It makes them nervous and they don't like the competition," Lerrante said. "I can't have them interfering with my work. Not now. Not while I'm *this* close!"

Marquand shrugged.

He had no idea what Lerrante was doing and didn't care one way or the other what happened to him. All he knew was that he was being well-paid to supply him with fresh, young bodies. Sure, it was illegal, but caretaking didn't pay very much and he had a gambling habit to support.

Lerrante often ranted about acting the part of god and resurrecting the dead or creating the perfect being. Marquand never paid too much attention to his rants. He figured Lerrante was crazy. He didn't care how crazy as long as the money kept coming. And the strangers just might put a stop to that extra income.

Dr. Francois Henri Lerrante himself was somewhat of newcomer. He'd arrived in Malta nine months earlier and purchased the old abbey on top of the cape. The title of "doctor" was mostly self-imposed. Although he'd had some formal medical schooling, he was forced to leave the university in Heidelberg under some very shady circumstances. Similar circumstances forced him to leave several smaller cities he'd attempted to set up his practice in. After 23 years, he managed to end up on Malta.

Marquand had met him at the local casino a month later. That's when Lerrante hired him to help make repairs to the abbey. Three months after that, Lerrante offered to triple his pay to steal fresh, young bodies from the graveyard. It was an offer the often-indebted Marquand just couldn't refuse.

If they got caught, Lerrante would be sent to a madhouse and Marquand would go to prison—and *that* would certainly limit his access to the casino.

Lerrante stepped back from the table and shook his head.

"This was one of your better acquisitions, Bernard," he said. "She was nice and fresh, too. I can harvest several organs from her. When can you bring me another?" he asked.

"That will depend on when and if someone else dies. How soon do you need one?" Marquand asked.

"I wasn't speaking of a corpse," Lerrante said with a grin.

"You don't mean—!" Marquand gasped.

"That's *exactly* what I mean. This one must be very fresh. Preferably still alive when you bring her," Lerrante said.

"That's impossible! Grave robbing is one thing and bad enough. Kidnapping is an entirely different matter! I could be *hanged* for such a thing!" Marquand said. "Why do you need a live one?"

"That is *my* business. Let's just say that there is one human organ that is totally useless once it dies. I need a live person from which to harvest it. Without it, my entire experiment, *decades* of work, are for nothing," Lerrante said.

"How about I bring you the next one an hour after he or she dies?" Marquand suggested.

"No! That will not do. It must be taken from someone while she's still alive. When can you bring her to me?" Lerrante said.

"I'm no kidnapper! I will not bring someone here so you can murder her for your experiments!" Marquand insisted.

"You have no choice. If you don't do what I ask, I will turn you in to the police—anonymously of course," Lerrante threatened.

"Try and I'll tell them you are the one who's buying the bodies from me," Marquand said defiantly. "If you want to kidnap anyone, send your troll to do it. I refuse. I'd turn myself in to the police before I'd do that and take *you* with me."

"So you have *morals* now?" Lerrante sneered.

"I don't have many but even *I* must draw the line somewhere!" Marquand said. "Bringing you corpses is one thing. They are already dead and beyond pain. You can't possibly do the dead any harm. But I will *not* be an accomplice to murder—no matter how much money you offer to pay or how many threats you hurl at me. I may be a drunk and a gambler and a grave robber—but a kidnapper I am not!"

"Is that your final word?" Lerrante asked.

"It is," Marquand insisted.

Lerrante smiled.

"Actually, I just realized that you don't have to bring me a live person," he said.

"Oh? And why is that?" Marquand asked.

Lerrante suddenly turned and stuck a syringe in Marquand's shoulder. Marquand pulled it out and threw it at him. Then he turned to leave and fell unconscious to the floor.

"Because *you* are *already here*, my friend," Lerrante said as he knelt next to him.

Lorena had followed Marquand ever since he left his cottage. She did so in total silence and melted into the shadows or blended into the scenery in ways that made her virtually invisible. It was a typical vampire stalking technique. One that put them at the top of the list of the world's most dangerous predators.

She followed several hundred yards behind him. He led her out of the town and along a twisting foot path that led to the foot of the rocky cape. She watched him make his way up the ancient road to the ruined abbey at the top of the cliff. When he entered the crumbling structure, she scaled the outer wall and stopped when she came to the window of the only illuminated room.

She listened to the entire exchange between Marquand and the strange doctor. It reminded her of a scene from an old horror novel she had read decades earlier. She watched as Lerrante stood over Marquand's unconscious body and laughed. Then she let go of the wall and dropped to the ground without making so much as a sound.

She almost laughed to herself as she made her way back to the inn. The entire scenario seemed somewhat comical to her. She could have burst into the room and dealt with the doctor and his hideous assistant, She could have rescued Marquand.

But she also knew that whatever the doctor had planned would most likely take several hours to prepare for. That gave her more than enough time to tell Hunter and DuCassal what she'd discovered.

After she returned to the inn, she found Hunter and DuCassal having dinner with Inspector Maisson. She sat down at the table and ordered a meal for herself and told them what she saw at the old abbey.

Hunter looked at her as if she'd gone insane.

"A mad scientist *hired* Marquand to steal bodies for his experiments?" he asked in a state of disbelief.

"I am not making this up, mon cher. I heard *everything*. When Marquand refused to bring him a live person, he drugged him and said that he'd use him instead. I think he plans to harvest one of his organs," Lorena said as she cut into her roast.

DuCassal laughed.

"It sounds like something Mary Shelley would have written," he quipped.

"Yes, it does," Hunter agreed. "Do you suppose this 'doctor' is trying to create his own version of the monster?"

Lorena shrugged.

"From their conversation, I have no idea what he's doing with those bodies. I do know that whatever he needs from Marquand he plans on taking it while he's still alive. So it must be an organ that ceases to function soon after death and can't be restored," she said.

"The human brain shuts down within minutes after blood ceases to flow into it and it can't be restored," DuCassal said. "Perhaps he plans on taking Marquand's brain."

"It would be a very poor choice," Maisson said. "Bernard's brain is ravaged by decades of alcohol abuse and concussions he suffered during his many and almost legendary bar brawls."

"Maybe he figures it's the best he can do under the circumstances," Hunter said.

"Beggars cannot be choosers," DuCassal added. "When do you plan on paying this doctor a visit, Charles?"

"Sometime after dinner. There's no rush," Hunter replied.

Darkness had already blanketed the island by the time they set out for the abbey. Since it was on the edge of the island, it took them the better part of an hour to get there another tem minutes to make their way up the slippery path to the structure. By then, a steady rain was falling.

Hunter glanced up the lone illuminated window just as a jagged bolt of lightning sliced through the sky.

"Look like a perfect night for monster making," he said. "Let's pay the good doctor a visit—unannounced, of course."

"Of course!" Lorena smiled as Hunter forced the heavy wooden door open.

The groan of the rusted hinges attracted the attention of the hunchback who came running into the entry room with lantern in hand just as they entered. He dropped the lantern and attempted to flee, only to be brought down by one of Hunter's shiruken. The hunchback fell to the floor amid a lot of gurgling sounds. They watched as a large pool of blood spread out beneath him and the eye ceased its sickening movements.

"An ugly sort, wasn't he?" DuCassal observed as he leaned over the body. "Do you think he was one of Lerrante's earlier experiments?"

"I'd say that was a safe wager, Jean-Paul," Hunter said. "Let's go find the doctor."

"There's a large door on the opposite side of the room," Lorena pointed out. "I sense heartbeats behind it. *Several* heartbeats."

"Let's see who they belong to," Hunter said as they walked to the door.

To their surprise, it was unlocked.

"What's that foul odor?" DuCassal sniffed.

"This place reeks of human waste and rotting flesh," Hunter said as DuCassal turned on his lantern.

"I'm ready," he announced.

"Are you sure?" Lorena asked.

"Well, I'm as ready as I'll ever be for what's down this hall," he replied as he led the way.

They found themselves in a long corridor with doors on either side. Each door was made of thick iron bars and padlocked. Each cell had a small window to admit air and light, straw strewn about the stone floor and a crude cot in the corner. And the cells reeked of urine and feces and rotted food.

"This looks like a dungeon," Lorena observed.

"That's *exactly* what it is. Let's see who he has locked up in these cells," Hunter said as they walked to the first door.

DuCassal shone his lantern into the room. They saw a pathetic, naked figure lying in fetal position on the floor. It was sobbing pitifully.

When it saw the light, it rolled over, jumped up and charged at the bars, snarling angrily as it reached for them. They stepped back and studied the emaciated, humanoid creature. Its body was covered with thick scars and clumps of hair protruded from the many boils that had erupted from its flesh. It had a lipless mouth filled with nasty-looking decayed teeth, a flat nose and eyes that didn't match. It clawed angrily at them and snarled and growled like an animal that's been caged too long.

"What is it, Charles?" DuCassal asked.

"If I had to guess, I'd say this is one of his earlier experiments that didn't turn out quite like he expected," Hunter said.

He drew his revolver, aimed it at the creature's forehead and fired. The shot blew out the back of the creature's skull and sent it to the floor. They watched it twitch a few times before going completely still.

"An act of kindness?" DuCassal asked as they continued down the hall.

"Something like that," Hunter replied.

In the next cell, they saw what appeared to be a woman. She was dressed in a filthy shroud and long, dirty unkempt hair. She was chained to a wall by her ankle and seated in an old metal chair. She looked up at them when she saw the light from the lantern. She had one eye where it belonged and a second eye on the cheekbone on the other side of her face. Otherwise, she looked normal.

She stood up and shuffled toward the bars.

"Do you have a name?" Hunter asked.

"I had one a long time ago. I don't remember it now," the woman said in a raspy voice. "I couldn't speak at first but I have been forcing myself to use words every day. Do you know who I am?"

"I'm afraid not," Hunter said. "When was the last time you had something to eat?"

"Two sunsets ago," she said after some thought. "It was not much. Only a raw potato and some water. He only feeds us scraps when he thinks about us."

"Stand back," Hunter said.

The woman stepped back into the room and watched as Hunter shot the padlock off the door and pushed it open. He walked over and shot the chain off her ankle. She smiled at him.

"You're free now. Go home if you remember where it is," he said.

"Th-thank you," she said as tears ran from her eyes. "Bless you."

At the end of the corridor was a flight of narrow stairs. DuCassal looked up and smiled.

"If I had to guess, I'd say these steps will take up to his laboratory," he said as they began their ascent.

The steps spiraled upward for at least 150 feet and ended at a door. Hunter held up his hand then put a finger to his lips.

"Let's listen awhile," he whispered.

They heard one man talking. His voice sounded almost oily.

"That's Lerrante," Lorena said.

In the background, they head a deeper voice. It was muffled. It was accompanied by the sounds of someone struggling against heavy chains and straps and the squeaking of heavy furniture.

"Sounds like he has someone strapped to a table," Hunter noted.

Lerrante was standing in front of an upright slanted operating table. He had a scalpel in his right hand and he was addressing Marquand who was gagged and strapped to the table by his wrists and ankles. A heavier strap secured his waist. He was staring at Lerrante in terror while vainly struggling to break free.

Lerrante just mocked him.

"Don't waste your strength. Those traps can hold a man ten times stronger than you, my friend. Just try and lie still during the operation. I would not wish to damage that precious brain of yours before I can make use of it," he said as he stepped closer.

Hunter looked at the others and nodded. He stepped back and kicked the door in. The racket stopped Lerrante in mid stride. He turned and glared at the "trespassers" in disgust.

"What do you think you're doing here?" he demanded.

"From the looks of it, we're just in time to prevent a murder," Hunter replied as he walked into the room.

DuCassal and Lorena were behind and to either side of Hunter. They fanned out when they reached the middle of the room. Lerrante glanced at each of them and sneered.

"Leave at once or I'll have Herman throw you out!" he snarled as he waved the scalpel at Hunter.

Hunter sized his wrist and gave it a sharp twist. Lerrante screamed and dropped the scalpel. Lorena picked it up, examined it, then tossed it over her shoulder. She smiled and bared her fangs at Lerrante.

"A vampire!" he gasped.

"Who is Herman?" asked DuCassal as he drew his Bowie knife.

"He's my assistant," Lerrante said. "Get out or I'll call for him!"

"He must be the hunchback you killed a few minutes ago, mon cher," Lorena said.

"If that's the case, you can call for him until you turn blue in the face. Where he is, he'll never hear you," Hunter said as he backhanded Lerrante across his face.

The blow sent Lerrante reeling a few steps but he managed to keep from falling.

"Cut him loose, Jean-Paul," Hunter said as he nodded at the table.

DuCassal cut the straps and freed Marquand. He slid off the table and pointed at Lerrante.

"He's mad! He was trying to steal my brain!" he accused.

"That's so small, you probably wouldn't have noticed it was missing," Hunter said.

"That's true. It's not as if you use it very much anyway," Lorena added.

Lerrante glared at them.

"You've ruined my experiment! All my years of hard work, of trial and error—for nothing because of your interference!" he screamed as the veins in his neck bulged.

"What experiment?" asked Hunter.

"I am trying to create the perfect being. One who will live forever. One who will be impervious to all known human failings and diseases. Perfect! I was almost finished. I was one small step away from achieving my dream. All I needed was a fresh brain from a living person. But you *ruined* it all!" Lerrante ranted as he started drooling.

"What gives you the right to think you can play god?" asked Hunter.

"The diary on my desk over there! It's been done before. I was trying to duplicate it," Lerrante said as he pointed to an extremely old book.

DuCassal walked over, picked it up and smiled when he read the cover. He tossed it to Hunter.

"*Frankenstein?!*" he almost shouted as he glared at Lerrante. "You were trying to duplicate the experiments in *here?*"

"That's right. I thought that if a doctor of the First Age could create life, I could, too. I came close, too. But like all such endeavors, there were *mistakes*," Lerrante grinned.

"We've met your mistakes," Lorena said.

Hunter gripped Lerrante's throat and picked him off the floor. He shook him until he turned blue and his eyes bulged.

"You maniac! You fool! Frankenstein isn't a diary, it's a *novel*. It was written by Mary Shelley centuries ago as a warning against playing god. But Frankenstein never existed and neither did his monster!" Hunter growled as he threw Lerrante to the floor.

"You lie! I *know* it's true! It *has* to be true!" Lerrante said as he slowly got up and rubbed his neck. "And if Frankenstein had been more specific about the details, I would not have made so many mistakes!"

"You truly believe that this is a diary?" Hunter asked.

"Yes!" Lerrante nodded.

DuCassal shrugged.

"You can't reason with an insane man, mon ami. This poor excuse for a doctor should be incarcerated before he actually kills someone," he suggested.

Lerrante sneered at them contemptuously.

"Go ahead and turn me over to the police! Prison doesn't frighten me!" he challenged.

"I have a better idea. A punishment that fits your crime perfectly," Hunter said as he grabbed him by the throat.

He shoved him against the wall. Lerrante steadied himself and glared at him.

"What do you mean? What sort of punishment?" he asked.

Hunter turned and nodded at DuCassal. He grinned and opened the door. Then he stepped back as Lerrante's earlier experiments shuffled into the room. Each was armed with an iron bar they had taken from their cell doors.

Besides the woman they had freed, there were three other poorly stitched together abominations they had passed in the other cells. Instead of trying to find her way out of the abbey, the woman had decided to liberate Lerrante's other projects and, collectively, they decided to repay the doctor for all of the misery he had caused them. The other three were males with uneven limbs, matted hair, swollen eyes and lips and various other deformities too numerous to count.

Lerrante's eyes nearly tripled in size.

"Oh shit!" he said.

"I think I'll let these good folks decide that," Hunter said as he stepped aside.

Marquand saw the expression of abject terror on Lerrante's face as his creations slowly moved toward him. He laughed. Hunter turned and backhanded him across the face as hard as he could. The blow sent him over the operating table and he landed on the floor next to Lerrante's feet.

The creatures looked at Hunter.

"He's as much to blame as the doctor. He's the one who brought you here so the doctor could experiment on you," he said.

Their expressions turned from quizzical to anger. They closed in on both of them. Marquand regained his senses just in time to see the creatures descend on him and the doctor with the iron bars raised.

Hunter turned and walked out of the room. Lorena and DuCassal followed. The screams of pain and the sounds of iron cracking into bone echoed through the old abbey as Lerrante's creations dealt out their particular brand of justice.

They stopped at the base of the cliff and looked back.

"That'll teach him not to play god," Lorena said.

"And all because he believed what he'd read in Mary Shelley's novel! He was indeed mad!" DuCassal said. "But what will become of those creatures, Charles? After all, it is not their fault they are like that."

"We'll tell Maisson about them. Maybe he'll figure out what to do about them," Hunter said. "After all, they *are* citizens of Malta."

They returned to the inn around midnight. Maisson was waiting for them at a corner table. They walked over and sat down. As they drank and ate a light meal, they told Maisson everything that had happened at the abbey.

"I sincerely thank you all for your service to my fair city. As for those poor wretches at the abbey, I have no idea what to do with them. You must admit, it is a rather unique situation for them and us," Maisson said after some thought.

He sighed and looked through the window at the storm.

"The first thing I must do is bring them food and clothing. I will interview them personally to see if they can think and reason as normal people. If they can, we will take whatever steps are necessary to reincorporate them into our society. If not, I will make sure they are safe and comfortable right where they are," he said after some thought. "What happened to them is no fault of theirs. We should not treat them any differently as we would ourselves. They are all citizens of Malta after all."

Hunter smiled.

He reached into his mantle and took out a thick envelope. He handed it to Maisson. The inspector opened it and was surprised to see several large notes of Vatican scrip.

"What is this?" he asked.

"Twenty thousand Vaticans. Consider it my donation to their welfare fund," Hunter said.

"Malta is a very wealthy place, Monsieur Hunter. This won't be necessary, I assure you," Maisson said.

"I insist," Hunter said. "Use it to restore the abbey and make it a more pleasant and comfortable place for them to live. If they don't want to stay there, use it to purchase another house for them. Or for anything else they'd like."

Lorena beamed with a sense of pride in his gesture.

Maisson nodded and stuffed the envelope into his coat pocket. Then he raised his glass and toasted them. They clinked glasses and laughed.

"I must bid you good-night, mes amis," Maisson said after another round. "I will make certain that your gift is put to the proper use. But may I ask you why you insist on doing this? After all, those people are not really your concern."

"But they *are*. All victims of such heinous crimes are my concern. They *should* be everyone's concern. Rescuing them only solved half their problems. They still need help and I want to make sure they get it," Hunter answered.

"They will. I promise!" Maisson assured him as they shook hands.

Two mornings later, Maisson drove them to the dock in his carriage. When they stepped out, they encountered a mob of well-wishers. Most applauded when they saw them. Hunter smiled and blushed.

"It appears that word of our deed has gotten out, mes amis," DuCassal said as he graciously accepted a bundle of flowers and hugs from several young women. "My word, Charles! It's like we've become *rock stars!*"

Hunter was too busy shaking hands and hugging women. Lorena was doing the same. Maisson watched and beamed. He knew that Slayers liked to do their work without fanfare or much public notice. Somehow, word of what happened spread throughout the city and everyone wanted to come out and see them off.

As he was shaking hands, Hunter noticed a slender young woman in a brown cloak making her way through the crowd. The cloak was pulled down in such a way as to conceal most of her features. He held up his hands and politely asked those around him to let her through. She walked up and put her arms around him.

"Maisson told us what you did. Thank you from the bottom of our hearts," she said softly.

"There's no need for thanks," he said. "Just live a good, full life. If you need us for anything, Giles knows how to get in touch with us."

She nodded.

He watched her disappear into the crowd. The steamer's whistle sounded three times. It was the signal to board. He tipped his hat to the crowd, turned and followed Lorena and DuCassal up the gangplank. They stood at the rail and waved to the people as their ship put to sea.

The steamship, Varadna, cut across the vast Mediterranean Sea and made stops at Sicily and Crete before ending its journey in the bustling Byzantium capitol of Constantinople. That part of the trip took nine days. Three days later, they caught an Egyptian passenger schooner for the port of Alexandria. They disembarked, unloaded their horses, and went overland the rest of the way.

It was a long and arduous ride through the lush Nile Valley and across the Great Western Desert to the mountain range known as the Great Gray Wall. This was the natural border of the Empire of Thule, although most of the desert was also part of its territory.

"The last time I traveled through this desert, it belonged to the old Ottoman Empire," Hunter said.

"Was that before you became a Slayer?" Lorena asked.

"I'm not sure. It was so long ago that the timelines have blurred. I had several occupations back then. I can't recall which I was doing when. At one point I held the rank of pasha in the army of Suleiman the Magnificent. I remember fighting in several battles under his banners. I was also a spice and silk trader in Basra and made several caravan trips into China. I've done so many different things over the centuries that I have trouble remembering them all," Hunter replied.

"I think I became a Slayer sometime after when I grew bored with trading. I still don't recall how I ended up at the Vatican or what drove me to go there. That was kind of an on again-off again-on again relationship," he added.

DuCassal laughed.

"I was during one of your off again periods that we met, Charles," he said. "And what grand adventures we had!"

"And *continue* to have!" Lorena said.

"This is my first time in this part of the world, Charles. What do you know about this empire?" DuCassal asked.

"Not much," Hunter replied. "From what I've read, it's ruled by a very enlightened emperor and a trusted inner circle of friends. It has a constitution that's based on the one written by the Founders of the United States in 1789 and it's one of the most modern and prosperous nations of the Second Age. We'll get to meet the emperor when we reach his palace," Hunter said.

"Is that where this Red Witch lives?" DuCassal asked.

"She's one of his closest advisors. That's where most of the members of his inner circle live," Hunter explained.

"Do you think she'll help us?" Lorena asked.

"There's only one way to find out," he said.

CHAPTER NINE:
Season of the Witch

The capitol city of Thule, one week later.

It was an unusual summer night in Thule as an uncharacteristic thunderstorm raged throughout the Valley. While most of the citizens remained indoors, three figures astride black stallions made their way through the wide streets of the city. The lead rider wore a wide brimmed black hat and black leather mantle. Next to him rode an exceptionally beautiful woman with flaming red hair and green eyes dressed in a black cape and hood. A few feet behind them rode the third member of the party. He was dressed in a long black duster and black hat.

Although the trio was a familiar sight in the streets of New Orleans, they were strangers to Thule. No one noticed them on this dark, wet night. If anyone did, they didn't pay much attention.

They made their way through the open gates of the rose garden and along the well-lit path until they reached the front doors of the palace. As soon as they dismounted, a stable boy dressed in rain gear hustled out of the side door and took the reins of their horses. Hunter nodded and thanked him.

"I'll make sure their patted down and fed, sir," the boy said as he led the horses to the stables.

They walked up the wide marble steps. Hunter used the heavy knocker to announce his arrival. A few seconds later, a plump but rather pretty maid opened one of the doors and peered at them.

Hunter smiled.

"We've come to see Gorinna," he said.

The maid squinted at them but let them inside.

"I'll go and get her. Please wait here," she said as she scurried off.

Hunter, Lorena and DuCassal looked around the foyer.

"It's very nice, but it really doesn't give me the sense of being in a royal palace," Lorena observed. "I see none of the usual trappings of state. It just looks like a comfortable waiting area I'd expect to see in a house in New Orleans."

Hunter nodded.

"The locals said their emperor didn't approve of such things and preferred to make his palace more like a family home than a center of power," he said. "They also said there were no official titles in Thule. No lords, ladies, earls—none of the so-called nobility one might expect to find in the upper classes of an empire."

"It sounds very much like the ancient United States during the First Age," DuCassal said.

"Yes, it does," Hunter agreed.

They heard a side door open and watched as a tall, black haired woman with deep green eyes approached. She was dressed in a simple red tunic with a leather belt and sandals. She stopped and studied her visitors while they, in turn, studied her. After a few moments, she decided that these strangers didn't come looking for trouble—but they had certainly brought some with them. When she saw Hunter, she could tell by his garb that he belonged to a very select group. It was a group that had, at one time, posed a threat to people like herself.

"I'm Gorinna. I was told that you asked to see me," she said.

"We did. It's a matter of great importance, too," Hunter said.

"Who are you?" she asked as she tried to read Hunter's thoughts.

To her surprise, she discovered that she could *not*. The stranger was able to block her and his will was very strong indeed.

She squinted at him.

Hunter smiled and removed his hat. His smile was quite disarming.

"My name is Hunter. This is my wife, Lorena and my friend, Jean-Paul DuCassal. We've been sent here on a mission and we need your help," he said.

"You're a Witch Hunter?" Gorinna asked.

"Sometimes. In our order, we're known as Slayers. Mostly I hunt *other* things. Things that are far more deadly than witches," Hunter said. "We hunt the things that escape from our deepest nightmares. Foul creatures that cross over from the darkest shadows into our world and must be killed before they can do much harm."

"How?" she asked.

Hunter smiled—*almost.*

"I *sense* them when they cross over—although I never know their exact locations until after they've committed some foul act. Sometimes, people in dire need *request* our help," he explained.

"Are you a holy man, Hunter?" she asked.

"Some say I am. Others call me a monster. It's a matter of perspective," he said.

"And which are you?" she asked.

"A little of both I think," he said. "I truly don't know anymore and it no longer matters."

"How is that I was unable to detect your approach?" Gorinna asked.

"We Slayers have natural, built-in cloaking abilities. It allows us to travel freely and without fear of detection," Hunter explained. "Many of the things we hunt can also read thoughts."

"Have you come here to hunt *me*?" Gorinna half-joked.

"Not at all. I've come to ask you to hunt *with* us," he replied. "We need your help."

"You need *my* help? This thing you're hunting must be highly dangerous," she said as they walked toward the living room.

"It's already killed two other Slayers, along with over a thousand innocent people from Berlin to Budapest. It was last seen moving toward Thule. The last message we received from the Slayer who was hunting it came from an area called the Yboe," Hunter said.

"What is it you are hunting, exactly?" she asked.

"I'm not really sure. I do know that it's evil incarnate and that we've been trying to kill it for decades. I don't know where it came from but it leaves nothing but death and misery in its wake. It's like your worst nightmare magnified a thousand times," Hunter said.

"If it's here in Thule, I'd better help you find it," Gorinna said with a smile. "But why would you need help? The three of you look formidable enough to handle just about anything."

"Normally, you'd be right. But this is something we can't do by ourselves. We need help. *Powerful* help so we can rid the world of this monster once and forever," Hunter said.

"I see. The last time anyone dressed like you came to Thule, I was one of his intended targets," Gorinna said. "Instead, you've come here to ask me for help. Doesn't that go against the grain?"

"Not in the least," Hunter said. "I'm not what you'd call conventional. I hunt and slay vampires along with my wife."

"Who is *also* a vampire," Gorinna said with a smile. "I knew that the moment I saw you, Lorena. Your lives are filled with ironies and contradictions. Doesn't that bother you?"

"Not in the least," Hunter replied. "What fool tried to hunt *you?*"

"His name was Bardax," Gorinna said.

"He was not from *my* order. He was a member of Opus Dei. We've had more than our fair share of trouble with that bunch over the years," Hunter said. "But they're gone now. The Cardinal found a way to destroy them."

"I know," Gorinna said. "And you'd be amazed at how he *accomplished* it."

"How did you know about that?" Hunter asked.

"You forget who I am," she said smugly. "What else do you know, Hunter?"

He smiled.

"Not as much as I need to and perhaps too much," he said.

She laughed.

"Do you ever give a straight answer?" she asked.

"Do you ever stop asking questions?" he countered.

Before Gorinna could say anything else, the side door burst open and a half dozen laughing, playing children poured into the room followed by a tall, muscular, dark haired man and two beautiful women. The one on his right arm was a short, slender Asian woman with long black hair. The one on his left was a taller, copper-skinned beauty with flowing black hair and amber eyes.

They stopped when they saw Hunter and his two friends.

"We have visitors," the man said as he extended his right hand to Hunter. "I'm Arka-Dal. I bid you welcome to our house."

Hunter shook his hand and introduced himself. He then introduced Lorena and DuCassal. Arka-Dal shook each of their hands then introduced the women.

"This is Mayumi," my first wife and Empress of Thule. "And this is my wife, Galya."

As Hunter moved to shake Galya's hand they stopped and started at each other.

"I feel that I know you. Have we met before?" he asked.

"Yes. Many times and under many different circumstances," Galya replied.

"Pleasant, I hope," Hunter said as he studied her carefully.

"That all depends on your definition of pleasant," Galya replied as she sensed that he was really struggling to recall their run-ins.

He looked into her eyes then smiled.

"Galya! You're Lucifer's daughter!" he said as recognition came to him. "It's been a long time."

"Nearly 450 years. I see that you still work for the Vatican. Why have you come to Thule?" Galya asked as they sat down.

"We've come here on a special mission for the Cardinal," Hunter said. "We received a report that a certain living nightmare has reached Thule. The report was sent to the Vatican weeks ago by one of our best Slayers. He'd been following a trail of its victims across Europe. He tracked it to Budapest where it killed another Slayer. From there, he followed it south and east. His last report said he was following it toward Thule. Then he vanished. The Cardinal believes he was killed by that thing right after he mailed that report. He believed it was headed for a region known as the Yboe."

Galya almost blanched at his reply.

"Is it the same thing that destroyed the villages in Italy 30 years ago?" she asked.

Hunter nodded.

"Then we must locate and destroy it before it can do more harm," Galya said. "That thing is dangerous beyond words."

"You know about it?" Gorinna asked.

"Father told me about it years ago. He lost interest in it when it dropped out of sight. I can't believe it's returned after all this time!" Galya said.

"If that thing is as dangerous as you say and it's here in Thule, then I'd *better* help you find it so we can rid the world of it. Any idea where it is now?" Gorinna said.

"No. The trail went cold after it reached the Yboe," Hunter said.

"Where *would* it go?" Gorinna asked.

"That all depends on how hungry it is. It feeds off living energies and leaves nothing but dried up husks behind. It usually heads for a populated area. The hungrier it is, the longer it lingers. It's been known to wipe out entire villages in a single night," Hunter said.

"The Yboe is sparsely populated. There are less than a handful of villages there. The area is mostly grasslands and rough ground. It's our cattle grazing area," Arka-Dal said. "There are several large and small ranches there."

"It also feeds on livestock," Hunter said.

"It sounds like the Yboe would be the perfect feeding grounds for this thing," Arka-Dal said.

"Does this thing use magic of any kind?" Gorinna asked.

"That I don't know. I can tell you that it moves slowly and sleeps after it feeds. It's been nearly impossible to track at times and we usually arrive on the scene after it's too late to stop it," Hunter answered.

"If it uses magic, it may be able to shield itself," Gorinna mused. "That would make it difficult to locate."

She saw the despondent look on Hunter's face.

"Difficult—but not impossible," she assured him.

Arka-Dal nodded.

"It looks like you have one Hell of a mission before you," he said. "You've arrived during our rainy season. Travel will be almost impossible until the rain stops and the roads dry. While you're waiting, you can stay here."

"That's most kind of you, Emperor," Hunter said gracefully.

"My name is Arka-Dal. We don't use titles in this house or anywhere else in Thule," he said with a grin. "We aren't very formal around here."

Hunter and Lorena laughed.

"And of course, you'll join us for dinner," Mayumi added.

"We would be delighted to dine with you," DuCassal said with a tip of his hat.

"Good! I'll have one of our servants show you to the guest rooms so you can wash the road from your bodies. We'll start dinner after you've refreshed yourselves," Arka-Dal said.

After a long, hot bath and a change of clothes, Hunter, Lorena and DuCassal walked down to the dining room. The long, oval table was already crowded with adults. The children were already feasting at a smaller table nearby. There were three empty chairs directly across from where Arka-Dal was seated.

The table was already laid out with platters of meat, fish, cooked vegetables, nuts, fruit and bottles of blue wine and ale. It was the most food Hunter had ever seen on one table and he thanked the Emperor for inviting them to feast with them. Before they began, everyone introduced themselves. As they ate, Arka-Dal and his friends exchanged their usual insults and bad puns while the women groaned, rolled their eyes or joined in. After a few minutes, DuCassal and Hunter also joined in.

Arka-Dal was more than a little curious about them and began asking questions.

"What is it like being a Slayer?" he asked.

"I like to think that we serve a real purpose. And it also pays very well," Hunter said with a grin.

Arka-Dal laughed

"Have you always been a Slayer?" Gorinna asked as she poured him another cup of wine.

"I've been around a very long and I've tried my hand at several professions," Hunter said. "I've been a soldier of fortune, an explorer, a trader, a merchant, pirate, bounty hunter and even a peace officer. Everything but a ballet dancer and a circus clown. How about you? Have you always been a witch?"

She laughed.

"Touché!" she said as she raised her glass. "You must think I'm being awfully nosy."

"Not awfully—but yes," he said.

"Forgive me, Hunter. But you intrigue me. I want to know what makes you tick," Gorinna said.

"My heart does the ticking for me," he joked.

Galya chuckled.

"I've always liked your sense of humor, Hunter," she said. "Some of the things you've said to me during our encounters still make me laugh."

"I'm glad I was able to provide you with a source of amusement. Now that I've gotten to know you better, I'm happy I never killed you," he said.

"It's not like you didn't *try*. But I could have killed you several times and quite easily at that," Galya said.

"Why *didn't* you?" Hunter asked.

"Father ordered me *not* to," she said. "He said that you were far too valuable to humankind and ordered me to avoid any further confrontations with you if possible."

"That's strange. The Cardinal also ordered me to leave *you* alone. I wonder why he did that." Hunter said.

"Guess!" Galya smiled.

"It sounds like the two of you have had many interesting battles," Arka-Dal said as he sipped his wine.

"But not as many as I've had with Merlin, my love," Galya said. "He wanted to rid the world of me so badly that he could taste it."

"I'm glad the two of you are good friends now," Arka-Dal said.

"Merlin still lives?" Hunter asked in surprise.

"You *know* Merlin?" Arka-Dal asked.

"We've met before. I guess it was sometime during the early 1500s in Trier," Hunter said. "I don't recall how it came about. There's much about those times I've forgotten."

Galya smiled knowingly.

"And most should remain forgotten," she said almost to herself.

"How much have you heard about Thule?" asked Arka-Dal.

"Quite a lot actually. I've also heard about *you*," Hunter said. "People compare you to Alexander the Great and say you cannot be defeated in battle. They also say that you're the legendary Arthur reborn and have returned to lift mankind out of the darkness. I've heard that you even have the legendary sword, Excalibur."

"They are wrong about everything but Excalibur. Merlin passed that on to me several years ago. He said I was meant to have it because I am nothing at all like Arthur and he said he hoped that I'd never become like him in any way," Arka-Dal said with a laugh. "If you have time, I'd be happy to tell you the *truth* about Thule—and myself—if you'd like."

As usual, the conversation around the dinner table lingered long into night. Arka-Dal and the rest of his inner circle, provided their guests with quite a bit of information on Thule, the diversity of its people, the government and some of the challenges they face almost on a daily basis.

What fascinated Hunter most was the fact that the Emperor had seven official wives, but only the first, Mayumi, was considered the Empress by everyone in the Empire. As such, she served as the ruler in Arka-Dal's absence—with the help of the other wives and Leo, the chief advisor.

Medusa, his second wife, was the last of the legendary Gorgons. She served as Leo's assistant and the translator of several ancient languages.

His third wife, Chatha, came from a dying parallel world. She also served as the commander of the Atlantean Regiment, which was part of Thule's Central Army.

Galya, his fourth wife, had come to seduce Arka-Dal. Instead, theirs became a mutual seduction and they wed soon after. She was also the official liaison between Thule and Hell and still served as the commander of some of Hell's more elite legions.

The other two wives ruled kingdoms elsewhere. Both bore children of Arka-Dal, who were heirs to the thrones of Egypt and Minos. The throne of Thule *could not* be inherited under Thulian laws. Whenever Arka-Dal decided to step down, the people would elect a new Emperor. They could also remove him from office the same way. Arka-Dal was elected "Emperor for life" by over 95% of the Thulian people. The Constitution contained a clause that would assure there would never be another such emperor.

"Leo came up with the title Emperor because we couldn't think of anything else to call me. I try not to live down to it, though," Arka-Dal joked. "My title is only used during official state functions. To me, personally, it has no meaning. It's a title of convenience at best."

"What do your people call you?" Hunter asked.

"Arka-Dal," he replied with a grin. "The title of emperor might make my people feel that I'm unapproachable or that I'm above them in some manner. I don't want anyone in Thule to think that way of me. Ever!"

"Originally, he was elected to serve a single ten year term. But the people pushed for an exception and demanded that Arka-Dal be elected 'emperor' for life," Leo added. "He wanted no part of ruling at all, but after we explained why the people needed him, he came around."

"The people of Thule have chosen me to serve them and serve them I will, to the best of my abilities, until such time as I'm no longer needed," Arka-Dal said modestly.

Hunter nodded as he allowed this to sink in. He'd met many rulers during his long life. They came in all shapes and sizes. All from different cuts of the cloth. This one was far different from any of them.

His wives had no official titles, either. Lorena was fascinated by their living arrangements and personal relationships.

All five of the wives who lived at the palace were closer than sisters and helped raise the mob of children that romped through the halls. And they all served on the Inner Council as advisors.

Unlike other kingdoms, there was no social caste system in Thule. No titles and everyone could rise as high as their talents and abilities enabled them.

"Thule is what Arthur wanted Camelot to be but he never achieved it. Centuries later, another great country emerged with similar ideals and goals. They came close to achieving them, but that nation, too, fell into ruins thanks mostly to greed and corruption at all levels of their society. Ancient Rome also had such ideals in the beginning until the Republic became an empire ruled by megalomaniacs. So far, Thule has come closest to becoming that 'shining city on the hill' that symbolizes freedom, equality and the rights of its people over the rights of the government," Leo explained.

"And it's all because of Arka-Dal," Galya said proudly.

Arka-Dal laughed modestly.

"I had help. Lots of help. I'm still learning my way around this," he said.

After dinner, everyone adjourned to the living room. Hunter was surprised to see several of the children busy at board games or playing with toy soldiers. Even the girls played with the soldiers. The area was littered with various toys and over a dozen cats of all sizes and colors lounged lazily on the furniture or chased catnip mice.

Arka-Dal poured several drinks into glasses at the bar and passed them out to his guests.

"This is our famous Thulian brandy," he said as Hunter sipped. "What do you think?"

"It's excellent. In fact, it's the smoothest I've ever tasted," Hunter replied.

"It comes from a region to the south and west of here. I've been told it's aged in great wooden barrels for 12 years. Just before it's bottled, they blend it with a touch of honey and roses. That's what gives it its distinctive flavor and aroma," Arka-Dal explained.

He then went on to explain where their famous blue wine was made and how Thule was the only place on Earth where those mutant grapes grew in abundance.

Their conversations lasted well past midnight. Then everyone bade each other good night and headed up to their rooms.

Upstairs, in the privacy of her chambers, Galya watched as Gorinna prepared for the trip. She took her saddlebags from a closet and placed them on the bed and began folding changes of clothing and slipping each inside. She turned and looked at Galya.

"You said that he hunted you," she said.

"Several times. But he didn't only hunt me. He went after all sorts of things that go bump in the night. He's the number one agent of the Vatican and has been on and off for centuries. Over the years, Father and

I slew many of their agents. Hunter is something else entirely. Something very special," Galya said.

"That pact he made with your father have anything to do with it?" Gorinna asked.

"Yes and no. We've had some very interesting encounters. Our last was over 450 years ago. He looks exactly the same as he always has," Galya said.

So, he *is* immortal?" Gorinna asked.

Galya shrugged.

"Nothing lives forever. Not even gods," she said. "We all have our expiration dates stamped on us somewhere."

Gorinna laughed.

"What about this thing he's hunting?" she asked.

"Father mentioned it to me several times in the past. It's not one thing—but *millions* of things that answer to a controlling entity," Galya said.

"What are those other things?" Gorinna asked.

"Some sort of demonic rats," Galya said. "That's the best description Father gave me. He said he wasn't sure who the controller was or where it came from. He did say that even though he does rule all of the planes of Hell, even he finds it impossible to know the type and whereabouts of all of its citizens."

Galya walked over and put her hand on Gorinna's shoulder.

"I advise you to be very careful with this one, Gorinna. If Hunter needs your help, this must be dangerous beyond words," she said softly.

Galya turned and left the room.

Gorinna thought about their conversation as she packed her saddlebags. Hunter's reputation had preceded him. His knack for getting seemingly impossible jobs done made him almost legendary throughout the world. He'd slain dozens, perhaps *thousands* of werewolves, vampires, witches and varieties of demons. He'd banished restless spirits and vengeful ghosts. He was fearless and resourceful—and relentless.

Until recently, he had accomplished this alone. His wife and friend now traveled with him and they, too, were more than equal to most any task.

Now, they had come to Thule to rid it of some sort of monster. And they had asked *her* for help!

She reasoned that if *they* needed *her* help, whatever they were after must be incredibly dangerous and powerful.

Just as she finished packing, her husband, Kashi entered and hugged her. She smiled and kissed him.

"Are you sure you can trust this Hunter?" he asked.

"He is who he appears to be. I sense no deceit in him or his companions. Besides, they all know my reputation and what happens to anyone who crosses me," she replied with a smirk.

He laughed.

"Don't worry. I'll be fine," she assured him.

"It's not *you* I'm worried about," he joked.

New Orleans.

It was nine p.m. Hannah was just about to close the store for the night when she heard the front door open and close. She stood at the counter and watched as three, dark clad, seedy-looking men walked up to her. From the way they looked, she knew they hadn't come to purchase anything.

"May I help you?" she asked.

The larger of the three pulled a thick-bladed knife from his boot and brandished it at her. The other two began moving toward both ends of the counter.

"Yeah, bitch," the large man said. "You can give us all the money in your cash box. While yer at it, take off those clothes so we can have a little fun."

Hannah simply smiled at him.

Her smile nearly unnerved the would-be robber. The others also drew knives and started to move around the counter. She watched them from the corners of her eyes and chuckled.

"What's so funny, bitch?" the large man demanded as he shook the knife at her.

"I was just thinking how silly you're going to look with that knife shoved up your ass," Hannah replied.

"Oh? And *who's* gonna stick it there?" he said bravely.

"Me!" she replied calmly.

That's when the man to her left tried to reach for her. The sound of bone snapping along with his painful scream rang through the store as he dropped to his knees. The one to her right got his windpipe shattered by a sharp kick. He fell to the floor as the blood gurgled from his open mouth. Like a shot, she leaped over the counter and grabbed the large man by his throat. He raised the knife only have it batted from his hand by a surprising hard punch to his wrist. It landed on the opposite end of the store.

Hannah picked him off the floor with one hand and shook him violently. When she set him back down, he was trembling with fear.

"What sorta woman *are* you?" he asked with a now quivery voice.

"Guess!" she said as she bared her fangs and sunk them into his neck.

The man with the broken arm cringed as he watched her drain his friend of every last drop of blood. Two minutes later, she let his pale, lifeless body fall to the floor. The other robber attempted to run for the door. Hannah seized him by the collar and slammed him to the floor.

"Stay put!" she commanded.

He rubbed the back of his head with his one good hand and watched as she walked over to the man with the shattered windpipe who was now drowning in his own blood. She knelt over him and smiled.

"I just hate to see so much good blood going to waste," she said as she sunk her fangs into his neck.

She stood and wiped the blood from her lips with the back of her sleeve. She walked over to the last remaining thug and pulled him to his feet.

"It's lucky for you that I'm full right now," she said as she pushed him toward the door.

"What are ya gonna do with me?" he asked.

"I'm going to march you over to Basin Street and turn you over to the cops. I'm sure that you'll love your all-expenses-paid vacation in Angola," she said as she pointed at the door.

The man sighed and opened it. Hannah told him to wait while she closed the shop then marched him to the station. He just looked at the ground the entire time and was real meek when she turned him over to Valmonde. She told him what happened.

Valmonde laughed as Sam took the thug down to the holding cell.

"They must have been from out of town. Everyone in New Orleans knows enough not to mess with you," Valmonde said.

"I'm sort of glad they did stop by tonight. I was feeling kind of hungry and these fools saved me the trouble of hunting someone down," Hannah said. "While I'm here, do you have anything for me?"

"Just this thorny missin' person's case," Valmonde said as he handed her the file. "We get a few each month. Normally, these folks turn up in a couple of days—after they recover. But we've been lookin' for her for the last five days with no luck."

Hannah read the file.

Collins, Lucille Anne

Age 24

Dark brown hair, green eyes

Five feet three inches, 118 pounds

No distinguishable marks

Lives at 383 Poydras Street

Husband reported her missing on June 23 when she did not show up for work.

"Where'd she work?" asked Hannah.

"Over at the Napoleon House. She was a barmaid there for three years. Her boss, Dave DuPont, said that she'd never missed a night. So when she failed to show up as usual, he got worried and asked her husband, Jack, where she was. That's when he filed the report," Valmonde said.

"Interesting. Anyone else go missing lately?" Hannah asked.

"Not that I've been made aware of," Valmonde said. "You takin' this one?"

Hannah nodded.

"I think I'll start by asking her husband a few questions and go from there," she said as she left the office.

She showed up at the Poydras address an hour later. A very distraught Jack Collins smiled with relief when he opened the door. He recognized her instantly.

"Hannah Morii! Are you going to help me find Lucy?" he asked.

"I'm going to try my best," she replied as she looked around.

"Thank God. If anybody can find her it's be you," Jack said. "What can I do to help?"

"I need to see a recent picture of Lucy and something she's worn recently," Hannah said.

"There's a photo of her on the fireplace," he pointed.

She picked it up and burned her image into her mind. She placed it back on the mantle. Jack went into the next room and quickly returned with a shimmery, white satin blouse. He handed this to Hannah and watched as she inhaled deeply several times to catch Lucy's scent. When she was finished, she gave it back.

"Thanks. Now tell me, what route did Lucy usually take to work?" she asked.

Jack told her the way his wife normally went to work. Hannah watched him closely and listened to his heartbeat and breathing. There was genuine concern in his voice. It was enough for her to rule Jack out as a suspect.

"She usually walked on clear nights. And the night she went missing was a clear one," Jack said. "I hope you find her, Miss Morii. I'm just about sick with worry. I just want Lucy home safely."

"I'll find her," she promised as she left the house.

She decided to walk the route to the Napoleon House that Jack had given her. She stepped out into the street and inhaled. After several attempts, she managed to pick up Lucy's trail and followed it down the block.

It was easy at first. Apparently, Lucy had not deviated from her usual route. Hannah soon reached Chartres. The Napoleon House was less than three blocks away. About a block from the bar, the trail suddenly veered south. Hannah stopped and concentrated. She saw two men accost Lucy. One put a knife to her throat. Then they escorted her down Iberville.

"She was kidnapped," Hannah thought. "Now, where did they take her/"

She followed the trail down Iberville to Decatur then onto Clinton. It ended in front of a boarded up building on Clinton and Bienville.

Hannah walked around the block and listened carefully. She heard three distinct heartbeats coming from inside the building. One was very slow, as if the person was heavily drugged. The others were obviously those of two strong men.

She went to one of the doors and pushed. It eased open then stopped. She looked at the old rusted chain, smiled, and kicked the door in. It made a loud sound as it opened. Hannah stopped and waited to see if anyone would come to investigate. When no one did, she followed the heartbeats until she came to a locked door in the back of the building. There was a light coming from beneath the old door.

Two men were talking inside.

Hannah stopped to eavesdrop.

The first man seemed nervous. "I think we overdid that shot. She's barely breathing," he said.

"So what? As long as she stays alive long enough for us to get paid, I don't give rat's ass," the second said.

"What do you suppose he wants with her? What so special about her?"

"Beats me. She's nothing special to look at. But she's the one he wanted so she's the one he gets. None of that matters. He paid us well enough, so stop asking so many questions."

"He said she wasn't the first. What do you think he meant by that?"

"He probably had other women snatched. If we play this right, he may throw more business our way."

That's when Hannah kicked the door open. The thugs leapt to their feet and drew their knives. There were two quick flashes of steel followed by the sound of two heavy bodies hitting the wooden floor. Hannah smiled at the pools of blood spreading out from beneath each body. She wiped the blade of her katana on one man's shirt then turned to the victim who was chained to the wall by her wrists.

Lucy stared at Hannah as she snapped the chains to free her. She was having trouble focusing thanks to the drugs she was given. Hannah helped to a nearby chair.

"Those men!" Lucy shouted.

"I took care of them. You're safe now," Hannah assured her. "Do you have any idea who they were?"

"I never saw them before they kidnapped me. How many days have I been gone?" Lucy asked as she shook her head to try and clear it.

"Five," Hannah replied.

"Five! Jack must be worried sick. I'd better get back to him," Lucy said as she tried to stand.

Unable to find her legs, she simply plopped back down.

"You'd better rest until those drugs wear off. I heard those men say they were expecting a visit from the man who hired them to grab you. I'll take you into the next room. You can rest there while I wait for their boss," Hannah said as she helped her out of the chair.

Hannah sat in the darkest part of the room while she waited. Three hours went by. She was just about to give up her vigil when she heard the sound of heavy boots moving across the ancient wood floor.

She listened.

The stride was definitely masculine. His walk was confident. Almost arrogant. She melted into the shadows and watched as the old door creaked open and a man dressed all in black entered the room.

He stood nearly seven feet tall, was almost gaunt in build and deathly pale. What bothered Hannah was the fact that she could detect neither a heart beating in his chest nor the sound of breathing.

"What the Hell *is* he?" she wondered.

The man stopped when he saw the bodies on the floor. He smiled and looked directly at Hannah.

"You did me a favor. At least now, I will not have to pay them," he said in a Slavic accent.

"And you're going to join them," Hannah said as she stepped into the center of the room with her katana drawn.

The man studied her carefully. His gaze was steady. Unwavering. His demeanor bothered her.

"That is highly unlikely," he said as they slowly circled each other. "You *cannot* kill me as I have been deceased for at least one thousand years."

"Who and what *are* you?" asked Hannah.

"My name is Harker Langven—or rather it *was* many centuries ago. As for what I am—well, your guess is as good as anyone else's," he replied.

"You don't *know*?" she asked.

"To me more precise, I do not *care*," he said with a shrug. "That does not matter after so many years. It is sufficient to say that I am."

"Why did you have those men kidnap Lucy?" Hannah asked.

"I fancied her. I had been observing her for weeks. After much consideration, I have decided that she was to me my next bride, for lack of a better word. She was to be the next bearer of my offspring," he said.

"There are *others* like you out there?" Hannah asked.

He smiled.

"That would be telling," he smiled. "Since you have set her free, you must take her place."

Hannah laughed.

He sneered.

"You dare to mock me?" he asked as his eyes turned red.

He launched himself at Hannah. She easily evaded his attack and struck him twice with her katana. Langven turned and looked down at the two deep cuts on his upper body. To Hannah's shock, no blood was dripping from them.

He charged at her again only to be cut twice more. The first slit his upper right thigh. The second severed his left hand at the wrist. He scowled as he examined the stump. Hannah bared her fangs.

Langven smiled.

"You are a vampire!" he said.

He barely dodged Hannah's attack which was aimed at his throat. Langven backed away as if he was unsure of how to handle this unexpected development. Hannah lunged again. This time, he seized her wrist, whirled her around and threw her at the far wall. She hit it feet first and launched herself back at him. Before he realized what happened, she sunk the katana into his chest all the way to the hilt.

Langven took two steps back, looked at her and smiled as he pulled the weapon from his chest and tossed it aside. He then held up his left arm. Hannah stared as she watched his severed hand slowly reappear on the stump.

"I grow weary of this little game. Until we meet again," he said as he vanished.

Hannah retrieved her katana, sheathed it and looked around.

"*What are you?*" she shouted.

She got Lucy from the back room and escorted her safely home to a very relieved and elated Jack. Then she headed down to Bourbon Street. She had to find Alejandro and tell him about Langven.

"Hunter, where are you when I need you?" she asked.

Thule

Hunter's night was interrupted by one of his usual dreams. It wasn't exactly a nightmare, but it caused him to wake suddenly. Unable to return to sleep, he dressed and walked downstairs to explore the palace. As he walked down the hall and turned a corner, he met Galya who was coming from the opposite direction.

"You're up early," she greeted.

"So are you," he said.

"I sleep but little. I'm mostly a creature of the night, though I've come to love the day since I've been here," she said. "It has stopped raining. I was about to go for a walk in the garden. Would you care to join me?"

"I'd be delighted," he replied.

They left the palace and followed the path into the large public area known as the Rose Garden. As they walked along the winding brick path, Hunter began to feel more at ease and he let himself enjoy the scenery and the delicate scents of the roses and other flowers that were all around them.

"I sense much uneasiness inside of you, Hunter," she said. "I also sense this has nothing to do with your mission. There is something eating away inside of you. Something that wants to come out."

Then why *doesn't* it?" he asked.

"You *won't* allow it to," Galya said. "Your subconscious mind suppresses it."

"Why?" he asked.

"That is something only *you* can figure out," she said.

"This is all so amazing," he said. "I never would have imagined that the two of us would be walking together like this and talking as if we're old friends."

"But we *are* old friends. You and I go back several centuries. Even though we've had many encounters, I've never borne you any animosity. In fact, I've always admired the way you handled things. I also figured that although you hunted me relentlessly, there was never anything *personal* to it," Galya said.

He laughed.

"The entire universe seems to have been turned inside-out," he said.

"I know. Isn't it wonderful?" Galya smiled.

An hour after breakfast the next morning, Gorinna saddled her horse and rode out of the rose garden with her new companions.

Arka-Dal watched from the front door until they were out of sight. He returned to the living room and smiled when he saw Gayla seated on the sofa with four of the household cats.

"Those might have been the three most interesting guests we've had here since you first arrived," he said as he sat beside her. "Lorena was especially fascinating. I never knew that vampires could wed humans."

"Why not? They're just a different type of human. Besides, you and I married—and most people would say that such a thing was impossible, too," she said. "I'd say that Hunter and Lorena are perfectly matched—in a most *ironic* way."

"What do you know about Hunter?" Arka-Dal asked.

"Just what I've learned during our encounters," Galya said. "Don't worry. Gorinna is in very good hands."

"I hope she knows what she's gotten herself into," Arka-Dal said.

"I hope Hunter knows, too!" Galya joked.

They left the city and followed the main road north to Osumel, Thule's second largest city. Along the way, they passed through several small towns and villages. Each time they encountered groups of people, they waved at Gorinna or engaged her in conversations. Halfway between the two cities, they stopped to dine at a small inn. While they ate, several of the local children ran up to meet Gorinna and she entertained them with some simple illusions and magic.

Hunter was amazed that no one was afraid to approach the Red Witch and that she was more than happy to pass the time talking with them.

"You're very popular," DuCassal observed. "You're almost like a rock start of the First Age."

Gorinna laughed at the comparison.

"The people have very favorable opinions of us and we like to keep it that way," she said. "Like Arka-Dal says, we serve the people. It's important to maintain their trust in us."

"That sounds like something Thomas Jefferson would have said," Hunter said.

"Arka-Dal has been compared favorably to him over the years," Gorinna smiled. "He has always admired Jefferson and the other founders of the last great nation of the First Age. In fact, he and Leo modeled our Constitution after theirs with very few modifications. Arka-Dal said there was no need to try to improve upon something that was nearly perfect."

"Thomas Jefferson was a remarkable man. Charles and I had dinner with him several times when we visited the capital," DuCassal said.

"That's right! We did! We met George Washington, too, as I recall," Hunter said with a smile. "We dined with him and Martha at Mount Vernon right after he retired from the presidency."

"I wish you had mentioned that when we were at the palace. Arka-Dal would love to hear about that," Gorinna said.

They left the inn and continued northward. About 15 miles from Osumel, they found themselves at a fork in the road. The main, well-paved road continued to the city. A smaller dirt road cut west across a wide grassy plain.

"This is the Yboe," Gorinna said as she pointed. "It runs from here all the way to the mountains in the west and north to the shores of Lake Po. It covers about 1,500 square miles and is mostly grassland. Yboe in the Osumel language means 'Great Plain'."

"It's getting dark. Let's camp here tonight," Hunter said as he slid from the saddle.

"That's fine by me. My ass is getting sore from all this riding," Gorinna said as she slid to the ground.

"I would be happy to rub the soreness from it," DuCassal offered.

"Try and I'll turn you into a vole!" Gorinna said as she rubbed her backside.

"A vole would be an improvement," Lorena said with a grin.

"Not for the vole," Hunter joked as he pulled his bedroll down from the saddle and spread it on the ground.

They watched as Gorinna waved her hand. A small campfire suddenly appeared. Lorena laughed and passed out the dried jerky and fruit, which would be their meal for the night. Hunter passed out canteens of water and sat down next to the fire.

"How is life as a Slayer?" asked Gorinna.

Hunter stared into the flames a while then answered.

"Before I met Lorena, it was lonely," he said. "My life was filled with endless nights and days of prowling graveyards, crypts, tombs and ruins and anywhere else the enemies of mankind lurked."

"What about family?" she asked.

"Lorena and DuCassal are my family. I have no memories of anyone else," Hunter said. "Nor do I need any."

"Were there any other women before Lorena?" Gorinna asked.

He smiled.

"Too many to count or remember," he replied.

"But no love?" she pressed.

"None before Lorena," he said as he smiled at Lorena.

"What place do you call home?" Gorinna asked.

"New Orleans," he said. "It fits me best. I'm comfortable there. I'm needed there, too."

"What about the Vatican?" she asked.

"I go there from time-to-time, but it was never home in the true sense of the word. It's where our pay comes from," he said.

"Our?" she asked.

"I also get paid," Lorena added. "The Cardinal named me an official Slayer last year and added me to the payroll. He said I was a most 'valuable asset' to their mission. I thought that was very generous and open-minded."

"And incredibly ironic," Hunter added. "The Vatican's agents and Cardinals have taken oaths to destroy all vampires. Yet the Cardinal appointed Lorena as a Slayer."

DuCassal laughed.

"He knew you and Lorena were partners and lovers and turned a blind eye to your relationship because she was helping you. I think he also expected you to marry eventually—same as I did, mon ami. Once you did, he had no choice but to make Lorena a Slayer," he said.

"What sort of weapons do you usually carry?" Gorinna asked.

"I usually carry two revolvers and a variety of different types of bullets, a katana, Bowie knife, shiruken, holy water and both wood and silver stakes. Sometimes, I add explosives to the arsenal. It depends on what I'm hunting," Hunter said as he bit into the jerky.

"I've heard that Slayers can use magic spells," Gorinna said as she stirred the flames.

"I'm the exception. I've never been able to use any sort of spells. I'm immune to vampire and werewolf bites and I heal rapidly. I can easily recover from wounds that would kill most men and I've survived even the most impossible situations," Hunter said. "I guess that's magical in a way."

"What makes you so effective?" Gorinna asked.

"I'm stubborn and relentless. I hate to give up and I keep going after things until they're destroyed and I don't care about the consequences," he said.

"You sound just like my husband, Hamid," she remarked.

"In that case, I don't feel the least bit sorry for him," Hunter said.

"Why not?" she asked.

"He has *you*," Hunter replied.

"Is that good or bad?" Gorinna asked.

"I'm not sure. What do *you* think?" he teased. "I see that you also carry a sidearm."

"Using magic saps my energies. Sometimes to the point where I can't cast spells for several hours. The pistol and short sword are backups and I've learned to become very proficient with both," she explained. "Even Merlin carries a sword into battle. Magical powers are *not* infinite. All magic users have limits."

"I figured *you'd* be the exception," Hunter said.

"Unfortunately, there *are* no exceptions—well maybe there's *one*," she said with a smile.

"The Devil?" he asked.

Lorena stood suddenly and looked to the north.

"I hear something," she announced.

"What?" asked Hunter as he stood next to her.

"A sickening, almost nerve wracking sound—like a swarm of rats. Millions of them," she said.

"I don't hear anything," Gorinna said.

"Vampires can hear things humans can't. Even things that are miles away," Hunter explained. "Especially on clear nights like this. That's when sound carries the furthest."

DuCassal nodded as he checked his shotgun.

"You will learn to trust Lorena's senses just as we do," he said.

"How far?" asked Hunter.

"Five or six miles to the north," Lorena said as they saddled their horses. "It's moving fast, too."

"What lies in that direction?" Hunter asked.

"A small village called Dorne. It's about three miles from here," Gorinna said.

"We'd better hurry," Hunter said as they galloped into the night.

As the cloud approached Dorne, the weird, high-pitched chattering sounds grew louder and louder. Most of the terrified villagers dropped what they were doing and raced inside and locked their doors and windows behind them to seal out the noise. Those who remained outside to watch out of curiosity clapped their hands to their ears and tried to flee to safety.

But it was too late.

The cloud and what hunted within it rolled through the streets and fields. Above the din, those inside could hear the horrified screams of those who were trapped outside. Before long, they, too, heard the ominous scratching on their walls and doors . . .

Hunter and the others arrived at the crest of a hill just in time to watch the cloud make its way through the stricken village. It obscured street and house lights, covered smaller homes and shops and swirled about like a tornado.

"By the Gods!" Gorinna gasped.

"It sounds like millions of rats are swarming through the village. I did not expect to see anything like this, mes amis," DuCassal said as he watched in horror.

"What *is* that thing, mon cher?" Lorena asked.

"No one knows. But we must find a way to kill it," Hunter said.

"This is where I come in!" Gorinna shouted as she spurred her horse down the slope at full gallop and headed straight at the cloud.

Two hundred yards away, she stopped and dismounted. She slapped her horse on the rump to chase it to safety, then she turned and faced the cloud. The others waited on the hill and watched. The cloud seemed to sense her presence and moved toward her, picking up speed as it did. The sounds grew louder and shriller. They became almost deafening.

Gorinna eyed the approaching cloud as she readied her spell. As soon as it came within 20 feet of her, she raised her hands above her head and loosed a powerful white bolt of energy right into the center.

To her astonishment, the cloud shrieked in agony and broke into smaller parts that moved around her and rolled away. Gorinna hit the closest part with another spell and watched as it burst into flames amid higher pitched screams and melted to the ground. Before she could hurl another spell, the cloud swirled around violently and suddenly vanished.

The others galloped toward her as fast as they could. Hunter reined up next to her. He looked down at the smoldering, malformed, and charred rats lying all around her.

Some oozed a putrid yellow slime.

Others lay smoldering with their tongues hanging out.

Some twitched hideously.

"You managed to kill part of it," he said.

"Not *it*. *Them*," she said. "That was a cloud of rats—just as Galya said. There are millions of them. They're ugly, malformed things that are not found in nature. They seem almost *demonic*."

"Anything else?" he asked as he dismounted.

"Yes. I sensed something. Something vile and dark. Something *evil*. It's strong and intelligent and it's filled with hatred for all living things," she said. "It's in the exact center of the rat cloud, guiding them."

"It's some sort of demon, probably from the lowest of the planes of Hell. How it got here is anybody's guess," Hunter surmised.

"But they did *not* attack you, Gorinna. They could have tried to swarm you, but they fled. Why?" DuCassal wondered.

"Maybe it's because I used magic to attack them. Maybe they *fear* it," Gorinna said. "That's only a guess on my part, though. I expected them to try and swarm over me, too. But they didn't. I'm as puzzled as you are, Jean-Paul."

"But where did they go?" asked Lorena.

"I don't know. They simply vanished into thin air after Gorinna attacked them. At least we kept it away from that village," Hunter said as he looked back at the cluster of houses. "Or *did* we? Let's check it out."

When they reached the village, they found themselves riding through a scenario of incredible horror. Dozens of twisted and dismembered corpses littered the streets and the windows and doors of every house and shop were shattered. Nothing moved. No cats or dogs.

No birds or insects.

Nothing.

The only things left in the village were the pitiful, gnawed upon skeletal remains that cluttered the streets and lay inside the buildings.

Stripped of flesh, sinew and anything else edible, they lay sprawled in hideous poses with mouths agape and stared up at the moon through empty eye sockets. Even their clothes were in tatters.

Hunter shook his head and cursed at the top of his lungs. They listened as his epithets echoed through the now deserted streets and faded into the nearby canyon. Gorinna wept at the devastation.

"We didn't help at all," she said softly. "We arrived too late. Everyone's gone. They're dead. All of them."

"Now you know what we're up against," Hunter said softly.

Her eyes flashed with hate and anger as she turned to Hunter.

"I don't know where they came from, but I swear by all that is holy and unholy in this world that I will destroy them. *All* of them, even if it takes the rest of my life!" she vowed.

"We're with you all the way, Gorinna," Hunter promised.

"But just *how* do we deal with millions of rats?" Lorena asked.

"Perhaps we could shoot them?" DuCassal suggested.

"Bullets would kill what's in the swarm but you'd need millions of rounds and you'd have to fire them at point-blank range. Before you could do them any real damage, they'd be all over you," Gorinna said. "The only way to get rid of the rats is to kill whatever's controlling them. I could attack him directly but the rats are too distracting. I can't concentrate on my spells."

"And that makes casting difficult at best," Hunter said. "We have to find a way to separate that monster from the rats long enough for you to cast an effective spell."

"And just *how* do you propose we do *that*, mon ami?" asked DuCassal.

"We need some kind of bait. Something tempting enough to lure the rats away from their master. Something that would be irresistible to them," Hunter mused.

"How about cattle? You said they attack livestock," Gorinna suggested.

"We'd need lots of cattle and they'd die horrible deaths," Lorena said.

"We don't have to use *real* cattle. I can create an *illusion*," Gorinna said with a smile.

"It would have to be realistic enough to lure the rats," Hunter said.

"*My* illusions will look, act, sound and even smell like real cattle," Gorinna assured him smugly. "They'd be good enough to even fool a Texan!"

Hunter laughed.

"In that case, let's try it," he agreed." If it works, the rats will attack the illusion and provide you with enough of an opening to take our friend down."

"What if it *fails*, mon cher? Then what?" asked Lorena.

"We drop back and punt," Hunter said flatly.

"Or we could resort to Plan B," Gorinna offered.

"Which is?" asked Hunter.

"There's someone *else* we can turn to. Someone all-powerful," she replied as they rode away from the village.

"Why not ask him to help us *now*?" asked DuCassal.

"I refuse to admit defeat just yet. Call it professional pride," Gorinna said with a grin. "I don't want to call on him unless we have no other choice. By the way, since this thing is so powerful, just how *did* you plan to kill it?"

"I didn't plan. I just figured we'd play it by ear," Hunter smiled. "We've tackled demons before and won. But this one is something *else*. Now you know why we asked you to help us."

"Thanks a lot," Gorinna said.

"Don't mention it," Hunter smiled.

"I won't," she said.

After a bone-numbing ten hour ride, they decided to make camp. Hunter gathered up some dry sticks and weeds and placed them in a pile. Gorinna watched as he ignited it with a match and added more sticks. In a few seconds, they had a nice little fire going and Lorena began to prepare the evening meal of rabbit jerky and small red potatoes. Hunter took the bottle of Absinthe from his saddle bag, took a long drink and passed it to Gorinna. She coughed as it burned her throat and passed it back.

"How far to the next village?" asked Hunter.

"Another day's ride. It's Marchama. It has less than 150 people. It's mostly a watering place for camel caravans but it has a thriving market each spring and fall," she said. "It's very old, too."

"As old as me?" he asked.

"No," she said with a smile. "Just how old are you anyway?"

"I was born in the year 1420," Hunter said. "In Romania. That makes me nearly 3,000 years old."

"You're not as old as Merlin," she said.

"No one is as old as Merlin," Hunter smiled. "Well, perhaps Galya is."

Gorinna laughed.

"I think Medusa is older, too," she said. "Gorgons are almost immortal."

"Immortality isn't what it's cracked up to be," Hunter said as he took another drink from the bottle. "In order to keep it bearable, you have to remain active. I think that's another reason I became a Slayer—among other things. How long do witches live?"

"That all depends on what type of witch you're speaking of," Gorinna replied. "I have no idea how long I'll live. I never gave it much thought. I'm more of a sorceress than a witch. I'm kind of a female version of Merlin."

Lorena saw Gorinna eyeing her and smiled.

"You seem to be fascinated with me," she observed.

"I am. I've never met a vampire and I have so many questions," Gorinna admitted.

"Feel free to ask them, I have nothing to hide," Lorena invited.

"What's it like to return from the dead?" Gorinna asked.

Lorena giggled.

"I cannot answer that. I have never been dead," she said.

Gorinna wrinkled her nose.

"But vampires are referred to as *undead*," she pointed out.

"It is such a silly word. After all, undead simply means *not dead* or alive. When someone is turned, he simply becomes a vampire. He does not die and rise from the grave later. In my case, I simply slept for a few days. I am not a reanimated corpse nor do I sleep in a coffin like the vampires in the old novels. My heart has always beaten and blood has always flowed through my veins the same as in any other person. I've always been very much alive. In fact, I am probably more alive than most people," Lorena explained.

"I meant no offense," Gorinna apologized.

"And I took none," Lorena assured her. "I get asked that same question quite often and people are always surprised with my answers. Being a vampire bestows a sort of cursed immortality on a person. And we remain immortal as long as we can replenish ourselves periodically with fresh human blood."

"How often do you—?" Gorinna began.

"Two or three times per month. When the hunger strikes, I hunt down some vicious, wanted criminal and feed on him and anyone else in his gang. Then I turn them in and collect any reward they may have on them," Lorena said.

"So you're also a bounty hunter?" Gorinna asked.

Lorena nodded.

Gorinna looked at Hunter.

"What about you? Were you always immortal or did you become so when you made the pact with the Devil?" she asked.

Hunter shrugged.

"I'm not sure. Six of one. Half dozen of another. At this point in my life, it doesn't matter," he said.

"I, too, am immortal. I was born that way by some strange, lucky chance. I have learned that there are only a handful of us left on Earth. Perhaps we are the remainders of an ancient race. I used to wonder about that centuries ago. Now, I don't care," DuCassal said as Hunter passed the bottle to him.

He had been listening in silence the entire time as he nibbled on some rabbit. Gorinna noticed that he was dressed more like a wild west lawman than a typical Slayer. She also felt that DuCassal was far more than meets the eye.

"Are you also a Slayer?" Gorinna asked.

"Unofficially," he replied. "Charles and I have been best friends since we met back in 1642. Where he goes, I go. I watch his back and he watches mine. I also get a kick from doing this."

They ate and talked a while longer. Hunter told Gorinna about some of his more dangerous exploits and how he and Lorena first met. DuCassal filled her in on their exploits in New Orleans and the Caribbean during the First Age, when they amassed the first of their huge fortunes.

"We dared anything and everything. Sometimes, we failed. Most of the time, we either doubled or tripled our fortune. We have had a most lucrative partnership," he said with a grin. "Of course, Charles had forgotten completely about all of that until he returned to New Orleans."

"So you remember all of your past life now?" Gorinna asked.

"Most of it. There are still a few gaps. Still some unanswered questions," Hunter said.

"Have you worked with anyone else besides Jean-Paul and Lorena?" Gorinna asked.

"About 40 years ago, I worked with an adventurer who called himself the Bard. He carried a lute around with him and was very good with a sword. He also knew how to cast some spells," Hunter replied.

"The Bard? Why that sounds like Arka-Dal's cousin, Mithra-Dal. Where did you meet *him*?" Gorinna asked.

"In Budapest. We were hunting the same demon at the time. When we ran into each other, we decided to team up. After we slew the demon and the fools who summoned it, he took off for parts unknown. I haven't seen him since," Hunter said. "What ever happened to him?"

"He was killed about 20 years ago while on a mission for Arka-Dal," Gorinna said. "We were shocked to hear of it."

"I'm surprised. I didn't think anything could kill him. Too bad. I was hoping to run into him again," Hunter said with a note of regret.

"Neither did he, I'm sure," Gorinna said. "We never did locate his body so we couldn't give him a proper send off. Arka-Dal said at least he died the way he wanted, with sword in hand."

They finished their meal and settled down for the night. Hunter and Lorena snuggled up close to the fire while DuCassal took the first watch. The night was quiet save for the occasional bark of a hyena in the distance. Gorinna watched as Hunter ran his fingers slowly through Lorena's red hair and smiled. They seemed so perfect together. She looked up at the stars and sighed.

Lorena detected a sense of longing in her sigh and wondered what troubled the famous Red Witch. Who or what did *she* long for and why? It was then she realized that Gorinna was in love.

They broke camp just after sunrise and continued their furious ride. They arrived in the tiny oasis village of Marchama late that afternoon. The village consisted of seventy stone and mud brick structures clustered around a clear pool of water that welled up from deep under the earth. The streets were wide and clean and almost every home doubled as a tavern, eatery or shop. A few of the locals looked up when they rode in and watched as they headed for the large, white structure at the northern end of the square.

"This is what passes for the town hall," Gorinna said as they dismounted and tied their horses to the rail in front.

A rather short, rotund balding man stepped onto the porch and greeted them with a big smile and large bottles of cold water.

"Gorinna! It's been a long time! Welcome back to our humble village," he said as they drank. "Who are your friends?"

Gorinna made the introductions as they stepped into the building. The front room was a large open area with comfortable chairs, a desk in the center, tables and book shelves. Their host, was Charvin Bey and he was the unofficial "mayor" of the village. He bade them to make themselves at home and tell him why they traveled so far off the beaten path.

Hunter and Gorinna explained everything. Bey whistled.

"Do you think it will work?" he asked.

"I do," Gorinna said confidently.

"And if it doesn't? What will happen to my village?" Bey asked.

"I'd hate to think about that," Hunter said. "It won't be pretty."

"Just in case, do you have a place you can evacuate to? I'd feel much better if we could get your people out of harm's way," Gorinna said.

"There are a series of caves in the mountains just west of here. They would be large enough for us to hide out in until this is over. I can take my people there if you like," Bey suggested.

"That thing is less than a day from here. How soon can you move your people to the caves?" Gorinna asked.

"I can start right now. It will take us about two hours to reach the caves," Bey said. "I'll have my men go from door-to-door to get everyone out."

"Thank you, Charvin," Gorinna said.

"In the meantime, you are all welcome to stay here. There's food, drinks and clean beds. Consider this to be your home for as long as you like," Bey said graciously.

Early the next morning, Bey and the other people of the village, packed some of their belongings and trekked towards the mountains to take refuge in the caverns. Hunter and the others watched their procession from the shade of the porch. Within two hours, the entire village was deserted, leaving it eerily quiet save for the occasional cries of the crows that circled overhead.

"That's the last of them," Hunter said. "It's time to work your magic."

Gorinna jumped down from the porch and climbed onto her horse. She picked up the reins and looked back at them.

"You coming?" she asked.

Hunter laughed and climbed into his horse. Lorena and DuCassal did the same. They all rode to the western edge of the village and stopped in the middle of a large meadow. Gorinna slid from the saddle and looked around.

"This will do nicely," she said as she waved her right hand in front of her.

Almost instantly, a large herd of black and white and brown and white cattle materialized in the meadow. They were transparent at first but slowly solidified into highly convincing three dimensional images that appeared to be living, breathing animals, complete with natural movements and sounds. They even smelled like real cattle.

Gorinna turned toward the others.

"How's that?" she asked.

"That's amazing. If I had not watched you create them from thin air, I'd swear they were real live animals. Are all of your illusions this convincing?" Hunter asked.

"Yes," she replied smugly. "Illusions are very simple for me, although this is one of the largest ones I've ever attempted. I'm glad that it meets with your approval."

"That it does," Hunter said. "But is it realistic enough to attract that horde of twisted rats?"

Gorinna climbed back onto her horse.

"I think so. Just to be sure, I added the smells and sound," she said as they rode back into the village.

"How long will it last?" asked Lorena.

"This one will last two full days then start to fade away," Gorinna replied. "My smaller illusions last indefinitely. A few have become actual realities over the years."

"I have to admit that was quite amazing," DuCassal said.

"Thank you. Now we just relax and wait for our visitors to arrive," Gorinna said. "Let's hope they take the bait."

They sat on the porch and sipped wine while they waited. Lorena told Gorinna how they managed to finally do away with their most dangerous adversary in a showdown in New Orleans.

"That's when I also found out who I am—or rather *was*. At first, I was almost horrified. Then I realized how long ago that was and what I'd done since. I no longer was that person. I was able to leave that life in the past where he belongs," Hunter said.

"I still say that you look nothing at all like the portrait that has become so popular, Charles," DuCassal remarked. "The man in the painting looks so much better than you."

Hunter laughed.

"And just *who* were you?" asked Gorinna.

"Vlad Tepis," Hunter replied.

"Vlad the Impaler? *Dracula?*" Gorinna asked in surprise.

Hunter nodded.

"I don't see any resemblance," she said.

"I *told* you so, Charles," DuCassal said.

Lorena stopped sipping wine and put her glass on the rail. She stood and looked toward the meadow.

"They're coming," she said.

"How close?" Hunter asked.

"Less than a mile," she replied.

"Let's ride!" Hunter said as he climbed onto his horse.

They others did the same and followed him to the meadow. The illusory cows were still grazing peacefully and the night air was slowly filling with the awful chitter-squeaks of the rat horde as it drew closer and closer.

Gorinna dismounted and looked up at the others.

"Wait here. I'll handle this by myself," she said.

"What if you fail?" asked Lorena.

"If I fail, ride like Hell back to Thule. But I don't *intend to fail*," Gorinna said as she walked through the herd.

She stopped about 200 yards to the left and watched as the cloud of rats crept closer and closer. She could sense the ominous dark figure amid the horde. The sheer evil it projected sent cold shivers down her back.

"Just what *are* you?" she thought as she mentally probed the swarm.

Hunter and his friends waited atop a hill and watched as the rats swarmed closer and closer to Gorinna. At the last second, they stopped and raced toward the grazing cattle, intent on devouring every last one of the illusory cows. Being rats, they had no idea the herd was a distraction and they abandoned the dark figure to feast.

The figure now stood alone in the middle of the field. He was nearly eight feet tall, lean and completely black save for the two burning red eyes and twin row of jagged white teeth that filled his evil grin. The eyes penetrated into Gorinna's mind and struck her nearly numb with a deep sense of dread and terror. She fought off the urge to flee and unleashed a spell directly into the center of the figure.

The figure burst into flames, bellowed angrily at her, then fell to dust and vanished. Before the flames died out, he suddenly materialized next to Gorinna. Startled, she turned to face him.

It was too late.

She never saw the blow that sent her flying across the meadow. She hit the ground hard, rolled several more yards and lay still.

Hunter leaped down from his horse and charged at the figure. He emptied both revolvers into him as he did but the bullets simply passed harmlessly through the figure. The figure shook his head and emitted a mocking, sinister laugh that chilled Hunter to the marrow. He stopped in his tracks and they stared at each other for several seconds as the horde of rats again swarmed around their master. Then, as suddenly as they had appeared, both the demon and the rat cloud vanished into thin air.

"Just what in God's name are you and how do I kill you?" Hunter wondered.

He holstered his pistols and ran over to Gorinna who was now up on her hands and knees as she shook the blow off. He helped her to her feet. She had a huge bruise on the side of her face and her cheek was swollen.

"That was quite a hit you took," Hunter said.

"I've had worse. Where'd he come from? I didn't see him until it was too late," she said as they walked back to the others.

"Well, at least your illusion worked. It drew off the rats just as you said it would," DuCassal said.

"That spell would have incinerated a hundred demons. He just shook it off like it was nothing more than a mosquito bite," Gorinna said as her head cleared.

She walked over to her horse and mounted.

"Now, we call in the cavalry!" she said.

"You mean the Devil? Why would he care?" Hunter asked.

"I'm sure he'll help us. After all, he *is* Arka-Dal's father-in-law!" Gorinna said as they guided their horses back toward the main highway.

As soon as they were out of sight of the village, the strange, black mist rose slowly from the ground in the center of the meadow and began to creep toward the next populated area some 75 miles to the east.

New Orleans—

It was just a little past two a.m. when a subtle shuffling sound woke Hannah Morii from a not-so-deep sleep. She had just finished her patrol of Treme an hour earlier and had decided to call it a night when she had no luck trying to locate her intended prey.

But vampires are light sleepers, especially at night. Even the softest noises sound like church bells ringing in their ears.

She turned over and listened.

The shuffling continued for another minute or two, then stopped. She sat up and reached for her katana just as she heard someone climbing the stairs. She walked to the door and listened.

The footsteps stopped right outside of her room.

She gripped the katana with both hands and waited.

Nothing happened for several minutes.

Hannah relaxed and lowered the sword. She never saw the blow that sent her hurtling across the room to her bed. She struck the mattress, bounced off and went into a fighting crouch. She looked around carefully.

The room looked empty.

But Hannah knew it wasn't.

She sensed that her attacker was still there. Watching.

She peered into a dark corner and saw the glow of his red eyes.

"I see you now!" she said as she attacked.

To her surprise, he seized the katana's blade and pulled it from her hands. She backed off and glared as he tossed it aside and stepped into the light.

Then her jaw dropped.

The man standing before her was her *father*.

"That's impossible! You're dead. I watched you die," she said as he stepped toward her.

She was momentarily frozen with indecisiveness as her brain tried to see through the disguise. It was enough time to enable her attacker to move in for the kill . . .

Thule—

Hunter and his group arrived at the palace late the following evening. Arka-Dal and several others were in the living room. The Emperor was seated at the chess table with Merlin while Leo and Medusa watched the game over their shoulders. Galya and the other wives were busy playing with the children while the huge Minotaur, Jun, dozed on the sofa. Everyone turned when Gorinna and her company walked in.

"Back so soon? I take it then that you've dispatched the menace?" Merlin queried.

"Not hardly," Gorinna replied as she led her group to the bar.

They all helped themselves to drinks. Arka-Dal and Merlin stopped playing and walked over to join them.

Merlin studied Hunter's face for a moment, then nodded in recognition.

"It's been a long time," he said as he extended his hand. "Did you ever find the help you sought?"

"Yes, I did—thanks to your advice. Thank you," Hunter replied as they shook hands. "I'm surprised to see that you're still very much alive."

"I've had a few close calls since our meeting, but I'm still intact. You look well, too," Merlin said.

"I am," Hunter assured. "But we came close to meeting the Maker two days ago."

"What happened?" asked Arka-Dal.

Gorinna and Hunter explained it to him. He shook his head and cursed. Hunter nodded.

"My sentiments exactly," he said.

"We can't handle that thing by ourselves. We need a *higher power*," Gorinna said.

Galya chuckled.

"I guess you mean Father, don't you?" she asked.

"Yes—*if* he'll help us, that is," Hunter said.

"He's helped you before. I don't see any reason why he won't help you now, especially since this cloud threatens Thule," Galya said.

Hunter raised an eyebrow at her comment. She giggled again.

"When Arka-Dal and I wed, Father vowed to protect Thule and its people for as long one of the Dal line walks this Earth. And as you well know, he always keeps his word," she explained.

"It appears that many things have changed since our last meeting," Hunter mused.

"In more ways than even *you* can imagine," Arka-Dal added. "Galya, can you inform your father that his help is needed once again?"

"I already have, my love," Galya assured him. "He is on his way."

"In fact, I have *already* arrived!" the Devil announced as he suddenly materialized in their midst.

Hunter, Lorena and DuCassal started.

"That was quite an entrance!" DuCassal remarked as he mocked putting a hand on his chest. "You just about frightened me to death!"

The Devil smiled.

"I know you. It's been a long time since our last meeting. Centuries!" he said as he extended his hand.

Hunter hesitated, then clasped it.

"The last time we met, you asked what I still feel is the most *unusual* favor anyone has ever asked. It was so unusual, I felt that I absolutely *had* to grant your request. I see that it has worked out quite well for you. The Cardinal told me that you and Lorena are his best Slayers," the Devil said as he walked to the bar and made himself a drink.

"You *know* the Cardinal?" Hunter asked.

"You're not the only one who makes requests of me," the Devil said. "He and I have known each other for many years now and I have great respect for him and the work he—and people like you—perform."

"You actually approve of what we do?" Lorena asked.

"Of course! Someone has to help maintain order in this sad world. I can't watch over everything by myself. That's why I created the Vatican agency. There are many things out there, *nasty, evil things that* prey on helpless humans. People like you help keep them at bay," the Devil explained.

Hunter was dumbfounded.

The Devil saw the look on his face and laughed.

"I am *not* the foul and evil being the church has made me out to be. If it were not for my interventions, humankind would not exist at all. The world would now be populated with a race of mindless puppets created to serve a very questionable 'god'," he said. "If you want proof of my veracity, you need look no further than the people in this house."

"The world I was born into was dark and nightmarish. I want to keep this world from becoming anything like it. If that means I must ally myself with the Devil, so be it!" Hunter said as he again shook the Devil's hand.

"I liked you back then. I *still* like you. You have become every bit as good as I expected," the Devil said. "Now, tell me why you had Galya bring me here."

Gorinna explained all that had happened in the Yboe. The Devil listened attentively as she described the cloud of mutant rants and the dark entity who controlled them.

"Your guess is right, Gorinna. That *is* a demonic cloud. From the way you've described it, I'd say it came from a level of Hell that is so low, I never bothered to number it. That's where I throw all of my, for lack of a better word, trash," he said. "Every once in a while, that trash manages to escape its confines. I suspect that is how they got here. Either that or some damned fool accidentally summoned them by playing with things that he shouldn't have."

"Can you get rid of it? Send it back where it came from?" Hunter asked.

"I can do better than that. I'll destroy it and everything that dwells within it," the Devil promised with an almost wicked grin. "It's quite annoying when something like this occurs without my knowing. Even though I did not create this problem, I must correct it before it gets too far out of hand. Unfortunately, I can't bring back those they killed—if I did, that would lead to *other* problems for you and the Vatican."

"What about that thing who controls them?" Gorinna said.

"The other demon?" Hunter asked.

"No. I got a very vivid impression that this entity is *not* a demon—at least not in the sense that we know them to be," Gorinna replied. "This entity is tall and very dark. Inside *and* out. And I sensed *power* and an evil that chilled me to my marrow. I've never felt anything so cold before. This thing actually *frightened* me!"

Arka-Dal whistled.

"I've never known you to be frightened of anything before," he said. "That thing must be evil incarnate."

"What really frightened me most is that I have no idea who or what it is or how it got here," she said. "I *do* know this much—it *controls* the rats in the cloud."

"That adds another wrinkle to this game entirely," the Devil said.

"It sure as Hell does," Hunter agreed. "Now what?"

"We proceed with my plan. We locate that demonic horde and send them all into oblivion. Once that's done, we'll identify who that other entity is and figure out how to deal with him," the Devil said. "One step at a time."

"Unfortunately, we have no way of knowing where it will turn up next," Gorinna said. "How fast does it move?"

"It's not fast at all. It took months for the cloud to reach the Yboe. It sort of just creeps along," Hunter replied.

"If it uses any sort of magical energy, I'll be able to locate it the instant it reappears," the Devil said. "Since you feel it is still in the Yboe, I think you should leave first thing in the morning. Position yourselves somewhere near where you last encountered it and wait for it to return. I'll be there the instant it does and deal with it."

"So we're the bait?" Hunter asked.

"If you prefer," the Devil said with a chuckle. "Since he's already fought with you, I suspect that he'll most likely try to finish the job."

Early the next morning, Hunter and his band left the palace and once again headed for the Yboe. After two days or riding, they selected an open flat space between two small hamlets and set up camp. The villages were the only inhabited areas within 100 square miles and both were likely targets for the demon and his horde of rats.

They gathered a pile of dry twigs, grass and anything else that would burn and started a rather large and obvious campfire. As the flames climbed high into the night, Hunter sipped from his canteen and looked around.

"If this doesn't get our friend's attention, nothing will," DuCassal said. "You can see our fire for miles."

"He'll find us. If I were him, I'd want to finish the job before we became too big a thorn in the side," Hunter said.

"Our lives have taken a very strange turn, Charles," DuCassal said as he warmed his hands over the fire. "We have actually called upon the Devil himself to help us do the Vatican's work. This is the irony to end all ironies."

Hunter nodded.

"This certainly blurs several lines I've always taken as givens. I've learned that God, or what most people thought of as God, wasn't exactly a kind and merciful lord and that Lucifer has done more good for mankind than all of the other gods combined. This kind of trashes one of my long-established belief systems," he said.

"Well, mon cher. *You* started it," Lorena said.

"How did I do that?" Hunter asked.

"You called upon the Devil and made a pact with him so you could do some good in this world," Lorena replied.

"Only he went beyond your original request and added a few touches of his own to make you more effective. The Devil remade you into an agent for good. You were the very first to make such a request of him, so it was *you* who started the ball rolling in this most bizarre tableau," DuCassal added.

"I never thought of it that way. Perhaps you're right," Hunter said.

Gorinna smiled.

"Lucifer always claimed he was a victim of bad press," she said. "A smear campaign."

"He may have been the first victim of the yellow press. I doubt he'll be the last," Hunter said.

Lorena stood and looked to the east.

"He's coming," she said.

"Let's prime the trap," Hunter said as he climbed onto his horse.

The others also mounted their horses. They rode in the direction Lorena indicated and stopped when they first heard, then saw the dark swarm moving toward them. They watched as it grew closer and closer.

The sounds became louder and louder.

Almost deafening.

It stopped fifty feet from them. The rats crouched in a swarm that was several hundred deep and glared at them with their sickly orange eyes.

The swarm parted as the tall, black figure strode forward and snarled at them. After a brief stare-down, Hunter drew his revolver which he'd loaded with high explosive bullets and fired it straight into the center of the figure. The bullets passed through him but struck the rats and detonated. The blasts sent several dozen sailing in all directions and kicked up quite a stir among the others.

Hunter holstered his revolver and swung his horse around.

"Time to go!" he shouted as they all galloped off into the night.

"Kill them! Kill every one of them!" the demon hissed as he pointed to the fleeing group.

The chattering grew louder as the rats swarmed after them, intent on adding them to the menu of their meal. As Hunter and his band disappeared over a hill, the Devil suddenly appeared in front of the horde of rats in burst of white light. The rats halted in their tracks and became quiet as their master carefully eyed the interloper.

"I command you to go no further," the Devil shouted.

The demon bared his jagged teeth as he grinned.

"I am Morthrane, Lord of Rats. Who are *you* to command *me?*" he demanded.

"I am your very worst nightmare," the Devil said. "I am one whom you *dare not cross*. Return to the fetid trash heap that spawned you and take your rats with you. If you don't, I promise you that you *will not* enjoy the consequences," the Devil said.

"My pets require sustenance. As they feed upon the flesh of their victims, I devour their souls so nothing is wasted and my power grows. *Nothing* can stop me. Not even the likes of *you*—whoever you are," Morthrane said.

The Devil simply smiled at him.

"Do your worst, maggot," he challenged. "Show me what you have— and it had better be good!"

Morthrane pointed at him.

"There stands your next meal, my pretties! Feast upon his flesh!" he hissed.

The quiet was suddenly shattered by thousands of chattering and squealing hideously twisted rats as they advanced toward the Devil.

Morthrane watched and laughed as they closed is. He expected them to make quick work of his arrogant adversary. But the Devil calmly stood his ground where all others had fled before the nightmare horde.

When the rats were less than 20 feet from him, the Devil waved his right hand. Morthrane ceased laughing as he watched his ravenous horde of rodents instantly morph into a harmless cloud of multi-colored butterflies which flew off in all directions.

"Impossible!" Morthrane gasped.

"*Nothing* is impossible—*for me*," the Devil said. "I know not what plane of Hell spawned you or what damned fool summoned you to this world. That matters not at this moment. But by all that is unholy, I vow that you will plague this world no longer!"

"Words cannot harm me!" Morthrane hissed as he raised his right arm to cast a spell.

To his horror, he was unable to raise it more than a few inches above his waist. As he struggled to break the Devil's hold, he shuddered in horror then began to wail painfully as inch-by-inch his arm began to turn unto a column of slimy, slithering, bloated worms which dropped to the ground and quickly burrowed out of sight. This continued until everything up to Morthrane's shoulder was gone.

The Devil laughed.

"I have decided to turn you into the vermin you truly are," he said. "At least in this manner, you shall nourish the earth instead of poisoning it."

Morthrane's knees buckled and also began to turn slowly into slithering worms. This transformation continued inch-by-inch until Morthrane's entire body changed. He couldn't stop it. He had no way to defend against it. All he could do is scream in pain as his bloated "offspring" vanished into the ground beneath him.

When only his head remained, Morthrane realized who he had dared to challenge.

"Lord Lucifer!" were the final words he ever uttered, then his head became a pile of worms and they, too, joined the rest of him deep beneath the earth.

When the last of the worms had vanished, the Devil turned and watched as Hunter and his party rode toward him.

Hunter, DuCassal and Lorena just sat on their horses and stared, awed by what they had just witnessed. Gorinna laughed.

"That was one of your better ones," she complimented.

"It was a minor spell at best," the Devil said. "I saw no need to waste anything good on such low-level trash."

"You call that a *minor* spell?" Hunter asked. "What would constitute one of your *major* spells?"

"You'd be amazed," the Devil replied. "Now that Morthrane's been dealt with, it's time for us to return to Thule."

Before Hunter or anyone else could take a breath, they found themselves seated astride their horses right in front of the palace.

"W-what just happened?" asked the startled DuCassal.

"We're home," Gorinna said as if such travel was normal for her. "Let's go inside. It's nearly time for dinner."

They walked into the palace just as everyone was headed for the dining room. Arka-Dal greeted them warmly and expressed surprise they had returned so soon. Over dinner, Hunter explained what happened and how Lucifer made quick work of the strange demon and his rat cloud.

"It was child's play, really," the Devil said modestly. "The most difficult thing was deciding exactly what to do with him. I'd still like to know just how he managed to find his way into this world and if he had help. He certainly wasn't powerful enough to do it himself."

"So he was *summoned*?" Arka-Dal asked.

"There's no other way he could have gotten here," the Devil replied.

"Who in his right mind would want to summon *him*? What reason would anyone have for bringing him here?" Hunter asked.

The Devil shrugged.

"I believe it was an accident. As you know, all sorts of strange things can enter this world when people fool around with things they don't understand. I feel that in this case, it was some drunken fools playing with a Ouija board or reading aloud a spell just to see what would happen," he said.

"Anyway, Morthrane's gone and that's the end of it," Gorinna said.

"Is it?" the Devil asked. "Imagine this, if you dare: what if it wasn't an accident that brought him here? What if someone summoned him and set him loose on purpose as a sort of test? Someone who wants to discover exactly how to do this and which ones he can control?"

"For what purpose?" asked Arka-Dal.

"The usual. Greed, power, revenge—," the Devil said. "Just to be on the safe side, I'll monitor the situation for a while."

"I'd appreciate that," Hunter said.

"We'd *all* appreciate it," Arka-Dal added.

After the meal, Arka-Dal, Galya, the Devil, Gorinna, Hunter, Lorena and DuCassal gathered in the living room. Arka-Dal shook their hands.

"Now that we've gotten to know each other, don't be strangers. Feel free to visit us any time you like—even if you're *not* hunting anything," he said.

"You can count on it," Hunter said. "Thule is a little out of the way for us, but I'd like to come back one day to explore this country of yours. I'd like to learn more about it."

"And please bring your friends," Arka-Dal said as he shook DuCassal's hand and hugged Lorena.

Galya gave them each a warm hug. When she hugged Hunter, they both laughed.

"This is far better than trying to kill each other, isn't it?" she said.

"Much better," he agreed.

She turned and left the room to tend to something that needed her immediate attention. Hunter walked over to Lucifer and extended his right hand. The Devil clasped it and smiled.

"Perhaps you can answer a question for me?" Hunter asked.

"No, I do not know who turned you," the Devil said with a frown.

"I'm surprised. I thought you knew everything," Hunter said.

"A common misconception. In fact, I don't care to know everything. Running my kingdom, writing contracts, and keeping those I love from being harmed already gives me enough on my plate. I have little time for anything else. That's why that thing I slew managed to escape my notice for so many years," the Devil explained. "I knew nothing of your existence until you summoned me and requested my assistance. The identity of the vampire who turned you is none of my concern."

"I see. I thought you were a divine being," Hunter said.

The Devil laughed.

"Immortal—yes. Omnipotent—perhaps. But divine? Never! I am *not* a deity, my friend. In fact, I still find it amusing that some people insist on worshipping me," he said.

He put his hand on Hunter's shoulder and looked into his eyes.

"Why trouble yourself over such a trivial matter? Why is this causing you so much torment?" he asked.

"I'm not sure, really. It just sticks in my mind and I can't get rid of it," Hunter said.

"Let it go, Hunter. Let it be as dead as the old you. Those days are long gone. Put them behind you and don't look back. That's the only way you'll find peace with yourself," the Devil suggested.

"Perhaps you're right," Hunter said.

"I'm *always* right!" the Devil said with a hearty laugh as he patted Hunter on the back.

Hunter laughed, too.

"Thank you—for everything," he said.

"I did only what our contract called for," the Devil said.

"I'd best pack. It's a very long trip back to New Orleans," Hunter said.

"I'll have you home in the blink of an eye," the Devil said as he snapped his fingers.

Seconds later, Hunter, Lorena and DuCassal found themselves seated astride their horses. They were in the Garden District and facing DuCassal's mansion.

"What a rush!" DuCassal exclaimed. "I wish I could travel like this all the time!"

Hunter nodded.

"The Devil saved us at least a month of hard travel," he said. "This is the first time I've ever been teleported anywhere."

"Coming home this way makes me feel as if our journey was only a dream. I feel as if we have never left New Orleans," Lorena added. "But it *is* good to be home."

"I'm hungry. How about joining me for dinner at Brennan's? I'll buy," DuCassal suggested.

"In that case, Jean-Paul, we will be happy to dine with you," Lorena said.

"Indeed!" Hunter added.

Far away in Thule, Galya walked through the living room of the palace and saw her father seated on the sofa before the fireplace. She walked over and sat beside him. He smiled.

"Where's Hunter?" she asked.

"I've sent them back to New Orleans. Why?" he replied.

"I wanted to give him something," she said.

"If you're referring to that strange-looking medallion, I put that in his pocket. He'll find it sooner or later," the Devil said.

"Good," Galya said.

"Why is that medallion so important to you?" the Devil asked.

"It's not important to me, but it may be to Hunter," she said. "I've wanted to give it to him since I found it over 400 years ago. It may provide him with some answers and perhaps peace of mind."

"Or with more questions and more tormented dreams," the Devil said. "There are some questions that are best left unanswered, my daughter."

Galya peered into the flames in the hearth and sighed.

"I hope we did the right thing, Father," she said softly.

When the Cardinal read Hunter's report two weeks later, he laughed out loud. He smiled as he passed it back to Fra Capella.

"The beast is no more, thanks mostly to some help from an old friend of yours. Mr. L. asked me to send his regards and added that you may feel free to call upon him any time you feel his assistance is needed.

We are already back home in New Orleans, again thanks to Mr. L.

—Charles D. Hunter"

"You may place this in the file with the rest of his reports," the Cardinal said.

"Yes, Excellency. But who is this Mr. L. he wrote of? I've never heard you speak of him before," Capella said.

"He is a very old acquaintance of mine," the Cardinal answered.

"Is he a Slayer?" Capella asked.

"No," the Cardinal replied. "But he has provided us with assistance from time-to-time. And that is all I will say on the matter."

Capella placed the report into the folder and excused himself. The Cardinal nodded and watched as he left the office and shut the door behind him.

He wasn't surprised at Hunter's report. Vatican agents had been keeping him informed of the important and strange events in Thule for decades now. In fact, when he learned of Arka-Dal's marriage to Galya, the Devil's daughter, he was dumbfounded. He had expected the worse from their union. Instead, to his amazement, Galya had almost completely changed her stripes. In fact, her union with the Emperor had greatly influenced her father in ways he never imagined were possible.

He smiled.

Once again, the ever resourceful Hunter had accomplished something that no other Slayer had been able to. And he did it by enlisting not only the help of the famous Red Witch herself, but the Devil as well. He realized that the beast would be far beyond his capabilities and had called upon higher powers to intervene.

He laughed.

"And that is precisely why he will always be our best Slayer," he said to himself.[2]

---

[2] For more about these characters, read The Avenger of Thule and other books in the series

CHAPTER TEN:
The Horror From St. Louis

Inspector Valmonde looked at the clock on the wall of his office. It was only five p.m. He had seven more hours left on his shift. So far, it had been a fairly quiet night in the Big Easy.

He poured himself a cup of coffee and sat down at his desk to read the bulletins. He had just opened the file when his door opened. He looked up and smiled as Hunter, Lorena and DuCassal walked in.

"Well, look what the wind blew in," he said as they seated themselves.

"Hello, Chief," Hunter said.

"When did you folks get back?" Valmonde asked.

"Earlier this afternoon. Anything happen while we were away?" Hunter asked.

"You mean besides the usual murders and attempted murders?" Valmonde asked.

Hunter nodded.

"In that case, plenty. Somethin's goin' around tearin' folks limb-from-limb on a regular basis," Valmonde said as he pulled the file from his desk drawer and passed it to Hunter.

"How regular?" Hunter asked as he started to read the file.

"Too damned regular. We've had 12 murders in the last five weeks. They were all slaughtered just like those folks we found at the Frenchman a couple of months ago. They died by the bunch, too," Valmonde said.

"Three on May 6th at the old mortuary. Two more outside of St. Louis Number Three. Three on the 20th at the Art Museum and four last week the Lamothe House," Hunter read. "That's quite a list."

"Whatever's been doin' this really seems to have it in for those folks," Valmonde said. "And it likes to stay busy."

"Too damned busy," Hunter said as he read deeper.

"This is interesting. According to your files, all 12 of the victims were from St. Louis—just like the group at the Frenchman. And they were all carrying so-called vampire hunting kits," he said as he passed the file to Lorena and DuCassal.

"Seems to me they came down here on some sort of huntin' expedition only *they* ended up bein' the hunted," Valmonde said.

"Whatever they're hunting doesn't like to be hunted. From the descriptions of the bodies, I'd say it really pisses him off," Hunter said.

"I never seen anybody butchered like those people were. They were killed with a vengeance," Valmonde added. "I've had my men out lookin' for anythin' that could have done this but so far, they haven't found a thing."

"It's just as well. They're not equipped to tackle anything as dangerous as this thing seems to be. They would have just ended up dead like the others," DuCassal said as he handed Valmonde the file.

"Anything else?" Hunter asked.

"Yeah. They were all vampires, same as the first bunch," Valmonde said.

"That makes this even more interesting, Lorena said.

Valmonde nodded.

"But none of the locals have been killed or attacked. Just this bunch. I even asked Tony if he knew or heard anythin' but came up empty," Valmonde said.

"Who else was looking into this?" Hunter asked.

"Miss Morii. Besides tryin' to track that thing down, she's been thinnin' out the local criminal population big time. She's good at it, too. Almost *too* good," Valmonde said.

"What do you mean?" Lorena asked.

"She's been killin' three or four each week. If she's tryin' to make New Orleans crime free, I'd say she's succeedin'," Valmonde said.

"We'd best drop by the Emporium and have a chat with her," Lorena said.

"Good luck with that," Valmonde said.

"Why?" asked Hunter.

"I haven't seen her around for the last eight days—and that's unusual," Valmonde replied. "She always keeps in touch. It's not like her to up and vanish like that."

Hunter looked at Lorena.

"Let's get over there," he said.

When they arrived at the Emporium, they were surprised to find the door unlocked. They stepped inside and called out several times.

"Looks like no one's home," Hunter said as he ran his fingers over the top of a display case. "From the looks of this dust, I'd say no one's been here for few days. Hannah always keeps this cases clean."

They walked to the back room and headed up the stairs. Lorena stopped halfway up and sniffed.

"I've just caught a very faint scent of something nasty and evil," she said. "Let's hurry upstairs."

The door to Hannah's suite was wide open. When they looked inside, they saw furniture and broken knickknacks scattered on the floor. The bed was disheveled and the room reeked of stale blood.

"Looks like there's been one Hell of a fight here," Hunter said.

Lorena walked to the bed. She picked up the blood-stained sheet and sniffed it. She tossed it back on the bed.

"That's Hannah's blood all right. There's no mistaking it," she said.

Hunter paced and took in every detail of the room. He saw her katana lying beneath the bed and retrieved it. He passed it to Lorena who examined the dark stains on the blade.

"This isn't her blood," she said as she tossed it onto the bed.

"That means she got at least one good shot in," Hunter said. "Hannah is strong, intelligent and lightning fast. For anyone to be able to do this, he would have had to take her completely by surprise."

"And *that*, mon cher, is nearly impossible," Lorena said.

"I know," he nodded.

"Do you think Hannah is dead?" DuCassal asked.

"No. If she were dead, I'd sense it because I'm the one who turned her," Lorena said.

"From the looks of the blood stains, I'd say she was badly wounded. But where *is* she now?" Hunter wondered.

"Perhaps whoever did this has taken her prisoner?" DuCassal suggested.

"Prisoner? Why would anyone want to do that?" Hunter asked.

"Find Hannah and we'll find the answers to all of our questions," DuCassal said.

"Lorena—can you *track* her?" Hunter asked.

"I can *try*," Lorena said.

She walked around the room and took several deep breaths. Once she caught Hannah's scent, she walked downstairs and out into the street. Hunter and DuCassal followed her as she walked around the corner and stopped. She turned and sniffed again.

"Nothing! Her trail ends right here," she said in frustration.

"That means she was put into a carriage," Hunter reasoned.

"And there are far too many carriage trails for me to just home in on a single one," Lorena said. "I'm sorry, mon cher."

"The one who took her will be a lot sorrier when I get my hands on him," Hunter said as they headed toward Bourbon Street.

"Hannah is no joke to deal with. Her martial arts skills make her a very formidable force. Whoever took her is very fast and very powerful enough to have taken her down. My guess is he somehow too her by surprise," Hunter said.

"Which is nearly *impossible*, mon cher," Lorena said. "You *know* how difficult it is to surprise a vampire."

"*Someone* managed to surprise her. There's no other way her could have taken her. The big question is *why?*" Hunter said.

Father Paul was sweeping the main aisle of St. Louis Cathedral as he did every afternoon. The aisle wasn't dirty or anything. He did it mostly to pass the time and it made him feel a little bit more productive. As he swept, he heard the heavy front door creak open then shut. He turned and watched as a tall, thin man dressed in the old style frock coat of Catholic priest walked down the aisle toward him. The man was pale and almost gaunt. He had slicked back black hair and deep, dark eyes.

Something about him just didn't feel right to Paul.

"Father Paul?" the priest asked.

"Yes. Welcome to St. Louis Cathedral," Paul said as he extended his right hand.

The priest simply bowed his head instead.

"I'm Father Tobias Fink. I manage the Old Cathedral in St. Louis," he said as they sat down in a nearby pew.

"What brings you to New Orleans?" Paul asked.

"I'm searching for some parishioners of mine. I have reason to believe they are here in New Orleans and against my advice," Fink replied.

"Oh?" Paul asked.

"Yes. There is a vicious fiend roaming the streets of St. Louis. Or there was. He tore several people completely apart, then fled south. Several of my flock decided to form posses and go after him but I fear they are sadly overmatched. I've come here to talk them out of this madness before they end up like the people in St. Louis," Fink explained.

"You say they've come here to hunt the killer down?" Paul asked.

"I believe so," Fink replied. "I was hoping that some of them might have stopped by here to ask your advice."

"No one's been here lately," Paul said warily. "But they might have gone to the police station on Basin Street for information. Perhaps you should inquire there," Paul suggested.

Fink smiled.

The smile made Paul's skin crawl.

"Thank you, Father. I shall go there next," Fink said as he stood and bowed his head.

Paul watched him leave the cathedral then realized that even though he was walking across an old marble floor, Fink didn't make a sound.

"A vampire," Paul thought. "I wonder why he's *really* here."

Paul waited a few minutes, then locked up the Cathedral and headed out in search of Hunter.

An hour later, Inspector Valmonde looked up from his morning paper and nearly jumped out of his skin when he saw the strange priest seated in the chair across from him. Valmonde composed himself and smiled.

"Excuse me, Padre. I didn't hear you come in," he apologized. "What can I do for you?"

"I am Father Tobias Fink. I've come from the Old Cathedral in St. Louis on a most urgent mission," the priest said.

"What sort of mission, Father?" asked Valmonde.

"I was told by Father Paul that you might be able to help me locate some misguided parishioners of mine," Fink said as he sat down. "There are about 15 of them. They traveled down from St. Louis over the last two months against my wishes. I've come to try and talk them into returning."

"You say they're from St. Louis?" Valmonde asked.

Fink nodded.

"In that case, I have something that may interest you, Father," Valmonde said as he produced the same folder and manila envelope he'd shown to Hunter.

Fink took the envelope and poured the contents out onto Valmonde's desk. The inspector and Lem watched as he slowly went through each wallet and looked at the ID cards.

"They are my parishioners. Where are you holding them?" Fink asked.

"I ain't holdin' them anywhere," Valmonde said. "Their over at the morgue."

"Come again?" Fink asked.

"Each one of your people was torn to pieces by somethin' that really detested them. I've never in my entire career seen anythin' like that before. Those folks were slaughtered. Whatever did this wanted to make damned well sure they were all dead," Valmonde explained.

"I *warned* them this would happen," Fink said. "That same monster has killed over two dozen people in St. Louis over the last year. When my parishioners learned that the local police had chased it out of the city and it might have fled to New Orleans, they decided to form posses and go after it. I warned them it was suicidal and that they were no match for this thing. But they refused to listen and this is the results I was afraid of."

"Just what is it you're hunting, Father?" asked Valmonde. "I know it ain't no vampire. I've seen folks that were killed by vampires and they were never torn to pieces like your people were. This looks more like the way a rougarou kills."

"Rougarou?" Fink asked.

"Werewolf," Valmonde translated. "Are you goin' to hunt that thing?"

"It seems that I have little choice now. But I'm not stupid like my parishioners were. I know I can't do this by myself. I need help. *Professional help*," Fink said.

"Anyone in mind?" Valmonde asked.

"Yes. Do you know of a Slayer called Hunter?" Fink asked.

"I do," Valmonde admitted.

"Good. Then perhaps you can arrange a meeting with him for me?" Fink asked.

"That should be easy enough. Where can you be reached?" Valmonde asked.

"I checked into the Lamothe House last night. You can reach me there," Fink answered.

"I'll let you know when I locate him," Valmonde said.

"Thank you, Inspector. I'll be waiting for your message," Fink said as he rose and bowed his head.

Valmonde and Lem watched him leave the station. Valmonde shook his head.

"That is one spooky old man," Lem remarked.

"I'll say. That fella makes my skin itch. I don't trust him as far as I can throw this buildin' either," Valmonde said as he got up and grabbed his hat.

"Let's go find Hunter," he said.

When Hannah Morii finally opened her eyes, she realized she was in pitch blackness. As her eyes slowly adjusted, she looked up to see several pine boards directly above her. She tried to stretch out her arms and hit more wood.

"I'm in a box," she thought. "A coffin! How on earth did I get in here?"

She summoned all of her strength, made a fist and drove it upward as hard as she could. The boards splintered and moist, dark earth began to pour in. She hit it again and again and again. Then dug her way out until she reached open air. She rolled out of the hole and took several deep breaths. Then she sat up and looked around.

She was in the middle of the swamp and surrounded by murky water. It was night. A full moon shone down on her as she looked around at the trees and tall reeds. Here and there, she saw the glaring red eyes of alligators as they watched her every move. That's also when she realized she was naked.

And hungry.

Very hungry.

She tried to think about how she got there.

Nothing.

She tried to recall her name and where she lived.

Another blank.

All she knew was that she was hungry and she needed to feed—*fast.*

She needed fresh human blood and she didn't give a damn who she got it from.

Valmonde and Len located Hunter, Lorena and DuCassal while they were at Pere Antoine's having dinner. When he told Hunter about the strange priest he simply nodded.

"I know about Fink. Father Paul told me he was here this afternoon. I figured you'd come looking for us, so I made sure we'd be easy to find," he said. "I also know he's a vampire himself, so it's unlikely that he's here for the reasons he said he is. If those people who were butchered were indeed part of his cult, then we're dealing with a possible vampire infestation."

"I am almost willing to bet that he had something to do with Hannah's disappearance," DuCassal said.

"Where's he staying?" Hunter asked.

"The Lamothe House on Esplanade," Valmonde replied. "He said he'd like to meet with you."

"And I certainly want to know what he really wants here," Hunter said. "Send him over to our place this evening. I'll decide what to do after I meet him."

"You got it. I'll send Lem over with the message right away," Valmonde agreed.

At six p.m., Fink arrived at Hunter's house. He spotted Hunter and Lorena, who were seated on the porch sipping wine after their evening meal. Fink walked up and introduced himself. Hunter nodded.

"Have a seat, Father," he offered.

Fink sat down in the chair directly across from him and smiled. The smile was more than a little disingenuous.

And creepy.

"I need your help in tracking down a most terrifying beast. It has terrorized St. Louis for months and when my and my parishioners closed in on it, it suddenly fled the city. We were able to track it to New Orleans," Fink said.

"What kind of beast are you talking about?" asked Hunter.

"A shape shifter. A demon from the very bowels of Hell. It tears people apart without mercy," Fink replied. "It's incredibly strong, fast and dangerous."

"What does it look like?" Hunter asked.

"It usually takes the form a young woman. But when angered, it becomes this fearsome monster. It has already killed several of my parishioners," Fink said.

"You mean the ones at the Frenchman?" Hunter asked.

"I see that Inspector Valmonde has told you of my visit," Fink smiled.

"That he has. I also saw what the creature did to your fist band," Hunter said as he sipped his wine. "It wasn't very pretty, to say the least."

"Have any similar murders occurred before then?" Fink asked.

"Not a one," Hunter replied. "Seems to me, the creature only went after the ones you sent to kill it. I'd call that an act of self defense," Hunter smiled. "I'd dot the same of they came after me."

"I see," Fink mused as he tried to read Hunter's expression.

"Before I go after this thing, I need to know more about it. What does it look like in human form? What are its habits? What form does it take when it's angered? Without that information, I'd be flying blind— and I won't do that," Hunter said as he leaned forward.

"The last known human form it took was that of a young woman. It goes by the name of Madison. I believe she came down here with the hope of blending into the scenery. Perhaps you've run into her by now?" Fink said.

"Can't say as I have," Hunter said. "Tell me more."

Fink went on to describe two other horrific murders and several others that he claimed can be attributed to Madison. As he spoke, he became more animated and the veins in his neck protruded as if they were ready to rupture. Lorena glanced at Hunter while she listened. Hunter winked, but kept his eyes on Fink as he continued to explain why he was in New Orleans.

"If at all possible, I'd like to capture this creature alive so we can study it and find out what it is and what makes it kill. As of now, I am the only remaining member of our parish. If that thing isn't dealt with immediately, I fear it may cut a swath of death and destruction through the very heart of New Orleans," Fink said.

"That's quite a story. If it weren't for the trail of mangled corpses all over New Orleans, I'd say you were lying," Hunter said.

"Every word of what I've told is the truth," Fink avowed. "Would a priest lie?"

"A *real* priest wouldn't," Hunter said.

Fink squinted at him.

"Will you help me find this creature?" he asked.

"I'll think about it," Hunter said with a smile. "I have quite a lot on my plate at the moment. I can only handle one case at a time. I'll contact you if I find out anything."

Fink nodded in frustration.

"Thank you for your time," he said as he rose and walked away.

"He's a *vampire*," Lorena said as Fink vanished around the corner.

"I know. I picked up on that immediately," Hunter said.

"Why didn't you call him on it?" she asked as he poured himself a glass of wine.

"I wanted to hear him out. I thought he'd tip his hand and we'd find out why he's really in New Orleans," Hunter said. "That story about his 'parishioners' is pretty feeble, especially when you consider that they were all vampires. It makes me wonder what in Hell they were hunting."

"Do you think he sent them?" Lorena asked.

"I *know* he sent them," Hunter said.

"He's no fool, mon cher," Lorena said. "He knows that I know he's a vampire. There was no way he could hide that from me," Lorena said.

"I know. Yet, he said nothing. He's playing his hand close to his vest. I want to know what cards he's holding and when he plans to play them," Hunter said.

"I also smelled something on him," Lorena said.

"Hannah's blood?" Hunter asked.

"Yes," she replied. "He is the one who attacked her. He knows where she is now."

"Can you back track his scent?" Hunter asked.

"I'm not sure. It depends on how fresh the trail is," Lorena said.

"Give it a try. Follow it as far as possible. Maybe we'll get lucky," Hunter said.

The trail led to a boarded up, crumbling mansion at the far end of Palmyra Street. The place had a sunken in porch and a grand gallery that was missing several floorboards. Weeds had claimed more than half of the structure, which looked pale and eerie in the light of the full moon.

They jumped down from the carriage and looked around. There was a ruined stone wall around the property. A live oak had sprouted right at the base of the wall near the front gate and knocked the post it was anchored to the ground.

Hunter drew his revolver and walked past the gate. Lorena walked next to him. DuCassal checked his shotgun and followed after them. Bats fluttered above the mansion noisily, engaged in a "dog fight" with the hordes of mosquitoes that were their food supply.

"What a charming place!" DuCassal joked.

"Yes. Kind of makes you want to spend the night, doesn't it?" Hunter said as they stepped onto the creaking porch.

"I'm picking up both Fink's and Hannah's scents," Lorena said.

"Are they still here?" Hunter asked as he gently pushed on the front door.

"No," she said. "I sense nothing but bats inside."

"Let's have a look around. Maybe you'll be able to pick up their trail inside," Hunter said as they entered the mansion.

The interior was a complete disaster. With every step they took, fallen plaster crunched beneath their boots. Lorena led the way to a small room just off the kitchen. Inside, they found a long, wooden table. There were chains attached to each of the four legs and several dark stains on top. Lorena ran her fingers through one of the stains and concentrated.

"My God!" she exclaimed as images of Hannah being brutally raped over and over again flashed through his mind.

"This is where he took her—and tortured the Hell out of her. I sense her terror. Her feeling of helplessness. And her hatred for her tormentor," she said. "I can't take it anymore!"

Hunter saw tears flowing down her cheeks and brushed them off with his fingertips.

"Where'd they go from here?" he asked.

"That way," Lorena said as she pointed north.

They hopped back into carriage. Lorena led them to the bridge that spanned Lake Ponchartrain. DuCassal ordered his driver to stop while Lorena caught her bearings. She looked at them and nodded.

"They crossed here alright," she said.

They crossed the bridge and stopped again. Lorena took another deep breath then pointed north.

"They headed into the swamp," she said.

It was nearly dawn when they reached the edge of the bayou. DuCassal stopped the carriage. They jumped out and looked around while Lorena tried to pick up the trail. After about 20 minutes, she screamed in frustration.

"It ends here! Right here at the edge of the bayou," she said. "It's as if they suddenly disappeared."

She tore up a tree stump and hurled it about 50 yards into the bayou. It splashed loudly and stirred up several birds that were nesting nearby. They voiced their displeasure at being disturbed as they flapped off into the morning light.

"There's nothing left for us to do but return to New Orleans and wait for Fink to play his hand," Hunter said as they climbed back into the carriage.

Hannah trudged through the muddy waters until she reached a stretch of high ground that was relatively dry and solid. Her stomach grumbled louder and her flesh began to feel dry. She had to feed and fast.

She walked on for another hundred years and spotted a small cabin hidden amid the trees. There was lights on inside and she could hear men laughing and cards being shuffled. She crept closer and peered through the window. She saw three rough-looking men seated around a table. There were beer bottles in front of them along with a pile of chips and cash in the middle of the table.

She decided to take the direct approach and knocked on the door.

The biggest of the three got up and opened the door. At first he stared then smiled at her lithe nude body.

"Looky here, boys! We got ourselves a visitor, She's cute, too! What can we do you for you, miss?" he asked as she stepped into the cabin.

"I need food and some clothes," Hannah said.

"I'm not sure about clothes but you can help yourself to the fried gator tail and some beer," he offered.

"That's not the kind of nourishment I need," she said as she bared her fangs.

"Holy shit! She's a vampire!" the big man shouted as he reached for the pistol in his pocket.

Before his hand got halfway there, she seized him by the throat and sank her fangs into his neck. The other men jumped up and armed themselves with tools from the fireplace and watched as their friend twitched helplessly as Hannah drained him. When he was empty, she tossed him against the far wall and charged at the others . . .

Once she had reached her fill, she sat down at the table and finished off what remained of the fried alligator and chased it with a bottle of warm beer. Satisfied on both counts, she decided to search the cabin for something to wear. She found a checkered, short sleeved shirt and a pair of jeans in the bedroom closet. They obviously had belonged to the smallest of the three men who were now pale and lifeless in the next room. Hannah slipped them on and left the cabin.

Although she still didn't know who she was, she instinctively headed west toward New Orleans. She didn't know how far it was or what she would do when she got there, but she thought someone might be able to tell her who she was and why she was inside that damned box in the middle of the swamp.

Images of being chained to a table by the wrists and ankles and being forced to gag down some vile pulpy concoction that robbed her of her senses popped into her mind. She saw a hazy, dark clad figure who laughed as he whipped her with a leather strap. She felt her legs being pried apart then a feeling of numbness as her captor used her over and over and over until she ceased to care anymore.

A chilling thought entered her mind. It made her feel sick and cold all over.

"What if that bastard *impregnated* me?"

Then a feeling of disgust and anger swept through her and she decided that if she was pregnant, she'd abort the bastard child—then she'd track down her tormentor and *abort him*.

The last thing she wanted was for her captor to be able to live on through a bastard child and she sure as Hell didn't want to be its mother.

Then a name popped into her mind.

"Lorena!" she said as she quickened her pace.

Hunter, DuCassal and Lorena walked into the Dragon and saw Madison tending the bar. They walked over and sat down. Madison hurried over to greet them and Hunter ordered a round of drinks. As Madison mixed their cocktails, Hunter asked her if she was familiar with a strange priest from St. Louis who was searching for a vampire in New Orleans.

Madison's face lost most of its color when she heard the name. She was obviously shaken and it took her several seconds to recover.

"Are you *sure* that's his name?" she asked.

"That's who he said he is. You know him?" Hunter asked.

Madison stared straight ahead and nodded.

"I know him all right. *Intimately*," she said after a while.

"Tell me all you know," Hunter said.

"To begin with, he's not a priest. He's a monster. A cold, heartless killer who lives only to satisfy his perversities. He dresses as a priest because people trust them. It makes it easier for him to choose his victims," she said.

"Like you?" Hunter asked.

"Yes. Like me. Some he kills. Some he keeps to satisfy his personal needs. He kept me as his personal sex slave. He used me at will and even pimped me out as bait to lure more victims into his trap. I had to take just enough blood from my clients to weaken them, then he'd move in and make the kill. If I didn't do what he told me, he'd beat me or withhold blood from me until I begged him for it. My life for the last six years has been a living Hell. A true waking nightmare that I never imagined possible," she said bitterly.

"How did you become involved with Fink?" asked Lorena.

"He snatched me right out of my bedroom one night. At first, I tried to fight him off, but he beat me and raped me and took blood from me until I became like him. That took ten days. It was the ten worst days of my life—or so I felt. What followed was far worse. He took me back home and made me watch as he killed my parents. By then, my will was broken and I just did what he ordered me to," Madison answered.

"Did you kill those people?" Hunter asked.

"Oh yes. Those were his disciples. Heartless monsters just like their master in all respects. They've killed and raped their way through St. Louis and nearby towns with impunity. The police were helpless to stop them, too. They have no one like you there," she said.

She sighed.

"I finally got the courage to break away from the pack," she said. "Fink gave me to three of his disciples so they could have their way with me. While they were doing this, this sudden rage surged through me and I fought back. When it was over, I had torn all three of them to pieces and drained each of their blood. Right after that, I decided to come to New Orleans. I'd heard about you and I thought I'd ask you to come to St. Louis and help me get rid of Fink and his disciples."

"Why didn't you ask for help when we first met?" Hunter asked.

"I don't know. I guess I wanted to be sure I could trust you," she admitted. "Before I could ask, I discovered that some of the pack had arrived in New Orleans. That's when I decided to take matters into my own hands."

She leaned back and took a deep breath.

"When I learned they were at the Frenchman, I arranged to meet with them on the pretense of returning to St. Louis. They invited me into the room. Three others of the pack had also arrived by then. When I saw them, I just allowed my rage to explode. You saw what was left of them," she said.

"What about the one we found in the tree?" asked DuCassal.

"I chased her down, drained her of her blood and threw her up into the branches," Madison said.

"You killed the others, too?" Hunter asked.

"Yes. I had no choice. It was either them or me. I don't want to kill anyone, but those monsters *deserved* to die. I thought I'd be safe after I'd killed all of the disciples. But now you've told me that Fink is here in New Orleans. I know him, Hunter. He won't stop until he's killed me. I'm not strong enough to defeat him by myself," she said.

"You're not alone now, Madison," Hunter said.

"You mean you'll help me?" she asked hopefully.

"Definitely," he assured her. "But, if he's as powerful as you say, we'll need some extra insurance."

"Alejandro?" Lorena asked.

He smiled and nodded.

"I have a plan . . ." he said.

Dave Montgomery and his ten year old son, Chris, were fishing from their flatboat. It was early morning and the low lying mist was beginning to burn off in the hot sun. As Chris dropped his line into the still water, he tapped Dave on the elbow and pointed at the beautiful young woman slogging toward them.

Dave waited until she was a few feet from the boat and greeted her with his usual friendly smile and a cheerful "morning miss."

"You lost?" he asked as she stepped onto the boat.

"Lost and hungry," the woman replied.

"We got some fried egg sandwiches and coffee in the cooler. Help yourself," Dave offered. "It ain't a lot but I'm happy to share."

The woman thanked him and opened the cooler. She took out one of the sandwiches and bit into it. As she ate, she looked them over. They did the same to her.

"How'd you get way out here?" Dave asked.

"To be honest with you, I really don't know how I got out here. I don't remember much of anything at all," she replied as she finished the sandwich.

"Well, who are you?" Dave asked.

"I don't know that, either," she said.

"Can you recollect anything?" asked Chris.

"I remember New Orleans," she replied. "I think I'm supposed to go there. Maybe that's where I live."

"Dang! That's nearly a hundred miles south of here," Dave remarked. "You *are* lost!"

"Can you tell me how to get there?" she asked.

"There's a dirt road on the other side of that hill over there. If you follow it, it will take you to a paved road. That should lead you to New Orleans. You look like you've had a rough time of it, Miss. Are you sure you can handle such a trip?" Dave asked.

"I'll be all right," the woman said with a smile as she fought off an urge to add both Dave and Chris to her meal plan.

"Why don't you take the rest of our sandwiches along with you? At least that'll give you something to eat along the way. There ain't many places along the way you can stop at," Dave offered.

"If I did that, you and your son won't have anything to eat," she said.

"That's okay. We can eat afterward. You look like you could use it more than us anyway. Go ahead and take them. I insist," Dave pressed.

Hannah smiled.

She picked up the other sandwich and stuffed it into her shirt. She was still hungry, but not for fried egg sandwiches. She needed blood. Human blood and she briefly considered taking what she needed from them. But even though her hunger was almost overpowering, she thought better of it.

"Thank you," she said.

They watched as she left the boat and climbed up the hill toward the dirt road. Dave dropped his line into the water as he watched her fade from view.

"I wonder who she is," he said.

"I don't know, Pa, but she sure is pretty," Chris said.

Dave laughed.

Forty miles to the east, Sheriff John Potts and three of his deputies closed in on the lone cabin with guns drawn. When they were within shouting distance, Potts held up his right fist. The deputies quickly surrounded the house and prepared themselves for a firefight. Instead, the house was quiet.

Eerily quiet.

Potts nodded at his deputies. They charged straight at the front and back doors with their weapons drawn and ready. Potts went to kick the front door in. To his surprise, it simply creaked inward. That's when he saw the three corpses lying on the floor. He holstered his pistols just as his deputies walked in. The cabin reeked of rotted flesh and flies were everywhere.

"They're all dead. Someone musta beat us to them," a deputy said as he looked around.

"Whoever did this, did us a favor. Most likely we would have had to kill them anyway. I'm sure they wouldn't have gave themselves up without a fight," Potts said as he knelt to examine one of them.

"Fang marks. Looks like a vampire got them," he said.

"They never had a chance," the second deputy said.

"Don't feel sorry for them, Roy. They got the same chance they gave those folks they robbed and killed last month. Don't bother to bury them. Just toss them into the swamp and let the gators have them," Potts said.

"Now what do ya have against gators, Chief?" asked the first deputy.

Fink sat in his hotel room and chuckled to himself. His plan, he felt, was moving along nicely. He would enlist the aid of Hunter and his cohorts to track down and kill his errant disciple. Since he realized they all knew he was a vampire (how could they *not* know that?) he figured they might refuse to help him.

That's why he had captured Hannah Morii several days earlier. In order to show how powerful he was, he'd spent the better part of a week beating her and drugging her into submission. Once he'd broken her will, he spent several more days finding new and more painful ways to rape her before locking her into a wooden coffin and burying her in the swamp. When he was through with Hannah, she had no memory of who she was or what had happened,

That's when he planted the *suggestion* in her subconscious mind. One that would be triggered the moment she heard the first eight bars of the Basin Street Blues being played. Two hours after that, she would be forced to carry out her orders no matter *who* stood in her way.

But that would happen only if Hunter refused to recapture Madison and hand her over to him. Of course, that meant he'd also have to kill Hunter and his entire team.

That's when he laughed out loud.

"That should be easy enough," he thought. "After all, they have never before had to deal with the likes of me!"

It was at that point he heard a light knock on his door. He rose from the chair, walked over and opened it to see Joe the hotel manager standing in the courtyard.

"This was delivered to the front desk a few minutes ago," Joe said as he handed Fink an envelope. "The messenger said it was real important."

"Thank you," Fink said as he took the envelope and shut the door.

Joe smiled to himself and headed back across the courtyard. Fink sat down and opened the envelope. When he read the note, he laughed softly.

"Meet me on the corner of Liberty and Cleveland at midnight tonight. It's time we talked. Madison."

"I'll meet you there, my pretty. But I will talk and you will listen and obey," he said as he crumpled the note and tossed it on the floor.

Midnight.

A very light mist fell upon the city and lent the streets an eerie luster. Fink walked down Esplanade past several hotels and old Creole mansions and clumps of club goers. When he reached Canal Street, he turned north to Liberty. The street was deserted at this point. He looked around casually, then walked north one black to Cleveland. As he reached the corner, he saw a small figure in a dark, hooded cloak standing next to a street lamp.

He stopped and listened.

When he recognized her heartbeat, he smiled and walked toward her, baring his fangs in a menacing manner.

As soon as Madison saw him, she fled down the street. Fink started to go after her but a voice from the shadows of a nearby doorway stopped him in his tracks.

"I would not go after her if I were you, my friend," he said.

Fink squinted as a tall figure dressed in evening clothes, a wide brimmed hat, a long black cape and an opera mask stepped into the street. He smiled at the man's outlandish attire.

"And who are *you* supposed to be? The Phantom of the Opera?" he sneered.

"My name is Alejandro—and I am about to become your very worst nightmare," the man said as he discarded his cape and hat with a theatrical flourish.

"We'll see about that, freak!" Fink hissed as he ran at him and swung his fist.

Alejandro not only blocked the blow, he seized Fink's wrist and gave it sharp, sudden twist which almost buckled Fink's knees. Fink screamed in pain. He screamed even louder when Alejandro stretched out his arm and brought his elbow down on Fink's elbow with all of his might. The sound of the bone snapping echoed through the deserted streets and Fink fell to his knees in agony. Alejandro laughed and gave the arm a hard wrench. It separated at the broken elbow and came off. As Fink screamed again and cursed, Alejandro tossed the limb over his shoulder.

"Now, you are mine!" he said as he came at Fink.

"That's what *you* think!" Fink replied as he delivered a backhand slap with enough force to send Alejandro into the wall of a building across the street.

As Alejandro rose and shook the blow off, Fink turned to run—only to be nearly gutted by the twin blast from DuCassal's shotgun fired at almost point-blank range. Fink fell to his knees and attempted to stand. Before he could get to his feet, Hunter kicked him in the face and sent him to the pavement. As he lay sprawled on his back, Hunter took a stake from his pocket and drove it straight into Fink's heart. It burst with a loud pop and sent blood flying in all directions.

As the light faded from his eyes, Fink smiled up at him.

"My nightmare is over but *yours* is just beginning," he said.

"We'll see about that!" Hunter said as he drew his katana and beheaded him with one deft strike.

He sheathed the weapon, then doused the body and head with oil and ignited it. They all gathered around to watch him burn until nothing was left but ashes.

"What did he mean by your nightmare is just beginning, mon cher?" Lorena asked.

"More importantly, mes amis, is where did he take Hannah?" asked DuCassal as they walked down the street.

"I tracked her to the edge of the swamp but her trail went cold. I'm sure she's still out there somewhere," Lorena said.

"Perhaps I can be of service?" Alejandro suggested.

"How?" asked DuCassal.

"In rougarou form, I can follow anyone's scent no matter how old and almost through any terrain—just like a super charged bloodhound. Please allow me to help you find her," Alejandro replied.

"You're on," Hunter agreed.

"We must find Hannah before something goes horribly wrong," Lorena said with a worried tone in her voice.

"Like what?" Alejandro asked.

"The worst thing possible," Lorena said. 'The *unthinkable!*"

Madison stepped back into the light and walked over to them.

"Thank you," she said sincerely.

"You're free now, Madison," Hunter said. "You can live without fear."

"I heard you talking about your missing friend. If Fink did take her, this isn't over yet," Madison said. "There's no telling what he did to her or what she's thinking right now. He was very good at *changing* people."

"Do you have any idea where he might have taken her?" Hunter asked.

"No. But I'd like to help you find her," Madison answered.

"As long as you can control your rage, I see no harm in that," DuCassal said with a grin.

"Another set of super keen senses is always welcome," Hunter added. "But if he did manage to brainwash Hannah, he must have programmed her to go after *you*. He wanted you back or dead. I believe he grabbed Hannah as sort of a Plan B—in case the others failed. No matter what happened, he probably wanted to make sure you didn't escape his vengeance."

Madison nodded.

"That's the way Fink always played things. That's why I want to help you find your friend," she said.

"Are there any more of those fiends roaming around?" DuCassal asked

"No. I've killed them all. Fink sent the entire congregation after me. I'm the only one left," Madison assured him.

"Unfortunately for *them*," Lorena said with a grin.

"Remind me never to piss you off," Hunter said.

"I second that," DuCassal added. "I would hate to end up like one of your pursuers."

"I only get that way when I'm terrified or very angry. With Fink and his 'family' dead, you've no need to worry about me, Jean-Paul," Madison said.

"Just to be on the safe side, I shall be very careful never to anger you in any way. I prefer to keep my extremities attached to my body," DuCassal said.

"When we first met, you said that something was tearing people limb-from-limb in St. Louis. Was that *you* by any chance?" Hunter asked.

"The only people I tore to pieces were two of Fink's disciples. As for the rest of the murders, I'd be willing to bet that they were committed by Fink himself," Madison said. "But I'm not very sure about that."

They climbed into DuCassal's carriage. He leaned out the window and instructed his driver to take them to the edge of the swamp. Then he pulled a leather case down from a compartment above Hunter's head, opened it and handed each of them a crystal wine goblet. He sat down and popped the cork off the bottle of champagne and filled each of their goblets.

"I thought this would be an occasion worth celebrating," he said as he raised his goblet.

The others clinked theirs against it and drank. By the time they reached the swamp, the bottle was empty. Alejandro refused to have more than one glass of the wine as he didn't want the alcohol to impair his senses. They climbed out and looked around as a very light mist rolled through the trees.

"I lost her trail about 200 yards further in," Lorena said as she pointed to the right. "Both hers and Fink's simply went cold and I couldn't pick either of them up again."

"Leave it to me," Alejandro said.

He removed his hat, mask and cape and handed them to Lorena. Then he walked out into the swamp and concentrated. They watched as he partially transformed himself into a cross between a human and rougarou. He stopped when he was halfway through. He looked back and bared his fangs as he attempted to grin. Then he squatted and sniffed the ground. After a minute ticked by, he turned and motioned for the others to follow him as he headed into the swamp.

"In this form, my sense of smell is one thousand times that of a blood hound. If Fink did not mask his trail, I will be able to follow it. Hopefully, it will lead us to where he too Hannah," he explained.

They followed the trail for one hour.

Then a second.

They slogged over the mucky landscape until Alejandro signaled them to stop when they came to a shallow pit.

"This is it," he announced as he pointed into the pit.

Hunter leapt into it and found himself calf deep in muddy water and surrounded by pieces of a long wooden crate. He picked one up and passed it to Lorena. She sniffed it and nodded.

"This has Hannah's scent on it," she said.

Hunter climbed out of the pit and looked around. Alejandro sniffed the ground around the pit, then shrugged and reverted to his human form. Lorena handed him his mask and watched as he tied it on to hide the nasty scars on his face. She passed him his hat and cape. He donned each with his usual dramatic flair and thanked her.

"Fink's trail ends here. Hannah's goes south," he said.

"That means Fink managed to capture her, put her into this crate and bury her out here. From the condition of the crate, it's obvious that Hannah managed to escape. But where is she? Where did she go?" Hunter asked.

"Her trail is heading south," Alejandro repeated.

"To New Orleans! If I were Hannah, that's the first place I'd go," Lorena said.

"Where else would she go but back home?" Madison asked. "I'd go home, too."

Hunter nodded.

"Her scent is several days old. If she headed for New Orleans, she should be there by now," he said. "Barring any detours."

"Detours?" DuCassal asked.

"Yes. I'm sure Hannah was *famished* when she clawed her way out of that box," Hunter said. "Let's just hope her hunger didn't lead her to do something we'll all regret later."

"Let's hurry back to the Emporium. Even if she's not there, we can wait for her. I'm sure she'll turn up sooner or later," Lorena said.

CHAPTER ELEVEN:
The Ghost of Jeromy Flowers

It was nearly midnight and a light, clammy mist drifted through the bayou. A very tired and hungry Hannah Morii trudged along the muddy path as it twisted its way through the ancient swamp. She hadn't seen another living being for two days and the urge to feed was driving her close to the edge. She briefly cursed herself for not feeding on the man and boy she'd met the day before.

Then laughed.

She didn't know why, but that thought had struck her as funny.

After another half hour, she came upon a ruined structure that was partially covered with vines and swamp reeds. She walked over and saw that it had been a church. From the looks of the tumbled-down steeple and cracked bell lying on its side amid the worm-eaten pews, it had been abandoned centuries ago.

It had no roof or windows and everything of value had been stripped from the ancient altar. But there were no signs of violence or even a fire. Whatever denomination had controlled it had simply walked away a long time ago due to a lack of interest.

Hannah wrapped her arms around herself tightly. Her body trembled with pain and hunger. She looked up at the sky and shouted to relive some her anxiety. But it only returned in force and caused her to tremble even harder. She cursed her circumstances.

She walked through the church and out the back door. She found herself standing in a very old cemetery with fallen headstones, moss covered crypts and tilted crosses. The stones were so old and weatherworn that most of the names and dates were illegible. As she neared a rather odd looking headstone, she stopped to look it over. To her surprise, she could plainly read the name and dates, despite that fact that it was as ancient as the ones surrounding it.

It read:

Here lies Jeromy Flowers, 1788-1820, May God Grant That He Lie Still.

"What a strange thing to put on a headstone," she said to herself. "But why isn't yours as badly worn as the rest?"

She ran her hand over the stone and started when she felt something surge through her. It felt like a light electric charge. It was then she began to feel cold.

Very cold.

Like ice.

Like death itself.

She shook her head to clear it and told herself she was suffering the effects of hunger. She also felt tired.

Bone weary.

She decided to sit down on the grave to rest. Her weariness quickly overwhelmed her. Before Hannah realized it, she was flat on her back. She watched helplessly as a large, black form materialized just inches above her. The darkness was cold and damp. It reeked of earth and rotted flesh.

Of death.

"You will do," it whispered hoarsely.

Hannah opened her mouth. She tried to say something. Tried to scream. But she couldn't utter a sound. Or move. That's when the darkness began swirling faster and faster and entered her body through her open mouth . . .

When she opened her eyes hours later, the sun was beginning to set. She sat up and looked around.

"I'm back home," she thought as she realized where she was. "But how?"

She tried to think about the last few days. She tried to concentrate. To remember something—anything.

Nothing came to her but small "snapshots" of people's faces and an old church. And the image of the thing that had attacked her. She stood and walked to the bathroom to shower. That's when she also realized she was naked.

She examined herself in the mirror on the bathroom door. Her body was covered with large welts—like whip marks—and dark bruises. Most had already healed. Images of being tortured and repeatedly raped and brutalized flashed through her mind. She saw chains on her wrists and ankles and briefly "tasted" the vile liquids she was forced to drink.

"How long was I gone?" she wondered. "And where is the bastard who did this to me? When I find him, I'll do the same to him ten times over! I'll make him suffer like no one in history has suffered before. Then I'll kill him."

As she dressed, a sudden hunger overcame her. She realized that she hadn't fed for a while and decided to remedy the situation. She threw on her black cloak and armed herself with her katana . . .

Hannah returned to the Emporium an hour after sunrise. She was just about to open the door to the shop when Hunter, Lorena, DuCassal, Alejandro and Madison walked up.

"You look like Hell," Hunter said.

"Thanks. It's nice to see you, too," she retorted as they followed her inside.

Lorena noticed a thin trickle of blood on her chin and smiled.

"I see you've been feeding," she said.

Hannah wiped the blood from her chin and nodded.

"Some damned fools tried to rob me earlier while I was walking through Pirate's Alley. Since I was already in bad mood, I made them pay the price," she said. "They got off easy compared to what I'm going to do to the bastard who buried me in that freaking coffin."

"We found your 'grave' last night. Do you know who did it to you?" Hunter asked as he sat down.

"I never saw him before. I know he's fast, real powerful and can shape shift. He momentarily caused me to lower my guard by taking on the form of my father. Once I did that, he had me," Hannah said. "I can't believe I fell for that!"

She went on to tell them about her experiences. She even described the incident at the abandoned church and cemetery and the name on the headstone that was still perfectly preserved even after centuries of weathering.

"Jeromy Flowers," she said.

"You've just described a possession," Hunter said. "If I'm right, Jeromy Flowers is now inside your body and he plans on using you for some unknown purpose. Whatever that is, I'm sure it's not going to be anything pleasant."

"I'm possessed?" Hannah asked.

"I'd be willing to bet on that," Hunter replied. "He picked you because you just happened to be at the wrong place at the right time. He was seeking a warm body to make use of and you just happened to come along."

"I don't want some dead guy inside of me. How do we get rid of him?" Hannah asked.

"First step is to find out exactly who this Jeromy Flowers was and what we're dealing with. The rest will be up to Minerva," Hunter said.

"What if we can't get rid of him?" Hannah asked.

"In that case, I'll just have to kill you. Nothing personal," Hunter replied with a grin.

"I never know when you're joking," Hannah said somewhat relieved.

"I'm not. But I'm sure it won't have to come to that. Exorcisms can be very rough on the possessed. It *could* put you out of action for a few days or even longer. When this is over, you may *wish* you were dead," Hunter said honestly.

"I'll take my chances. It can't be any worse than what that other bastard did to me," Hannah said.

"By the way, you don't have to worry about the one who attacked you any longer," DuCassal said.

"We rid the world of him and his followers two nights ago. But he said something that troubles me. Perhaps you can shed some light on that?" Alejandro said.

"What did he say?" asked Hannah.

"He said that his nightmare was over but ours had just begun," Alejandro said. "I feel it might have something to do with you. He kidnapped and brutalized you for a specific reason. Do you have any idea what that could be?"

Hannah thought for a few moments, then shook her and shrugged.

"I can't remember anything other than what I've already told you. Sorry," she replied.

"Perhaps it will come to you later," Madison said. "Fink was a real monster. He knew how to bend people to his will and use them. He never did anything without a reason. I know how you must have felt, Hannah. He did the same thing to all of his disciples. It was his way of breaking them of their free will."

"In other words, he brainwashed you?" Hannah asked.

"But it didn't take. Not completely. I think I was the only one ever to escape from his cult. It pissed him off royally that anyone could break his spell. That's why he and his disciples hunted me down. They wanted to bring me back into the group. Unfortunately for them, I decided I didn't want to go back," Madison said.

"Oh?" Hannah asked.

"She killed every single one of the disciples," Lorena said.

"In fact, she tore them to pieces," DuCassal added. "It was so brutal that it was almost *poetic*."

"As in *poetic justice*," Hunter said.

"Over the years I was with them, they each took turns raping and torturing me. Fink had made me their play thing. Then, one night, I just snapped and returned the favor in spades," Madison explained.

"You're a *vampire*!" Hannah suddenly realized.

"And she has killed over a dozen other vampires," Hunter added.

"You're just like Lorena and me," Hannah said.

"But I don't feed on humans. I just drink a lot of bloody cocktails and visit blood banks," Madison said. "I've never fed on a live human. I'm almost afraid to."

"We understand," said both Hannah and Lorena.

"I also do not feed on humans. I take my nourishment from the rougarous and vampires I slay. And I drink lots of cocktails," Alejandro said with a grin. "Perhaps you could join me in my nightly prowls? There are more than enough creatures of the darkness to satisfy us both."

"Maybe some other time, Alejandro," Madison said with a smile. "If my cravings grow too strong, I'll take you up on your offer."

"What about the three you killed earlier?" asked Lorena.

"I took their heads to Leon. It turned out that two of them were wanted for robbery and murder in Chalmette. The third was just a minor thug who happened to be hanging with the wrong crowd," Hannah said. "I made $2,000 in bounty money."

She reached into her till, took out $1,000 and handed it to Lorena.

"Please give this to Father Paul when you see him," she said. "He'll know who it's from."

Hunter laughed.

"Let's go have breakfast first. We'll visit Paul after we've eaten," he said. "Would you care to join us? I'm buying."

"In that case, I'm eating!" DuCassal said with a grin.

"You can count the rest of us in, too," Alejandro added.

"Where are we going?" asked Lorena.

"I'm really hungry. How about Brennan's?" Hunter suggested.

After breakfast, Alejandro and Hannah went their separate ways. Hunter, Lorena and DuCassal walked over to Jackson Square. They walked into the Cathedral just as Father Paul was preparing to do his morning cleaning. He smiled and greeted them with handshakes.

"What can I help you with?" he asked.

"We need some information," Hunter said as they followed him to the archives.

"On what?" asked Paul.

"Not what—but who. What can you tell us about Jeromy Flowers?" Hunter asked.

Paul thought for a moment and shook his head.

"Not a blessed thing. Why is he so important to you?" he asked.

"It was the last thing Hannah Morii remembered before waking up back in her own bed. She said it was on a headstone in an abandoned church yard about 75 miles from New Orleans," Hunter explained.

"Does she remember the dates on the stone?" Paul asked.

"She said the dates were 1788-1820," Lorena replied. "She also mentioned that all the other headstones were so worn out they were illegible. But his was in perfect condition."

"Now *that's* interesting. It makes me think that some sort of magic was involved," Paul said.

He led them to the oldest section of the archives and pointed to four large books on the middle shelf.

"You might find something in these," he said. "The first two are birth and death records from the 1750s to the 1830s. The other two contain newspaper articles from the 1820s. I somehow get the feeling that Flowers made one of the local papers and not in a nice way."

"I doubt he belonged to the local benevolent societies," Hunter quipped.

"Or t" he Rotary Club," DuCassal added.

Paul laughed.

"The archives are all yours for as long as you need them. Good hunting!" he said as he left the vault.

Hunter picked up the first book and opened the ancient leather cover. It was filled with old newspaper articles. DuCassal grabbed the birth and death register while Lorena started leafing through the second book of news articles.

After a few minutes, DuCassal pointed something out.

"It says here that a son was born on August 8, 1788 to a Mr. Robert LeFleur and his wife, Eileen. They named him Jeromy," he said.

"LeFleur means 'Flower' in French," Lorena said. "Isn't that Tony's last name?"

"Yes it is. I wonder if he's from the same family." Hunter asked.

"It's quite possible," DuCassal said. "Tony's family was among the founders of New Orleans."

"If it's the same Jeromy, why'd he change his name?" Lorena asked.

"It was common for people with French names to change them to English. It made it easier to conduct business after the Americans took over the Louisiana Territory," DuCassal said.

"Either that or he wanted to distance himself from the rest of the family for some reason," Hunter added. "Or they *forced* him to change it because he *disgraced* the family in some way."

"Interesting," Lorena said.

"What is?" asked Hunter.

"This article dated September 11, 1809 in the Times-Picayune," she said as she showed it to them.

"Jeromy LeFleur was arrested in a Storyville brothel early this morning. He was taken into custody by three police officers and taken to the Basin Street Station where he was charged with the murder of Angelina Beigne, an Octoroon from Natchitoches. Angelina's naked corpse was found in St. Louis Cemetery Number Two on the night of July 7. She had been badly beaten and stabbed several times. The medical examiner reported that her heart was missing. Police speculated that LeFleur, who is deeply involved with the darker side of voodoo, used it to perform a ritual.

He is scheduled to appear before Judge Harlan David Crowe in Municipal Court on Sept. 13."

Hunter whistled.

Lorena turned several pages and stopped when she came to September 13th.

"Judge Harlan David Crowe ordered Jeromy LeFleur to stand trial for murder one week from today. LeFleur plead 'not guilty' which prompted the need for a jury trial.

When asked if he had an attorney to defend him, LeFleur said that he had asked his family to help find one but they declined. His uncle,

Charles LeMay LeFleur, a prominent trial lawyer, has also refused to represent him.

"They've turned their backs on me, but I promise, they will be very sorry," said LeFleur."

Hunter shook his head.

"He must have been a very bad apple for his family to do that," he said. "It makes me wonder just what else he did and managed to get away with."

They kept searching. Another article, dated October 31ˢᵗ, caught their attention.

"After three days of deliberation, the jury found Jeromy LeFleur guilty of murder in the first degree. Judge Harlan David Crowe sentenced him to ten years hard labor in the state penitentiary, which is the maximum allowed under the law.

LeFleur laughed like a demon. Then he faced the jury and said that none of them would be alive come Christmas. When the judge ordered the guards to take LeFleur away, he laughed even louder.

"And you, my dear judge, will not live long enough to see the sun rise tomorrow!" he said as they led him from the court."

"He only received ten years for murdering that girl?" Lorena asked.

"That was because she was one eighth Negress," DuCassal said. "People of Color were treated as less than human by the laws in those days, even free ones. The most any white male could expect to get for murdering a person of color was ten years in prison."

"How incredibly unfair!" Lorena remarked.

"Yes it *was* unfair. But those were the way things were back then. It was far worse if you were a slave," DuCassal said.

"Did you ever own slaves?" Lorena asked.

"Never. Charles and I detested that institution. We did *purchase* hundreds of them but only so we could free them immediately after," DuCassal explained.

"That was very noble of you both," she said.

"We didn't do it to be noble, Lorena. We did it because it was right. People are people no matter what color their skin is and no one has the right to own another. Ironically, we purchased several slaves from Black owners," Hunter said.

"Here is another article," DuCassal pointed out.

"My God!" Hunter exclaimed as they read it.

"Judge Harlan David Crowe was found dead in his home at 1100 Poydras by his servant as 4 am this morning. He was 54 years of age and, according to his wife, was in perfect health."

"LeFleur's curse got him," DuCassal said.

"Let's look up the names of everyone who served on that jury and check their names against the death register for that year," Hunter suggested. "If none of them made it past Christmas, we'll know that LeFleur's curse worked."

After another hour of searching and checking, they discovered that all 12 of the jurors had met their ends prior to Christmas day of the same year. Ten of the 12 died when the riverboat they were on exploded near Memphis. The other two were found dead in their beds.

"Those were either incredible coincidences or that was one Hell of a curse," Hunter said.

"Let's keep going. Maybe we'll find articles dealing with what happened when he was released from prison," DuCassal said.

It took another hour and a half, but eventually, Lorena found an article dealing with LeFleur's release from prison on November 4, 1819.

"Mr. LeFleur, in an effort to put his past behind him and separate himself from his estranged family, legally assumed the name of Jeromy Flowers. He moved into a small house in the Lower Garden District."

"Anything more?" Hunter asked.

"Yes. There is another article dated February 21, 1820," Lorena said as she showed it to him.

"After a heated exchange in a saloon on Bourbon Street between Jeromy Flowers and his estranged father, Robert LeFleur, Flowers removed his gloves and slapped LeFleur across the face. He then demanded the usual satisfaction and a duel was arranged for the morning of the 23rd. The site chosen was the Trinity Church in Monte Maurice."

She turned to the article of the 23rd.

"The two met just after sunrise. Mr. Flowers arrived alone. Mr. LeFleur was seconded by his youngest son, Martin. The pair exchanged formalities, selected their pistols and walked ten paces, turned and fired. Mr. LeFleur was struck in the left shoulder. Mr. Flowers was struck in the throat and fell bleeding to the ground.

Witnesses carried him into the church and placed him in a pew. A doctor was quickly summoned but before his arrival, Mr. Flowers expired.

Rather than inter him in the family vault in St. Louis Cemetery Number One, Mr. LeFleur had Mr. Flowers buried in the small cemetery next to the Trinity Church, where he would rest "as far away from other members of the family as possible and not curse them with his remains."

Mr. LeFleur paid a minimal sum to the church for the burial and headstone and said neither he nor anyone else would attend."

Hunter shook his head.

"What a sad and deserving end," he commented.

"Do you suppose he was related to Tony?" Lorena asked.

"LeFleur is a common name in these parts," DuCassal said.

"There's one way to find out. Let's ask Tony," Hunter said. "If they're related, he may be able to shed some light on this curse."

"I wonder which is stronger—Fink's programming or Flowers' curse?" Lorena said.

"Or Hannah's urge to feed?" DuCassal added.

"I'd guess all of the above," Hunter said as they left the vault.

They thanked Paul for his use of the archives and stepped out into the street. A light rain was falling and, as is typical for New Orleans, the sun was shining brightly.

"Where to next, mon ami?" asked DuCassal.

"The Dragon. I want to talk with Tony about his family tree," Hunter said.

Ten minutes later, they were in the Dragon sipping cocktails.

"What can you tell us about an ancestor of yours named Jeromy Flowers?" Hunter asked.

"I haven't heard that name in centuries," Tony said as he leaned on the bar. "Sure, Jeromy was one of my ancestors. From what I remember he was a real nasty sort who thought his family's wealth could buy him immunity, even from murder. Too bad for him things didn't work out that way. Hell, his own father killed him in a duel. But that was all over 150 years before I was even born."

"The old newspaper stories claimed he was into voodoo and not the nice kind. Any truth in that?" Hunter asked.

"Beats me. My folks never spoke about Jeromy Flowers except to curse him when things went wrong. They blamed him for everything. According to them, he put a curse on the entire family just before he died. He even vowed to come back from the grave and kill anyone who was related to him," Tony said with a chuckle.

"Do you think he can?" Lorena asked.

"This is New Orleans. Anything's possible," Tony said. "Why are you so interested in him anyway?"

Hunter explained what happened to Hannah and how he felt that Jeromy had taken possession of her and would try to use her as his instrument of vengeance.

"If what you're telling me is true, I'd better watch my back," Tony said.

"Why is that?" asked DuCassal.

"I'm the last of that line of LeFleurs. My last existing relatives died during the yellow fever epidemic 175 years ago. The only reason it didn't take me is because I'm a vampire," he said.

"Since you're the last one, that makes you his likely target," Hunter said.

"And you know me, Hunter. I'm not going to hide. I've got businesses to run. If Flowers looks for me, I won't be hard to find," Tony said as he refilled their glasses.

"I don't expect you to hide or run, Tony. That's not your style," DuCassal said.

"Just how powerful was Flowers?" asked Hunter.

Tony shrugged.

"Old family legends say he was able to give Marie Laveau a run for her money," he replied. "They probably knew each other back then."

"Which means that I probably did as well," Hunter said. "But the name doesn't ring a bell."

"Unless you had a personal run-in with him, you wouldn't know him except by his reputation. He gave the family a real black eye," Tony said.

Hunter thanked him and finished his drink. Then he, DuCassal and Lorena walked over to the Emporium to tell Hannah what they'd learned.

"Great! This just gets better all of the time! Now I'm possessed by someone who knew how to use the worst kind of voodoo spells. Any other good news you want to tell me?" she asked sarcastically.

"That's about it for now," Hunter said with a smile.

"So what should I do?" she asked.

"Go about your life as usual. Just make notes of any unusual feelings or compulsions that come up. If Flowers' is inside of you, then he'll try to use you to carry out his vows to kill every last member of his family," Hunter said.

"Tony?" Hannah asked.

Hunter nodded.

"He's the last of the LeFleur line," he said.

"I don't want to hurt Tony. He's a friend of mine," Hannah said.

"I'm sure Tony would be happy to hear you say that," DuCassal said.

At sunset, Hannah closed her shop and went out to dinner. After what proved to be a light snack, she returned and donned her usual patrol attire and headed back into the street.

The hunger was getting to her again.

She didn't bother to control it now. What would be the point? If she got too ravenous, she could always find some lowlife criminal to feed on. She decided to head over to Basin Street and check the wanted posters.

When she walked in, Valmonde smiled and handed her a poster. She looked it over and smiled.

"Where was he last seen?" she asked.

"Bayou St. John. That's where my men chased him to anyway. That was a couple of days ago. We haven't been able to track him down, but I know that *you* can," Valmonde said as he leaned back and folded his hands across his chest.

"How bad do you want him?" Hannah asked.

"Real bad. Harlan Mackay is a real heartless scumbag, too. He buried a sledge hammer in his grandmother's skull and made off with the money in her purse. Anybody who's that heartless doesn't deserve to live," Valmonde said.

"He won't," Hannah promised as she left the station.

Valmonde chuckled.

"I'd hate to be anybody she goes after," he said.

At two a.m., Hunter took his usual stroll along St. Ann. Almost on cue, a low fog rolled in and obscured everything but the glare of the street lamps. Hunter stopped at the corner and waited. A few seconds later, a familiar figure emerged from the fog.

"Good evening, Marie," he said as he tipped his hat.

"Good evening, Hunter," Madame Laveau said with a smile. "I see you are out walking again. But this time, something other than a dream troubles you. You have questions."

"You're perceptive as always. I hope you have some answers," Hunter said as they walked side-by-side down the street.

"You want to know about Jeromy Flowers," she said.

Hunter smiled.

"I suppose you knew him?" he asked.

"I knew *of* him. We met exactly twice, both on St. John's Eves during the festivals. I tried to steer clear of Jeromy Flowers," she said.

"You *feared* him?" he asked.

"I *respected and detested* him," she replied.

"Why?" Hunter asked.

"I respected him because he was a man of great power and knowledge. I detested because of the ways he used both," she said.

"Should I respect him?" Hunter asked.

"You should be *careful* of him. Flowers was one of the nastiest, most black hearted and vile things ever to slither on this Earth. He has insinuated himself into the mind and body of Hannah Morii. You must drive him out before he smothers her personality and forces her to do his bidding. You *know* what needs to be done, Hunter. Don't waste time," she warned.

Hunter nodded.

"But Flowers is the *least* of your worries. There are worse things coming down the line. *Unspeakable things!*" she added.

"What sort of things?" Hunter asked.

Before he could even finish his question, both Marie Laveau and the fog were gone. He smiled and continued his patrol.

"I'd better talk to Minerva," he decided.

At six a.m., a sated Hannah Morii strode up the steps of the Basin Street station and dropped a severed head with a terrified expression near the front door. A second later, Valmonde pulled up in his carriage. He looked at the head and laughed.

Hannah smiled.

"I see you bagged him," he said.

"It was a piece of cake, Chief," Hannah said.

"He only had a thousand on his head," Valmonde said.

"In that case, give it all to Father Paul," Hannah said. "Besides, I've *already had* my reward."

"Somethin' else came in last night. A little girl was found under a park bench in Metairie around one. She had bite marks on her neck, but they were small. There wasn't a drop of blood in her, either," Valmonde said.

"That sounds like that vampire who killed Amanda Lowry," Hannah said. "But most don't prey on children."

"This one does," Valmonde said. "That makes two little girls he's killed. I'd appreciate it if you could see to it that he doesn't do this again."

"Any clues?" she asked.

"Not a damned one, but it's the same M.O. Anyone who'd do such a thing is real vermin in my book," Valmonde said. "Both murders were in the Old Metairie neighborhood, so you might want to start there."

"I'll get right on it, Leon," Hannah promised as she left the station.

CHAPTER TWELVE:
It Must Be True 'Cause I Read it in the Paper

It was early Tuesday morning when Lawrence Vaner, vice president of the Trans Atlantic Steamship Company, walked into his office on St, Louis Avenue. His secretary, Margery Chin, greeted him with her usual perky smile and handed him his usual cup of coffee and the edition of the Times-Picayune. He thanked her and retreated to his large, hand carved mahogany desk and sat down.

Although he didn't usually bother, something compelled him to turn to the obituary section on the next to the last page. His sipped his coffee as he scanned the column—and nearly choked when he read his own name.

He sat back and read the article.

The more he read, the more puzzled and upset he became. After he finished his coffee, he decided to head down to the newspaper offices and speak with Fred Crandal, the managing editor.

When he arrived 15 minutes later, Fred was proofreading the next edition. He stopped and smiled.

"Hello, Larry. What brings you here on this fine morning?" he greeted.

"This," Vaner said as he handed him the paper and pointed to his obituary.

Crandal read it and shook his head. Then he laughed.

"According to this, you're dead—or you're going to be by this time tomorrow," he joked. "It's some sort of mistake, Larry. Or someone's idea of a joke."

"A joke?" Vaner asked.

"Sure. This is some sort of a gag newspaper. I assure you that I never had anyone print your obituary," Crandal said. "We didn't print this, Larry. I'll prove it to you."

Crandal reached over to the shelf and picked up a copy of the paper. He turned to the obituaries and passed it to Vaner.

"See? It ain't in there," Crandal said.

Vaner folded the paper and passed it back. Crandal was right. His name was not listed in the column at all. He scowled.

"Hey, here's something strange. Look at this sentence here," Crandal said as he reread the paper Vaner had brought. "According to this, you died on October 17 at 9:35 PM of unknown causes. Anything strike you about the date?"

"Why, that's *today*. I never noticed that!" Vaner said as he grabbed the paper and read it again. "It says that I'm going to die tonight. That's crazy!"

"It sure is, Larry. That's why I think it's someone playing a prank on you," Crandal said as he leaned back.

"But who'd want to do that? It sure as hell ain't finny. At least, not to me!" Vaner said puzzled.

"Beats me. Whoever it is, went to a lot of expense. What puzzles me is how he managed to copy every article in today's edition *before* we even went to press. Look at it. He got the same headlines, article placement and even the same pictures and ads. We didn't even get some of these ads until one hour before we printed it. It's uncanny," Crandal pointed out.

"And *impossible*," Vaner said as they looked through it carefully. "You sure you didn't print this, Fred?"

"I'm positive, Larry. First of all, this ain't my style of humor. Second, it would have been too expensive to print just one special copy to play a joke on you. I'm in the news business, not the novelty business. Whoever did this, did a remarkable job and went to a lot of trouble and expense. You know anyone like that?" Crandal asked.

Vaner shook his head.

"Not a soul," he said. "Now what?"

"I wouldn't worry about it. It's just someone's idea of a joke. Just toss it away and go about your business like usual," Crandal advised.

"I guess you're right. Sorry I bothered you, Fred," Vaner said as he tucked the edition under his arm and extended his right hand.

Crandal shook it and bade him farewell. Vaner went back to his office and slid the paper into his middle drawer. Then he poured himself another cup of coffee and went to work. At six, he closed shop for the day and headed home to his mansion on St. Charles. He'd all but forgotten the article by then. After all, he had more important things on his mind than some gag newspaper.

At seven, he had dinner at his house with his wife, Emily and their two small sons. Feeling tired, he kissed Emily good-night and went upstairs. When she went up to join him an hour later, she saw he was curled up tightly into a fetal position. Normally, he slept on his back. Thinking he was ill, she reached over and shook him. When he didn't respond, she shook him harder.

And harder.

Then she let out a scream.

It was 9:35 . . . .

At two a.m. that morning, Tony was tending bar at the Dragon as usual when Hannah walked in. He greeted her with a smile as she sat down at the bar. He saw that she was dressed for battle.

"Morning, Hannah. What are you having?" he asked.

"A double Bloody and keep them coming," Hannah said.

"You've got it," Tony said as he mixed the drink.

It was two parts plasma and one part vodka. Hannah only drank them when she hunted other vampires. They controlled her hunger and kept her focused. He placed it in front of her and watched as she took a sip.

"Hunting tonight?" he asked.

"Yes. You've heard about the murders in Old Metairie?" she said.

"Yeah. Three victims in one week. Word on the street says there's a new vampire in town. He must be a man because his victims have all been young women," Tony replied.

"Girls. The oldest was only 12 years old. They found her body in an empty lot last night. Have you seen Hunter?" she said as she sipped.

"Not since they started their patrol last night. I heard that you ran into an ancestor of mine," Tony said as she passed him the empty glass.

"Oh. So Flowers *is* one of yours. What can you tell me about him?" Hannah asked as Tony handed her a second drink.

"Not much. According to family legends, Jeromy Flowers was a real piece of work and a disgrace to the LeFleur name. He was imprisoned for murder. He embezzled money from the family businesses and supposedly practiced voodoo—and not the good kind. He was finally killed in a duel by his own father and buried in that churchyard where you met him. That's about all I know," Tony said.

"Is the voodoo part true?" Hannah asked.

"Hunter seems to think it is. Since he lived at the same time Marie Laveau did, she'd be the one to ask about that. I asked Minerva last night but she said she wasn't familiar with him," Tony said.

"Madame Laveau only appears to Hunter and only at her discretion. He's the only one who can ask her about Flowers," Hannah said as she finished her drink.

"Want a refill?" asked Tony.

"No thanks. I'd better get out to Old Metairie. I want to find that vampire before he kills another girl," she said as she got up and left.

"Hannah's got troubles and they have nothing to do with that vampire," Tony thought as he cleaned off the bar with a towel.

Hannah reached the neighborhood of Old Metairie an hour later. Along the way, her mind was filled with dark voices and bleak images or tormented souls, demons, and an underlying current of fear. She began to sweat and even trembled at times. She shook her head in an effort to clear her mind, but the darkness and images and voices came back even stronger.

As she walked along the crumbling street, she had trouble concentrating on her quarry. She just kept following the street until it led to the grounds of the cemetery and stopped at the rusted iron fence. During the First Age, this was a college campus. When the college tumbled to the ground after a fire, the campus was abandoned and the city council decided it would make an ideal spot for a graveyard.

Like most cemeteries in and around New Orleans, people buried their dead in above ground vaults and ornate crypts. Some of the crypts were quite large and, even though they were badly weathered, Hannah could tell they were the final resting places for some very wealthy families.

Most of the vaults were overgrown with weeds and their roofs were cracked. Trees sprouted from many and the marble facings had fallen off several more, leaving the crumbling coffins exposed.

The conditions of the vaults reflected the conditions of Old Metairie. About half of the area had been abandoned decades ago after yet another disastrous flood. Only the homes on the high ground remained, along with several churches and two schools.

Hannah's mind momentarily cleared. It was long enough for her to detect something lurking in the shadows between two of the larger crypts. She looked around, spotted something moving about a hundred yards away, and walked slowly toward it.

That's when the voices and images again flooded into her brain.

While she was distracted, her quarry leaped out the shadows and rushed straight for her. Before Hannah realized it, both hands were around her throat and she had been slammed against the wall of the vault directly behind her.

She drew her Katana and slashed at her attacker. The figure seemed to dance out the way of the blade with surprising ease, then somersaulted over her and seized her by her long, black hair. Hannah tried to stab her with a backward thrust, but the attacker twisted nimbly out the way. At the same time, she yanked downward and slammed Hannah into the cracked pavement. It happened so fast that Hannah was momentarily stunned.

While she tried to regain her senses, her attacker danced around her and laughed in a high-pitched voice—just like a small girl would.

Hannah looked around and was surprised to see a very young girl in a billowy white gown dancing in the moonlight like a ballerina. She was laughing and singing. Hannah attempted to stand only to be sent back to the ground by a sudden and incredibly swift kick to her forehead.

She attempted to kick her again but Hannah seized her foot, twisted it sharply and drove her to the ground.

"I've had just about enough out of you!" Hannah said angrily.

The girl sprung back to her feet, giggled and bared her fangs. Hannah responded in kind. The girl smiled.

"You're just like me! You're a vampire, too!" she said.

"And I'm going to kill you," Hannah threatened.

"Hahaha! Catch me if you can!" the girl taunted as she whirled around and leapt high into the air.

At the height of her arc, a larger, faster figure caught her and brought her violently to the ground. Hannah heard the girl scream. Hear the deep growl and the sounds of bones being crushed by large teeth. She hurried over with her katana drawn, but stopped when she was Alejandro standing over the mangled corpse of the vampire. He was wiping blood from his lips with a handkerchief.

"Good evening, Hannah," he said with a grin.

"Hello, Alejandro," Hannah said as she sheathed her katana. "That was quite an interception. She never knew what hit her."

"The nasty little bitch got precisely what she deserved, wouldn't you say?" Alejandro said.

"In spades," Hannah agreed. "What are *you* doing out here? Were you following her?"

"In all honesty, Hannah, I was following *you*," he replied.

She looked at him.

"Oh?" she asked as they walked away. "I don't recall asking for a babysitter."

"You didn't. But Hunter did. It is very apparent to us all that you have not been yourself since your encounter with Fink and that spirit. Hunter feared that you might become distracted. That could be dangerous, even for you. In some cases, it might even prove fatal. So he asked me to watch your back for a few nights," Alejandro explained.

Hannah nodded.

"Hunter's right. I'm not myself. I feel like I'm trapped between two warring entities who want to take control of me. It's all I can do think straight and my dreams are filled with nightmares that leave me shaking all over. Both of these entities are urging me to let them take control. They want to use my body to carry out some sort of vendettas. So far, I've kept them at bay, but they're getting stronger by the day. I'm glad you were watching. You saw what happened. She caught me by surprise because I wasn't able to focus on her. I've never let that happen before," Hannah said.

She looked down at the vampire.

"She looks so innocent. No one would ever guess she's a vampire. I wonder who she is and where she came from? Who are her parents? Who made her?" she asked.

Alejandro put his hand on her shoulder.

"Your last question is the most important. The others will answer themselves or not once we find her creator," he said.

"Even though you did a number on her, I still have to make sure she doesn't return," Hannah said as she drew her katana and beheaded the girl with one quick stroke.

Alejandro watched as she doused her with oil and ignited it. They stayed until the flames completely consumed the tiny body. When nothing remained but ashes, Alejandro noticed something shiny and metallic among them. He reached down and picked it up.

"It appears to be a medallion of some sort," he said. "She must have been carrying it. It seems to be quite ancient."

Hannah took it from him and turned it over several times.

"The symbols are Cyrillic. I can't read any of them, though. This is from Europe. I'd say probably from the Baltic region," she said.

"Perhaps it has something to do with the child's history," Alejandro suggested. "I doubt that it came from any of her victims here."

Hannah nodded and slid the medallion into her pocket.

"With any luck, this will lead us to who made her," she said.

"If not, at least you will have an interesting souvenir," Alejandro said.

"I think I've already enough souvenirs, Alejandro," she said.

"You sound tired," Alejandro observed.

"I am. In fact, I'm exhausted," Hannah said.

"My carriage is just down the street. Please allow me to take you home," he offered.

"Thank you," she said.

"Who do you suppose that vampire was?" Alejandro asked as they walked toward the carriage. "It is rare for one so young to seek out victims."

"It's more common than you think," Hannah said. "That explains why she targeted other little girls. They were naïve and made easy victims. But the real question is, who turned her?"

"That's true. When a vampire chooses to attack a child, he usually kills her. He doesn't keep her over seven nights to turn her into a vampire. It is a cruel joke to force someone to live eternally as a child. What purpose does that serve?" Alejandro said as he held the carriage door open for her.

"Whoever did that has a sick, sadistic streak and a very twisted sense of humor. That makes him very *dangerous*, too," he added as he climbed in after her.

By the time he sat down, he realized that Hannah had fallen into a deep sleep. He smiled and leaned out the window.

"Take us home, Peter," he said to his coachman.

Five days later, Barton Radcliff, vice president of operations at the Trans Atlantic, marched into Fred Crandal's office. When Fred looked up and saw the expression of his face, he knew that Radcliff was definitely not a happy camper. Before he could utter a word, Radcliff too the issue of the Times-Picayune from his jacket pocket and spread it open on the desk.

"What's the meaning of this, Fred?" he demanded.

Crandal looked down and stared. The paper was open to the obituaries and, right at the top of the column, was an article announcing the "sudden and untimely departure of Baton Radcliff at 7:45 p.m. on the evening of October 22nd."

"Is this some kind of a joke? If it is, I'm not laughing," Radcliff fumed.

"I don't know what to say, Bart. I do know that we didn't print this. If you check the edition on that shelf behind you, you'll see that this article is nowhere to be found," Crandal said.

Radcliff looked at the paper on the shelf and shrugged.

"Hey, you're right. I'm not in this edition," he said. "Wait a minute. This one says I died on October 22nd. That's tonight! How can that be? Who's your editor? Nostradamus?"

Crandal laughed then stopped and stared at him.

"I just remembered something—this exact same thing happened to Larry. Somebody sent him a paper with his obituary in it announcing his death," he said.

Radcliff sat down and looked at him.

"And Larry died in his sleep that same night at the exact time the obituary had," Crandall continued.

"How can that be, Fred? Is it some kind of witchcraft or something?" Radcliff asked.

"I have no idea. Maybe it was just a coincidence," Crandall said after some thought.

"Tell *that* to Larry," Radcliff said. "I'm sure *he* doesn't think it was a coincidence right now."

"Don't get all worked up about it, Bart. You know such things aren't possible," Crandal said, although he really didn't sound too convincing.

Radcliff sighed.

"Just in case, I'm going to be real careful for the rest of this day. This is New Orleans, Fred. You and I both know that anything is possible here," he said as he got up and left the office.

He went back to his house in the Lower Garden District and locked himself in his study. He told his wife not to disturb him for any reason until eight o'clock. He reasoned that as long as he was safe inside his den, nothing could hurt him. He curled up in his wing backed chair to read a novel he'd purchased earlier that day.

He never got to finish.

At 7:45 on October 22nd, Barton Radcliff took his last breath . . .

When Crandal heard the news of Radcliff's death, he walked over to the Basin Street station. He saw Valmonde outside giving last minute instructions to his patrolmen.

"Hi, Fred. What brings you here this mornin'?" Valmonde asked.

"I need to speak with you, Leon. It's real important," Crandal said.

"Alright. Let's go to my office," Valmonde said.

"Uh, I think you'd best send someone over to get Hunter. What I'm about to tell you is so weird, I'm sure he'll want to check into it," Crandal said.

Valmonde nodded.

He pointed to Sam and told him to fetch Hunter.

"Might as well step inside and have some coffee while we're waitin'," he said.

Hunter, DuCassal and Lorena arrived a half hour later. Crandal introduced himself then explained why he was there. He told them about the two obituaries and how both Radcliff and Vaner had both died at the exact times that were listed in the columns. Hunter listened intently.

"I figured their deaths were more than a coincidence and whoever had those papers made up didn't do it to play a joke on them," Crandal said.

"Even so, how can anyone accurately predict the exact date and time of someone's death?" Lorena asked.

"I'd say whoever did this sent those obituaries as a warning. He wanted both men dead and went out of his way to make sure they died at the times in the obituaries. To be able to do anything like that, he'd have had to plan this far in advance and time it perfectly," Hunter said. "What were the official causes of death?"

"I don't know. But we could check with Julia down at the morgue," Valmonde said.

"Let's go," Hunter agreed.

Twenty minutes later, they arrived at the morgue in DuCassal's carriage. They found Julia seated behind her desk and sipping coffee. She scowled when they walked in.

"It's too early to talk with you. I haven't had my coffee yet," she said as she out the mug down. "What can I help you with, Chief?"

"We need to know the cause of deaths for Vaner and Radcliff" Valmonde said.

"It's too soon for Radcliff. We haven't received the body yet. But I did one on Vaner a couple of days ago," she said.

"What killed him?" Hunter asked.

"A very bad aneurism," Julia said.

"Aneurism? Hunter asked.

She nodded.

"Yes. A person never knows he has one until it bursts. When that happens, it's usually too late. Death comes quick. Vaner never knew what hit him," she said. "Why the interest?"

Hunter told her what Crandal had said. She whistled.

"So you want me to find out if Radcliff died from the same cause?" she asked.

"That or any other cause," Hunter replied. "I want to know if there's some sort of a connection."

"There is one big connection," Valmonde said.

"They were both executives of the Trans Atlantic Steamship Company," Hunter said. "They were friends of Jean-Paul's. He introduced them to me a few weeks ago."

"They were nice fellers, too. Good families. They did a lot of charity work. Their great grandfathers founded the company over 150 years ago, but they had to learn how to do every job in the company before they could move into the front office. Nothin' was handed to them," Valmonde said.

"Were there any other founding partners?" Hunter asked.

"There were two others. One died in an accident aboard one their ships a long time ago. The other one's great grandson is the company treasurer now. His name is Ferguson Moore," DuCassal said. "Do you think he may be the next one listed in the obituaries?"

"If he does get listed, we'll know that someone is targeting the executives of the Trans Atlantic for some reason," Hunter said.

"I'll get in touch with Moore and tell him to contact me if he gets one of those papers," Valmonde said.

Tony left the Dragon at two a.m. He walked down Toulouse toward Royal to go home. As he crossed the street, he became aware that someone was following him. He slowed his pace as he waited for his would be attacker to make the first move.

She watched him carefully. She saw his muscles grow tense, like a cobra poised to strike. She tried to stop herself. Tried to use her will to break the spell.

But the spirit of Jeromy Flowers was too overpowering.

Hannah attacked

Tony lashed out with a back kick, which she easily avoided.

"I read that," she said as she moved to the right.

Tony swung his fist twice. Hannah blocked both blows.

"I read *that,* too!" she said as she punched at him.

Tony batted her fist aside and smacked her square on the chin with heel of his hand. The blow knocked her back a few steps.

"You didn't read *that,*" he smiled as he deftly avoided another punch and spin kick.

They traded blows and counter blows for several seconds, with neither of them able to connect. Hannah drew her katana. As she swung, Tony struck her wrist with the toe of his boot and knocked the weapon from her grasp. Before it hit the ground, he seized it by the hilt and tossed it aside. Hannah rushed at him. He sidestepped her, grabbed her by the hair and jerked her toward him. She tried a back kick but missed. He spun her around, grabbed her by the throat and slammed her to the sidewalk. Before she could recover, he straddled her chest. Hannah tried to throw him off without success. Tony saw the evil glint in her eyes and slapped her as hard as he could across the face to break the spell.

Hannah shook her head and stared at him.

"Tony! What's going on? Why are you sitting on me like this?" she demanded.

"How else would you like me to sit on you?" he joked as he stood up and helped her to her feet.

"What's going on?" she asked as he picked up her katana and returned it to her.

"Oh, nothing much. You just attempted to kill me," he said with a smile.

"I was?" she asked.

"Yes. If I had been anyone else, you would have succeeded. But you don't get to live for centuries like I have without learning a few tricks," he said. "Let's go back to the Dragon. You look like you can use a few drinks."

They reached the Dragon just as Hunter, DuCassal and Lorena arrived. Tony led them to the bar and made them drinks as he explained what had happened.

"That settles it. We're going to see Minerva right after breakfast," Hunter decided.

"You're fortunate that Tony recognized you. If he hadn't, we would not be having this conversation right now," DuCassal said.

Hannah nodded.

Tony's reputation was well-established in New Orleans.

"Trust me, Hannah. The outcome of our little fight was never in doubt," Tony said as he handed her another drink. "I would have been wracked with guilt for a long time had I been forced to kill you."

"How long?" Hannah asked.

"Oh, at least a day or two," he said.

She laughed.

"What if I had killed *you*?" she asked.

He grinned at her.

"I *never* lose," he said without a hint of smugness.

They walked over to a table and sat down. DuCassal ordered another round of drinks. It was time to relax.

Hannah sipped her Bloody Mary.

"I heard you killed that vampire a couple of nights ago," Hunter said.

"Alejandro actually killed her. I just added the finishing touches. She was just a kid, Hunter. She must have been around five or six years old when she was turned. I felt really sad for her," Hannah said.

"Do you have any idea who she was?" asked Lorena.

"None. But there she was wearing this strange medallion," Hannah said.

Hunter sat up.

"What sort of medallion?" he asked.

Hannah took it from her pocket and handed it to him. He reached into the inside pocket of his vest and took out the medallion Galya had slipped into his mantle just before they left Thule. He placed both side-by-side on the table.

"They are *identical!*" DuCassal said.

"Where'd you get yours?" Hannah asked.

"I think Galya, the wife of the Emperor of Thule slipped it into my pocket before we left. I didn't pay too much attention to it. But now, it appears that I'll *have* to," Hunter answered.

"If Galya slipped it into your pocket, she had a very good reason. Perhaps it's something to do with an event of long ago?" Lorena suggested.

"What is the writing on it?" asked Hannah.

"It's a very ancient form of Cyrillic," Hunter said. "It reads: vitajie, cinste, crutare. Courage, honor, mercy. This was the form used in ancient Romania, between 1100 and 1645 of the First Age."

"That's the same region you are from, Charles," DuCassal said. "If that little vampire was carrying a duplicate, she must have also come from there."

"Or maybe she was turned by someone from Romania?" Hannah asked.

"Even if she was, what does that medallion have to do with it? Or anything for that matter?" DuCassal asked.

"They both have a winged dragon etched into them along with other strange markings. I believe these medallions were awarded to knights who earned acceptance into the Order of the Dragon," Hunter said.

"There may have been hundreds of such medallions floating around Europe back then, Charles. This does not necessarily mean the two are connected in any way," DuCassal said.

"True. But you have to admit that this is one Hell of an intriguing coincidence," Hunter said with a smile. "Especially when you take my original family name into consideration and its roots."

"Dracula?" Hannah asked.

"Yes. In Romanian, Dracul has two meanings. The first is dragon. My father was awarded the surname of Dracul. His children had the letter 'a' added to the end, which signified we were his offspring. Dracula means son of Dracul in Romanian," Hunter explained.

"So is it son of the dragon or son of the devil?" Hannah asked.

"I think it should be more like son of a bitch," DuCassal smiled. "That's what most of his opponents call him."

They all laughed.

"After seeing this, I think there may be some sort of connection between myself and that little girl. It's too bad we don't know anything about her. Even her name would help," Hunter said.

He sat back and ordered another round of drinks.

"Galya slipped that medallion into my pocket for a reason. That vampire was also carrying one for a reason. Now, it's up to me to find out what that reason is," he said. "But I'll worry about that later. Taking care of Hannah is more important."

The next morning, they walked over to the voodoo temple on Chartres. Minerva was already waiting in the parlor with tea and cakes. She nodded when they walked in sat down.

"I've been expecting you," she said. "I've heard about the fight."

"Then you know why we've come?" Hunter asked.

She nodded. She looked at Hannah and patted the seat next to hers.

"Sit here, child," she instructed.

Hannah did as she was told. Minerva peered into Hannah's eyes. As she did, she mentally probed her for signs of anything unnatural. Anything that didn't belong there. She probed deeper.

Deeper.

And deeper.

When she made contact, it was with an entity so dark and so foul that it caused her to recoil in horror. She closed her eyes and shook her head from side to side to clear it.

Hannah looked at her.

"Am I possessed?" she asked.

Minerva sat back and nodded.

"You're possessed alright," she said. "I sense someone else inside your body with you. I'd say it was Jeromy Flowers. If that's him inside of you, we'd best get him out as fast as we can."

"You mean an exorcism?" asked Hannah.

Minerva smiled.

"That's the only way, child," she said. "We can do it on the first night of the next full moon when my power is strongest. And I'm going to need all the power I can summon up to deal with that bastard."

They looked at her.

"Oh, I know all about that one," she said. "I did some reading up on him. Jeromy Flowers was as evil as they came and he *detested* his entire family. Knowing about him as I do, I'm sure that hatred extends to all of the family's descendants. Since Tony is the last of the LeFleurs, which means Flowers is out to kill him, too."

"He's the target now," Hunter agreed.

"And Tony *knows* that, too, Charles," DuCassal added. "There's no way that he doesn't."

"But Flowers isn't alone. There's something else inside of you, child. Something that might me much worse than Jeromy Flowers," Minerva said as she looked into Hannah's eyes.

"Tobias Fink?" Hunter asked.

Minerva shrugged.

"Most likely. Whoever it is, he makes Flowers look like a choir boy— and that's not easy," she said.

"Now that we've established that Hannah is indeed possessed, what's your next step?" Hunter asked.

"Let me think," Minerva said as she sipped her tea.

"The first night of the full moon is four days from now," Hannah said. "Are you sure that you'll be able to get rid of Flowers before he forces me to act?"

"I'm pretty sure. But first I need to gather up a few things. Most of the things I can get from my own temple. But I need something from Flowers. Something *personal* I can trap him with. It can be anything at all as long as it touched his body in some way," Minerva said.

"That means we'll have to go to that graveyard and exhume Flowers' body," Hunter said. "Think you can find that graveyard again, Hannah?"

"I can try," Hannah replied. "I have an idea where it probably is."

"I'll go with you," Minerva said. "I don't want any of you contaminating anything."

They climbed into DuCassal's carriage and hour later and headed out toward the bayou. When they left the city limits, they turned north for few miles then east. They stopped to eat a small fishing village, then continued their journey. An hour later, the sun sank behind a ridge of trees to the west and they had only the moon to light their way through the swamp. Around midnight, they could barely make the ruins of a church against the deep, purple sky.

"That's it," Hannah said. "That's the church."

They stopped the carriage and jumped out. The night was unusually quiet.

"Kind of creepy little place, eh, mon ami?" DuCassal said.

"Definitely," Lorena said.

Hannah led them through the ruins to the old graveyard in back of the church. Jeromy Flowers' grave was easy to find as the headstone was free of moss and erosion and glowed slightly.

Minerva held her hand above the stone.

"This place is evil. I can feel it," she said. "Let's get to digging."

Hunter and DuCassal got shovels from the trunk of the carriage and started digging. The ground was soft and moist, as if the grave had only been dug the day before. After a few minutes, their blades struck something hard. A few minutes later, they uncovered a perfectly preserved wooden casket. The casket was a crude pine box that had been thrown together without much thought for its occupant.

"Jeromy Flowers was trash so they treated him like trash," Minerva said as she looked at the box. "They just wanted to bury him and forget him."

Hunter used his shovel to break open the lid. He reached down and pulled away the broken boards and tossed them aside. Then he stared in disbelief at the perfectly preserved corpse inside. There was not even the slightest evidence of decay and the cruse suit he was buried in seemed to be in excellent condition.

"Step aside," Minerva said as DuCassal helped her into the grave.

She reached down. As soon as she touched the corpse, it crumbled to dust and the suit fell into tatters. She winced and tore two buttons from the jacket.

"This will do nicely," she said as she shook the dirt from it and placed it into a handkerchief.

She reached up. Hunter took her hand and helped her out of the grave. She smiled then looked back down at the skull of Jeromy Flowers that now stared up at them with its empty sockets and open mouth.

"We'd best cover him back up," she said. "There's no telling what he might do if we leave him like this."

It took Hunter and DuCassal ten minutes to fill in the grave. As they climbed back into the carriage, Hunter glanced back at the headstone. To his surprise, it looked as if had aged more than 500 years.

"The only hold to this world he has now is through Hannah," Minerva explained. "When his body fell to dust, his spell of preservation was broken. Now his grave is as it should have been."

When they returned to the temple, Minerva used a small, silver hammer to break the button into several pieces. She then put them into a clear glass bottle. They watched as she took a mandrake root from an old wooden box and placed into a small bowl. She added red colored oil and some sea salt then used a mortar to crush it all together. She then added this to the button fragments inside the bottle then poured two fingers of dark rum over it all.

She held the bottle up to the light and smiled.

"I'll let that soak for the next two days. That will give it time to blend," she said.

"Then what?" asked Hunter.

"You bring Hannah back here just before midnight on the night of the full moon so I can work my magic," she said with a smile.

"Will it work?" Hannah asked.

"Do you *believe* it will work?" Minerva asked.

Hannah nodded.

"Then it will," Minerva smiled. "Meantime, you best tell Tony to stay out of sight until this is over—just in case."

"Will do," Hunter agreed. "I'll see you in a couple of days."

She watched as they left the temple and sighed.

"A priestess' work is never done," she said.

Ferguson Moore was 54 years old and liked to keep himself fit. He lived in a large house that was known as the Wedding Cake House on St. Charles Avenue and was widely known for his charity work. His grandfather and father had spent most of their live accumulating a vast fortune. Ferguson had spent the last 20 years trying to give it away.

So when he spotted his name in the obituaries, he went over to see Fred Crandall and the two of them stopped by and paid Hunter and Lorena a visit. DuCassal was seated on the porch with them drinking wine as usual when Crandall and Moore rode up in a carriage.

"I received this a couple of hours ago," Moore said as he handed Hunter the paper.

Hunter read the column.

"According to this, you'll meet your maker at 11 pm. That's 14 hours from now," he said.

Moore looked at him.

"I don't feel like dying tonight or any time soon," he said.

"It says that you died on your way home from a masked ball when your carriage overturned. Are you planning to go out tonight?" Hunter asked.

"Sally and I are attending the annual charity ball at the Cornstalk this evening. We attend it every year," Moore said. "Should I cancel?"

"No. What costumes were you planning to wear?" Hunter asked.

"We were going as Louis XVI and Marie Antoinette. It's kind of our little inside joke," Moore said.

"Jean-Paul is about your size and I'm pretty sure that Mrs. Moore's costume will fit Madison," Hunter said as he looked at DuCassal.

"So we are to be the bait, mon ami?" DuCassal asked.

"Yes. You'll take their places at the ball. Lorena and I will watch your backs the entire time," Hunter said.

"What about me?" asked Moore.

"I don't want you to set foot outside of this house until after midnight," Hunter replied. "Just to be on the safe side, I'll ask Hannah to keep watch on you and your wife."

"Alright. I put myself in your hands. Do you think whoever's behind this will take the bait?" Moore asked.

"Once Madison and I don the costumes, he will not be able to tell the difference," DuCassal assured him.

"I need one more thing from you," Hunter said.

"Name it," Moore said.

"I want to know who hates the board of your company enough to kill you. Whoever's behind this elaborate scheme is going through an enormous amount of trouble to make sure you're all dead," Hunter said.

"Hell, I can't imagine anyone who'd want us dead," Moore said after some thought.

"It doesn't have to be anyone from the present time," Hunter said. "Your company's been around for decades. Think back to when your great grandfathers started it. Maybe it's someone they pissed off or wronged. Someone who felt they gave him a very raw deal."

"I'll go through the company archives this afternoon. Maybe I'll turn something up," Moore said. "I can say one thing for a fact—none of our ancestors who started this company could be considered boy scouts, if you know what I mean. They knew what they wanted and they didn't care who they hurt to get it done. They were real ruthless bastards—and that especially goes for my great grandfather, Arlen Moore."

"Sounds like you've got a lot of work to do," Hunter said.

"Well, since I'm not going to the ball, I'll have plenty of time to get it done," Moore smiled.

When Hunter told Madison what he wanted her to do, she smiled.

"Sounds like fun. I've never attended a masked ball before," she said. "I'm sure I can handle it."

"But can you handle Jean-Paul?" asked Lorena.

DuCassal feigned offense.

"I assure you that I will be the very model of propriety," he said to Madison.

"And I'll grow long ears and become the Easter Bunny," Hunter joked.

DuCassal squinted at him.

"I don't see you as the Easter Bunny, Charles. Perhaps the Tooth Fairy or even King Zulu but never the Easter Bunny," he said.

"How about Santa Claus?" asked Lorena.

"Now you are being ridiculous!" DuCassal said.

At eight that evening, Hunter and his team arrived at Moore's mansion. The maid showed them to his study. Moore had a pile of papers on the desk in front of him and he smiled when he saw them.

"The costumes are in the next room," he said.

"Thanks," DuCassal said.

"Did you find anything out?" asked Hunter.

"Back when the company started, my grandfather and his business partners needed several acres of land on the riverfront so they could sue it to build their steamships. They went about buying up about 100 acres at prices that were hard to resist. They managed to get several small businesses to sell out to them. But one family, led by Henri Terrance, refused to sell. They had just come down from Canada and they established their business the year before. So, granddad and his partners upped the offer several times. Each time, Terrance refused.

Since his property sat square in the middle of the land they'd bought, they *had* to have it or their entire enterprise would have been lost," Moore said.

"How'd that work out?" Hunter asked.

"Like most things did back in those days," Moore replied. "There were several accidents that left Terrance's workers either dead or maimed for life, followed by his own mysterious death and a fire that took out his house and business. His wife and youngest son survived the blaze. The other five kids were burnt to death. Desperate to get on with her life, Mrs. Terrance offered to sell the land to the company. Only this time, they had her over a barrel. She was deep in debt and had no other resources."

"So they made her an offer she couldn't refuse," Hunter said.

"You got it. She was forced to sell for just enough to cover her debt. After that, she left New Orleans and was never seen again," Moore said. "But as far as I can tell, she's the only one they did that to. It was a crying shame no matter how you look at it, but granddad was known for being ruthless. So were his partners."

"If anyone has it in for you and your partners, it would be someone from the Terrance family," Hunter said.

"You think any of them are still around?" Moore asked.

"I'd be willing to wager on that," Hunter said. "If it is a descendant of the Terrance family, that still leaves several questions as to how he's able to do this."

"Black magic?" DuCassal suggested. "Or a curse of some sort?"

"If it is, it's a spell I haven't seen in centuries," Hunter said. "Whoever's behind this is going through an incredible amount of trouble to make those obituaries come true. If it's magic, it's a strange and powerful type of magic."

Lorena looked at the wall clock.

"It's getting late. Hadn't you better change into your costumes?" she said.

"Let's do this," DuCassal said as he and Madison headed into the next room.

"While we're dancing, Jean-Paul, I suggest that you keep your hands to yourself—if you know what's good for you," Madison half joked.

"I will be the perfect gentleman," he assured her. "I promise that I will not try anything unless *you* want me to."

"That'll be the day!" she said as they closed the door behind them.

They arrived at the ball around eight thirty and mingled as inconspicuously as possible with the other guests. There were over 100 couples in attendance along with a ten piece orchestra. After dancing, chatting, dining and drinking, they left the ball at 10:40 and climbed back into the carriage for the trip back to the Moore mansion.

As George turned and steered the carriage up St. Charles, their attention was captured by a loud creak that came from the left front side. The creak was almost immediately followed by a loud snap as the wheel broke away from its axle and caused the carriage to pitch violently.

"It's time to leave!" DuCassal shouted as he grabbed Madison by the hand.

They jumped to safety and watched as the carriage rolled several times, taking the startled horses with it. When it finally came to rest upside-down, pieces of it were scattered all over the street and nearby lawns. They saw one horse lying motionless on its side while the other one managed to stagger back on its feet.

"That was quite nasty!" DuCassal remarked as he surveyed the wreckage.

Hunter and Lorena ran over to them.

"Are you alright?" he asked.

"I'm a little dusty from landing in the street, but otherwise unharmed," DuCassal said.

"I was speaking to Madison," Hunter smiled.

"Hmmph!" DuCassal said as he feigned being snubbed.

"What time is it now?" asked Madison.

"It's 11 p.m.," Lorena said.

"That's exactly when the obituary predicted it would happen," Hunter said as they explored the remains of the carriage.

At that point, George limped over to them.

"That was too damned close," he said as he dusted himself off. "It's lucky I landed in the grass in front of that house or I'd be just like that horse now."

"Indeed," DuCassal said as he patted him on the shoulder. "For a moment, I was afraid that I would have to hire another driver and you know how difficult it is to find good help these days."

"Working for you sure ain't boring, Jean-Paul," George said. "Especially not since Mr. Hunter showed up in New Orleans."

Hunter smiled.

"Oh, well. At least this time the carriage is *not* mine," DuCassal said. "Shall we go and explain this to Mr. Moore?"

"Let's," Hunter agreed.

They walked the six blocks to the mansion. The maid showed them into the study where Moore was busy reading by the fireplace. He put down the book and greeted them with handshakes, then noticed the rather disheveled condition of DuCassal's costume.

"What happened?" he asked.

"First, I think you'll need a new carriage," Hunter said.

He went into an explanation of what had happened. Moore listened and shook his head afterward.

"If you had been in that carriage, you would most certainly have been killed—just as it said in the obituary," Hunter said.

"We never saw it coming. There was no warning. Not even a hint it was coming," DuCassal said.

"The good news is that if this is some sort of a curse, this might have broken it. You're still alive and well and whoever's behind this probably won't be able to use a similar spell again," Hunter said.

"So I can relax?" Moore asked hopefully.

"No," Hunter replied. "Whoever's behind this *wants* you dead."

"So he'll come after me again?" Moore asked.

"I'm *counting* on it," Hunter answered. "Do you still have that newspaper?"

"It's right here in my drawer. You can take it if you want," Moore said as he opened the drawer, too it out and handed it to him.

Hunter rolled it and stuck it into the pocket of his mantle.

"I want Minerva to see this. If this is some sort of spell, it may be attached to the newspaper itself and when you touched it, it transferred to you," he explained.

"Is that even possible?" asked Moore.

"I've heard of it being done many times," Hunter said. "In the meantime, I suggest you stay out of sight and whatever you do, don't read the paper."

Moore laughed.

"You don't have to tell *me* twice," he said.

They went straight to the voodoo temple on Chartres. Minerva was just opening up when they arrived. She greeted them with her usual, knowing smile.

"I've been expecting you," she said as she led them inside.

"I have something I need you to examine," Hunter said as he handed her the paper. "I think it may have some sort of transference spell on it."

Minerva placed the paper on the table and unrolled it. She opened it to the obituaries and ran her fingers over the print. When she came to Moore's obituary, she stopped and pulled her hand away. Her fingertips were glowing.

"You're dead on about that spell," she said as she held up her hand. "It's a nasty one, too. I can feel the power in that print. Whoever did this is no amateur. This is a very rare and difficult spell."

"Is it voodoo?" Lorena asked.

"No. It's some sort of ancient and dark magic. More like old witchcraft," Minerva said as her fingers slowly returned to normal. "This is the kind of spell that causes people to die in exactly the way the spell is written. Is Moore dead?"

"No. We switched Jean-Paul and Madison for Moore and his wife. The spell triggered as it was written but they were able to avoid injury," Hunter explained.

"That means whoever created this will try again," Minerva said. "Unless we can find out who that is and stop him. Do you have any ideas?"

"Does Henri Terrance ring a bell?" Hunter asked.

"No," Minerva said. "Should it?"

"He was the last holdout when the company expanded. Moore said his grandfather and his partners made their lives miserable until they were forced to sell. It wasn't a pleasant situation," Hunter replied.

"I don't know of anyone with that last name in New Orleans now," Minerva said. "Maybe you'll be able to find something in the archives?"

"That's our next stop," Hunter said. "Can you locate the source of the spell?"

"I can try. Give me a few hours," Minerva said.

Minerva took the newspaper to her altar in the back of the temple and used a pair of pure silver scissors to cut the obituary out. She them placed the clipping on a silver tray and sprinkled a few drops of sacred oil over it while saying a prayer.

"Oh Gods of the four directions, I beseech you to show me the source of this dark spell. Reveal to me its place of origin so that I may undo the evil that spawned it."

She then invoked the names of each of the major gods as she sprinkled a pinch of her special blend of magic powder on the obituary. She then lit a red candle, passed it over the tray once for each direction as she prayed to each individual god for help. This done, she ignited the powder with the candle.

She stepped back and watched as the clipping burst into flames and a white wisp of smoke rose to the ceiling. When the smoke dissipated, she blew out the fire and watched as the remaining ashes formed the letter N in the tray.

"Thank you, Lord of the North," she said softly.

When Hunter, Lorena and DuCassal returned two hours later, Minerva told them what was revealed to her.

"Now that we have a direction, how do we locate the spell caster?" Hunter asked.

"We drive around until the source reveals itself to me," Minerva replied. "It's best to do this late at night when the city is mostly quiet. That way, nothing will interfere."

"We'll be back at ten," Hunter said.

They headed straight for the St. Louis Cathedral in Jackson Square. When father Paul saw them enter, he rushed over to greet them. He looked at Hunter and smiled.

"What do you need?" he asked.

"Any information you can give us on the Terrance family," Hunter replied. "I especially need to know if any of them were practitioners of magic. Dark magic."

"Give me a few minutes," Paul said as he hurried down to vault.

He returned with a hand-scribbled legal pad. It contained names and dates of every member of the Terrance family since they arrived in New

Orleans over 175 years before. Hunter read down the list and did a double take when he came to the name Robert Edward Terrance.

"That's interesting. It says here that he died while in Haiti at the age of 34. His widow brought his body back to New Orleans where he was buried in the family plot. That was in 198 S.A. There's no further mention of her afterward. What happened to her?" he asked.

"Her name was Henrietta. After she buried Robert, she left New Orleans and was never seen or heard from again. From the records, I'd say that the Terrance line ended with Robert as there are no mention of any children," Paul said. "Why the interest in the Terrance family?"

"You've seen the records about how they lost their business and other property to the founders of the TransAtlantic Steamship Line and how two of the three remaining board members ended up dead," Hunter replied.

"You think Robert Terrance had something to do with it?" Paul asked.

"Stranger things have happened," Hunter said with a smile.

Paul laughed.

"Especially in *this* city!" he said. "Well, good luck with this one. If what I've heard is true, this is bizarre even for New Orleans. But I will say this—Robert Terrance and his wife spent several years in Haiti. And we all know what that place is famous for."

"If it's what I think it is, I hope Minerva can help us deal with it before Moore joins his fellow board members in the city morgue," Hunter said. "Thanks, Father. You've been a big help as always."

"You're welcome, Hunter. I wish I could do more," Paul said as they shook hands.

"Haitian voodoo?" Lorena asked.

"It's the strangest and darkest kind," DuCassal said. "There's no telling what Terrance learned down there."

"This case gets more interesting as we go along," Hunter said. "Let's get your carriage, Jean-Paul."

"First we must dine. I refuse to do battle on an empty stomach!" DuCassal insisted.

At the appointed hour, they picked Minerva up in DuCassal's carriage. Minerva sat back, took several deep breaths and concentrated.

"Take Canal Street," she instructed.

DuCassal looked up at his driver and nodded.

"Go slowly so I don't miss it," Minerva said.

"Yes Ma'am," George said as he snapped the reins.

When he reached Canal Street, he turned north and slowed down. They rode past restaurants, bars, old stately buildings and clumps of late night party goers. Those who recognized the familiar carriage shouted and waved.

Hunter gazed through the window at the scenery. For the most part, they were following the street car path. And the crowds were thinning out as they neared the end of the line. They crossed over Carrolton to City Park Avenue. Minerva leaned out the window and shouted.

"Stop at Holt."

George pulled up in from of an ancient cemetery that was unlike any other in New Orleans. Minerva opened the carriage door and stepped out. Hunter and the others followed as she led them through the gate. The place was filled with what appeared to be burial mounds.

"There are no tombs here," Hunter remarked as they looked around.

"Just one," Minerva said. "This is where you get buried when you're poor. These are what we call coping style graves. Most of the markers are hand-made and the graves are outlined by stone walls, concrete blocks, iron rails—whatever folks could afford. This is on high ground, so almost all the people here are buried in the earth."

"This is the only such cemetery in the city limits, Charles," DuCassal added. "It was established in 1879 or the First Age."

"This cemetery has no caretakers. The relatives of the folks buried here tend the graves and keep the place clean. This is where they come to celebrate the Day of the Dead every November first. It's a very personal cemetery," Minerva said as they walked past several headstones, some of which leaned precariously to the side or backward. One of two lay on the ground in pieces.

Holt was well kept.

It's twisting paths were lined with stately live oak trees with Spanish mosses dangling from their branches and waving in the breeze like ghostly fingers. Besides the wind, the only sound was an owl hooting in a nearby tree.

Minerva stopped in front of a large grave and pointed at the hand-carved marker. Hunter read the name and nodded.

TERRANCE FAMILY

"Those flowers look fresh," Lorena said as she pointed to the neatly arranged urn at the foot of the grave.

"Someone still tends this grave. That means at least one member of the Terrance family still exists," Hunter said.

"Maybe," Minerva hedged. "Or maybe there's something *else* at work here."

"What do you mean?" asked Hunter.

"I'm not sure yet," she replied. "I think we'd best find a comfortable spot and wait and see what turns up."

Lorena walked around the grave and read the inscriptions carved into the stone wall.

"That's odd," she remarked.

"What is?" Hunter asked.

"The last name on here is Robert Edward Terrance. According to this, he was buried on October 31, 198 S.A. There are no other names on this wall," Lorena said.

"That means that Robert was the last Terrance," DuCassal said. "According to the old customs, even if his family had come into money, they still would have been buried here in the family plot. Since there are no other names, the line ended with Robert."

"What if the family had left New Orleans?" asked Lorena.

"That would be an entirely different matter," DuCassal said. "In that case, they would not have been returned to New Orleans to be buried in the family plot unless, of course, they requested it."

They walked to a grave that was flanked by oak trees and sat down on the wall. DuCassal pulled a flask from his inner pocket, in capped it and took a sip. He passed it to Hunter who did the same, then handed it back. DuCassal offered it to the ladies. Minerva took it, sipped, coughed several times and offered it to Lorena.

She wisely refused.

"Just what in Hell is in that thing?" Minerva queried after she cleared her throat.

"This is one of the finest locally distilled whiskeys," DuCassal replied as he took another sip. "But I'm not sure what it's called."

"I can think of a few names for it," Minerva said.

Lorena laughed.

They settled back and continued their vigil. Around midnight, clouds obscured the moon and cast a dark curtain over the cemetery. A breeze suddenly kicked up and swirled the dry leaves and other debris around as it blew through the graveyard.

Minerva shivered.

"Damn, that's cold!" she remarked.

"Almost like ice," Hunter agreed. "I have a feeling that we're no longer alone."

"We're *not*," Minerva said.

The wind stopped right at the Terrance grave. As the windborne debris settled back to the earth, a tall, dark figure suddenly blinked into view. The figure was dressed in long robes with a hood and resembled an ancient monk. His robes were as black as the night around him.

They watched in silence as he walked to the grave and looked down. That's when they heard the strange, disembodied voice. It sounded as if someone was speaking at the end of long tunnel.

"Embrassons nous, mon fils. Prendre ma force pour que ne puisse prendre ma vengeance sur coux qui nous lese."

(Let us embrace, my son. Take my strength so that we may take our vengeance on those who wronged us.)

The man in the hood opened his arms.

"Utilisez moi comme vous voulez. Pere. Faire de moi votre instrument de la justice. Faire de mois votre epee!"

(Use me as you will, Father. Make me your instrument for justice. Make me your sword!)

The disembodied voice once again replied.

"L'acte doit etre accompli. Nous ne manquerons pas exact de la vengeance que est legitimememnt le notre!"

(The deed is done. Let is now exact the vengeance that is so rightfully ours!)

The man in the hood bowed his head and wrapped his arms around himself.

"Il sera fait, Pere!" he cried.

(It shall be done, Father!)

The figure turned and walked away from the grave. They watched as he left the cemetery. He climbed onto a small buggy and rode east. They jumped into DuCassal's carriage and followed at a safe distance.

"Did you catch any of what was said, mon ami?" DuCassal asked.

"Most of it. My Cajun's still a little rusty," Hunter replied. "Did we just witness a willing possession?"

"We sure did," Minerva said. "The voice that came from the grave called him 'son'. If so, that would make him a member of the Terrance family."

"Apparently, that line hasn't gone extinct like we thought," Hunter said. "Robert wasn't the last."

"And the desire for revenge reaches from beyond the grave," Lorena added.

They followed him out of the graveyard and back into the heart of the city to the office of the Times-Picayune. They waited until he vanished inside, then silently followed him down to the basement where the paper was printed each morning.

The man walked over to the large typesetting board, changed a few things and printed a single page. He picked it up, looked it over carefully, smiled and walked over to a stack of papers that were to be delivered first thing in the morning. He took one from the top, opened it, pulled out a page and inserted the one he'd just printed. Then he rolled it and tucked it under his arm. They waited until he left, then entered the room.

Hunter checked the typesetting board.

"According to this, Moore and his entire family will die at 3:35 this morning when their house explodes. That's just two hours from now," he said.

"We'd best get over there in a hurry and prevent this," DuCassal said as they raced back to the carriage.

Thirty minutes later, Hunter pounded on the front door of Moore's mansion. A weary-looking main opened the door just as Moore and his wife stumbled downstairs in their robes.

"I need you to leave this right now," Hunter ordered.

"Why?" Moore asked as he started to wake up.

"I'll explain everything at 3:36," Hunter said. "Just get out."

"Where can we go at this time of morning?" asked Mrs. Moore.

"You can wait in my carriage. My driver will take you a safe distance from here," DuCassal offered. "He'll bring you back when this is ended."

The Moores nodded.

"One more thing—where's your gas meter?" asked Hunter.

"Out in back of the house. You can't miss it," Moore replied as he and wife went toward the waiting carriage. As the carriage vanished around the corner, DuCassal checked his pocket watch.

"It is nearly time," he said.

They walked around to the rear of the house and secreted themselves in the gazebo. Less than a minute passed when they saw the hooded man enter the yard and walk toward the meter with a tool box in his right hand. He looked around, then knelt on the ground and opened the tool box.

"Je ne le ferais par si," (I would not do that if I were you.) Hunter said as he stepped into view.

The man stood and faced him. DuCassal and Lorena moved to either side to cut off his escape. He sneered at them.

"Jetais vous. Je doit fuer, il est destine. Il doit payer pour sa famille de crimes," (I must kill him. It is destined. He must pay for his family's crimes) he said.

"Ceux qui vou cherchentdes crosses sont morts depuis longtemps. Leurs peches sont morts avec aux. Qu'il soit," (Those who wronged your ancestors are long dead. Their sins died with them. Let it be) Hunter said as the circled each other warily.

"Jamais ses peches doivant etre effaces. Moore doit mourir!" (I cannot let it be until his line is erased. Moore must die!) the man insisted as he drew a revolver from his robe and aimed it at Hunter.

Hunter drew his weapon and aimed it at the man's forehead.

"Drop ou mourir!" (Drop it or die!) he shouted.

The man pulled the trigger.

So did Hunter.

The man's shot missed.

Hunter's shot didn't.

The man fell onto his back and stared up at the stars. With his last breath he cried,

"Pardonnez-moi, le Pere! Jenais pas vous!" (Forgive me, Father. I have failed you!)

At that point, Moore and his wife, Sally, came running into the yard. They gathered around the dead man and studied his face.

"Just who in Hell *was* he anyway?" DuCassal asked.

"He looks familiar. I think he works down at the newspaper. I'm sure I saw him down there a few times when I went to talk to Fred," Moore replied. "But he'd be the best one to ask."

He turned and shook each of their hands.

"If not for you folks, he would have blown our house up with us in it. You really saved our hides tonight. Thank you," he said.

Sally walked up and gave each of them a big hug.

"Thank you! You're like angels," she said with tears of thanks in her eyes.

"That is the very first time anyone has called me an angel!" DuCassal said.

"Don't let it go to your head," Lorena smiled.

"I'll send our butler over to fetch Inspector Valmonde so he can cart this poor soul away to the morgue," Moore said.

"Thanks. I think we'd better drop in at the newspaper tomorrow morning and talk to Crandall. Maybe he can identify this man and help us make sense of this," Hunter said as they took their leave.

The next afternoon, Hunter, Lorena, Minerva and DuCassal dropped in on Fred Crandall at the Times-Picayune. They found both him and Ferguson Moore in the office. They both shook hands with everyone. Crandall invited them to have a seat and had his secretary bring in some hot coffee.

"Ferguson here tells me that he dodged a bullet this morning— thanks to you," he said.

"We were lucky," Hunter said modestly.

"You have no idea *how* lucky!" DuCassal added. "We were in the right place at the right time."

"Luck or not, you saved my hide. Thank you. All of you," Moore said as he raised his coffee mug in a toast.

"What can you tell me about Bonterre?" Hunter asked.

Crandall sat back and shook his head.

"Nestor Bonterre was our head typesetter. He walked into this office about a year ago and asked for the job. I didn't even have an opening at the time, but I hired him on the spot. Damnedest thing, too. He had no references. No resume. He just walked and told me to hire him—and I *did*. It was like he *willed* me to do it."

"He actually did. He needed to have access to your press so he could put his plan into motion. He altered the obituary on a single newspaper, cast a contact spell over it and delivered it himself to his chosen victims. As soon as they touched the paper, the spell activated," Hunter explained.

"Bonterre didn't have the knowledge or the power to cast such a spell. He had no training in the black arts. But his ancestor *did*. Somehow or other, perhaps it was predestined in some way. Robert Terrance managed to bring Bonterre to New Orleans. Then he possessed him so he could use his physical form to manipulate the press and carry out his plan for revenge," Minerva added.

"I'm not sure if Bonterre willfully returned to New Orleans to fulfill his legacy or Robert forced him to do it. Bonterre's not in any condition to tell us now," Hunter said.

"Since he was the last member of the Terrance line, the spell died with him. Robert will have to suffer for eternity knowing that he has failed," Minerva said. "You're safe now, Ferguson."

Moore nodded.

"I'll make sure that Bonterre is placed in the Terrance family plot at Holt," he said. "And I'll personally tend the grave each year so they won't be forgotten. After what my granddaddy did to that family, it's the least I can do. It ain't much, but I'd like to atone for my family's sins in some small way."

"I'll go to the funeral with you, Ferguson. I'll do a crossing over ceremony at the grave. That should put the family at peace," Minerva offered.

"We'll all be there," Hunter promised.

Two nights later, the large pale moon shone down on the ancient city. Hunter, Lorena and DuCassal escorted Hannah to Minerva's temple at 20 minutes to midnight. Minerva let them.

"You're right on time," she said. "The potion's ready."

"Now what?" asked Hannah.

"You come to the back with me. You three can wait our here," Minerva instructed.

Hunter took off his hat and sat down. He poured himself a glass of iced tea. DuCassal plopped down in the chair across from him and picked up one the spice cakes while Lorena sat next to Hunter.

"I feel bad for her," she said. "Somehow, I feel this is all my fault."

"There's no need to kick yourself, Lorena. What happened to Hannah is the doing of Tobias Fink and a long-dead asshole," Hunter said. "You had nothing at all to do with this."

"Do you think she'll be alright?" Lorena asked.

"I'm sure she will. Hannah's in good hands," Hunter said soothingly.

Minerva led Hannah to a piece of furniture that resembled an old psychiatrist couch. This one had several heavy straps attached to it.

"Lay down here, child. Make yourself comfortable," Minerva said.

Hannah did as she instructed. As soon as she was positioned properly, Minerva strapped her wrists, waist and ankles down.

"You'll be doing a lot of thrashing about. This is so you won't hurt yourself—or me," she explained. "The straps should be strong enough to hold you for a few minutes anyway. I just hope it's long enough."

She stood over Hannah and uncapped the bottle.

"Open your mouth," she said.

When Hannah did, she poured about half the liquid into it. She then placed the open bottle next to her on the floor. Hannah felt the liquid start to burn in her stomach. The rum—and whatever else Minerva had blended it with—was incredibly strong.

And somewhat vile tasting.

Minerva placed one candle at the head of the couch and lit it. She placed a second one at the foot and lit that, too.

"We're going to exorcise Jeromy Flowers from you and try to trap him inside this bottle," she explained. "I have to warn you that you'll probably feel pretty sick."

"Sicker than I do now?" Hannah asked as her stomach began to churn.

"Oh, yes," Minerva smiled.

She put a cigar in her mouth and lit it. She took several puffs to get it going, then inhaled deeply. She then exhaled and blew the smoke all over Hannah from head to toe. She repeated this three times. In between, she intoned a prayer and asked the gods to expel the evil spirits from Hannah's body.

Hannah coughed and moaned as the ceremony progressed. She felt herself trying to vomit.

"Let it out, child! Don't try to hold anything in!" Minerva shouted.

Hannah couldn't have even if she wanted to. She opened her mouth wide to vomit. To her surprise, only smoke came out.

Ugly black smoke.

It swirled above her for a few seconds, twisted and sparkled then slowly got sucked into the bottle where it mingled with the rest of the liquid and the crushed button and finally disappeared.

Minerva quickly capped the bottle and held it up to the light.

"I've got you, Jeromy Flowers. You're going to a place where you won't be able to harm anyone ever again," she said with a smile.

Hannah took several deep breaths.

"It's over now, Hannah. You can relax for a while," Minerva said as she undid the straps.

She helped Hannah to her feet and led her out to the front parlor. She was surprised to see Madison seated with the others. Hannah moved to an empty chair and sat down. Lorena passed her a glass of tea.

"That wasn't as bad as I thought it would be," Hannah said weakly.

"I must admit that this was one of the easiest exorcisms I ever did," Minerva said. "I expected more of a fight from Flowers. I guess he wasn't as powerful as I thought."

"Are you alright?" Lorena asked.

Hannah nodded.

"I just feel drained—and a little hungry," she replied as she sipped the tea.

"That takes care of Jeromy Flowers," Minerva said as she nearly collapsed into her chair. "Tobias Fink will be much more difficult."

"How so?" asked Hunter.

"Fink didn't possess Hannah, so there's nothing for me to exorcise," Minerva explained. "I think he planted something deep inside her mind which he'll force her to act out as soon as something triggers it."

"A psychosomatic suggestion?" Hunter asked.

Minerva shrugged.

"That I can't tell you. I'm not a psychiatrist. I don't know what will trigger it or what's she'll do when that happens. You can bet on one thing, Hunter. It won't be anything nice."

"You've got that right, Minerva," Madison said. "Fink was as evil and cruel as they come. He lived only to satisfy his own urges and anyone who tried to cross him in any way paid a terrible price. He came after me. Even though you killed him, I won't feel completely safe until we break his hold on Hannah."

Lorena put an arm around Madison's shoulders to comfort her. She felt her tremble with fear.

"Don't worry, Madison. We'll protect you *and* Hannah," she assured her.

Hunter leaned back. He took a spice cookie from the tray and bit into it as he studied the abject terror in Madison's eyes.

Was Fink *that* powerful?

And if Hannah did act out what he programmed her to do, would they have to take extreme measures to stop her? Just how far *would* they go?

He knew that Hannah was fighting a triple threat inside her mind and body. She had been rid of the nasty spirit of Jeromy Flowers, but now she had to try and deal with what Fink had placed in her mind and her constant urges to feed. She was being pulled in multiple directions. Was she strong enough to handle it?

Minerva poured some tea into a cup, sipped it and sat back.

"The good thing about this—*if* you can call it good—is that once it's triggered and she tries to act it out, it's over with. When that happens, Hannah won't remember anything about it. Her nightmare will be over."

"Unless Fink planted more than one suggestion in her brain," Hunter said. "It's possible he programmed Hannah for multiple purposes. Each would have its own unique trigger."

"How many suggestions are we talking about, Charles?" asked DuCassal.

"The possibilities could be endless," Hunter replied.

"Perhaps that's what Fink meant when he said that our nightmare was just beginning, mon cher," Lorena said.

"I don't want to be yours or anyone else's nightmare," Hannah said as she opened her eyes and sat up. "I heard everything you said for the last minute or so."

She looked at Lorena.

"There's no telling what that monster did to me. If I become a threat to you or anyone else and you feel I'm out of control, I want you to do all in your power to stop me. Even if you have to kill me," she said flatly.

"I'll do as you ask, but only as a last resort," Lorena said.

"We'll try everything else we can think of first," Hunter added. "But if you start ripping heads off innocent people, we'll take you down—*hard*."

Hannah nodded.

"I wouldn't expect you to treat me any differently than we treat the monsters we have to deal with," she said. "Like you always say: it goes with the territory."

"I think it would be best that you deal with each problem as it arises and not fret over what may or may not happen next," Minerva suggested. "We could be dead wrong on this."

Hunter nodded.

"I'm famished," DuCassal said. "Let's all go out for dinner. I'm buying."

"I'm for that," Hunter said. "How about Pere Antoine's?"

"Let me get my scarf. I'll go with you," Minerva said.

After dinner. A very exhausted Hannah attempted to get some sleep. But in the middle of the night, her entire body suddenly stiffened. Try as she might, she couldn't move her arms or legs. A panic began to set in. She tried to scream but no sound came from her open mouth.

As she lay helpless, her body became racked with intense, searing pains that felt as if she were being beaten with a heavy whip or strap. After several agonizing minutes of this, the pains ceased. That's when something rolled up her night gown and forced her legs apart. She trembled with horror as something long, hard and icy cold penetrated her and she felt it moving in and out.

Faster and faster.

She couldn't fight it off.

Couldn't escape.

All shoe could do was lie there, immobile, and take it.

Again and again and again.

Despite it all, her body responded in kind. She began to move her hips in time with her attacker's thrusts as waves of excitement raced through her quivering body.

Faster and faster.

Harder and harder and harder.

Her heart pounded as she moaned softly.

The she came.

It was a hard, long and very powerful one. Her body responded to the intense pleasure as her libido went into overdrive.

The trusts continued.

She moaned louder now, totally lost in the sensations as she came a second and a third time.

Then suddenly, the thrusting stopped and she was able to move again.

She say up and looked around. Her room was quiet and empty. Her body ached as she dragged herself to the bathroom and stared at her reflection in disbelief. She was covered with welts and bruises from her shoulders to her thighs. It was just the way Fink had left her in that casket after days of excruciating torture.

She forced herself to dress then went in search of Hunter. She found him, DuCassal and Lorena having brunch at Brennan's as usual. She joined them at the table and explained what happened.

"At least the sex was great," she tried to joke. "I really didn't mind that part of it. I just can't take another one of those beatings."

"Madison told us that Fink was a real sadistic bastard," Hunter said.

"I thought you killed him," Hannah said as she sipped her coffee.

"We killed his *physical* body. Apparently, we still have his spirit to contend with," Hunter said.

"Now what?" asked Hannah.

"First, we tell Minerva what just happened. Maybe she'll be able to come up with a remedy," Hunter said.

Minerva listened to Hannah's story and sighed.

"I was afraid of this," she said. "Fink's hold on you is stronger than I thought it might be. This is going to take some real careful planning. But I have to warn you, child. This is going to be *very painful* for us both."

"I don't care how painful it will be, Minerva. I want this bastard out of my body. Just do whatever you have to but get rid of him," Hannah said. "I don't want to go through the rest of my life getting raped by some phantom."

"But you said that sex was great," DuCassal joked.

Hannah glared at him.

"I can't take the beating that comes with it," she growled.

"You know the old saying—you always hurt the one you love!" DuCassal quipped.

Hannah reached out and backhanded him off the chair. Hunter shook his head and smiled as he picked himself off the floor and sat back down.

"Most likely, he put some kind of trigger in you that will cause you to attack Madison," Minerva continued.

Madison looked Hunter in the eyes.

"I don't want to spend the rest of my life looking over my shoulder, worried about what might trip her trigger.

If I'm attacked, I'll be forced to defend myself and I can't be held responsible for what might happen if I go into a rage. You saw what I did to Fink's people," she said.

"Yes. And it wasn't pretty, either," Hunter said. "We'll try to watch both your backs, but sometimes, that might be impossible. If Hannah does anything, it might be too quick for us to intervene."

"If it comes down to me or Hannah, I choose me," Madison decided.

"I haven't actually seen you in action, but I'd be willing to wager that it would be the fight of the century. Perhaps we could sell tickets?" DuCassal said.

"Is there anything you can think of that Fink may have implanted in Hannah's mind as a trigger? Like a favorite song or phrase? Anything you can think of might prove helpful," Hunter said.

"No. Fink probably selected something very random. Maybe something that caught his ear or eye on the spur of the moment. He liked to remain unpredictable," Madison said. "You have to remember that he was more than a little bit insane. That's what made him so dangerous."

"How dangerous I'm just finding out," Hannah said.

CHAPTER THIRTEEN:
Moon Stalker

Lafayette was a medium sized city in the heart of Cajun country. It was 137 miles west of New Orleans and, like most places in Louisiana, it was a city that time forgot. Life was slow and easy in Lafayette, which was known for its rich culture, zydeco music and festivals. It was surrounded by swamps and bayous, which gave the city an air of mystery.

And it was as old as New Orleans.

Older if you counted the local Indian settlement it was built on top of.

It had about 125,000 residents and almost no crime. It was an ideal place for the easy going Cal Hobson, who had been the sheriff for the past 30 years. Cal was six feet tall, broad shouldered and had a slight paunch from all the rich Cajun and Creole cuisine he liked to eat. He kept his head shaved because he didn't like to fuss with what little hair he had left.

His department consisted of ten deputies who patrolled the city in two twelve hour shifts. Usually, the only "criminals" they had to contend with were the local drunks who disturbed the peace or got into brawls.

Nothing really bad ever happened in Lafayette.

Nothing, that is, until the first night of the full moon in July.

That's when two of his deputies came upon a sight that made them sick to their stomachs. The police station was located in the old city hall just off St. Mary's Boulevard. At midnight, which was the shift Cal usually worked, he sent his five deputies out on patrol. Ten minutes later, two of them came rushing back into the station. Cal looked up from his evening paper and saw they were as white as sheets.

"What's wrong, boys? You look like you've seen a ghost," he asked.

"What we just found is a lot worse than any ghost, Cal," one said. "You gotta come and look."

"Where?" Cal asked as he got up and grabbed his hat.

They led him six blocks south. As they approached the intersection, Cal saw what he hoped wasn't real. But the closer he got, the more he realized that it was real. And it made his blood run cold in veins.

Dangling upside down from a lamp post was the headless corpse of a large man. Cal looked up and fought off the urge to vomit. Never in all of his years had he seen anything like this.

"Mother of God!" he said as he walked around the lamp post.

He shook his head and told his men to cut the body down. He watched as one of them shinnied up the post and cut the rope that was around the corpse's ankles with his pocket knife. The body hit the pavement with a dull thud right in front of Cal. He knelt down and looked at the neck.

"That's a clean cut," he said. "This was done by a blade of some sort. I don't think it was an ax. Whatever did this was real sharp."

"There's no blood anywhere, Cal," said the deputy. "Not even a drop."

"Maybe a vampire got him?" the other deputy suggested.

"There hasn't been a vampire here for a hundred years," Cal said. "Go to the hospital and have them send a wagon over to fetch the body. Maybe we'll know more after they do an autopsy."

Cal walked slowly back to the station. This was the first murder case he ever had and it was unusually gruesome. He wondered who did it and why the killer took the head. He also wondered who the victim was. Without a head, he'd be hard to identify. And why was there no sign of any blood?

When he reached his office, he went into the toilet and puked his guts out.

But the nightmare had just begun.

The very next night, the same deputies found another headless corpse dangling from the exact same lamp post.

Faced with something beyond his understanding, Cal sat down and wrote a letter to Hunter, asking for his help.

It took two days for the letter to reach Hunter's house in the Garden District. When he opened it and read it, he handed it to DuCassal who was seated next to him on the porch.

"I know Cal Hobson quite well, mon ami. He is a very level headed and logical man. He has never requested any sort of help before, so this must be beyond his abilities to handle."

"We'd better get over to Lafayette," Hunter said. "How soon can you be ready?"

"Give me two hours to pack," DuCassal said. "I'll have George prepare my carriage for the trip."

That same night, two other deputies found yet a third victim. Like the two before, he was headless and hung upside down from the same lamp post. Cal had the body brought over to the morgue and waited for help to arrive.

Three days later, it did.

Cal greeted Hunter, DuCassal and Lorena with warm handshakes and had them sit down in his office. Then he told them all about the strange and gruesome murders.

"Have there been any others since?" Hunter asked.

"No. As soon as the moon passed out of its full phase, they stopped. It's been creepy quiet since," Cal replied. "Nothing like this has ever happened in the entire history of Lafayette. It's normally pretty peaceful here. This kind of thing is new to us."

"Have you identified the victims?" Hunter asked.

"Because their heads are missing, we were only able to identify one. That was the last. We were able to find out who he was because he had a prison tattoo on his right arm," Cal said.

"Who was he?" asked DuCassal.

"Jose Valejo Barca," Cal said. "He served 22 years in Angola for rape and robbery. He was paroled only a week before we found him."

'Interesting," Hunter mused.

"Very," DuCassal agreed.

"What about the other two? Anyone in town turn up missing?" Hunter asked.

"I'm still working on that. I'm trying to match the victims to our missing persons reports. So far, I've had no luck. No one in town's been reported missing in over a month. I figure those two weren't from around here," Cal said.

"Tourists?" Lorena asked.

"We get our fair share of them, Ma'am," Cal replied. "Mostly, folks stop by on their way to New Orleans unless we're having a festival."

"Lafayette is known for its festival and fine food," DuCassal explained. "This is the heart of Cajun country after all."

"Jean-Paul and I used to visit Lafayette several times each year back in the First Age. That was a long, long time ago yet the city looks pretty much the same as it always has," Hunter said.

Cal smiled.

"Folks around here hate change. When something gets knocked down, we rebuild it and make it look exactly as it did before. That gives us a sense of place, I guess," he said.

"The Great Disaster went unnoticed here," DuCassal said. "As it did in a handful of cities in North America. In fact, those places managed to carry on as if nothing had happened. They even thrived."

"Nothing keeps us Cajuns and Creoles down for long. We just pick ourselves up and go one with our lives like always. We're pretty resilient and we take pride in our way of life," Cal added. "We usually handle things without outside help. But when something disturbs the natural order of things, we call in the cavalry."

"That's *us*," Hunter smiled. "Can you take us to where you found the bodies?"

"I sure can. It's just up the street a few blocks," Cal said as he grabbed his hat.

They walked over to the house and watched as Lorena concentrated. She shook her head and squinted at Hunter.

"What's wrong?" he asked.

"I've picked up three different trails," she replied.

"Track them one at a time and see where they lead," Hunter said.

She nodded.

They followed her through a small patch of woods to the edge of a pond. Lorena stopped and looked around. Then she shrugged.

"It ends right here, at the edge of the water," she said.

"Let's try number two," Hunter said.

They went back to the house and started again. The second trail led straight to a nearby park and stopped right in the center of a playground. Lorena walked around several times and finally gave up.

"This is crazy! It's like whoever make this trail just vanished into thin air," she said.

She followed the third trail six blocks west and into an ancient cemetery. They followed as he led them along a twisting path that ended in a small, flat, open field.

"It ends right here," she announced.

"Let's check the area and see what we can turn up," Hunter said as they fanned out.

"I think I may have something," DuCassal shouted as he pulled the grass away from a large, marble slab.

They rushed over.

"It's an old gravestone," Cal said. "It looks like it's been covered for centuries."

"Herein lie the remains of Col. John Larkin Capstan, 2nd Louisiana Cavalry, CSA.

Born July 5, 1798 Natchitoches, La. Died July 5, Gettysburg, Pa. May God keep his souls at rest." Lorena read.

"Fascinating. Why would the trail end here?" Hunter wondered aloud.

"He was killed during the War Between the States," DuCassal said. "Gettysburg is over a thousand miles from here. But if he was originally from Natchitoches, why on Earth was he buried here?"

"And what, if anything, does he have to do with the murders?" asked Cal.

"We have several good questions but no answers," Hunter said.

Lorena looked at Cal.

"Is there a town historian?" she asked.

"Sure is. His name is Arlington Spears. He knows just about all there is to know about Lafayette," Cal replied.

"Take us to him," Hunter said.

Arlington Spears lived in a big, old white house at the end of the main street. He was sitting on his front porch sipping a mint julep when they walked up. Spears was tall, broad shouldered and had a rich head of white hair and a goatee to match. He looked like a typical southern gentleman.

Cal made the introductions. Spears poured each of them a mint julep and told them to make themselves at home. Hunter explained what they wanted to know. Spears leaned back in his armchair and folded his fingers across his considerable girth.

"Off hand, I can't rightly explain how Capstan ended up here. The family name doesn't ring a bell at all. But that doesn't mean they didn't live here at the time. Those were pretty chaotic years in Louisiana. Thousands of families passed through here looking to get away from the fighting up north. Some stayed. Some didn't. I'll have to do some research," he said.

Hunter nodded.

"We'd really appreciate anything you can tell us," he said.

"Anytime. I'm always happy to help," Spears said as they shook hands.

That night, they decided to patrol the area where the bodies were found. Hunter wanted the Colonel to make another appearance so he could see exactly what they were up against. He walked the street near the cemetery. DuCassal covered the nearby parks while Lorena walked up and down the streets.

All remained quiet until three a.m.

As Hunter passed the cemetery, he felt the ground rumble beneath his feet. He stopped and looked in the direction of Capstan's grave and waited. Seconds later, he stared as a tall man clad in a Confederate uniform and mounted on a black horse, came galloping straight at him. He was waving a cavalry saber and emitting the old rebel yell. Hunter drew his katana just in time to parry the blade that hissed toward his head.

The colonel wheeled his horse around and charged again. Again Hunter parried the blow and attempted one of his own. His blade struck the horse's flank but did no damage. The colonel laughed, turned and charged again. Hunter raised his katana and braced himself.

The blow sent vibrations coursing through his body and sent him to the ground. Hunter stayed down and watched as the shadowy rider vanished into the night air. When it grew quiet, he picked himself and retrieved his hat. DuCassal and Lorena hurried over to him as he dusted it off and put back on.

"Now what?" asked Lorena.

"We can't kill him—he's *already* dead. That would be redundant," Hunter said as they walked back to the police station.

A light rain began to fall and what little light there was became obscured by the rolling clouds and fog that drifted in from the nearby swamps.

"The colonel was buried here for a reason. No one transports a corpse all the way from Pennsylvania unless they *wanted* to bury him here. But why?" Hunter asked.

"We need to find out the answers to those questions so we can figure out how to send the colonel back into whatever Hell he rode out of," DuCassal said.

"Since he's already killed three men, I'd guess someone *brought* him back. Maybe it was to fulfill some sort of vendetta," Lorena suggested.

"But why now? And what, if anything, do the victims have in common? Are the related to each other in any way?" DuCassal asked.

When they walked into the station, Cal handed each of them a hot cup of coffee. Hunter told him what happened. Cal seemed to lose all the color in his cheeks as he sat back down.

"So far, I don't have any positive I.D. on the other two victims. When that bastard made off with their heads, he made that part of it kind of difficult. Why do you suppose he took them anyway?" Cal asked.

Hunter shrugged.

"Trophies?" he suggested.

"But their blood is also gone. Every last drop of it. If the colonel is a ghost, why would he take the blood? What sort of ghost drinks blood anyway?" Cal asked.

"Ghosts do not need human blood in order to manifest themselves," Lorena said.

"Maybe this one *does*," Hunter said.

"Huh?" asked DuCassal.

"Maybe he's under some sort of curse and whoever brought him back needs the blood to control him," Hunter said.

"Control him?" DuCassal asked.

"It's just a guess," Hunter said. "But I have the strangest feeling that someone *summoned* the colonel."

"Voodoo?" Lorena asked.

"Possibly," Hunter replied. "Cal, do you have a voodoo queen here?"

"Doesn't every city in Louisiana?" Cal replied. "Her name is Cassandra Bowman. She has a small temple over on Jefferson."

"Let's go!" Hunter said.

Cal led them to the northern side of town and down a narrow street that backed into a swamp. There was a small voodoo temple on the far end. They walked up and knocked. The old door creaked open and a middle aged, dark skinned woman grinned at them and let them inside.

Cassandra looked him in the eyes.

"I *know* why you've come," she said. "The spirits told me."

"And what do the spirits say about the murders?" asked Hunter as he leaned on the counter.

"Nothing. They are strangely silent," she said.

"Silent?" he asked.

She nodded.

"They're afraid of what lies behind the behind the murders," she said. "I sense there's something dark and very evil behind this. Something so wicked, it makes my stomach ache to think about it."

"What is it, then?" Hunter pressed.

"I don't know. But I do know that whatever it is, it's very angry and filled with hatred. A strong and deep hatred. It's been here before, too. A long, long time ago. After centuries of sleep, it has awakened and it wants blood," she said. "Your blood."

She leaned closer.

"You've met him, Hunter. You and he have crossed paths several times before, both while he was alive and later when he was dead," she said.

She had a wild look in her eyes.

"If I did, I don't remember," he said.

"You will," she assured him.

"Why did he come back? What's he after?" Hunter asked.

She stared directly at him. Her gaze made him feel cold all over.

"It's *you*, Hunter. He's come back for *you!*" she said.

"Him? But what about the victims?" Cal asked, now more perplexed than ever.

"They was only bait," she said. "Something to lure Hunter back to Lafayette."

"Bait?" Lorena asked. "What hideous bait!"

"You took something from him, Hunter. Something that meant everything to him. He never forgave you for it and swore he'd get revenge, even if it took him forever. Once it's returned, he'll rest easy. But here's the problem—you *can't* give it back. It's gone forever. So you'll have to confront him and put him back in his grave where he belongs—if you're able," she said.

Hunter thought for a moment and shook his head.

"I have no memory of anything. What does he want from me?" he asked.

"Only *you* know the answer to that, Hunter. Search your soul. It's hidden there," Cassandra said.

"What about our horseman?" Hunter asked.

"If you take care of the one, the other will go away. The colonel is his instrument. He does his bidding," she said. "The colonel was a perfect choice for him as both are evil incarnate and filled with hate. Their hearts are blacker than the pits of Hell itself and both love to kill."

A brief image of himself facing off against a Confederate officer in the midst of battle flashed through Hunter's mind. He could see the office's twisted, hate-filled lips and large, deep, dark eyes as they circled each other with cavalry sabers. Then the image was gone.

Cassandra smiled knowingly.

He looked into her eyes and realized she saw it, too. Or perhaps, she *put* it there?

"No, Hunter. That came from deep *within*," she assured him. "You met him on the field of Gettysburg. You purposely sought him out so you could kill him. You *knew* what he was."

Hunter shuddered.

"I fought at Gettysburg?" he asked as he looked at DuCassal.

"We *both* did, mon ami. We rode with George Custer," DuCassal replied.

Hunter thought for a moment, then nodded.

"That's right. We chose his outfit because he was reckless and unafraid of anything. We took on Stuart's cavalry and turned them back even though we were badly outnumbered. Custer charged when another commander might have retreated and his audacity worked," Hunter recalled with a smile. "But where did the colonel fit in?"

"His name does not ring a bell," DuCassal said. "That was very long ago and I have rarely given those days much thought since the war ended."

Hunter stood and paced.

"What about the one who's behind this? If I did take something from him, what could it be? And why did he wait so many centuries to come after it?" he asked.

Lorena shrugged.

"We are dealing with the supernatural, mon cher. It doesn't have to make sense," she said.

Cassandra looked at him.

"Somehow, the dark one has sensed that you've returned to Louisiana and he lured you here by having the colonel murder those men. Now, you must find a way to send them both back to the Hell that spawned them," she said.

"But why use Capstan? What does he have to do with me?" Hunter asked.

"Again, that's something only you can figure out. Perhaps the two of you met in battle that day and it was you who sent him to his grave." she suggested.

"That's it!" DuCassal shouted.

Hunter looked at him as he slapped himself on the knee.

"We joined that battle because we *tracked* him. He left a trail of bodies from New Orleans to Virginia and back again. Most were women and children. He murdered them indiscriminately and dared us to catch him. Think, Charles. I'm sure it will come to you if you concentrate," he said.

Hunter had an epiphany.

"He was a *vampire!*" he said.

"Bravo! I knew you'd remember," DuCassal said with a nod.

"But we *killed* him. I remember running a stake through his heart and beheading him," Hunter said as the imaged flashed through his mind. "Unfortunately since we were in the heat of the bloodiest battle in American history, we never got the chance to cremate the body."

"His men must have gathered up his corpse and had him transported back here to Lafayette for burial. We aren't dealing with a ghost, Charles. We are dealing with a vampire that has been resurrected. That's why those men had no blood left in them. Capstan *fed* on them," DuCassal said.

"Whoever is behind this knew that Capstan would make the perfect bait to bring us here. And that Capstan would be eager to exact revenge," Hunter said.

"Now what, mon cher?" asked Lorena.

"We finish the job I started at Gettysburg," Hunter replied. "Since Capstan was actually brought back from the dead, he has to return to his grave and sleep in his coffin in order to replenish his strength—just like the vampires in Stoker's books."

"You think he's there now?" asked Cal.

"There's one way to find out," Hunter replied.

"Let's go and pay the colonel a visit," DuCassal said as he donned his hat.

After purchasing two shovels at the local general store, they rode out to the cemetery and stopped beside Capstan's grave. Hunter stepped out of the carriage and examined the soil. The others followed.

"The ground has not been disturbed," DuCassal observed.

"How is that possible?" asked Cal.

"The same way he appears on his horse each time. He's a *supernatural* being. He simply *wills* himself into existence above his grave without disturbing it or his corpse inside. This is a classic Stoker vampire with a slight twist," Hunter explained.

"Can he be killed?" Cal asked.

"No. He's already very dead. But if we destroy his corpse, we may be able to force him to move on. He has to return to his corpse each time. If we deprive him of that refuge, he may simply fade into nothingness," Hunter replied as he started digging.

Cal picked up the other shovel and helped. After an hour, they finally managed to reach the ancient coffin.

Lorena marveled at the near perfect state of preservation.

"It looks as if it were just buried here yesterday," she said. "There is not a sign of decay."

"Step aside," Cassandra said as she held a strange, twisted root above the coffin.

"Just as I feared. There's some serious magic at work here. Dark magic," she said as she stepped back. "He was placed here with the help of a voodoo priest. But the spell seems to be one of *containment.*"

"You mean it was meant to keep him inside?" Hunter asked.

"Yes. Whoever did this wanted Capstan to stay put. That's why the coffin is still intact. Whoever brought him back, managed to break the spell," Cassandra said. "That means he's real powerful."

Hunter and DuCassal wrestled the heavy coffin from the ground and opened it so that its contents would be bathed by direct sunlight. To their surprise, the corpse was also perfectly preserved.

"He should look good considering all the blood he's gorged upon," Lorena said. "Ones like him give us vampires a bad name."

DuCassal laughed.

"You're a vampire?" Cal asked.

She smiled and nodded.

Cal laughed.

"For the record, someone as pretty as you is welcome to bite me anytime!" he joked. "I heard the stories about you but I never believed they were true. I have a lot of questions for you if you won't mind my asking."

"I'll be happy to answer all of them—when we're through with our mission," she replied graciously.

Hunter took a wooden stake from his mantle and drove it through Capstan's heart. It popped like a water balloon and splattered blood in all directions. Capstan's chest heaved and he emitted a growl. Hunter drew his katana and beheaded him.

"That's the second time I've had to do this to you. I swear by all that's holy, it will be the last!" he said as he doused him with oil.

He dropped a match into the coffin and jumped back as it burst into flames. They watched until the fire died out, then gathered up the ashes and placed them into a small metal box. Cassandra dropped the root into it, added a small cross and some blue powder, then locked it.

"I put two containment spells on that box. Capstan won't be able to make another appearance anytime soon," she said.

"Let's toss it into the river and let the currents take it away from here," Hunter said.

After this was done, they destroyed Capstan's marker with sledgehammers, tossed the pieces into the hole and covered them up.

"Now what?" asked Cal as they headed back to the hotel.

"Now we wait for his master to contact us," Hunter said.

They didn't have to wait very long.

At sunset, the hotel manager spotted them dining in the restaurant and walked over. He handed Hunter an envelope.

"I just saw this in the mail box. It's addressed to you. I have no idea where it came from. It appeared out of nowhere," he explained.

Hunter opened it and read the letter out loud.

Now that we have each other's mutual attention, there is something important we need to discuss. Meet me in the old Mouton Plantation at midnight.

"It looks like your plan worked, mon cher. He wants to meet with you," Lorena said.

"Mouton Plantation?" Hunter asked. "Any idea where that is, Jean-Paul?"

"I believe it is the house that was built by Alexander Mouton's father. I'm sure you'll recognize it once you see it," DuCassal replied. "It's just outside of the city."

"Anyone live there now?" Hunter asked.

"No. That house has been standing empty for more than 150 years, Charles. The last time I saw it, it was a museum dedicated to the lives of the families who once lived there," DuCassal replied.

"It sounds like the perfect place for a meeting," Hunter said as he finished his drink.

They left the hotel at eleven and followed the main street to the edge of the city. The street then became a dirt road which wound through the swamp and ended right at two large, brick pillars topped with the welcoming pineapples. A tarnished brass sign was still in place on one of the pillars.

"MOUTON HOUSE MUSEUM" it read.

They left the carriage at the gate and walked onto the grounds. The front lawn was cluttered with knee-high swamp grasses and twisted weed trees and live oaks draped with frightful strands of moss.

The plantation had been abandoned for more than 150 years. It had been built in the latter part of the 18th century of the First Age as a rice plantation. No one could recall who the original owners were or why the plantation was abandoned. During its long history, it had changed hands several times and served many purposes. The last was that of a museum.

It had been built in the Greek Revival style and was considered quite elegant. Even in its current state, it looked almost grand as it stood quietly in the swamp and defied Time to finish it off.

Hunter, DuCassal and Lorena rode up to the house. When Hunter looked up at the paneless windows, images of a grand ball flashed through his mind. He stopped and tried to capture them, but the quickly slipped away. He stepped out of the carriage and looked around.

Swamp grasses and other vegetation had tried, with some success, to claim the structure. The great double doors were still on their hinges. One was slightly ajar. DuCassal and Lorena joined him as he stepped onto the veranda.

"I seem to recall this place," Hunter said as he pushed the door open.

"You should, Charles. We attended a wedding here in 1844. It was a magnificent affair, too. The bride's name was Melodie Elsbeth Harper. Since her father had been killed only a week before the wedding, Mrs. Harper asked you to give the bride away," DuCassal said as they looked around.

There were still some ancient pieces of furniture and artifacts in glass display cases. All were covered by layers of dust. The huge, marble fireplace was still intact. Above it hung a portrait of a young woman with long red hair. Hunter stared at her face and saw himself dancing with her at the party.

"Was that Melodie?" he asked.

"No. That was her mother, Louisa," DuCassal said. "That was painted when she was only 30 years old. She looked very much the same at the wedding. You danced with her that evening."

"I'm starting to remember," Hunter said.

Another image flashed through his mind. This was of a mangled corpse of a middle aged man. He was lying on his back on the steps of the house. His throat had been ripped open and he had a look of terror in his eyes. Hunter closed his eyes to capture the image, then opened them and shook his head.

"Harker Langven!" he almost growled as the name came to him.

DuCassal stared at him, then smiled.

"I have not thought of that name for centuries!" he said. "You think he is behind this?"

Hunter shrugged.

"Anything's possible, Jean-Paul," he said. "We chased that monster all over the continent and beyond for years."

"As I recall, he was the one who murdered Royce Harper when he tried to prevent Melodie's abduction. He would have taken her, too, had we not arrived seconds later," DuCassal said.

"You chased him away?" Lorena asked.

"Charles did. Langven wanted no part of him but he vowed to return to claim what was his," DuCassal said.

Hunter had a brief flash of aiming a pistol at the chest of a young woman. It went as quickly as it had appeared.

"If it is Langven, we could be in for a long night," Hunter said.

"Who *is* he/" asked Lorena.

"He is the living embodiment of the word 'monster'. He preys on young, beautiful women. He tortures and rapes them until he grows bored, then either kills them or leaves them old and withered. I don't know how many women he's done that too. He's been around for centuries," Hunter said.

"I first encountered in Romania in the year 1620. The Vatican assigned me to slay a vampire. But Langven proved to be something far worse."

He walked across the room and looked through the large broken window at the full moon.

"The last time we fought was on a night like this. When I was over, Langven was lying beneath a pile of rubble and I was barely able to stand. I sat down on a pile of debris and watched his lone hand that stuck out of the rubble. When it didn't move after several minutes, I left."

He walked back to them and smiled.

"I thought I'd killed him. I guess I was wrong," he said.

"How can you be sure it was him who sent that note?" asked Lorena.

"I can't. I just have this feeling," Hunter replied.

"And your feelings are never wrong, mon cher," she smiled.

"Now, we relax—and wait," DuCassal said as he checked his pocket watch.

As the full moon rose above the swamp, it flooded the interior of the house with a strange, ghostly light. Hunter was about to open his flask when they heard the steady, heavy footsteps echo through the house. He slipped the flask back into his pocket and motioned for Lorena and DuCassal to melt into the shadows. When they were hidden, he watched the door and waited.

The footsteps stopped. After a few seconds passed, the door creaked inward. Hunter watched as the tall, dark man entered. He walked to the middle of the room, stopped and smiled as Hunter stepped into the light.

"We meet again, Charles," he said. "It's been such a long time."

"It wouldn't have hurt my feelings at all if we'd never met again," Hunter said as they slowly circled each other. "I thought I'd killed you."

"And I thought I had killed you. It appears that we were both mistaken," Langven grinned.

"You won't be so lucky this time. This time, I promise that you *will* die," Hunter said.

"I am not certain if someone like me can actually die," Langven said.

"Everything dies," Hunter said.

"Really? Then why are *you* still here?" Langven asked.

"I'm just lucky, I guess," Hunter joked. "Just what *are* you, Langven? Are you a vampire?"

Langven shrugged.

"I am not quite sure. After so many centuries, it doesn't matter. I am. I exist and that is all that has meaning. After our last meeting in 1856, I thought I had finally rid myself of you. I left America and returned to Romania. Others like yourself, came after me. One after another after another. The last two nearly did me in. They didn't kill me, but I was so badly injured that I was forced to seek refuge inside a deep cave of the Carpathian Mountains. There, I fell into a long, deep sleep. When I woke, the entire world was in chaos. That chaos enabled me to feed, murder, and sow my seeds at will for over 1,000 years," he said.

"You mean there are others like you?" Hunter asked.

"There are hundreds. Perhaps even *thousands*. Honestly, I have never bothered to count," Langven replied smugly. "I have walked this Earth for thousands of years. I have had many brides and each has borne me a child. Some even gave themselves to me willingly. Others I took by force. In each case, I abandoned them. How my offspring turned out was of no concern to me."

The idea that there were many others like Langven roaming the Earth angered Hunter. He wondered how many were doing exactly what their father had been doing. How many generations had they spawned?

"It boggles the mind, doesn't it?" Langven asked when he saw the expression on Hunter's face.

He looked into the shadows and laughed when he made eye contact with Lorena and DuCassal.

"I see you've brought along your friends," he said. "You may as well show yourselves."

They stepped into the light. Langven studied Lorena.

"You are a vampire," he observed. "Just like the young lady I encountered in New Orleans a few weeks ago. She ruined my plans just like you did, Charles. I will make her pay *after* I settle the score with you."

He took a step toward Hunter, expecting him to flinch. Instead, Hunter stood his ground and glared at him. Langven nodded.

"In your letter you said there was something to discuss with me. What is it?" Hunter asked.

"Long ago, you took something from me. Something very precious. I wish to have it returned," Langven said. "Immediately!"

Hunter laughed.

"That was over 2,000 years ago. If I ever did have something of yours, it's long gone now," he said. "What makes you believe that *I* took whatever it was?"

"I was there when you took it! I saw you take it. Now, I want it back!" Langven almost growled as he stepped closer.

Hunter backhanded him across the face. Langven snarled and returned it with equal force and the fight was on.

Lorena and DuCassal watched as the two exchanged punches and vicious kicks. At one point, Hunter seized Langven by the arm and whirled him around and into a nearby wall with enough force to crack the ancient plaster and rain dust down on them both. Langven responded by picking Hunter up and slamming him to the floor so hard that he cracked the marble tiles. He jumped back up, pulled his revolver and fired point-blank into Langven's chest. The shots caused him to reel backward. Hunter drew the second revolver and shot him in the face. That one knocked Langven to the floor. Hunter realized that despite being shot several times, Langven wasn't bleeding and his face looked intact.

Langven leaped up, grabbed Hunter by the front of his mantle, lifted him over his head and hurled him into the wall as hard as he could. The impact brought down most of the wall and part of the ceiling and Hunter found himself buried beneath the rubble.

"Just like old times, eh, Charles?" Langven said.

"Too much like them!" Hunter said.

Langven laughed as Hunter tried to extricate himself from the pile of plaster, wood and dust. He turned and walked toward the door. Just before he could make his exit, Lorena sized his head from behind and gave it sharp, violent twist. The sound of his neck snapping echoed through the mansion as he dropped to his knees. His head was now twisted all the way past his left shoulder and the pain was incredibly intense. He glared at her.

He reached up and twisted his head back. The bones snapped and popped ominously as he winced in agony. Lorena kicked him in the face with all of her might. The kick sent him skidding across the floor and into the next room. Langven cursed vehemently the entire time, angry with himself for letting his guard down.

Hunter finally got back to his feet, then he, Lorena and DuCassal chased after Langven who was dusting himself off. His head was still leaning toward the left. He sneered at them defiantly.

That's when Lorena launched herself straight at him. She seized him by the throat, dragged him to the floor and shook him as hard as she could. Langven screamed and cursed as he tried to throw her off. In the middle of their struggle, she leaned over and sunk her fangs into his throat. She felt them penetrate his surprisingly icy flesh. When the frigid liquid in his veins entered her mouth, she recoiled in disgust and spat it out. He laughed at her reaction.

She backhanded him so hard to spun his head around to the right. Langven yowled as the pain seared through him. In all of his many battles, this was, by far, the worst injury he'd ever suffered.

Lorena stood and stepped away from him as she wiped his horrid fluid from her lips.

"That is by far, the most vile thing I have ever tasted!" she declared. "You taste like raw sewage!"

"I apologize for leaving such a bad taste in your pretty mouth, but that is what you deserve for trying to bite me," Langven said weakly as he attempted to get up.

Hunter stepped forward and sized him by the front of his coat. He dragged him to a seated position and slit his throat with the Bowie knife. The foul liquid gurgled from Langven's ruptured throat. He smiled at Hunter and placed a hand on the side of his face.

"Remember!" he whispered.

It was as if a bolt of lightning struck Hunter. He released Langven and was suddenly hurled across the room by an unseen force. He struck the wall and landed on the floor face-down. Lorena saw the smoke rising from his body and raced over to him. He was smoldering.

Langven laughed.

He fell onto his back with his arms akimbo, burst into flames, and slowly vanished from sight. Hunter managed to get to his knees. His head pounded violently now and his body tingled and ached like never before.

"Are you alright, mon cher?" Lorena asked worriedly. "I thought he had killed you!"

"I'll be alright in a few days," he said with a smile. "At least I've stopped smoking. I don't what he hit me with but it hurt like Hell."

Lorena and DuCassal helped him to his feet. They looked at the spot Langven had fallen. All they saw was a scorched outline on the floor. The room smelled like sulfur.

"Is he dead?" Lorena asked.

"I hope so but I wouldn't bet on it," Hunter said as he retrieved his hat.

"What did he say when he touched you?" DuCassal asked.

"All he said was 'remember'. Then the pain hit me and I ended up across the room on my face," Hunter said as they left the mansion. "I still have no idea what this was all about or what he wanted me to remember."

"Maybe it will come to you later, mes ami. Like a bolt from the blue," DuCassal joked.

"Please! I don't think I can handle another such bolt. That one was bad enough," Hunter said.

"You still don't know what he wanted?" Lorena asked.

"I haven't a clue," Hunter insisted. "After all this time, I don't think that matters. At least we rid Lafayette of the colonel so the people here can rest easy for a while. Let's go back to the hotel and get cleaned up. We'll try to explain this to Cal in the morning—after we figure out what happened."

He looked back at the old mansion.

"Whatever happened to Melodie?" he asked.

"She and her husband, Philippe, moved to Baton Rouge where he began his rather successful medical practice. Philippe died of a brain tumor in 1883. Melodie died in St. Louis in 1927. She never remarried as far as I know," DuCassal said.

"Did she have any children?" Hunter asked.

"None that I am aware of. I did not keep in regular contact with them after they left Lafayette," DuCassal said.

"What about the mother?" Hunter asked. "What happened to her?"

"You don't remember?" DuCassal queried.

"No," Hunter replied.

"Poor Louisa committed suicide in that very house in 1851. She hung herself from the railing of the third floor landing. Her servants found her suspended by the rope in the main hall," DuCassal said sadly.

Again the image of him pointing a pistol at a beautiful woman flashed through his mind. This time, he lowered the weapon and shook his head. The woman seemed to be begging him to kill her. Then, the image melted away.

"Why did she do it?" he asked.

"It was a sad state of affairs. Rumors began to circulate that she had become pregnant after several midnight liaisons with an unknown lover. When she realized she was with child, she told him. Instead of doing the honorable thing, he supposedly walked out on her. Rather than become the object of scorn and scandal, she did what any woman of her station would have done at that time. You and I attended her funeral. She's interred in the family vault in back of the mansion with her husband," DuCassal explained.

Hunter saw himself standing in front of Greek Revival style tomb with his head bowed as six pall bearers carried the ornate casket inside.

"I remember her funeral. Were the rumors true?" he asked.

DuCassal shrugged.

"That I cannot say, mon ami. If she was pregnant, then the unborn child was interred with her," he said.

"Then the child might have been alive in her womb at the time? That's terrible!" Lorena said.

"That was the way things were in those days," DuCassal said matter-of-factly. "Family name and honor took precedence over what was right. A scandal could actually ruin a family. Why so much interest in the Harpers, Charles?"

"I just can't shake the feeling that Langven's demands are connected to them," Hunter said. "It's another hole in my memory that I'm having trouble filling."

After explaining everything to Cal as best as they could, they took their leave of him and headed back to New Orleans. Hunter remained almost silent most of the trip as he tried to search his memories for any sort of hints that could lead him to what Langven wanted.

"What did I take from him that was so precious?" he wondered. "What did Langven want him to remember?"

He had a feeling that if he ever did find the answers to those questions, he probably wouldn't like them. He also felt that he'd not heard the last of Langven and wondered if he'd ever be able to rid the world of him.

"Don't bother yourself about it, mon cher," Lorena said. "Things always have ways of working themselves out in the end."

"Who's end? Mine or his?" Hunter asked.

"That remains to be seen, mom ami," DuCassal smiled. "Do not worry. I will be there to ensure that you have a proper burial. I think a traditional jazz funeral would be most appropriate in your case."

"Thanks. Just don't plan on arranging one for me any time soon," Hunter said as they slapped hands.

CHAPTER FOURTEEN:
When the Music Plays

Hannah was on her nightly patrol when she passed Preservation Hall. As usual, the place was packed with locals and tourists and several more were standing outside listening to the old fashioned jazz band play. She stopped to listen for a little while. They were just finishing the last few bars of *My Blue Heaven*. Without missing a beat, they segued into the *Basin Street Blues.*

A strange sensation came over Hannah. She listened until they finished the tune, they continued her patrol. For some reason, she made her way back to Bourbon Street. When she reached the corner of Bourbon and Toulouse, a blast of icy air stopped her in her tracks. She shivered and looked around. The immediate area had turned pitch black. That's when she heard the voice whisper in her ear.

"Now!"

Ten minutes later, she was standing in front of the Dragon and watching the front door. A few minutes later, Madison emerged. Her shift was over and she was heading back to her apartment. Hannah raced up to her and knocked her to the ground with her elbow. Madison stared at her.

"What did you hit me for?" she demanded.

Hannah glared at her and drew her katana. In a voice that sent child up Madison's spine she said:

"It's time, bitch!"

Madison jumped to her feet and took off down the avenue. Hannah raced after her. Madison ran down alleys, leaped over fences and even scaled walls in an attempt to get away, but Hannah stayed right on her heels the entire time.

Frustrated and angry, Madison decided that she'd had enough of this game. She stopped and faced her tormentor.

"Okay, bitch! Since you want a fight so badly, I'll give you one!" she almost growled.

Hannah grinned and bared her fangs.

Madison emitted an almost diabolical laugh and tossed aside her cloak. Her eyes took on a bright amber gleam and her pupils narrowed into dark slits like a cat's. She twitched and snarled as her fingernails extended slowly into long, hooked claws and her fangs elongated until they extended halfway down her chin.

Hannah realized that Madison wasn't just a vampire. She was something different. Something strange and terrible.

And deadly.

She stopped and raised her katana, then went into her defensive stance. Madison hissed, crouched and sprung at her. Hannah dodged beneath her leap and swung the katana. To her shock, the blade sent off sparks when it struck Madison's body. Madison landed on her feet, turned suddenly and leaped again. This time, she managed to knock Hannah off balance and send her to the ground. But Hannah managed to roll away from her next two strikes and come back up, ready to fight.

As their battle raged, Madison began to look less and less human.

The sounds of their struggle echoed through the almost empty streets of the French Quarter and caught the attention of Alejandro who had just exited his favorite bar on Burgundy. Curious, he hurried toward the sounds. When he reached Dauphine, he saw Hannah engaged in what appeared to be the fight of her life against a creature that made his blood run cold.

Without hesitating, he tossed aside his cape, mask and hat and morphed into his rougarou persona. He entered the fray just as Madison decked Hannah with a swipe of her powerful claws. The blow tore Hannah's shirt and splattered her blood everywhere. Madison crouched and leaped at Hannah, intending to finish her off. Alejandro also leapt. He seized Madison around the neck, twisted around in mid-air and brought her to the pavement with him. She kicked free, jumped to her feet and snarled at him as he positioned himself between her and Hannah.

"I've no quarrel with you, Alejandro," Madison growled.

"Madison?" he asked.

Before he could react, she knocked him to the ground with a kick to the chest then took off down the street. She ran so fast that she was out of sight by the time he got back on his feet.

He reverted to human form and scratched his head. He turned to help Hannah only to discover that she, too, had left the scene.

He retrieved his clothes and headed down to Bourbon Street. The brief battle had worked up a thirst. He decided he look up both ladies the next morning to find out what had happened.

As Madison's heartbeat slowed to its normal rate, she returned to her human form. She felt achy and exhausted. The transformations always drained her. As she walked back to her apartment on Conti, she hoped that she didn't do too much damage to Hannah.

Hannah limped back to her shop and forced herself to climb the stairs to her apartment. He clothes were ripped in several places and she was still bleeding from the wounds on her stomach, back and left thigh.

Ten minutes later, the bleeding stopped and the wounds slowly faded. It would take several days for the deeper ones to completely heal. She peeled off what remained of her outfit and tossed it into a trash basket as she prepared to shower. Before she stepped under the warm water, she glanced in the mirror.

She stared as a dark figure appeared in the glass and turned. There was no one behind her at all, but she sensed a presence. Something foul and unspeakably evil. Then she heard a voice whisper in her ear.

"Better luck next time," he said.

"There won't *be* a next time if I can help it," she said.

That's when she heard the sinister laughter and realized it would be another long and painful night.

When Alejandro dropped in on her the next morning, he noticed that she was moving especially slowly.

"You look terrible this morning," he remarked.

"I feel much worse than I look. Thanks for coming to my rescue last night. You really saved my neck out there," she said. "It's my fault, I guess. I heard that tune at Preservation Hall and everything went red. The next thing I knew, I was chasing after Madison. I wanted to kill her, Alejandro. I couldn't stop myself."

"Are you still suffering from the effect of the battle?" he asked.

"No. That bastard returned. He beat me then he raped me. Just as he's done every night for the past two weeks. I can't do anything about it, either. I can only lay there and take it. I guess it's his way of showing me that he's the boss. I don't even dress for bed now. I just lay there with my legs apart and let him use me," she said as she choked back her tears.

"Oh, God, Alejandro! I just want it to stop! I want this freaking nightmare to end!" she sobbed.

They heard the bell above the door tinkle as someone entered the shop. They watched as a very anxious looking Madison walked up to them.

"Thank God, you're alright! I thought I'd mortally wounded you last night," she said as she hugged Hannah.

"I'm so very sorry I tried to kill you," Hannah bawled. "So, so sorry!"

"It wasn't your fault. It's that bastard Fink's. We have to find a way to break his hold on you before one or both of us gets killed," Madison said.

"Perhaps we should go and speak with Minerva?" Alejandro suggested.

When they arrived at the temple, they found Hunter, Lorena, DuCassal and Tony seated in the parlor, sipping tea and laughing. The room grew quiet when they walked in. Minerva smiled.

"We were just discussing what happened last night," she said.

"Already?" Hannah asked.

"News travels like lightning through this city. You know that," Minerva replied as they sat down.

Alejandro explained what happened and why they had come. Minerva simply nodded as she stirred her tea and sipped from time-to-time.

"I'll have to try an exorcism. One more powerful than any I've ever tried before," she said.

"Will you need to strap me down or something?" asked Hannah.

"Definitely," Minerva said. "For your own safety and *mine*."

"How dangerous is this?" Hunter asked.

"Very. We'll need someplace she can't escape from, like a strong iron cage," Minerva said.

"You can use the cage in the basement of the Sultan's Bar," Tony offered. "Those bars are good and thick."

The Sultan, as he now called it, was Tony's second biggest bar. Two years earlier, Hunter and Lorena had to rid it of a very malevolent spirit.[3]

---

3   Read: Hunter: Nightmare in New Orleans

"I don't know about that, Tony. The negative energy and anger might reopen some old wounds and force us to do another cleansing," Hunter said.

"I could have my craftsmen construct such a cage inside one of my warehouses," DuCassal offered.

"Aren't you afraid of the negative energy being set loose there?" Lorena asked.

He shrugged.

"Not at all. The place is already haunted. A little more negative energy won't make much of a difference," he said.

"How soon can your men build it?" asked Hunter.

"Two, perhaps three days. I'll have them work around the clock," DuCassal said.

"Let's do this," Hunter agreed.

Two days later, DuCassal walked over to Hunter's house and knocked on the front door. Hunter opened it.

"It's done," DuCassal said.

They climbed into his carriage and drove over to the Emporium. When Hannah saw them enter, she nodded. She knew why they had come and she knew it was something she needed to do. She closed the store and they drove over to the Temple. Minerva was waiting in the parlor with six small white bags tied with long, golden strings.

"I've been expecting you," she said as she handed each of them a gris-gris bag and a St. Anthony medal.

"Put these on and keep them on until I say it's safe to take them off," she instructed. "This should prevent Fink's spirit from possessing one of us during the ceremony."

"You make this sound dangerous," Lorena said as she donned the amulets.

"More than you know, child," Minerva said. "When we trip Hannah's trigger, almost anything can happen. This won't be pretty and I promise that you'll never forget it."

"How long will this take, Minerva?" Hannah asked.

"As long as necessary," Minerva said.

"Will it work?" Hannah asked.

"I don't know. I've never tried anything like this before," Minerva said. "If it doesn't, Hunter can always kill you."

"Now *that's* comforting!" Hannah said.

"In that case, you better hope this works," Hunter said.

They drove over to the old warehouse. DuCassal told his men to leave for the day and escorted them to the back room. A large, heavy iron cage stood in the middle of the floor. There was a heavy, leather padded platform in the cage with several thick straps attached to each side.

"Shall we?" Hunter asked.

He, Hannah and DuCassal entered the cage. Hannah laid down on the platform and took a deep breath and exhaled as Hunter and DuCassal strapped her down. They turned and left the cage.

Minerva nodded and stepped inside. DuCassal locked the cage door behind her and stepped back with the others.

Minerva opened her satchel. She took out a clear glass bottle and a cork. She then shoved a mandrake root and a chicken bone wrapped with a black ribbon into it. When this was done, she added several other ingredients and filled it one third of the way with holy water she had gotten from the Cathedral. She handed the bottle and the stopper to Hunter.

"My basic spirit trap. I just made it a lot stronger. When I say cork it, do it fast," she explained.

"Why me?" Hunter asked.

"You're the strongest. Fink won't be able to possess you because your will is like steel. If I do this right, he'll have no other place to go but into the bottle," Minerva said.

"How will we know if it didn't work?" asked DuCassal.

"You'll know when you see me run out of this place as fast as I can go," Minerva answered.

She took out a set of handcuffs and ankle cuffs and placed them on Hannah. After she was certain they were secure, she handed the keys to Lorena.

"Now, everybody out of the cage," she said. "As soon as you're all outside, I want you to lock me inside with Hannah. No matter what you see or hear, don't interfere. Don't open this cage or disrupt the ceremony in any way. Understand?"

They all nodded and left. Hunter looked back at Hannah.

"Good luck," he said.

She made Hannah lie down on the floor. When she was in the right spot, Minerva drew a circle around her with sea salt. She then placed four candles, one for each direction of the compass, on the line and uttered a spell. They watched as the candles suddenly flickered to life. Minerva then took out a vial of sacred oil and drew a cross on Hannah's forehead. The oil sizzled ominously and Hannah moaned.

Minerva smiled.

Now she was sure Fink was inside of her. She didn't detect him earlier because he was hidden behind the strong persona of Jeromy Flowers which partially kept him at bay. The moment she'd expelled Flowers, Fink took over and Hannah's long nightmare began in earnest.

Minerva took out four Guinea peppers, licked each of them, and placed one next to each candle. As she did, she made the sign of the cross and prayed. This done, she took a bottle of rum from the satchel, uncorked it and took a long swig. She corked the bottle and placed it next to the candle that was on the northern part of the circle. She also took out a cigar, placed it into her mouth, lit it and puffed until the end glowed a deep red. She placed this next to the rum.

These were offerings to Baron Samete to invoke his protection. Now, she was ready to begin the long ritual.

She raised her hands high above her head and prayed. As she prayed, beads of sweat appeared on her forehead and her voice grew quivery and hoarse. She prayed for what seemed like an eternity as she petitioned the Baron to lend her the power she needed to drive the evil from Hannah's body.

An hour dragged by.

Then a second.

Hannah trembled uncontrollably and bled from her eyes, ears, nose and mouth and other orifices. The bleeding started as a light trickle and gradually grew more profuse. It dripped to the floor and mingled with Hannah's sweat as she writhed and groaned and cursed at the tops of her lungs. Now, deep red welts began to appear on her body. As each welt appeared, she screamed and begged it to stop.

But the ritual continued.

Minerva was also bathed with perspiration. Her knees trembled. Her head ached and her throat was getting dry. She was beginning to feel weaker and weaker but she forced herself to continue, despite having a nearly overpowering desire to flee from the cage.

Outside the cage, the others were also covered with sweat as the negative energies bombarded them relentlessly. Even Lorena perspired— something that vampires don't normally do.

By then, Hannah lay quivering in a poll of sticky muck and she slipped into a strange, almost surreal form on consciousness. She was now oblivious to the pain and everything else that was happening inside her body and she began to feel colder and colder as her body grew numb.

Minerva senses that Fink's spirit was on the verge of being expelled from Hannah's body. She reached into her satchel, took out a small box filled with red powder and blew it all over Hannah. It spread out in a filmy red cloud then slowly settled onto Hannah. She screamed and bounced violently up and down as the powder covered her and her body took on a bright orange glow. Minerva said another prayer and raised her hands above her head as she called up all of the voodoo deities to help her rid Hannah's body of the evil inside. Gradually, almost fitfully, a small ball of dull yellow light emerged from Hannah's chest. It hovered above her as she fell still. Minerva seized the ball and hurled it at Hunter. It stopped about two feet in front of him, hovered a few seconds, and then slowly entered the bottle.

"Now!" Minerva shouted.

Hunter slammed the cork into the bottle and held it up. The mandrake root took on a dull green glow and he felt a strange vibration through the thick glass.

Minerva stumbled to the door of the cage. DuCassal unlocked it and she collapsed into his arms. She was trembling all over.

On the floor behind her, Hannah lay quiet.

DuCassal helped Minerva to a nearby chair and handed her a flask of water. She drank deeply and wiped her lips with the back of her hand.

"Look like we bagged him, Minerva," Hunter said as he held up the bottle.

Lorena rushed into the cage, uncuffed Hannah's wrists and ankles and cradled her in her arms. She was sound asleep.

"She's alive!" Lorena called out.

"Of course she is, child," Minerva said with a smile. "Now, let's finish that bastard off."

She led Hunter and DuCassal out to the carriage and climbed in. Hunter handed her the bottle. She smile d and placed it in the pocket of her apron.

"Are we going to throw the bottle into the bay?" DuCassal asked.

"Not this time. I need to make sure this monster won't bother us again. Take us to the morgue," she said.

"The morgue?" DuCassal asked.

"You heard me, Jean-Paul," Minerva said.

He leaned out the window.

"Take us to the morgue, George," he said to the driver.

When they reached the morgue, the night man, Mark Colter, greeted them at the door.

"What can I do for you?" he asked as they walked in.

"We need a recent unclaimed corpse," Minerva said. "You have anyone like that here?"

"Sure. We got an unclaimed. He was found last night near Bayou St. John," he said as he led them over to one of the drawers.

"We figured that a couple of 'gators nailed him. He's pretty chewed up and there was no ID on him and nobody's tried to claim him. So if you need him, he's all yours," Mark said as he slid the drawer out.

"Wrap him up, Mark, We'll take him with us," Minerva said.

Mark shoved the body into a large burlap sack. Hunter picked it up and tossed it into the trunk of the carriage. Minerva looked at the driver and told him to drive to City Park. Once there, they stopped in a large open field. Hunter dragged the body out of the trunk and placed it on the ground. He used his Bowie knife to slash open the sack.

"He'll do," Minerva said. "Now, slit him open. I need to shove this bottle inside the body."

Hunter nodded and slashed the body open from neck to stomach. The air became filled with noxious gases and the pungent aroma of rotting flesh. Minerva shoved the bottle as far into the corpse as possible then uttered a prayer over it.

"Burn it," she instructed. "Make sure there's nothing left."

Hunter doused it with two bottles of sacred oil and ignited it. They watched as the flames quickly consumed the entire body and the black smoke rose high into the night sky. After about 20 minutes, they heard the glass shatter. This was followed by a loud, mournful scream that echoed through the entire park for several minutes before it faded away.

They waited until the flames died down. Minerva walked over and kicked at the ashes. Nothing but a few bone fragments remained. There was no sign of the bottle.

"He's gone," she announced.

"Are you certain?" DuCassal asked.

She smiled.

"Have I ever lied to you before?" she joked.

They pulled up in front of the warehouse just as Lorena was helping an obviously worn out Hannah through the door. Hannah smiled at Minerva as she climbed aboard the carriage.

"Thanks, Minerva," she said in a shaky voice. "Damn! I feel like I could sleep for an entire month! I've never felt so tired in my life."

"Perhaps a late dinner at Broussard's will help restore your strength?" DuCassal suggested.

Hannah smiled.

"Sounds great, Jean-Paul. I'm also famished," she said as she sat down beside him.

She fell asleep the second her head touched the cushion.

CHAPTER FIFTEEN:
That Voodoo That You do

It was a rainy Tuesday afternoon. Valmonde had just finished his po' boy and chased it down with a glass of sweet tea when a wet, puffing David Knight walked into his office. David was the janitor at the Maison Dupuy on Toulouse. He'd been there for at least 35 years and wasn't given to flights of fantasy.

"What can I do for you, Dave?" Valmonde asked.

"There's been a death at the hotel, Leon," David replied. "I found the body not ten minutes ago in the courtyard."

"One of your guests?" Valmonde asked.

"No. A guy from the neighborhood named Luther Terry," David said. "I found him face-down next to the pool."

Valmonde grabbed his hat. He and David jumped into his carriage and rode over to the hotel. David led him through the lobby and out the back door into the courtyard. Kyle Harris, the hotel manager, was standing next to the body with an umbrella. He nodded when Valmonde walked over.

"That's Luther alright," Valmonde said. "He lives over on Royal and Marigny with his girlfriend, Amy Dawes. How'd he get here?"

"Be damned if I know, Leon," Kyle said.

Valmonde turned him over and winced at the poll of blood beneath the body. He looked up at the second floor gallery.

"Looks like he fell," he said. "Or jumped."

"A suicide?" Kyle asked. "Why would he do that? He seemed to have everything going good for him lately."

Valmonde shrugged as he went through the man's pockets. He found an envelope in his left inside jacket pocket addressed "To the police."

Valmonde opened it.

After he read the first paragraph, he turned as white as a sheet.

"Dear God!" he remarked as he began to sweat.

"What's wrong, Leon?" asked Kyle. "You don't look so good right now."

"You wouldn't either if you saw what's in this note," Valmonde said. "You boys keep an eye on the body. I'm goin' to fetch Hunter."

Kyle and David watched as Valmonde hurried back to his carriage and drove off. They looked at each other then back down at the body.

"What do you suppose was in that letter?" asked David.

"I don't know but it sure scared the shit out of Leon," Kyle said.

Valmonde rode up to Hunter's house in the Garden District an hour later. Hunter, Lorena and DuCassal were on the front porch drinking wine. They stopped and watched as Valmonde climbed up the stairs and sat down in the empty chair.

"What's up, Chief?" Hunter asked.

"A possible murder-suicide," Valmonde said.

"Anyone we know?" Lorena asked.

"Luther Terry," Valmonde said.

"I know that name," Hunter said. "Why bring it to us?"

"Because of this note Terry had on him," Valmonde replied as he handed him the folded paper. "It just doesn't make sense."

"I offered my life to make amends for the life I took. I'm sorry, Amy. You didn't deserve to die like that. No one does. Please forgive me. I just couldn't stop myself."

Hunter handed it back to Valmonde.

"Amy?" he asked.

"His live-in girlfriend," Valmonde explained. "They were both musicians. They were well-known in the clubs on Frenchman. They played rock mostly."

Hunter nodded.

He'd seen them perform a couple of times at local festivals. They were inventive and liked to play heavy, dark rock. The last time he'd seen them perform was at the Creole Food Festival on Decatur a month earlier. He noticed then that their usually bleak music had taken a more decidedly darker tone.

"I see why you came to us," he said.

"Those two were just about at the top of their popularity. They had everything goin' for them," Valmonde said. "This just doesn't make sense."

"Murder-suicides don't have to make sense, especially if passions are involved, Chief," Lorena said. "Perhaps an argument got out of control?"

"Or maybe he caught his girlfriend with another man and confronted her about it?" DuCassal added.

"We can stand here and make speculations all night. That won't get us the answers we need," Hunter said. "Let's go check out the hotel. After that, I want to search their apartment. If he killed Amy, there has to be a body someplace."

"I'll send Lem and Sam on over to their apartment to check it out and secure it before we get there," Valmonde said. "We don't need any nosey neighbors snoopin' around and messin' things up."

After checking out Terry's suicide scene at the hotel, they decided to head over to the apartment. It wasn't exactly in a nicer part of town and the building was very old, run down and the windows and the doors of the lower floor were boarded up.

"They lived in the apartment upstairs," Valmonde said as he led them around to the back.

There was a flight of wooden steps that led up to a gallery that was virtually covered with potted plants. Hunter noticed that most were of the variety that most local musicians liked to smoke.

Lem greeted them as they approached the front door.

"This is the most god-awful crime scene I've ever been to in my whole life," he said. "When you sent us over here, Chief, we never expected to see anything like *this!*"

He opened the door and they stepped inside.

The entire apartment reeked of incense mixed with decaying flesh and flies seemed to be everywhere. Lem nodded at the two large pots on the stove.

"You ain't going to believe what's in those!" he said.

Hunter walked over and picked up the lid from the largest pot. Inside was a soupy, oily muck with chunks of meat floating in it. He grabbed a ladle from the nearby sink and raked it through the muck. He just about jumped when he pulled up a very boiled-looking human hand. One finger still had a ring around it.

Hunter dropped it back into the pot and shook his head. He then took the lid off the second pot and looked inside. He stepped back to allow DuCassal, Lorena and Valmonde to have a look.

"Mother of God! That's a human head!" Valmonde exclaimed in disgust.

"It looks as if it has been boiled for several hours. Most of the flesh is peeled off," DuCassal said as he fought off the urge to puke.

"It's the head of a woman—or was," Hunter said.

"Have a look inside the oven, Chief," Sam suggested.

Valmonde pulled the door open and reeled back as the aroma of rotted flesh suddenly permeated the entire room. Hunter looked inside and saw the upper half of a woman's torso lying on the grate. It was charred but still recognizable.

"Cannibalism?" he asked.

"I don't know what this is, Hunter," Valmonde said. "I've never in my life seen anythin' like this."

"And that's saying a lot for New Orleans," Hunter said as they walked to the large refrigerator. "Want to be the rest of her is inside?" he asked as he grabbed the handle and pulled the door open.

They stood and stared at the arms, thighs, lower torso and other body parts that filled the entire appliance. Hunter noticed something shiny on top of it. He reached up and took down a bloody hacksaw.

"Now we know what he did it with," he said. "The question is, was she still alive at the time?"

The others gaped at him in disbelief.

"That's the sickest thing I ever heard!" Valmonde said. "I sure as Hell hope she wasn't alive. If she was, this would be one of the most brutal crimes in the entire history of New Orleans."

Hunter nodded.

"Now we know for sure that Terry murdered his girlfriend—and why he committed suicide," Valmonde said.

"But most of the pieces are still missing," Hunter said. "We don't know why he killed her or why he cut her into pieces and cooked her like he did. Even if he killed her in a drunken rage or the heat of an argument, that doesn't explain why he did these things to her afterward. Was Terry known to use drugs or alcohol?"

"Hell, he was a musician. They *all* drink and use drugs here. It goes with the territory. But I've never known anyone to go off the deep end like *this*," Valmonde said as they stepped outside onto the gallery.

'Nor have I, Charles," DuCassal added. "And I have lived here for centuries."

Hunter leaned over the rail and saw that the windows of the lower floor were boarded up.

"What was in the lower part of the building?" he asked.

"Beats the Hell out of me, Hunter. This place has been boarded up like that ever since I can remember," Valmonde replied.

"Is it important?" Lorena asked.

"Perhaps," Hunter said. "Let's check the records at the Cathedral."

"I'll have my men search the apartment from top to bottom. I'll make sure they don't miss a thing—even if they have to tear up the walls and floors," Valmonde said. "First, I'd better have the boys from the coroner's office come over and cart out the body parts. Maybe the Doc can tell us how she really died."

"Too bad she doesn't have much left to work with," Hunter said as they walked downstairs.

He stopped in the middle of the street and looked back at the building. Even the boards over the windows were rotted from age weather.

"This looks familiar somehow," he said. "I feel like I've been here before."

"It seems familiar to me as well, Charles. But for the life of me, I can't recall what was here before. Maybe we'll find something in the archives?" DuCassal said as they walked to Valmonde's carriage.

Father Paul was carrying out the trash when they pulled up in DuCassal's carriage. He dumped the bundle into a trash can and greeted them. He saw the expression on Hunter's face and nodded.

"I take it that this isn't a social call?" he asked as they walked into the Cathedral.

"Not hardly, Hunter said. "What can you tell us about the old building at 307 Marigny?"

"Make yourselves comfortable while I check the real estate records. How far back do you want me to go?" Paul asked.

"To the year the place was built," Hunter replied.

"There's some whiskey in my desk drawer. Help yourselves. This might take a little while," Paul said as he went down to vault.

He returned an hour later with several notes he had scribble onto a yellow pad.

"I think I have what you're looking for," he said as he sat down behind his desk. "That house is one of the oldest in the entire city."

"How old is it?" asked Lorena.

"According to this, the house was built in 1760 by Louis Marquand LeSec. He and his family occupied the property until the yellow fever epidemic in 1817 killed the entire family.

It was then sold at auction and converted to a voodoo temple the following year with an apartment above. It doesn't say who purchased it. It was done through a third party proxy. He was a local attorney named Guy Fashion," Father Paul said.

"Anything else?" Hunter asked.

"The register is bank until 1896. That's when the city, for whatever reasons, changed the numbers on every house in the city. Then it became 708 Marigny and was owned by James Ruthermen and his wife, Marie until 1955.

Hey. Here's something interesting. And kind of ironic in a way," Paul said.

"What?" Hunter asked.

"That place became a voodoo temple once again in 1958 and remained active until the monster hurricane of 2005 almost wiped out the city. According to this, it's been vacant ever since," Paul said.

"That *is* interesting How did Terry get hold of it?" Hunter asked.

"He probably claimed it under the city's old squatter laws. Lots of people do that. It's legal to occupy an abandoned building as long as you go through the expense of restoring it. After five years, the city inspector comes out to examine the building. If he decides you've done a good job, he signs it over to you free and clear. If not, he has the police evict you and the house goes up for auction," Paul explained. "That law's been on the books here forever."

"Is there anything that says Terry was the legal owner?" Hunter asked.

"Not a thing," Paul said. "It was due to be inspected this summer. I guess Bill Whitten hasn't gotten around to it yet."

Whitten was the only city inspector. He was nearly 80 years old but still spry and sharp. And he took his job seriously.

Hunter wondered if Whitten would have approved Terry's kitchen. He also wondered why Terry never bothered with the lower floor of the house. Or did he?

"Who ran the last temple?" he asked.

"Naomi Trinidad-Mays," Paul said as he reread the ledger.

"What happened to her?" DuCassal asked. "After Hurricane Katrina, I never saw her again."

"I keep forgetting how old you two are," Paul smiled. "Nearly 1,600 people perished in that hurricane. Many were never found, so they never got a proper burial or send off. My guess is that Naomi was among those unfortunate souls."

"Naomi was from the Caribbean, Charles. She practiced as slightly different type of voodoo than we do here. I recall that she was a generally pleasant woman with a great, wide and infectious smile. But she also had a very quick temper and did not forgive anyone who she believed wronged her in any way," DuCassal said.

"But that's not why the house looks familiar. There's something else there, Charles. Something very old and dark. I know that you sensed it, too," he added.

"Maybe it's still there, mon cher. Perhaps that's what drove Terry to murder his girlfriend?" Lorena suggested.

"Or it may be a combination of things," Hunter said.

He looked at Paul and shook his hands.

"Thanks for the help, Paul," he said. "It's been an interesting afternoon."

"Glad I could help," Paul said as he closed the ledger and escorted them outside.

They looked up at the darkening sky.

"Looks like we're in for another storm," Paul said.

"Or something worse," Hunter said.

They decided to walk back to the Basin Street station to see if Valmonde had turned up anything else in his search of the apartment. They found him seated behind his desk shaking his head as leafed through a black, leather book.

"What's that?" asked Hunter as he sat down across from him.

"It's Terry's diary. It's just about the sickest thing I ever read in my entire life, too," Valmonde said as he slid the diary to him.

Hunter opened it and almost blanched. He could hardly believe what he was reading. Terry gave detailed descriptions of everything he'd done to Amy on the night of the murder. It seems they'd been drinking heavily most the night when Amy "decided" to start an argument.

"One thing led to another and next thing I knew, my hands were around her neck and I was choking the Hell out of her. I knew I was doing it. I tried to stop but something inside of me wouldn't let me. My, God! That wasn't me! That wasn't me! Why couldn't I stop?"

"It sounds like something had possessed him," DuCassal said.

"But what?" Hunter asked as he kept reading.

The more he read, the more disgusted he became.

Terry wrote how he had taken Amy's clothes off and placed her in their bed. Then, after drinking very heavily each night, he had sex with her corpse several times over the next week.

"One day, I woke up and realized that she was making the house smell awful. I knew I had to do something. I didn't want anybody to know what I did. I didn't want to get caught and be sent to Angola. I had to get rid of her. I knew I couldn't just take her out and bury here somewhere. Somebody might see me and tell the cops. As I sat there drinking Scotch and looking at her, something came over me again. I got my hacksaw and cut her into pieces. Then everything went black.

When I came to, I saw that two pots were on the stove and they were boiling away. The room smelled like cooking meat. I went to the stove and looked into the pots. That's when I heard that weird laugh inside my head.

I turned off the stove and knew my life was over. I had to make amends for this horrible crime. Forgive me, Amy! I didn't mean to kill you. But that wasn't me! It wasn't me! Dear God! What have I done? I have to make amends. I have to do something before I kill anyone else. God help me!"

Hunter shook his head.

"He goes on to say why he decided to commit suicide. Something about it was the only right thing to do. The only way to beat the thing that was inside of him. He was either demonically possessed or totally insane," he said as he put the diary down.

"I did notice one thing that struck me kind of odd," Valmonde said. "If you look at the handwriting on the first few pages of the diary, you'll see that it's a lot different from the rest. It's like two different people wrote it."

"Two very different people," Hunter agreed. "The last few pages were written by someone who had a lot of anger inside of him."

"Now what? This case is closed as far as my department is concerned," Valmonde said.

"I want to check out that abandoned temple. I think Terry not only entered it, but he found something that wasn't meant to be found. We'd better bring Minerva with us, too. If voodoo is involved, she should be able to tell us how to deal with it."

"Do you think Terry actually would have eaten Amy?" DuCassal asked.

"Can you think of a better way to dispose of a body?" Hunter asked.

"Now *that's* revoltin'!" Valmonde said.

An hour later, Hunter, Lorena and DuCassal walked into the voodoo temple on Chartres. As usual, Minerva was seated at the table in the front parlor, stirring her tea. She smiled as they sat down and helped themselves to the spice cookies.

"What can I do you for today?" she asked.

Hunter explained what they'd just seen.

Minerva looked at him.

"That place is cursed," she said. "Royally and truly. It reeks of dark magic. It's in every board, every single brick and nail."

"What do you know about it?" Hunter asked.

"Terry wasn't the first one to go mad in that place. About forty years ago, so I was told, a young woman from up north tried to restore that place. She spent one month there and left in the middle of the night. Nobody knows where she went.

After her was a middle aged man who wanted to turn the place into a bar. The police found him hanging from a tree in City Park three weeks later. They said he committed suicide," Minerva said.

"Interesting," Hunter said. "Anyone else?"

"Not that I know about. You know how it is with abandoned buildings in New Orleans. All kinds of transients, some good, some bad, use them for temporary shelters. Luther Terry and Amy were the last who tried to restore it. They were there for a long time, too. At first, I thought the place wasn't cursed. And maybe the other things were just coincidental. Then I found out what happened. Now, I *know* it's cursed," Minerva said.

"But by what?" Hunter asked.

"To learn that, I'd have to go there," Minerva said. "But it has to at the time of day when the spirits are weakest of at the height of a full moon. That's the time when all the channels to the spirit world are wide open."

"That won't be for another week," DuCassal said.

"Six days, to be exact," Minerva said. "In the meantime, I'll do some research on that house. It has a very long, dark history—like most places do in New Orleans. I might find mention of it in some of these old books of mine."

"Happy hunting," Hunter smiled.

"Thanks. I'll let you know if I find out anything," Minerva said as she escorted them to the door. "Watch your backs," she warned as she shut it behind them.

They stepped into the busy street and watched the crowds of tourists explore the city.

"Some things never change, eh, mon ami?" DuCassal said.

"Especially here in New Orleans," Hunter agreed. "The city's always been a big magnet for travelers. Some of them even stay here because New Orleans gets into their blood or they find something here they've always sought. Some return over and over again. And a few even end up dead. It's strange, mystical, magnificent, timeless and downright dangerous, but people still go out of their way to come here."

"And some of us even come back to stay," DuCassal smiled.

Hunter laughed.

"I know that I'm never going to leave this city," Lorena said. "New Orleans is home now. It always will be home."

"I doubt these good people would allow us to leave even if we wanted to," DuCassal said. "When they see us walking around, it gives them a sense of security. Even the vampires like having us here."

Hunter laughed and slapped him on the back.

"And that is a bit of irony that must be driving the Cardinal crazy!" he said.

Two a.m.

It was a clear, somewhat cool night. Hunter was out on his usual nightly patrol through the French Quarter. He walked down Chartres past the Cabildo and the Cathedral and turned left on St. Ann. When he crossed Royal, a heavy mist began to roll in from the river. By the time he reached Dauphine, the only things he could see were the dull gleaming lights from the street lamps.

He stopped at the corner and waited.

Before long, a familiar woman dressed in a white blouse, long blue skirt and wearing a blue scarf around her shoulders, emerged from the mist. She stopped in front of him and smiled.

"Good evening, Marie," he said as he doffed his hat.

"Good evening, Hunter. I've been expecting you," she replied. "You want to know more about a certain house on Marigny, don't you?"

"Right as usual, Marie. It has a long, dark and now bloody history. I need to know what's inside," he replied.

"What is inside is a evil you can't even imagine. That house was cursed a long time ago and we *both* knew the one who cursed it," she said as they walked together.

"You mean Flowers? Jeromy Flowers?" he asked.

She nodded.

"It was he who built that place and made it into his private voodoo temple. He had it all done through a third party proxy while he was in prison. It was there he learned a different kind of voodoo. A dark voodoo. He had several followers, too. Most of them disappeared. The rumors going around at that time were horrific. Some even accused Flowers of using his followers for human sacrifices in black masses. Some accused him of boiling and eating their organs and burying their remains somewhere beneath the house," she said. "If ever evil took on a human face, Flowers was that face."

"But there was another voodoo temple there in the 20th century," Hunter said.

"And she also practiced that same dark voodoo. That ran in the family," Marie said.

"Family?" Hunter asked.

Before he could blink, both Marie Laveau and the mist were gone.

Hunter shook his head.

"Marie said it ran in the family," he thought. "Was Naomi Trinidad-Mays *related* to Flowers? Looks like it's time to see Father Paul again."

The next morning, Hunter, Lorena and DuCassal walked over to the Cathedral. They arrived just as Father Paul returned from an early breakfast. He greeted them with his usual warmth and led them inside.

Hunter explained what had happened. Paul whistled.

"I suppose it's possible," he said. "I don't know if we have anything on her in the archives but you're free to look."

They headed down to the vault and spent the next few hours going through the ancient ledgers. They found a small note that stated Mrs. Naomi Trinidad-Mays, a native of Port Au Prince, Haiti, had purchased the crumbling building on May 12, 1959. She also obtained a license that same day to open and operate the property as a place of worship.

There were no birth records or any other information on her.

"Just as I expected," Hunter said in frustration. "If we want to learn anything at all about her lineage, we'd have to go to Haiti."

"I doubt we'd find anything there either, mon ami," DuCassal said. "Even when there was an actual government running that place, they weren't very good at keeping records of any sort. Such a trip would be a complete waste of time."

Hunter nodded.

"Unless Minerva can come up with something, we're at a dead end," he said.

At ten the next morning, they drove up to the temple in DuCassal's carriage. As usual, the cookies, cakes and tea were set out on the table. Minerva smiled pleasantly as they sat down and helped themselves.

"Anything?" asked Hunter.

"I think the best way for me to understand what's in that place is to go there myself and try to make contact with it," she said.

"Alright. When do want to go?" he asked as he nibbled on a spice cake.

"Right now," she said. "I want to contact whatever's there while they are at their weakest. So morning is best."

Hunter nodded.

They finished their snack and climbed into the carriage. Thirty minutes later, they pulled up in front of the building. Minerva jumped out first and closed her eyes. The others climbed out after her and waited while she concentrated.

She blinked and looked at Hunter.

"I can't sense anything from out here. Do you have the keys?" she asked.

Hunter produced the keys he'd gotten from Valmonde and opened the rusted lock. As the door swung open to admit a beam of sunlight, they watched the dust particles sparkle within it until their eyes adjusted to the dim light. Minerva nodded and they walked inside.

The main room contained and ancient altar that was covered with dust-covered statues and other voodoo paraphernalia. On a shelf to the left were jars of various shapes and sizes and some strange bottles. Several large, leather bound books lay atop a nearby table. One was opened.

"This is a voodoo temple alright," Minerva said as they walked around.

"You mean was, don't you?" DuCassal asked.

She shook her head.

"I mean *is*. Once a temple always a temple," she said as she stepped toward the book.

As she reached for it, the pages ruffled and the ancient cover slammed shut. She jumped back and stretched out her hand. Then she suddenly drew it back as if someone had slapped it.

"I sense the presence of *bokun*," Minerva said after a few seconds.

"What are bokun?" asked Lorena as she felt a sudden chill in the room.

"Spirits who were summoned from the other side," Minerva said.

"For what purpose?" Hunter asked.

"They have several purposes. It depends on who summoned them and what that person had in mind. You might call them *soldiers*. They can be guardians or they can be sent to punish someone. They can even kill them if they are strong enough," Minerva explained.

"Are they good or evil?" asked DuCassal.

"Both and neither. When kept under tight control, they are neutral. But if left unfettered and to their own devices, things can get interesting. Bokun like to feed off the psychic energies of human beings. They especially enjoy strife and anger and they can stir it up and intensify it," Minerva said as they continued to walk around.

"Are they responsible for what Terry did to his girlfriend?" Lorena asked.

"Definitely," Minerva replied.

"How many are here now?" asked Hunter.

"At least ten. Perhaps more. I can sense them all around us. They're watching us, trying to get a reading on us to see if they can use our energies to grow stronger. Don't let your guards down. Not even for a second," Minerva warned.

"Can you make contact? Find out why they're here?" Hunter asked.

"Perhaps indirectly," Minerva said after some thought.

"What do you mean?" Hunter asked.

"If I try to directly contact the bokun, I'll have to let my guard down. That will put me in a battle for my soul. These bokun have been in this house for *centuries*, Hunter. They are very old and very powerful. I might lose. I can't risk that," Minerva said as they left the building.

Once outside, she shivered and fought down an urge to vomit. When she regained her equilibrium, she looked at Hunter.

"They just gave me a sample of what they can do. I can't risk making direct contact with them. I'll have to try to contact the spirit of whoever summoned them and bound them to this place," she said.

"Is that dangerous?" Lorena asked.

"Yes. But it's safer than messing with the bokun. This is H*aitian voodoo* and not the good kind. I'm not really sure how to deal with it right now. I need some time to figure this out," Minerva said as they climbed back into the carriage.

That evening, as Hannah resumed her normal patrol of the city, she decided to stop off at the Dragon for her usual cocktail. She saw Madison tending bar and walked over. Hannah sat down on a stool and smiled. Madison walked over.

"Hi, Hannah. Feeling better?" she asked.

"A lot better, thanks. I slept for nearly five straight days. At least my scars and bruises are gone now," Hannah said as she watched Madison mix her cocktail with a double shot of plasma.

"Listen, I'm really sorry about what happened. I really had no control of myself," Hannah apologized. "If Alejandro hadn't shown up, there's no telling what might have happened."

Madison smiled.

"We wouldn't be talking right now. You'd be *dead,*" she said. "Alejandro pretty much saved your life when he tackled me. It broke my rage enough for me to see things clear and get away."

"I won't argue that point with you. You nearly had me that night," Hannah admitted. "I can deal with vampires and rougarous but *you're* different. Just what *are* you, anyway?"

"To be honest, I really don't know. What did I look like?" Madison asked.

"Like a cross between a human and a mountain lion, only nastier," Hannah said. "When you changed, it scared the Hell out of me. I wanted to run, but Fink held me in place and forced me to keep fighting."

"Well, that's over with. We're both very much alive and we can get on with our lives. That monster's gone for good now," Madison said.

"Friends?" Hannah asked.

Madison laughed and nodded.

"Friends!" she said. "I see you're in battle mode tonight. Where are you headed?"

"I'm going up to the Station to see if Leon has anything for me to hunt down," Hannah replied. "If not, I'll just make a sweep of Treme and Storyville. It's been kind of quiet lately—except for that Terry incident."

"The Inspector ruled it a murder-suicide and closed the case," Madison said. "That was in yesterday's paper. Hunter is investigating the cause to prevent anything like it from happening again."

"Has he been by tonight?" Hannah asked as she finished her drink.

"Not yet. It's kind of early," Madison replied. "They usually come in around four."

"Maybe I'll run into them tonight. I'm curious to know what they've found out," Hannah said. "Later!"

Madison smiled as she watched her leave.

Hunter was sitting on the front porch drinking wine with Lorena and DuCassal when Hannah came up the walk. They greeted and invited her to sit with them while DuCassal poured her a glass of wine. She sipped it and told them about her talk with Madison.

DuCassal shook his head.

"I always felt that she was not a woman to be trifled with. But I have never heard of anything like that," he said.

"I have—in Hindu mythology," Hunter said.

"Oh?" Hannah asked.

"In ancient Hindu mythology, there are beings called rakshasa who can take the form of tigers or other beasts of prey. Most of the time, they are ordinary human beings but when they are angered, their animal nature comes out and anyone who crosses them usually gets torn to pieces," Hunter explained. "I never thought they existed until you just told me what happened. Since Madison is also a vampire, that makes her doubly dangerous."

"Wow! I might not have had a chance against her!" Hannah said.

"Probably not. I guess you could say that Alejandro saved *your* life that night," Hunter said as he refilled their glasses.

"Not to change the subject—" Hannah began.

"You notice that when someone begins a sentence with that phrase, they *always* change the subject?" DuCassal said.

Hannah laughed.

"Touche!" she said as they clinked glasses. "What have you learned about those medallions?"

"Nothing. I checked the archives at the Cathedral but, as I expected, there's nothing there. I also haven't had any luck finding out the identity of the girl. No missing child report within the last 50 years matched her description. That means she certainly wasn't from Louisiana," Hunter replied.

He sat back.

"My father and his before him belonged to the Order of the Dragon and membership was bestowed by the Catholic church at that time. I've decided to send a drawing of the medallion to the Vatican to see if there's anything in their archives," he added.

"That sounds like the best place to start," Hannah said. "But I still wonder why that child was wearing it. Who was she and where did she come from?"

Hunter shrugged.

"We'll probably never learn the answers to those questions, Hannah. I'm not sure it's all that important at this point in time. Right now, it's all just part of a fascinating puzzle that may or may not have something to do with my past," he said.

"I just hope that this doesn't become something that will bite us all in the ass later, mon ami," DuCassal said. "Your past has an annoying way of intruding on our present."

Hunter laughed.

"Doesn't it, though!" he said.

Three days later, Minerva asked Hunter and his friends to meet her in front of the house. At three in the afternoon, they rolled up in DuCassal's carriage. Minerva was waiting on the sidewalk across the street. She had her valise with her. She smiled grimly as they walked over.

"Are you sure you're ready for this?" Hunter asked.

"As ready as I'm going to be," Minerva replied. "That house has to be cleansed and I'm the only one who has the power to do that."

Minerva doused herself with holy water and made the sign of the cross. She took a deep breath, exhaled slowly and looked at Hunter.

"Whoever bound those spirits to this building was what is known as a boku. That means someone who practiced what you would call black magic. In the old days, a person could actually hire a boku to put a curse on someone. They were feared and hated. So they practiced their arts in secrecy. It was said they could create zombies with special drugs but I think the bokun were often mistaken for zombies.

Anyway, this won't be easy. I advise you to stay outside. No matter what happens, don't enter that house. If the doors and windows shatter, run like Hell," she said.

Minerva steeled herself and opened the front door. She was immediately hit by a blast of air that was so frigid, it chilled her to the marrow. She shuddered from the cold and stepped inside and pulled the door shut behind her.

The room was dimly illuminated by shafts of sunlight streaming through the broken and missing boards on the windows.

"I know you're here. I can *feel* you," she said as she felt the bokun moving in on her.

She opened her satchel and took out a bag of sea salt and drew a circle on the floor around herself. As she did this, she said a prayer of protection to keep the bokun at bay so she could complete the ritual. When the circle was completed, she took out a large piece of chalk and drew a pentagram inside the circle. She then added symbols for each direction and each of the five major voodoo deities. This done, she took out five white candles. She placed one at each point of the star and lit it. As she did, she invoked the names of each deity and asked for protection.

She could sense the bokun standing just beyond the glare of the candles and smiled at them. The barrier had worked. None of them could cross the circle unless she invited them—which she definitely would never do.

She then took out a bottle of rum, opened it and took one deep drink. She then placed it by the candle belonging to Baron Samete. She then took out a cigar, placed it into her mouth and lit it. She puffed three times and placed this next to the bottle. These were her offerings.

"Baron Samete hear my plea. In the name of Lord Jesus, I call forth from beyond the shadows the one who bound these spirits to this place. In the name of Baron Samete, I command you to step forward and speak with me!" she called out.

The bokun begin to stir and writhe. They cursed her and taunted her. She stood her ground and waited. When nothing else happened, she repeated her demand. This time, the ancient logs in the fireplace suddenly sparked to life. She heard a creaking sound and saw that several boards had exploded from the windows and out into the street. The room got colder. It was so cold, she could see her breath.

"I command you to appear before me!" she shouted.

She watched as a wisp of smoke began to swirl just outside the circle. It grew larger and larger and began to take on human form. As it solidified, she saw that it was a thing, black skinned woman dressed in typical Haitian attire. The woman's eyes were bright and piercing and filled with hatred and anger. An anger so strong, it made her feel sick to her stomach.

"Who are *you* to command *me?*" the woman asked in a voice that echoed from the grave.

"I am Minerva DuPres, High Priestess and Queen of the Believers. What is your name?" Minerva replied with shaky knees.

The woman smiled through jagged teeth.

"I am Naomi Trinidad-Mays, High Priestess of Voudou and mistress of the bokun," she said. "This is my temple. My house. You are not welcome here. Leave if you value your life."

"This hasn't been your house or temple for centuries. Your time is past. I command *you* to leave and take your vermin with you," Minerva said as she fought down an urge to run for the door.

The spirit *projected* fear.

A deep, intense, bone rattling kind of fear.

"Bold talk from a worm! If you want me to leave, *force me*—if you have the courage and the power. If not, leave this place or die!" the spirit said with an evil, almost snake-like hiss. "This is my house. It was my great great grandfather's before me. My roots run deep here. Are you strong enough to pull them out?"

"Yes!" Minerva said defiantly.

The spirit laughed.

"It's your funeral. Let's see who is strongest!" she said.

Hunter, Lorena and DuCassal had seen the boards fly off the windows. DuCassal took a step forward but Hunter restrained him.

"She said not to interfere—no matter what," he reminded him.

DuCassal nodded and stepped back.

They watched as the building began to shake harder and harder. Some already loose bricks fell from the walls and crashed into the street. More boards exploded from the windows and lights appeared in every opening. They heard moans, groans and creaks. They heard insane laughter.

And curses.

And crashes.

And explosions.

Parts of the gallery fell away.

The stove in the upstairs apartment burst through the wall and landed in the middle of the street as a crowd gathered to watch the bizarre spectacle.

Hunter knew that inside that building, Minerva was engaged in the fight of her life. He wondered what she had encountered and if she was strong enough to come out alive.

The battle raged for hours.

The entities launched attack after attack at Minerva to drive her out of the protective circle. Some were mental attacks designed to cause her to panic and flee. Others were physical and ranged from thrown objects, blasts of frigid air, intense heat and even flames to being pelted with swarms of insects and ice.

Minerva was just as determined to remain within the circle as she used everything she could think of, from prayers, to spells, to threats, to drive the bokun and their mistress from the building and force them back across the river.

Bits of plaster fell from the ceiling as walls cracked, floors creaked and wallpaper peeled and burst into flames. Anything breakable in the building burst into pieces and the very foundation shook as if it were the center of a powerful quake.

Minerva was bathed with sweat. Her arms and legs ached like Hell and her joints felt like they were on fire. But she held her ground and fought back with every ounce of strength, ever bit of faith and every bit of divine help she could summon.

By now, hundreds of locals had gathered across the street to watch the strange spectacle unfold. Most brought food and drinks and treated the event more like a picnic. Others prayed the rosaries or held up crosses and other holy symbols as if they were attempting to channel their own energies to Minerva to help her win this grim battle.

One hour passed.

Then three.

Then five.

Soon, the sun set and the city grew dark. Then the streetlights flickered on one-by-one.

An hour after sunset, they heard a woman scream at the top of her lungs. The scream echoed throughout the city streets and faded away in the night. It sounded like a combination of a scream, wail and death rattle and left most of the people on the street visibly shaken.

Then the house became quiet.

Eerily quiet.

They watched anxiously as the front door opened and an obviously bone weary Minerva stumbled out. She sat down on the steps to catch her breath and smiled as they ran over to her.

One-by-one, people began to applaud and cheer. Soon, the entire crowd was shouting their congratulations to Minerva and an impromptu block party began to take form. Someone handed them each a cold beer. Minerva smiled as she accepted the libation and downed it in one gulp.

"I really needed that!" she said.

"You look like Hell," Hunter said.

"Thanks," Minerva smiled. "I feel worse than I look."

"Did you win?" Lorena asked.

"That depends on what your definition of win is, child," Minerva said. "I met with the desired spirit and persuaded her to move on and take her bokun with her. She placed them here as protection after Katrina drove her from the city. She intended to return so she could control them, but was murdered on the way back by two thugs who wanted her money. That's why the bokun were left behind. You know the rest."

"Anything else?" asked Hunter.

"She said the house had belonged to her great-great grandfather, whoever *he* was," she said.

"Jeromy Flowers?" asked DuCassal.

"Who can know for sure, Jean-Paul? Flowers made several trips to Haiti to learn voodoo. No doubt, he laid several women while there. Maybe one was the great-great grandmother of Naomi Trinidad-Mays. Since there are no records, we'll never know," Minerva said as she stood up.

As they walked down the street, she lowered her head scarf.

Lorena stared.

"What's wrong, child? Why are you looking at me like that?" Minerva asked.

"Your hair! It's turned white like snow!" Lorena said.

Minerva stopped and looked at her reflection in a store window. As she did, she ran her fingers through her hair and laughed.

"So it is!" she said. "Yours would be, too, if you'd gone through what I just did. A little bit of dye will bring the color back. Or maybe I'll just leave it like this. It makes me look wiser somehow."

"It does sort of become you in a way," DuCassal said. "But do you want to go through the rest of your life looking like your own grandmother?"

"That's better than looking like *your* grandmother!" Minerva joked. "I'll worry about my hair later. Right now, I'm hungry enough to eat a horse."

"How does Le Meritage sound?" DuCassal asked.

"Are you paying?" Minerva asked.

"But of course!" DuCassal said.

"In that case, Le Meritage sounds great!" Minerva said.

As they climbed into the carriage, the crowd let out another loud cheer. Minerva leaned through the window and waved in appreciation. As they headed back into the French Quarter, the block party went into full swing. It didn't end until midnight of the following day.

"What will become of that building now?" Lorena asked over dinner. Minerva shrugged.

"As long as no one else tries to use it for a temple, I don't care what happens to it. We don't need some damned fool gating something else in that we'll have to deal with later," she said.

"It would make a good saloon," DuCassal said after some thought. "Perhaps I'll purchase it from the city. I already own several small saloons in Louisiana, so one more won't be a problem."

"Good idea. What do you plan to name it?" Hunter asked.
DuCassal smiled.

"There is only one thing I *can* name it now," he said.

"And what would that be, Jean-Paul?" asked Minerva.

"The Voodoo Lounge, of course!" he replied.

They all laughed and clinked their glassed together.

Two weeks later, the new Voodoo Lounge had its grand opening . . .

The Vatican, two weeks later.

The Cardinal was seated at his desk, picking at the side of questionable green slush that sat menacingly close to the leathery chicken legs on his lunch plate. He heard the door creak and looked up to see Fra Capella peek in. He put down his fork and motioned for him to enter and be seated.

"I'm sorry to interrupt your meal, Excellency," Capella said as he sat down.

The Cardinal pushed his plate aside and smiled.

"A meal such as this is better when interrupted. You may have come just in time to save me from a most horrible fate," he said.

"I take it that our new cook is not working out?" Capella asked.

"I am positive that condemned prisoners are served better meals than this," the Cardinal said.

"Shall I fire her?" Capella asked.

"No. I'm hopeful that her skills will improve with enough practice," the Cardinal said.

"And if they don't?" Capella asked.

"Then I shall consider these meals as God's punishment which is being bestowed upon for unspecified transgressions," the Cardinal joked.

Capella laughed.

"In that case, Excellency, God is punishing us *all*," he quipped. "Oh, I almost forgot why I came. We've received a request from Father Challons in Quebec. It's in his letter. I think it's important."

He handed the Cardinal a white envelope. He opened it, took out the letter and read it over carefully. When he was finished, he passed it back to Capella.

"Father Bruno Challons is an old friend of mine. I have not heard from him in many years. He is not one who is given to fantasies," he said.

"So you believe he is telling the truth?" Capella asked.

"Without question. If such things are indeed happening in Quebec, I feel we must send him the help he requested and the sooner the better," the Cardinal said.

"Whom shall we send?" asked Capella.

"Whom else?" the Cardinal asked.

"I'll prepare the letter for your signature immediately," Capella said.

"Be sure to include the necessary travel expenses. It is a long journey from New Orleans to Quebec and especially difficult at this time of year. Anything else?" the Cardinal asked.

"Yes. We've also received a request for help from Father Alvaro in St. Augustine," Capella said as he handed him the letter.

The Cardinal read and passed it back.

"Assign Ricardo and Carmelo O'Shea to this one. They're in Savannah. When they've finished, have them join Hunter in Quebec," he said.

Capella raised an eyebrow.

"Do you think the situation in Quebec calls for five Slayers, Excellency?" he asked.

"It may require every Slayer on Earth before it is over. I have a very bad feeling about Quebec. Very bad indeed. I want those letters on my desk within the hour," the Cardinal instructed.

Capella nodded.

"Oh, there's one more thing, Excellency," he said as he handed him an envelope. "This arrived this morning. It's from Hunter."

The Cardinal opened and took out a letter and a folded paper.

"Hunter wants to know if we can shed some light on this medallion he's found. He thinks it may be something important," he read.

When he unfolded the paper, he raised an eyebrow. Without another word, he refolded it and slipped it into his inner pocket.

"What is it, Excellency?" Capella asked.

"It's just a sketch of an old medallion. It's nothing," he replied. "Now hurry and get those letters written."

Capella rose and hurried off. As he walked back to his office, he wondered just what was on that slip of paper and why the Cardinal slipped it into his pocket.

"What is he hiding?" he asked as he sat down at his desk.

With Capella out of the office, the Cardinal took another look at the drawing Hunter had sent. It was something he'd been told about when he first arrived at the Vatican. It was something that he never expected to see. He rose from his chair, walked over to the fireplace and tossed the drawing into the flames.

"Just how did Hunter come across that medallion and why does he want to know about it?" he thought.

He knew it was the crest of the Order of the Dragon, an exclusive society of powerful and brave knights who had sworn fealty to the Pope. He also knew that the Order was later eradicated by the papal armies because it had become a source of fear. And there was a darker, more horrific history attached to its most renown family.

"But what does any of that have to do with Hunter?" he wondered.

He decided to sit down and write him a personal letter containing all of the information he had about the Order. If Hunter thought it was important enough to inquire about, then he deserved a response.

His stomach grumbled to remind him he hadn't eaten. He looked back at the food on his plate, picked it up and shoveled it into the wastebasket next to his desk

NEXT: QUEBEC